HUSH

HUSH

Kate Maxwell

virago

VIRAGO

First published in Great Britain in 2022 by Virago Press

1 3 5 7 9 10 8 6 4 2

Copyright © Kate Maxwell 2022

The moral right of the author has been asserted.

'Snow' from *Collected Poems* by Louis MacNeice (Faber & Faber),
reproduced by permission of David Higham Associates.

A CIP catalogue record for this book
is available from the British Library.

Hardback ISBN 978-0-349-01508-8
C format ISBN 978-0-349-01507-1

Typeset in Perpetua by M Rules
Printed and bound in Great Britain by Clays Ltd, Elcograf S.p.A.

Papers used by Virago are from well-managed forests
and other responsible sources.

Virago Press
An imprint of
Little, Brown Book Group
Carmelite House
50 Victoria Embankment
London EC4Y 0DZ

An Hachette UK Company
www.hachette.co.uk

www.virago.co.uk

For my parents

World is crazier and more of it than we think,
Incorrigibly plural. I peel and portion
A tangerine and spit the pips and feel
The drunkenness of things being various.

From 'Snow' by LOUIS MACNEICE

One

He looks nothing like me. That's what surprises me most. I expected to find something familiar in his features: my wonky earlobes, perhaps, or barely there top lip – something that says: half of you is me. But when the midwife passes him to me and we stare at each other, his eyes inky, it seems, with reproach, I don't recognise him at all.

They take us to a ward sliced into six cubicles and leave us there. I peer at the tiny stranger through the walls of his plastic cot, exhausted but incapable of sleep. Three a.m. Beyond the hospital's frosted windows the wheels of London continue to turn. Rain begins to fall like polite applause.

My mother comes first. She stumbles into the ward, arms outstretched, tears on pale cheeks. 'Does he have a name?' she asks as he snuffles and stretches, opens his dark eyes, then howls. I shake my head and she picks him up and sways from one foot to the other as I did the day before when he was still inside me. I unwrap a soft, striped jumper she has knitted for him and a sweatshirt from my middle sister, Rebecca, that has 'MAMA' printed on it in big letters.

My mother takes photos with my phone, and when she leaves I post one online. There I am, in a faded T-shirt, maternity leggings and a smile I don't mean, and there he is, swaddled in a muslin, his face crumpled with crying. I wonder what to caption the photo. A jaunty 'Here he is!', with a summary of his vital statistics? 'So in love!' and a trail of heart symbols, as a member of my antenatal group had done a week previously? I settle on one word, even though it feels like a claim I can't substantiate, even though it seems hopelessly optimistic. 'Us.'

If the midwives wonder, they don't let on, though I wouldn't blame them if they did. I'd be drawing family trees in the condensation on the windows if I were them; making up stories involving slammed doors and raised voices. Did he leave her as soon as the double lines loomed on the plastic wand? Did she steal his sperm on a one-night stand? Was it a heart attack, a car crash?

Or maybe they find nothing out of the ordinary about a lone woman in her late thirties screaming out a baby in a birthing pool. Because the tables have turned, haven't they? It's not teens getting pregnant any more – you can't make a baby on Snapchat. It's the late adopters you have to watch; the metropolitan midlife crises who enter the maternity ward as one and leave as two.

The five couples I share my quarters with certainly take note. I catch their eyes darting as they trudge to the loo; hear them speculate through the fabric walls when they think I'm sleeping. 'Poor woman,' says one, more than once. 'I couldn't do this on my own.' I don't mind. I live in limbo, caught between the before and an after I don't yet know. It interests me to hear who they think I am and will become, and I enjoy looking into their worlds, which might have been mine.

It isn't all bliss for them, I'll tell you that much. Beneath the cooing and future gazing there is tension that creeps like a red wine stain. The twenty-something who sobs into her phone after the father takes one look at the pleather armchair that serves as guest bed and departs. The angular French woman trying to coerce her husband into a multi-syllable name that would fail Rebecca's could-you-shout-it-in-the-park test and offering him the middle one, which everyone knows is only for christenings and weddings, as compensation. The negotiations that never end have begun.

I lose my own name during those thirty-six hours in the post-natal ward. 'How's Mum?' the nurses say as they take my pulse or squish him into the 'rugby ball' position, legs dangling somewhere near my armpit, to encourage more efficient nipple clamping. I want to tell them that my body feels like a series of snapped rubber bands, but that seems melodramatic, so instead I ask when I'm likely to stop bleeding. When they say three to four weeks and that I should inform them immediately if any foreign object larger than a fifty-pence piece emerges, I try to look neutral.

The baby, who has no name to lose, they simply call 'Baby'. Not 'your baby' or 'the baby', just 'Baby'. You'll start to recognise Baby's cry, they tell me, but his strained mewling sounds like all the others in the ward. When he isn't crying, fixing me with his affronted gaze, or feeding, such as it is, on the globs of royal jelly I produce, he lies swaddled in his transparent box, his presence a dull hum. From time to time, I forget he is there.

On the second day, at around one o'clock, when the lunch-goers begin to tap-dance on the pavement, they release us.

I pack my things, strap the baby into the car seat and heave us down the corridor. It hurts to walk; everything aches and rattles. A nurse leans out of a ward – 'Can I help? Is anyone picking you up?' – and I try to stand up straight, look capable.

'I'm fine,' I tell her, wishing I'd accepted Rebecca's offer to meet us, holding up the baby: look, he's light as air.

I'm amazed we don't set off alarms as we pass through the

3

hospital's double doors, into the October afternoon, that no one stops us. I set the car seat beside the kerb and he scrunches his tiny eyes, bunches his fists and opens his mouth, but I don't hear him because the traffic is screaming past. A woman walking by with a pushchair throws a stare of disapproval as I stand there, bewildered, looking between the baby and the oncoming cars, waiting for a taxi with its light on.

Two

August in the East Village. The moon hanging low like a street-lamp; the air overripe with sidewalk trash and vomit. Everyone at the beach but Nathan and me. I walked one block west, two south and found him in the queue for a lobster roll at a new place with fishing net strung over one wall and cans of Old Bay seasoning on the communal tables.

Lobster rolls were the menu item of the summer; the hot, new-old food thing. That spring, Manhattan's chefs went wild for ramps – skinny, foraged leeks with the lifespan of the mayfly. Last winter, there wasn't a menu in the city without a Brussels sprout on it. The lobster's star turn was, I'd read, due to its proliferation in the warming waters around Maine.

'Climate change tastes good, right?' said Nathan as he demolished his roll in three bites and eyed mine.

I shielded my plate. 'What've you been up to?' I asked.

'Hanging with Brice and the mutts. Planning a shoot.'

'Who are you influencing this time?'

'New mail-order razor brand. Hot founder. *Very* lucrative.'

It took me two large glasses, around the corner in a wine bar, but I hijacked a pause in the conversation and told him. 'I'm moving home,' I said. 'I'm going to do it. The London club – it's happening, and Lex wants me to launch it. It'll mean I can do the whole baby thing – donor, IVF – there. It makes sense. It's time.'

He shook his head. 'You belong *here*; you can do all that *here*.'

'Yes, and I was going to—'

'I'm sorry, Stevie, really, I am. So, have you told Jess?'

'Not yet.'

'Until then,' he said, 'I won't believe you're going.'

On Sunday evening, I took the 6 Train down to Canal Street to see Jess, my much older sister. Her Tribeca apartment was a study in restraint, everything the colour of stone, from the rug on the parquet living-room floor, to the L-shaped sofa, to the blinds. No ornaments or photographs, none of the detritus that I had gathered over the last half-decade, just a pair of purple-and-black swirl paintings on one wall.

I sat on the sofa, twirling my hair.

'You look as if you're about to tell me something, kiddo.' She smiled as she closed her laptop, kicked off patent pumps.

'Not really, just wanted to see you.'

We talked about the start-ups Jess's company was investing in, the non-profit whose board she was joining. About Mickey, the girl she had mentored since she was eleven – the same age I was when Jess moved to New York – taking her out every other weekend, to a museum, the movies, steering her towards college.

'Has Sam been in touch?' Jess asked.

'Why would he have been?'

'I just thought . . . '

'You liked him. You thought he was good for me. But we're not getting back together. It's been months and months.'

'OK.'

'You know I've been in New York almost five years now?'

'I do.'

'I can't remember how to say "water" properly.'

'Happens to us all eventually.'

I took a deep breath.

'Jess, I'm moving home. We're opening a club in London and Lex wants me to run it.'

She looked out of the window at the galaxy of lights. 'Oh,' she said. 'I know you've been thinking about it, so I can't pretend it's a complete surprise.' She sighed. 'I've loved you being here, Stevie, I hope you know that. We don't see each other enough but just knowing you're a few blocks away . . . '

'It's a great opportunity. A big step up. Total autonomy, Lex said. My gig.'

'It sounds like it. Seriously, I'm proud of you, kiddo. It's just . . . Gosh. I'll miss you so much.'

She opened her arms and I stepped towards her. They lasted now, her hugs, there was confidence in them. I thought about when she moved to New York and I wondered if this was payback, what I was doing, if I was punishing her. We'd come so far, the last five years, and here I was, retreating.

'There's another thing, Jess.'

We never talked about children. Jess had what she needed. A stellar career and causes. Loyal friends. Money and the time to enjoy it. I'd always imagined she thought procreation rather predictable. An unnecessary distraction from the business of living. That there were better ways to leave a mark.

I'd expected disinterest when I told her. I'd hoped she wouldn't take offence. Hers was not the life I wanted: she would know that now.

So, when I said it, when I told her I wanted to have a baby and I had a plan for how to get one, and her glass fell from her right hand and smashed in slow motion on the wooden floor, it took me completely by surprise.

I found paper towel and a dustpan under the sink. I filled another glass with water. The doorbell rang and the delivery guy thrust a brown paper bag into my hand.

I watched as Jess dipped a slice of raw tuna into the soy sauce and it turned from pink to brown.

'I don't know what came over me, Stevie. I'm sorry. It's a lot to take in. A big decision.' She folded her arms. 'I'm glad. Really, I am.'

'I'm going to do it on my own,' I said, unnecessarily.

'And the father?'

'I'll use a sperm donor. It'll be like internet dating without the rejection – or the sex, obviously.'

'You've worked it all out.'

'I've been thinking about it for a while.'

'I'm sorry you didn't . . . Does Mum know? Dad?'

'No. There's no point in telling them until it actually happens. It might well not, at my age.'

A thin, deliberate smile. 'A baby,' Jess said.

I nodded. Yes.

Three

We've been home from the hospital three days by the time I run out of excuses.

Rebecca bangs on the door with her trademark rat-a-tat-tat.

'Hi, Mama! Love the sweatshirt on you!' she says when I open it. I congratulate myself for putting it on when she texted. 'Where is he?'

I gesture to my bedroom. 'Asleep.' She stage-tiptoes and I follow, then trace her gaze to his basket.

'Oh, Stevie,' she says. 'He's beautiful.'

He stirs and begins to cry, and when I don't pick him up, Rebecca bends down. 'Could he be hungry?' she asks, cocking her head as if it is a genuine question. I check my phone. Half an hour until the next feed, two and a half hours precisely after the last. *Breastfeed your newborn baby between eight and twelve times a day*, the internet had told me, and I had taken the average: ten.

'It's not time,' I say.

Rebecca's salt-and-pepper hair, too long for a woman pushing fifty, swishes back and forth as she rocks him, a semaphore of disapproval. 'I think you should feed him when he wants at this stage, Stevie.'

Reluctantly, I unhook my bra, take him from her, open his

mouth with my fingers and place his lips around my blistered nipple. Rebecca puts the cupcakes she has brought on a plate and fills the kettle.

'No one told me breastfeeding would be this painful,' I say, inhaling sharply and leaning away from him. 'Do you think I'm doing something wrong?'

Rebecca pushes her tortoiseshell glasses down to her nose and examines my chest from the right and then the left. It reminds me of my father sizing up cows in the milking barn. 'All looks fine to me,' she says. 'Have you asked a midwife about it?'

'Yes, one came yesterday. She checked for a tongue-tie.'

'A tongue-tie? That's new.'

'It stops them sticking their tongues out, apparently. She said everything looked fine and I'd get used to it. Did it hurt you this much?' I ask, guessing the reply.

'I can't honestly remember, but if it did it wasn't for long. I loved it. I fed Lily for a year and Penny for eighteen months. Didn't want to stop. People in cafés were giving us weird looks by the end, but I didn't care.'

My sister, mother superior.

'I'm afraid your boobs will never be the same again, though,' she says brightly. 'I can tell you that now. If we all knew how much our bodies changed after pregnancy and childbirth none of us would do it. How *was* the birth? It must have been tough on your own, Stevie. I don't know why you didn't let me come – or hire a doula. Someone.'

I shrug. 'I wanted to do it on my own. But it was excruciating, if you really want to know. I thought I was going to breathe him out, but that hypnobirthing stuff I did was bullshit.'

'It worked for me.'

'I tried to inhale through my nose and exhale through my mouth, to focus on opening like a flower and the light at the end of the cave, or the tunnel, or whatever that hippie con artist said on the podcast. But when I closed my eyes all I could see was a black hole. And my breathing was all over the place. I felt like a novice scuba diver. Every time I thought I had things under control another contraction would hit and I'd hyperventilate. I was so far from the zone I was in a different hemisphere.'

'Why didn't you have an epidural?'

'I'd heard all these stories about not being able to push and the baby coming out floppy. So many people have them naturally. You did.'

I hadn't wanted Rebecca to beat me at birth. And how hard could it be? When I was pregnant, I met someone at a party who compared labour to a particularly challenging barre class: 'You know, when sweat drips into your eyes, pools on the floor, when everything aches and if you stretch one more inch you know you'll rip something and you don't think you can do it for another second, but then it's over and you feel high, intoxicated, *ecstatic* – and it makes it all worthwhile?'

I thought of that woman often during the day and night and day that felt like a year in the grey room with the inflatable ball and the blinds drawn, while I was writhing, howling, pleading him out. The lies we tell each other.

'And so did you,' replied Rebecca.

I skip the part where the midwife left the room, left me when I needed her most. How long was she gone? An hour? A minute? I know that if I dwell on it now, I will be there for ever, a needle on a scratched record.

'I was screaming for the forceps by the end,' I continue, 'but the midwife told me he'd be out if I gave one more push and thank God she was right because I was ready to give up. I looked down and the water in the birthing pool was bright red, like the aftermath of a whale kill.'

Well done, Mum! the midwife had said. *Here he is! Here's your boy!* And I didn't have time to ask whether there'd been a mistake – I was having a girl, I was sure of it – before she passed me a baby, a boy, a baby boy, kicking, screaming, living, so big, far too big to have come from inside me, and I reached out to take him.

After I feed him, I hand him to Rebecca and he falls asleep in her arms.

'When's Jess coming over?' she asks.

'In a few weeks. She sent flowers. And that.' I point to a huge box with a picture of a highchair on the side. 'And she's arranged for a night nanny to come in a couple of weeks.'

'A *night* nanny, wow.' She made it sound like a visit from the Queen. 'I was surprised Jess didn't come when you were pregnant, to be honest.'

'She did want to. I was the one who dissuaded her: I told her she should wait until there was actually something to see.'

'Right. It must be strange for her. It's just so different, isn't it, from her life, her lifestyle – a baby, I mean. The *responsibility*. Having something that needs you.'

'She has that. Her company, her team; Mickey . . . '

Rebecca sighs, then smiles. 'You'll see,' she says.

No question who was the responsible one when Jess and Rebecca were teenagers. She was so studious, Jess, so serious; lamplight and silence emanating from her bedroom in the evenings when she was home from school. I would lie on my stomach on the carpet outside, drawing, hoping she'd come and look.

Rebecca would lean against the door frame, fanning her split ends with one hand, pulling at them with the other. 'When you've finished your homework, will you do mine?' I remember her asking Jess, and when she refused, she'd threaten, 'Then I'll

12

tell!' What or whom I didn't know, and the door would open, and a hand would reach out. 'Give it to me.'

Rebecca gets up to go. 'You know, you're going to be a great mum, Stevie. It won't be easy, but I'll help you. I'm not far away, and the girls are dying to babysit.' I nod.

'Goodbye, Mama,' she says. 'Goodbye, sweet baby boy. I hope you'll have a name the next time we meet. He will start to look like you, Stevie. Babies just look like babies for the first six months.'

As she pads down the stairs and closes the door behind her, he starts to cry.

Four

I hadn't asked Jess to meet me at the airport when I moved to New York, but she had my flight details and I'd hoped, given the significance of the occasion, that she would.

The arrivals hall was loud with accents and unfamiliar languages. I walked slowly, scanning the hand-scribbled signs and hotel boards, peering between the balloons and new babies.

She wasn't there.

Just in case, I circled again, stalled, got a coffee: I was exhausted; it was eleven at night in London. Blinking away tears – did she actually want me in New York? – I looped the arrivals area one more time. Then, reluctantly, I made my way to the taxi rank.

The cars on the expressway were so big they made the clapboard houses we passed look like beach huts. Soon we were limboing under the arches of Brooklyn Bridge, the light and shadow making a stop-motion movie of our drive, Manhattan to the right, skyscrapers clawing the sky. For a few minutes I forgot about Jess because I was there, *I was there*, and my heart was hammering.

The driver put my suitcases on the kerb. I rolled them up the ramp to Jess's building, buzzed, waited.

When the elevator doors opened into the lobby, she pushed caramel hair behind an ear and stepped towards me, her arms outstretched.

'*Stevie.*'

We stood together in a brief embrace before she stepped back again. 'You're here,' she said.

As time went on, I felt better about Jess's no-show; I forgave her for it. She must have had an important meeting, a doctor's appointment, something she couldn't move. Or perhaps she just had an aversion to airport meet-ups, all that high-stakes emotion, perhaps they weren't her thing. *I'll find out what her thing is*, I thought, *I'll get to know her better.* That was one of the reasons I'd come.

Anyway, now was no time to hold a grudge: we were flatmates; I was staying at her apartment until I found a job with a visa and my own place.

'I keep having to tell myself that you're not on a two-week vacation this time,' Jess said soon after I arrived.

We were strolling through her neighbourhood with take-out coffees and she was pointing out the spots that had surfaced since my last visit – a concept store, a coffee shop, two cocktail bars – it was restless, this city, it was relentlessly self-improving.

'I hope it's OK, staying in your apartment while I find my feet? Living here?' I replied, trying not to sound needy.

'What – are you crazy?' She stopped, turned to face me. 'We've – well, *I've* – been planning this for years.'

An image of my first visit to New York, my best friend Mira and me sharing a cigarette on a cobbled street, twenty-one, everything in front of us. Jess had been to a gig with us, paid for the drinks. When it had finished, I'd watched her leave, a flash of yellow and red taillights, and Mira had taken the cigarette from my mouth and said, 'You're going to move here, aren't you? One day you're going to move here.'

'Am I?' I replied, because it hadn't occurred to me before; I'd always been waiting for Jess to move back. But she wasn't going to, I realised that then. And here was New York and perhaps Mira was right.

'Don't forget,' I said to Jess, 'I'm only staying if I find work.'

Jess liked a project and I, at that stage, was it. Finding me a job was her mission, and she sprinkled our conversation with mock interview questions. 'What did you enjoy most about your last role?' she said as we checked the listings outside a movie theatre. 'Where do you want to be in five years' time?' while we waited in line at a salad bar. I laughed. 'I don't know, Jess,' I said, 'New York. Can I say *New York*?'

'You know, you underplay it, your experience, you're too British about it,' she said one evening at the apartment. 'You've worked on some great TV programmes – you don't want to do that any more, I get it, but production is so transferrable – there are a ton of companies that would kill for your skillset.'

She picked up her BlackBerry. 'Hiring?' she said out loud as she filled in the subject line before typing out an email to her network, and I cringed and thanked her, again.

Then, 'I know!' she said. 'Lex.'

I met Lex two days later. He was a 'serial entrepreneur', Jess said, and he was launching a membership club for New York's start-up industry – Silicon Alley, she called it.

The club's building was, Lex said, 'in progress', so he suggested meeting at a brand-new speakeasy, hidden at the back of a laundrette. I walked past floor-to-ceiling bundles of folded clothes in transparent bags to a phone booth. 'Hello? I'm meeting Lex Adler,' I said.

At the end of the zinc-topped bar was a man hammering the keys of a BlackBerry.

'Lex?'

'Stevie! Thanks for meeting me in this *crepuscular* den!'

'This place is amazing – I'm used to pubs with sticky carpets.' I draped my parka over a stool and sat down.

'What do you drink? Gin? Whisky? Vodka?'

'Gin, please.'

'Then you have to try one of these.' He pointed to his drink. 'Two more,' he said to the barman. 'So, you've been here, what, a week? Are you loving it?'

'I am,' I said. 'I feel as if I'm on a permanent adrenalin high; I don't know whether it's all the coffee I've been drinking, or the bright-blue sky – London is so grey and rainy at this time of year. Actually, at every time of year.'

'Someone once told me that Manhattan is built on rock that's charged with an off-the-scale amount of energy – something to do with the way the molecules are bonded. That's why we're all a little crazy here, apparently.'

'Is that right?' I took a sip of my cocktail. 'This is delicious.' It tasted of violets and woodsmoke, a prairie at night.

'OK, so let me tell you about the project,' Lex began. 'It's essentially a members' club for the digital age, but what we're really trying to do is build a community, a tribe. We have this awesome building in Flatiron we're renovating, and during the day it'll be a co-working space with sofas, comfy armchairs, trestle tables – plus bookable rooms for meetings and retro phone booths for calls. The office is becoming obsolete, particularly for the kind of entrepreneurial folks we'll be attracting. And, you know, the downturn is in our favour here because people don't want to invest in big spaces right now – it's a *great* time to start this kind of business.

'So, everyone will be tapping away on MacBooks – coding the future. Drinking coffee. Taking breaks to play ping-pong. Then, in the evening, there'll be a seasonal menu with an insane burger, craft beers, music . . .'

I told him about the club I'd belonged to for a year in London, a birthday present from Jess. The panelled rooms became, for a time, our late-night go-to, Mira's and mine. I thought about the faces I'd nodded to at the bar, how good it had felt to be admitted to their gang, to press the buzzer and say my name and hear the door click open.

'Great spot!' said Lex. 'Big inspiration! Love what they've done over here, too.'

'I haven't been yet. Anyway, this sounds like a different crowd – tech instead of creative industries.'

'Well, *creative tech*, really, but yes, exactly that. And a different emphasis: work meets play, rather than the other way around. We *celebrate* work. You want to be on your laptop at ten p.m.? That's fine.'

'Right,' I said uncertainly, momentarily nostalgic for London, where you logged in and logged off, where the boundaries were unblurred.

'But it won't work without the right people, and that's where you come in, Stevie. What I'm looking for is someone to head up membership for the community, bring people together. I want start-up folks, some tech people, but not on-the-spectrum development guys you can't have a conversation with. And it has to be the right kind of start-up: music, fashion, food, art. Founders with proper backing. The odd venture capitalist – not too many. Cool people. Aspirational. Fun. People like us. What's your network like in New York?'

'Good,' I said. 'I know loads of people who've moved here from London, and I worked with Americans in London who've come back. It's that NYLON thing, it's a revolving door.'

It was sort of true: I had a few contacts and there were friends of friends, but mainly I knew Jess, and Jess seemed to know everyone. Lex must realise that. Perhaps that was why I was there.

'They're all fun, clever people,' I continued, 'and they'd love this.'

Lex ordered tater tots – 'like, fried potatoes' – and they arrived in a cardboard box with a pool of melted cheese the colour of egg yolk. He dipped one and I did the same.

'Jess has told me a lot about you, and your experience is very impressive,' he said.

I thought about the makeover Jess had given my CV. 'Just turning it into an American résumé,' she'd said and smiled. 'You know, you can't just list your title and the name of the programme and expect people to fill in the blanks, Stevie. You need to say you've *led teams*. You need to say you've *won awards*.'

'A producer is exactly what I need for this role,' Lex continued, 'but here's my question: who *is* Stevie? What gets you up in the morning – apart from caffeine, obviously? Why are you right for this?'

Without a visa, I'd be on a plane back to Heathrow in eighty-one days' time. I remembered Jess's coaching.

'You know what, Lex, I've made a few things I'm proud of, but what I like most about my job is the process of gathering talented people around an idea, selling it into a network, creating and nurturing a team. That, essentially, is what you're doing here.'

Lex nodded. 'Couldn't agree more. OK, final question. I'm a prospective member. Tell me why I need to join.'

'Sure.' What would Jess say? 'I only have five hundred founder spots and they're filling fast,' I began. 'Several big players have

19

already signed up – I can't name names, but I *can* say the club is shaping up to be where the decision-makers from your industry are going to congregate. And founder membership comes with extra privileges . . . I'll even knock off the joining fee.'

'Nice pitch. I need smart people like you to come on the journey with me, Stevie. I've got a few more candidates to see but I think you'd be great for this. And the British thing . . . you guys invented the members' club! The investors will love it.'

He looked at his watch, said something about another appointment and asked for the check. 'Six months from now, I want there to be a waiting list out the door.' He smiled. 'Or at least for people to think there is.'

Five

The microwave pings. I get up from my armchair, walk four paces to the kitchen, turn the time dial to five minutes and the heat from defrost to high and walk back. The week before the birth, Rebecca stacked my freezer with homemade stews and soups in Tupperware containers, and every day, at noon, I take one out and microwave it. The fact that she failed to label any of the containers makes roulette of every lunchtime. Two minutes in, whatever it was begins to waft its school dinner smell around the flat and I take a guess. Today is leek and potato soup, again.

Between the freezer, sporadic online shopping and my hoard of cupboard staples, I can survive indefinitely. My flat is my world now, seven hundred feet square. I know every knot of every floorboard, every scuff on every white wall.

The days and nights are dissected into three-hour periods. A forty-minute feed, the gunshot agony now a sharp sting that tapers each time to a wince before a dull ache. A nappy change, the black treacle of the first few days now wet sand.

Then an attempt at winding, his tiny torso on my knees; the heel of my hand pushing from the small of his back to his shoulders or bicycling his legs as the midwife instructed when she had appeared, unannounced, again, the previous day. The rewards are

21

rare: occasionally he emits a pathetic little belch; more often, he spends the next hour and a half pulling his legs to his chest and kicking and caterwauling.

I do my best to soothe him, holding him close, turning away from his head so that I can't smell its strange earthy odour, ramming the dummy back in his mouth every time he spits it out. If he keeps crying, I lay him in his basket in my bedroom with the door shut, hope the neighbours can't hear and wait for the cycle to begin again. Then I resume my post in the window, on an old armchair spewing horsehair that I meant to upholster in animal-print velvet and now never will, and conduct my neighbourhood watch through bloodshot eyes.

I live in a first-floor flat at the end of a terrace of Victorian, four-storey houses, identical except for the colour of their doors and the degree of peel on their woodwork. There are usually a couple of skips parked between the Ford Focuses and VW Golfs, piled high with chipped basins, plywood planks and copper piping. 'Always a good sign, skips,' Rebecca had said when I showed her the flat after I'd put an offer on it, a month after I moved back. 'Gentrification.'

My road's weekday routine is bookended by the pop of car fobs and the jangle of keys in locks. The school run at eight thirty, the redheaded boy struggling to catch up with the father who never turns around; the mother shooing pigtailed girls into the car. The postman with his red trolley at noon, the builders' billowing fag break at two, the teenagers swearing home at three forty-five.

After dark, electric cars sigh up and down the road, picking up and depositing passengers. And in between, at every time of day, the coming and going of the delivery vans that facilitate my hostage situation.

As I finish my soup, the baby sleeps on. Across the street, a man in a brown delivery uniform opens the back doors of his van and takes out a small cardboard box. He zaps a barcode and rings the doorbell. No answer. He places the parcel behind the wheelie bin. I could make a fortune from stolen packages if I could only leave these four walls.

I reach for my phone and tap an app. A photo of a pink-faced newborn in a striped hospital hat materialises at the top of the screen. *She arrived fashionably late*, said the caption, *and is named Clio after the muse of history*. A pop of guilt. My own baby remains nameless, the list of potential candidates growing when they should be shrinking.

I scroll down. An overhead shot of a bowl of oatmeal and blue-berries: breakfast in New York. A toddler mid-twirl. A couple looking down, laughing. Two texts from friends. Then the white envelope mail icon winks.

My out-of-office bounce-back has been remarkably effective. In the time I have been off work the email torrent has reduced to a trickle, which has dwindled to two, maybe three a day.

Every time I log on, I am reminded of the card Lex gave me on my last day before maternity leave, an illustration of a man look-ing at a computer screen that read: *You Have No Fucking Emails*. 'Enjoy your break!' he wrote.

Still, the impulse is impossible to suppress. I allowed my personal email to languish soon after I started at the club and over the last half-decade, messages from friends and family had become muddled up with status reports and all-company announcements. Here are two new emails, neither work-related. One a round-robin from Rebecca with photos from Lily's sushi-sleepover birthday party. The other from my friend Jenna in New York.

STEVIE! I'm sorry I haven't been in touch. I've been meaning to write since I saw your Insta pic a couple weeks ago.
Congratulations!! He's gorgeous. You must be over the
moon. What's he called? How is it going?? I've heard such
varied accounts of the first few weeks ... Are you getting
any sleep? How do you FEEL? Have you had that hormonal
love rush people talk about?

So many questions ... No pressure to write back – I know
you have no time. What I really wanted to say was I'm thinking about you, and I keep remembering the time we talked
about this at the beach. You did it, Stevie, you did it on your
own, and I'm proud of you.

Jenna xoxo

He has embarked on his first wail of the afternoon. I close the
email, bend over his basket and lift him up. His eyes, dry since
birth, have started to spit hot tears like lead pellets. I hold him at
arm's length and look him up and down.

'My boy,' I say aloud. It sounds like a question. I put him back
in his basket. I take a dummy from the steriliser by the kettle.
He gives it two sucks, then spits it out. I walk over to the radio
and turn up the volume.

If the days feel like purgatory, the nights are hell. When the
shutters are closed and the street is quiet, my flat becomes a
cave. Babies, I have read, need to learn when is day and when is
night, so I keep the lights off. Are those huge black eyes of his
casting around for information about the dry, cold world he has
recently entered? No, they are clamped shut. But his mouth is
like a tyre stretched around a bicycle wheel. His red lips gape in
a permanent roar.

At night, he is a tyrant. His screams are the whine of a hundred fireworks. He can keep up the performance for four, five, some-times six hours.

But not tonight.

Tonight, he is indefatigable. Tonight, after a seven-hour mar-athon, when I feel as if I have tried most of the internet's million and a half *How to make your baby sleep* suggestions – mummified him in case he's cold and stripped him in case he's hot, turned the lights back on, rocked him, cooed at him, rifled through my memory bank for lullabies to sing at him, proffered my boobs again and again – tonight, when every cell of my body craves rest, when the sun has begun to show, I open my bedroom cupboard, shine my iPhone torch inside, kneel on the floor, grab shoes and fling them behind me as if I am digging a grave.

A pair of patent stilettos, a stacked-heel knee-length boot, four-inch platform sandals. Relics of a departed life. I keep going until the bottom of the cupboard is empty. Then I pick up his Moses basket from beside my bed. He looks at me, startled, and stops crying. I pause. He starts again. I walk to the cupboard, put the basket in the space I have made and close the door.

Six

'You're gonna have to hustle,' said Lex.

We were walking down 8th Avenue on our way to an interior design meeting. It was December and I was a month into the job. I had fifty members signed up and Lex wasn't happy. By the time the club opened early next year, he wanted six hundred members: six hundred membership fees. A month ago, my target was five hundred. I was beginning to realise that moving goalposts was Lex's MO.

'Talk me through your process,' he said, as he strode, looking straight ahead, his skateboard under one arm. My head was still turned by every frozen yogurt bar, every *Cat in the Hat* chimney belching steam, every taxi driver shouting, 'Fuck you, asshole!' A trillion-dollar island with potholes and jagged pavements, spilling its grime and guts.

'I'm going to tech meet-ups, start-up mingles, holiday cookie-and-pitch gatherings,' I said. 'I'll get there, Lex, I'll get you your six hundred. You don't have to worry. I told you, I'm a grafter.'

We waited at the traffic lights. 'I love your boots,' said a woman to my right.

'Thanks,' I replied. I'd never get used to the compliments New Yorkers bestowed on complete strangers. I told her I bought the boots at the discount shop for a third of their original price. They were part of my new uniform, an attempt to assimilate with the city, to look glossy, groomed.

'Thanks for the tip!' she said.

How hard could it be, in this city where complete strangers struck up conversations, to find six hundred friends-of-friends-of-friends to join 'the first offline community for the digital age'?

'What are people saying?' continued Lex. 'Do they love the concept?'

'They do, but they want to see it in the flesh. They keep saying it's like buying an apartment off-plan from a first-time realtor.'

'But they know me? My track record?'

'Yes, but they say it's different, what you've done before. It'll be much easier when we start the hardhat tours. Showing them the PowerPoint and the address isn't really enough.'

'OK. Let's push the designers today, get them to bring things forward a few weeks.'

'That would help.'

'The other thing you need, Stevie, is a bold-faced name. It's like the movies, right? You snag the lead and the rest follow. Who's your George Clooney?'

'I'm working on that,' I said.

'Get him, or her, by the end of next week,' said Lex.

As we waited in the lobby, I texted Jess. 'Feel like a run in the morning?'

The designer, Rob, pulled out a large board pinned with swatches of velvet and tartan fabric and photos of chandeliers, chesterfield sofas and antlers. The predominant colour was womb red. Bordello-meets-Scottish-hunting-lodge. I watched Lex's eyes travel around the board twice, anticlockwise.

'So, your brief to us was to create a membership community for the digital age,' said Rob.

'Riiight,' said Lex.

'So, we researched the London gentlemen's clubs of the eighteen hundreds. And then we threw in a bit of American pioneer, a bit of Midwest settler – they were the start-up generation of their era, right? Which is where we got the plaid and the antlers.'

'*OK*,' said Lex slowly. 'Stevie, what do you think?'

'I mean, it feels very now; it has that vintage-y, retro feel a few bars and restaurants I've been to downtown have.'

'Exactly,' said Lex. 'I see Americana; I see British. I see that homesteader thing that's going on.'

'Great!' said Rob.

'I don't see digital,' said Lex.

Lex tipped his coffee to his lips, then gestured to the board. His voice ascended half an octave. 'Where's the digital here, Rob?'

'Well, we've integrated a ton of sockets and there are retractable partitions that turn the second floor into a series of meeting rooms . . .'

'I need to *see* digital, Rob, I need to *feel* it. I need more than places to plug in my laptop. All these dark colours and velvet upholstery say *social* members' clubs to me. Remember, the club is work-meets-play. It's for the tech community to ideate by day and network by night. It's not just somewhere to get wasted, right, Stevie?'

'Right.'

'I don't object to the homesteader vibe *per se*, but I need you to modernise it somehow. I want contemporary art on the walls, not antlers and oil paintings. And motivational slogans, but like, made into *art*, with super-cool fonts. "What would you do if you weren't afraid?" That kind of thing. Right?'

'Got it.'

'We're going to need final designs this side of the Holidays now. Think you can do that?'

'Not a problem. I want you to be happy, Lex.'

When we left the building, Lex raised his left hand in a good-bye salute and paddled off on his skateboard, dodging cabs and parting pedestrians on his way uptown. I watched him until he disappeared.

I wasn't a runner until I moved to New York. Jess had suggested I join her the first Saturday after I arrived and when I shook my head and said I'd never run anywhere, OK, maybe for a bus, she'd looked so disappointed that I'd relented.

To my surprise, I found I enjoyed running: time with Jess with no pressure to talk, an introduction to parts of the city I hadn't known. I'd told myself I'd mend my sofa-slouching ways when I left London and here was the solution. I wheezed and then jogged and then ran most mornings after that – with Jess, and then without her.

'It's giving me a new lease of life, your being here,' Jess said when we met the morning after my meeting with Lex, 'a new perspective on the city. I'm envious of you, starting over, making fresh tracks.'

'What would you do differently if you had your time here again?' I asked.

'Oh, I don't know,' she said, looking serious all of a sudden. What memory had I sparked? Then she smiled. 'Have I told you about the fortune-teller-hair-stylist?'

'You mean a fortune teller who was also a hairdresser? Definitely not. I'd remember that.'

'Well, she was recommended by a friend a couple of months after I moved here, and she read my tarot cards and then cut my fortune into my hair.'

'She did what?'

'She cut my fortune into my hair.'

'I thought that's what you said.'

'Wild, right? I can't remember what my cards said — you've come a long way, that kind of thing — but the results were *not* flattering. I walked in with shoulder-length hair and left with ear-to-ear bangs and a rat-tail.'

'Wow. I was going to ask for her number, but . . . '

'I don't know whether the makeover said more about my prospects or her haircutting skills. She gave me a pack of matches when I left — I was supposed to light one every evening while looking in the mirror and *self-actualise*, that was what she said, but all I could do when I saw my reflection was cry. And it took *two years* to grow out those layers. So, there you go, I'd ditch that haircut if I had my time here again. I wouldn't take the recommendation.'

'It's a great story, though.'

'Memorable, for sure. Only in New York.'

'Who was the friend who introduced you?'

'Ah, Celia. I miss her, crazy as she was.'

'What happened?'

'Our paths diverged. Another friendship lost to the mists of time. I'm not very good at hanging on to people.'

'What are you talking about? You've known Lex for years; you've got hundreds of friends here.'

'I do.' She nodded. 'But some of the people I, well . . . a conversation for another time, perhaps. Shall we run?'

'Tell me more about your first few months here, Jess,' I said, puffing behind her. She seemed more open than usual; perhaps it was the endorphins. I wanted to take advantage of it. 'New York in the late eighties, your eyes must have been on stalks.'

'Oh, God. Such a long time ago, so much is a blur. But yes,

they were. It was a different city then; you'd barely recognise it. Dangerous, parts of it, intimidating, you could feel it. Graffiti everywhere, on the buses, even in the subway carriages.'

'By artists that hang in MoMA now.'

'Ha. That's right. I wasn't exactly part of the subculture with my midtown job, my suits, apart from the occasional run-in with a fortune teller. I wish I could tell you I was hanging out in paint-spattered Soho lofts, but the closest I got to that scene was reading about it in the style section of the newspaper. A lot of the stuff you hear about New York at that time . . . it felt as if it was happening somewhere else.'

'What about the party scene, the nightlife?'

'I went out, of course,' she said, then paused – was she summoning the repetitive beats of a long-lost night? – 'but you don't want to hear about that.'

'Why not?'

'Me, partying, back in the day. It's like,' she took a breath, she was running faster now, I was struggling to keep up, 'it's like dad dancing, isn't it?'

'Not at all. Tell me.'

'I suppose it was my misspent youth, in a way,' she said at last, 'a sort of second adolescence. I'd been so sensible in London. I didn't know anyone at first, apart from work people, and, well, management consultants aren't renowned for dancing on tables.'

'You must have been lonely.'

'I was. But I met people. Slowly, and then all at once.'

'All at once?'

'Yes. Celia was one of them.' I could hear the full-stop at the end of the sentence. I knew better than to press her. We were getting somewhere, I told myself.

I hoped we'd still have these conversations when we didn't live together any more. Because it was time I moved out, moved on.

I'd been sleeping in Jess's spare room for two-and-a-half months. I needed to give her back her space and find my own.

'Wasn't there something you wanted to talk to me about?' Jess asked, as we turned into her street, walking now. 'Something to do with work?'

'Well, yes, if you're sure you don't mind. You've helped me so much already.'

'Don't be silly,' she said. 'I like to feel needed.'

'OK, it's the membership. I don't know how I'm going to make Lex's numbers. I told him I had a great network in this city, and, well, I'm looking at it.'

'Stevie, you got the job because Lex liked your creative perspective, he could see you'd be a fantastic ambassador for the club – and selling membership to something that isn't built yet isn't that different from selling an idea to a TV network.'

'Yes, you're right, I can do that stuff. It's just ... the *pipeline*. That's what Lex calls it. Where do I find all these potential members?'

'Oh, that's easy,' she replied, pushing open the door of her building. 'Leave it to me.'

Seven

The day that follows Jenna's email is a black day. Endless tears — mine as well as his — a split-bank roar. Exhaustion so profound my skin, my bones, my eyeballs ache.

I wanted him so badly. I went to such lengths to get him. I want to give him back.

I close my eyes. Step forward and show my green card. 'Welcome home, Ma'am.' Roll my carry-on to the line of yellow cabs. Drive past the rows of white tombstones, on to the red bridge.

No. I do what I am supposed to do.

I talk myself off the window ledge above the buckling pavement. I open my eyes. I resume my duties.

Still, the next day, and the day after that, and the day after that, lookalike days spreading out into infinity, I am relieved that I have at least felt something.

'You sound low, Stevie.'

I have called Nathan because he is the only one without an agenda or a parenting track record.

'What have I done?'

'What do you mean? You've had a baby. You've made a life.'

'I want my old life back.'

'You don't, Stevie.'

'I don't know who I am any more. I miss work, I miss *people*. Conversation. Feedback. Meetings, even. Wearing actual clothes. Can you believe the London club has opened and I haven't even seen it?'

'You've just *given birth*, Stevie. And you wanted more than a career. You wanted this.'

'I look at him and I feel nothing.'

'Come on, don't be so hard on yourself. I'm no expert, but I'm sure plenty of people don't bond immediately.'

'I thought I would. I thought that would be the easy part. Do you think it's harder to love someone when you don't know the other half of them?'

'All of this is harder because you're on your own.'

'I feel like a fraud. I can't tell anyone except you. You and the internet.'

It was a fickle friend, the internet. When I googled *not bonding*, *failure to bond*, *not in love with baby*, the answers would seem, at first, supportive, reassuring. It's OK, they'd say, many women struggle, don't blame yourself, your googling is evidence that you're a good mum. You may not care, but you're concerned about not caring. A checklist of explanations for my condition would follow and I would wonder how many of them I could reasonably tick.

Dearth of oxytocin-boosting hugging in the final trimester – yes.

Protracted labour – yes.

Traumatic birth – well, weren't they all?

After that, there'd be an invitation to 'seek help' and a list of

Freephone numbers and contact emails and I would press the back button on the website and click another page.

But if I delved too deep, the internet turned. If you fail to pour love into a child from minute-one, it said, you risk inflicting life-long damage. If you don't lock eyes, sink yourself into a perpetual, one-sided, coo-laden conversation; if you don't wind yourselves in a permanent naked embrace, you cut that child's tap root. It will think itself unlovable for ever.

When I landed on those pages, I would close my laptop and call Nathan.

'I want you to keep telling me about everything, Stevie, about how you're feeling,' Nathan says. 'And as far as anyone else goes, fake it till you make it.'

'Do you think he knows? I feel as if he's judging me.'

'*Of course* he doesn't know.'

Nathan pauses long enough for Manhattan's early-morning car horns to chorus down the line. It is twelve o'clock in London, time for the membership meeting, five of them gathering in the nook on the second floor. Will they talk about me? I wonder. Will they debate what I'd say about so-and-so's application, her networking potential? . . . *Would Stevie say she was in or out?*

'Anyway,' Nathan continues, 'we're talking about him as if he doesn't have a name. What is it? I can't believe you haven't told me.'

'He doesn't have a name.'

'He's almost three weeks old!'

'He doesn't need one yet. You don't have to register babies until they're six weeks.'

'So what? Don't you want to call him something *now*?'

'I can't decide. I'm not capable of deciding. I thought it'd be

35

easier to name a baby if there was no approval process, no one to say, "Rex sounds like a dog; Spike's ridiculous – what if he wants to be an accountant?" But I think it's harder.'

'I think you're scared of giving him a name.'

'Why would I be?'

'Because giving him a name will make him real.'

The baby's arms are raised above his head, his mouth is open in sleep. He seems real enough.

'I don't feel I know him yet,' I say.

'Whoever he is, he will become his name. Come on, Stevie, what's on your shortlist?'

'Jonah, Noah, Gabriel . . . '

'Well, it *was* an immaculate conception. Hang on a second.'

The click of a door opening.

'Hey, man, how's it going? Latte, please.'

He is at the coffee shop on Tompkins Square Park now, the one with the 'Unattended children will be given an espresso and a free puppy' sign.

'Get one for me, too,' I say.

'Ha.'

I went there most mornings after running along the East River, watching the first rays light the wooden stumps that rose from the water. I'd walk back to my apartment clutching my takeout cup like a sabre, riding the caffeine and endorphin high. On Saturday mornings, Nathan and I would meet, take our coffees to a park bench and dissect the departing week.

'Nathan, I'm serious. Can't you decide for me? Twenty per cent of parents regret the names they give their children, I read that somewhere.'

'You want me to take the blame?'

'You are his godfather.'

'I am? Did I know that?'

'I thought I'd told you. I can't remember anything any more. Are you OK with it?'

'Sure, I love kids.'

'You don't, but you love me.'

'That's true.'

'It's a ploy to keep you in my life for ever.'

'You don't need a ploy, but thank you, Stevie, I'm honoured. Seriously.'

'At least that's sorted.'

'OK, here's an idea: Asher? I swiped right on an Asher the other day. And you like biblical.'

'I wish you hadn't told me that. I do like it, though. It's unusual. Or Ash, as in tree.'

'Perfect. Does he look like an Ash?'

'I think he could. Ash Stewart. It sounds good.'

'Try it on him. See if it fits. Call him Ash for the next couple of days and report back.'

'I will.'

'In the meantime, are you getting out?'

'Do you know what it's like to have a newborn, Nathan?'

'Answer the question.'

'I've seen people. I had a few visitors the first few days: Rebecca, Mira . . . '

Mira came with Beatrice, her daughter, a few days after Rebecca. '*A meeting of mums!*' she'd said in the text. But it hadn't been like that, it hadn't felt like that, it was as if we were two critics with day and night opinions of the same play. The conversation was stilted, 'You must be so tired,' she'd said, plugging another pause, and she'd asked about the happy hormones and I'd said, 'Yeeesss,' lingering on the vowel, lying through the consonant. Thank goodness Beatrice was there. Darling Bea, so sweet with him, better than me, even at four years old.

'Well, that's a relief,' says Nathan.

'You know, they all said the same thing?'

'Why doesn't he have a name?'

'They wanted to smell his head, and then they all said they wished they could bottle it – the smell, that is.'

'That's weird.'

I hear the door to his block slam shut and the whirr of the approaching elevator.

'So how many times have you left the apartment?'

'I haven't.'

'Stevie, I mean, what the hell? You haven't left the apartment in THREE WEEKS?'

'I have everything I need here. Anyway, it's impossible.'

'What do you mean it's impossible? I can imagine the logistics are challenging, but it's not impossible to put a baby in a stroller and wheel it down the road, is it? I'm talking to someone who led a team of, what, thirty people – thirty high-maintenance millennials – until a few weeks ago.'

'I'm not that person any more, Nathan.'

'You are.'

'I'm so tired. Last night he barely slept at all.'

'Show me a new mom who isn't tired.'

'I'll go out when the night nanny comes, when I've had a decent rest.'

'Go out now, Stevie. Today. Go to the bodega for a start. Christ's sake, your wi-fi probably stretches that far – we could FaceTime the whole way. You'll go completely insane otherwise. Do it for me, the godfather. OK?'

In the end, it is an empty milk carton that smokes me out.

He – Ash – and I walk fifty yards to the corner shop. I don't trip on the doorstep. He doesn't suffocate in his cloth sling. He doesn't cry and no one stares. I lift a bottle of semi-skimmed from the fridge and the shopkeeper doesn't ask where or who his father is when I pay for it. Then we walk back to the flat and unlock the door with the key I haven't dropped.

Eight

Blocks of days-old snow, greying and speckled with grit, divided the sidewalk from the road. Yesterday, the temperature dropped to minus eleven.

I was waiting for a dozen prospective members and a journalist outside our West 21st Street building, which was beginning to look less like a burned-out parking lot and more like a series of supersized living rooms.

'Hey, are you Stevie?' A tall, slim man, his narrow face half-obscured by a floppy, dark brown fringe, approached.

'Nathan Walker?'

'That's me,' he said, pushing his hair out of his eyes and reaching for my hand.

After I'd quizzed her on prospective club members, Jess had sent me a spreadsheet of names, emails and phone numbers, scores of them, with a personal note on each: 'Tell her her yoga buddy says hi!' 'Say Jess will be in touch about that lunch.'

Almost every email I sent with Jess's name on it received a reply, and one of the positive responses turned out to be Lex's movie lead, the female founder of a health food start-up with a record amount of investment.

Then, the hawks began to circle. Nathan Walker was

writing a feature to run in a lifestyle magazine the day the ribbon was cut.

'This place is fancy!' he said. His eyes travelled along the curve of a vintage Danish sofa, then up to the montage of modern art on the wall behind it. Its centrepiece was a sampler cross-stitched with the words: *You miss a hundred per cent of the shots you don't take.*

'What are your criteria for entry?' Nathan asked. 'Do you *actually* vet every member or is it really just a case of show me the money?'

'*Of course* we vet them,' I said, narrowing my eyes.

It turned out Nathan's audacious line of questioning was a signature move. I imagined him feeling comfortable asking a soldier how many people he'd killed during his last tour of duty. By the end, he'd asked how much Lex made when he sold his last company – 'Was it money-money or fuck-you-money?' – what I earned, and whether my boss was straight or gay.

'Do you think this place will double as a pick-up joint?' I heard him enquire of one of my prospects.

'Let's have a look at the rooftop bar before the sun sets!' I interjected loudly.

It wasn't until the tour had ended and I'd collapsed into one of the lounge chairs that I noticed Nathan was still there, sitting on a ping-pong table, scribbling in his notebook. He gave me a thumbs-up.

'Good job!'

I laughed.

'Seriously, when my editor sent me to cover this I was like, *Uh-oh, I know how this goes, bunch of techies and a keg in a conference room!* But this is a classy operation. It's going to be a hit.'

'It might be if you write something nice about it. And if you haven't put everyone off with all your questions.'

'Ah, come on, just doing my job. Anyway, they know I'm not part of the package. Unless you're offering me free membership?'

'Don't you have some sort of journalistic code to adhere to?'

'Rules are meant to be broken! Can I buy you a drink to make up for it?'

We walked to a bar and slipped into opposite sides of a booth.

'I feel as if I'm on a date,' I said.

'You are,' Nathan replied. 'But it's a friend date, so don't go falling in love with me, OK? I bring all my new recruits here. The Negronis are killer.'

'How long have you been in New York?' I asked, glancing at the menu.

'For ever. I went to NYU and never left. You?'

'Four months. I keep thinking I came twenty years too late.'

'What, because you missed the crime and the crack and Andy Warhol? There's never a bad time to come to New York. Sure, it's a little shinier than it was a decade or so ago, and no, there isn't as much *death* – personally, I'm devastated about that – and you spend two-thirds of your pay-check on rent and everyone's moving to Brooklyn. But it'll always be the most creative, ass-kicking city on the planet and there'll always be rats in the subway.'

'Rats the size of cats. Where are you from originally?'

'Iowa. Heard of it?'

'Of course. It's a flyover state, isn't it?'

'Ha!' he exclaimed. 'That's not generally how I describe it – "flyover" isn't exactly a compliment.'

'I suppose not, sorry.'

'Don't worry, it's fairly accurate. Not much worth touching down for. Corn and cows, basically. Negroni?' he asked.

'Yes, please. Did you grow up in the country?' I asked.

'Yup. My family grows corn – and children, there are five of us.'

'Mine are farmers, too. Dairy, mainly.'

'Well, isn't that a coincidence.'

'Do you get on with your family?'

'I wouldn't say we're close. I'm kind of the black sheep. They're not too comfortable with my sexual orientation. What about you?'

'I'm straight,' I said.

'I didn't mean that! But good to know. How are you finding our dating scene?'

'I haven't tried it yet.'

'So much to look forward to. And what about you, are you close with your family?'

'Yes and no. My big sister, Jess, lives here. I've been staying at her apartment in Tribeca.'

'Roomies.'

'Yes, but I'm about to move into my own place.'

'Where's that?'

'The East Village.'

'That's where I live!'

I didn't tell Nathan that I hadn't spoken to my roomie in five days – that we hadn't even discussed the apartment I had found.

I'd sent Jess an email with the subject line: 'Look out, East Village!' a week before, and I hadn't heard back. Nor had I seen her. She'd cancelled our early-morning runs – breakfast meetings, she'd said – and either she or I had been in bed each night by the time the other came home.

She was probably just sick of me, of my clothes in her washer-dryer, my food jostling with the almond milk in her fridge. Poor Jess, she'd lived alone for so long. *At last!* I imagine she sighed when she opened my email. *About time!* No reason why she should have dignified it with a response.

I would see her tomorrow, I reminded myself. She'd invited me to a dinner she was hosting, some sort of charity thing.

We stayed until the bartender ejected us at three.

'Just trying to bring old-fashioned values to the big city,' Nathan said, when I thanked him for finding me a cab. 'Anyway, we'll be neighbours soon.'

Would he call? Should I call him?

The following afternoon, my mobile rang. It was Nathan.

'Hey, girl, what's going on?'

We spoke, emailed, messaged, pinged or poked each other every day that followed.

Nine

People often ask me when I first knew I wanted a child. It's a question directed at single mothers more often, I'm sure. Either way, does anyone wake up one morning and think, *I need a baby!* Perhaps, but not me. There was never a time I didn't.

My own childhood was both happy and unhappy. I arrived eleven years after my sister Rebecca – a mistake, clearly, though my parents never said, never would say. The nappies and all-nighters must have been a distant memory, and then they were plunged back in.

My father, I think, resented me. He tried to be kind, but it didn't come easily. I could always sense the effort: a slight bite to his voice; a forced smile.

If he tried, I tried harder. Waiting for him outside the barn with a flask of tea at four. Swallowing notes and dates and quotes at school – a desperate, and, it turned out, successful attempt to exceed my teacher's modest expectations and propel myself to the top of the class. Education mattered to my dad – education and religion. He'd had too little of one and too much of the other.

But whatever I did, he kept his distance, a tree on a country road that never drew closer, no matter how far I walked towards it.

He wasn't that way with everyone. He wasn't like that with

Rebecca, even when she was averaging her O levels, smoking Silk Cuts out of the bathroom window and playing Spandau Ballet so loud the windowpanes shook. Rebecca the not-quite rebel. For Dad, she was pure joy. His face flushed when he heard her voice.

My father was from a family of tenant farmers. My mother, two years older, was a grammar school girl, a smart cookie whose dreams of a career were postponed when she met Dad at the races one Boxing Day, the excitement of the occasion no doubt colouring her judgement. Five years later, they were married with two children.

When I was a teenager, prospective careers miraging before me, I asked Rebecca why Mum had never worked. 'She started veterinary training when Jess and I were at school; when she had time,' she had told me. But then, when she was thirty-seven, I came along, and she never finished it.

They moved to a new farm across the county border, a ten-minute drive from the nearest village. 'The tenancy ended,' was all Mum said when I once asked why. Rebecca left for school at seven every morning. Jess, for whom A grades came as easily as breathing, was sent to boarding school on a scholarship soon after I was born. My father worked from before dawn until after dusk. For most of the time, we were alone, Mum and me, a woman and child in a window.

I often think of her when I sit in my armchair, the baby in my arms. I wonder whether she felt what I can't.

Ash is asleep. I pick up my phone and dial her number.

'Hello?'

'Mum, it's Stevie.'

'Darling girl, I've been meaning to . . . Have you decided on a name?'

46

'Ash.'

'Ash. Like the tree?'

'Like the trees on the farm.'

'Ash Stewart. It is Stewart, isn't it?'

'Of course. What else would it be?'

'That's lovely, darling. Shall I tell Dad?'

'Yes.'

'I'll tell him tonight. Ash. He'll love it. How are you both?'

'He's growing, changing. He has new hair like the fuzz on a peach. Yesterday, dirt appeared under his fingernails, as if he'd been burrowing in earth.'

'I remember that happening to you.'

A pause. Through the window, the bin men are collecting the rubbish.

'It's hard, Mum.'

'I know. You're all on your own, I wish I could . . . '

'I'm not asking you to help, and anyway, there's a night nanny coming in a couple of days, Jess arranged it.'

'A night nanny?'

'She stays the night, takes over, so I can get some sleep. She's coming for five nights.'

'Oh, right. That *will* help.'

'Jess says all her friends have them in New York, whether they're on their own or not. I've been thinking, Mum, about what it must have been like for you when I was born. Dad working so hard; Jess away at school.'

'I remember feeling exhausted. Washed out. You were never a sleeper. I was almost the same age as you are now when you arrived – did you know that?'

'I did. You must have been a breastfeeding pro by then, at least,' I say.

'Darling, I . . . ' I imagine her twirling the white cord of the phone around her fingers, looking through the kitchen window to the hill that rises sharply from our garden, the herd silhouetted at the top.

'I didn't breastfeed you, actually,' she says. 'It had gone out of fashion; formula was so good by then.'

'Oh.' I am suddenly conscious of the milky weight and taut skin of my breasts.

'I'm sorry; I thought I'd told you. Rebecca wanted to help; it was a way of involving her. You know she gave you your bottle every day before and after school? You don't mind, do you? It certainly didn't do you any harm.'

'Of course not, why would I?' I am breastfeeding him, but she didn't breastfeed me.

I decide I will give up, I will prise his lips permanently from my bloody nipples, never mind the mastitis the health visitor promised. I will give up before the night nanny arrives. I will feel more like myself after that.

'Mum?'

'Yes, darling.'

'Did you love me straightaway? Or did it take time?'

'Oh, Stevie.'

'I'm sorry, it's just . . . It's a stupid question. Forget I asked.'

'Stevie. *Darling*. It was love at first sight.'

I will think of that phrase often in the weeks and months ahead. She has never given me any reason to doubt it. Her hugs, like lit brandy on Christmas pudding, fast and fierce, 'Darling, come here!' Her pleasure at my tiny achievements: drawing ten fingers on a stickman, a house with four windows, 'Stevie, clever girl!'

But our interactions seemed to become less frequent as I grew older; the spaces between them seemed to swell. I spent more time on my own.

'Will you play with me, Mummy?' I'd say, when she was sitting on the sofa with a cup of tea or stirring something on the stove, and sometimes she'd get to her feet and we'd rearrange the furniture in Rebecca's old doll's house or make pizzas out of Play-Doh and I'd never felt happier.

But soon, too soon, she'd push herself up from the floor with a sigh, leaving me looking up at her, wanting more. Or I'd catch her staring into space, wondering, perhaps, what she might have done, who she might have been.

I understood, even then. She was tired; she had years on my friends' mothers, and thirty-seven was older then. She had done it, the Lego, the homework, the parents' evenings, the ballet recitals. She had done them all, she hadn't expected to have to do them again.

And then there was my father's shadow. 'Indulging her, are you, Mary?' I'd hear him say, like a pair of shears hovering above apron strings.

But I always knew that if something bad ever happened she would run to my side, stroke my hair, press my freckles with the tips of her fingers, 'Magic buttons, these, Stevie.' She loved me, I could see she did; all my life I've been able to see it.

Still, sometimes, as I got older, I wondered if you could love someone and prefer your life without them there. If you could prefer your life before they arrived. Sometimes, I wondered if both things could be true.

Ten

The hotel where Jess's charity dinner was being held had a door-man in a peaked cap who pointed me up the stairs to the private dining room. I'd made a point of being early: an opportunity for us to talk before the guests arrived.

'You look amazing,' I said to Jess. She was wearing a short black dress with an asymmetric neckline and her hair and make-up were immaculate – impossible to believe she was approaching fifty. I regretted my capped sleeves, my knee-length hem, too dowdy, too London. Everyone would think I was the older sister.

'Thanks for coming, Stevie,' Jess said, leaning in to kiss me, but her voice sounded flat. Her eyes looped the room; she fiddled with the gold bangles on her right wrist. She's probably just dis-tracted, I told myself. She's not thinking about me, she's thinking about her guests.

'Anything I can do?' I asked.

'Oh, no. Everything's under control.'

'Drink? Calm the nerves?'

'I never drink at this kind of thing,' she said. 'Honestly, I'll be fine once everyone's arrived.'

'You know, this will be the first time I've seen you in action,' I said. 'I mean, in a work setting.'

'Yes. I hope I won't be a big disappointment.'

'Who's coming?'

'High-flying business and creative types with deep pockets,' she said. 'They don't know each other,' she added. How odd, I thought, to sit at a table with a group of people you'd never met.

'Look, Jess,' I said, 'can we talk really quickly? I wondered if you'd seen my email about moving out. I know it's been a long time coming.'

But before she could reply, an actor walked in. I recognised him immediately, the Ken Doll good looks; anyone would have. He must have the wrong room, I thought as he shook off his coat, passed it to a waiter, but then he bellowed, 'Jess!'

Jess whispered, 'He invests in tech; talk to him about the club.'

Next came a movie director who told me his name as if he needed to, and before long, there we all were, ten New York power players and Jess and me. For the next half-hour, I watched her glide among them, placing hands on shoulders, making introductions, while I shuffled between twosomes and threesomes, offering awkward hellos.

By the time we sat down, the room was as noisy as a school playground. As I listened in, Jess's strategy revealed itself. Everyone had something in common: the artist had a business idea, the businesswoman collected art; the editor-in-chief was just back from Marfa where the director's next movie was shooting.

I picked at my duck salad, listened to the founder counselling the TV anchor about his failing marriage, to the actor telling the editor she should open a magazine museum, so close was her industry to extinction. 'What do you do?' he asked me when the chortling subsided. 'I hope it's something with a future.'

When the conversation eddied again, it occurred to me that what was enabling the evening, allowing Jess's guests to be so open with one another, wasn't just a mutual interest in start-ups or in art, it was their shared experience of success. They lived at the same altitude, breathed the same air. You could hear it in the even pitch of their voices: they understood each other.

And Jess – the daughter of a dairy farmer, who had sat silently at the end of the table at family meals, who was evasive and unpredictable, and often shy with me – was deep in conversation one minute, head back, laughing the next; she was in her element. Jess was one of them.

She tapped her glass with her knife and stood.

'Thank you, *all of you*, for coming,' she said, her voice soft; you always had to lean in to hear her. 'It's a great pleasure to see you enjoying each other. I hope you've met my sister, Stevie, and heard about the members' club she's opening with Lex Adler, whom some of you know.' I blushed, nodded to the waiter hovering with wine, mouthed 'Thank you' across the table to Jess, but she was looking down at her notes again; she didn't see.

'Now, *one* of the reasons you're here is because I wanted to tell you about the foundation I chair,' she continued. 'And, you know, I have a whole bunch of talking points,' she waved a stack of cue cards, 'but I'm not going to use them. Because what I really want to tell you about is Mickey, the young woman I met through the foundation.'

As she spoke, I forgot about the other guests. I couldn't lift my eyes from Jess, none of us could. My sister, arms thrown open, the room in her hands.

'Congratulations, Jess,' I said when everyone had left. 'What a night! Your speech . . . I can't wait to see Mickey again. And I knew you had friends in high places, but that, as Lex would say, was *off the clock*. He'll be livid when I tell him.'

'He can come to the next one.'

'Well, thank you for asking me. And thank you to whoever dropped out and let me in.'

'No one dropped out, Stevie.'

'Jess, can we talk?'

'Now?'

'My email about the apartment I found – did you get it?'

'Yes, I'm sorry I didn't reply; it's been so . . . '

'Busy. I know.'

'Do you need help with the deposit? I know what they're like, realtors, when you don't have credit history.'

'I'm fine, thank you, I used my savings. Lex offered to be my guarantor.'

'He did? You should have asked me.'

'I've asked you for so much, Jess.'

'When do you move out?'

'Sunday.'

She paused, exhaled. 'You know, Stevie . . . '

'What?'

'You could have stayed.'

'Stayed with you?'

'Yes.'

'I thought . . . '

'I never expected you to stay for ever, and I know we never discussed dates, how long you would, but, well . . . I thought you'd be with me for at least six months.'

'Jess, I thought you'd want your apartment back,' I said. 'I didn't want to push my luck.'

'What gave you the idea you were pushing your luck? You know, I was hurt when I got your email; really hurt. You hadn't even told me you were looking for a new place. I couldn't understand it.'

'I didn't want to bother you after everything you'd done for me, Jess, letting me stay, magicking me a job . . . I thought I'd do something on my own for a change and tell you when it was all sorted. I thought you'd be *pleased*.'

She nodded, took off her bangles and placed them on the table beside her.

'Look, I'm sure I can get out of it,' I said, 'get my deposit refunded . . . '

She shook her head. 'No. You need your own space, your own life. I understand that. I shouldn't have said anything; it was unfair of me. I'm pleased you've got somewhere you like, Stevie, a good apartment is hard to find.'

'I'm not sure if *good* . . . '

'It's a great area. Much younger than Tribeca. Perfect for you. It's my old stomping ground, the East Village.'

'The dad dancing?'

'Ha, some of it. I expect there's even a bit of edge left, if you go far enough east.'

'We'll see each other all the time,' I said, scrabbling, I was losing her again. 'We'll see each other more than we do now *because* we don't live together – we'll have to make an effort.'

'Yes.' She didn't believe me. She looked at her watch. 'I have a breakfast meeting at seven thirty. Let's go.'

Eleven

You wouldn't think from the way I prepare for the night nanny that I will be spending the entire evening asleep. I stop short of lipstick, but I cover my cadaverous skin with foundation, brush my hair, change my clothes. She has come to save me, to give me the ultimate gift: ten uninterrupted hours. The least I can do is make an effort.

As for my flat, if you ignore the scuffed paintwork and worn furniture, it is a show home. She will be used to nurseries with rocking chairs and jungle wallpaper, and I cannot offer that in my one-bed, so I am compensating with neat and tidy.

Wet patches are beginning to appear on my T-shirt. I gave up breastfeeding three days ago, but so far, my boobs have refused to surrender. When Ash whimpers they inflate, and so I find myself pumping at the same time as bottle-feeding, attempting to seduce him with a plastic teat while he squirms, mouth ajar, in the direction of my nipples. Surely, tonight, when he and I are in separate rooms, my breasts will acquiesce.

Nine o'clock. The doorbell rings. *Yes.* I allow myself a victory lap of the front room before I answer.

I'm not sure exactly what I was expecting, but the night nanny is not it. She is a giant, filling the doorframe, blocking the light from the hallway, enclosing my hand in her own when she shakes it. She makes me feel like a child, she makes Ash look like Thumbelina when she cradles him.

Still, she seems gentle, despite her stature, kind. She is no disappearing midwife like the one in the hospital. As she rocks Ash from side to side, strokes his fuzzy head, whispers things I can't hear, hard as I try, he relaxes.

At the same time, I can feel myself tensing. Even though I don't want my baby in my own arms, it is strange to see him in someone else's.

'He looks very comfortable,' I say, hoping my displeasure is not obvious.

'Well, I've been doing this a long time.' Jess said they called her 'the baby whisperer' in the testimonials. 'Would you like to hold him?'

'No, no, you carry on,' I say, as I memorise the angle of her arm, the pressure of her hand on his head, picking up tips to use later.

'So, how have the first few weeks been?' she asks.

'Good, thank you,' I reply, my voice clipped. What am I supposed to say, that I am hanging on by a thread?

'You must be tired, though? Your sister told me you were on your own.'

'I think that goes with the territory, single mum or not.'

'Of course, and that's why I'm here. So, tell me about Baby's night-time routine.'

'Routine?' This is beginning to feel like an exam and I don't have the answers. 'He doesn't really have one. I generally give him a bottle around nine thirty and take it from there.'

'I can help with that,' she says. 'I can try to get him on a schedule.'

'Yes, please.'

'Tell me, do you swaddle him?'

'No, should I?'

'Some babies really enjoy it; it makes them feel snug, like being back in the womb. And it can help them settle.' Something else I've neglected to do.

'Can you show me?'

'Of course.' She places Ash on a muslin, and, like an origami expert, folds it deftly around him with her huge hands. 'There,' she says, 'a baby burrito. We can do it together a couple of times in the morning if you like.' She checks her watch. 'Well, I think it's your bedtime,' she says, and it takes me a moment to realise she means me.

I give a concerned-sounding do-I-really-have-to-leave-him sigh as I approach the Moses basket. 'Goodnight, darling,' I say to Ash. It is the first time I have called him that.

'He'll be *absolutely* fine, Mum,' she says, and I respond with a last, brave smile as I open my bedroom door and close it behind me. Relief. I get into bed and slip into sleep.

I wake at four, boobs hard as ball bearings, my pyjama top soaked. I rush to the kitchen and take the pump from the steriliser. The night nanny is sitting on the sofa, staring into the Moses basket.

'Everything OK?' she whispers when she sees me.

'I don't know why the milk's still coming,' I say.

'You said it had been three days since you stopped feeding him?'

'Yes, and I started by dropping a couple of feeds each day. I suppose pumping just encourages it.'

'You must, though, you might get mastitis otherwise. Do give me the milk when you finish, so it's not wasted. Nothing worse than pouring it down the drain.'

For the next hour, I sit on the bathroom loo, feeling the intermittent tug and release of the suction cones on my nipples, listening to the aggressive purring of the pump. I think about the nanny, her vigil in the next room. How content Ash seemed with her. The walls are thin and I have not heard a peep from him since I went to bed. Will she stay awake all night, her arms outstretched, ready to soothe him the moment he opens his eyes?

I hand her the bottle of expressed milk just as Ash is stirring.

'Perfect timing.' She smiles, and I stand behind her as she starts to feed him with it. I shouldn't, it feels like rubbernecking, but I can't stop. There is a noise in my head, faint but shrill, like the chirp a smoke alarm makes when the batteries run flat, on and on. Perhaps I'm getting a migraine.

'Would you like to do this?' she asks gently.

'No, thank you,' I reply. 'I must get some sleep.'

Before I get into bed, I write a text to Jess. *Can you cancel the night nanny? Sorry, so thoughtful of you, but not working.*

Then I feel the emptiness of my bedroom, its silence. The noise has gone. There is no baby breathing, no baby screaming. It is worth that. Almost anything is worth that. I delete the message and shut my eyes.

I awake again to curtains being drawn, the smell of toast. Am I back in hospital?

'Morning, dear,' the night nanny says, towering over me, putting a plate on my bedside table, passing Ash to me. 'Here he is. He's been such a good boy.' He looks at me, sighs. *You again.* 'I'll be off, then. See you tonight?'

I pause. Despite the interruption, I feel refreshed. I must have slept for eight and a half hours altogether. Eight and a half hours!

'Yes. Thank you.'

I will make the most of my new-found energy, I tell myself when she leaves. I'll try out the tricks she has taught me. I attempt, again and again, to swaddle Ash, but even with YouTube's help, I can't do it – he thrashes and kicks until the muslin lies around him like crumpled chip paper.

Instead, I coo, stroke and rock him, exactly, I believe, as she did, but once more, I am a poor substitute for a professional. Ash flexes and waves his fingers as if casting a spell, as if willing me to vanish and her to appear. Whenever I try to hold him close and cuddle him, he stiffens and jerks, a lobster being held above a pot.

'How are you feeling today?' the nanny asks when I let her back in that evening.

'Much better, thanks,' I say; I don't want to admit my failures.

'Good,' she says, picking Ash up. He softens in her arms. 'It changes everything at this stage, when you've had a decent rest, I remember it well.'

'You have children?'

'One, yes. A daughter. Thirty-two now!'

'Grandchildren?'

'Not yet. I live in hope. Oh, Ash, do you need a clean nappy?'

'I'll change him,' I say, embarrassed. I can't even tell when my baby has soiled himself; I am incapable, incompetent.

'It is tough, doing it all by yourself,' she says, as I pull wipes from the packet. I wonder how she would know, but I am surprised to feel my eyes filling.

'I was on my own, you see,' she says.

'Were you?'

'Yes. Not by choice.' Memories skitter across her face.

'How was it?'

'Overwhelming, at the beginning, if I'm honest. The *responsibility*. And lonely. You have to take every offer of help, every offer of company you can get. That's my advice. But, you know, having her all to myself, it was a blessing, in the end. We were so close. We *are* so close. You'll have that. You'll be everything to each other.'

I can't sleep that night. This time, the silence isn't calming, it is oppressive. I have been conditioned to react to every whimper and when I hear none, I am triggered into high alert. *A blessing,* I hear her say. It will come. I will try harder with him and it will come.

But my mind is obstinate, restless, it pushes me back to New York, to the double thud of the taxis crossing the manhole covers on Avenue A, the showgirl exuberance of the sirens. To where I would rather be.

In the early hours of the morning, when I know it is time for his next feed, I open my bedroom door, quietly, quietly, and tiptoe to the kitchen for a glass of water.

She sees me and puts her finger to her lips. Ash is drinking from the bottle, his eyes closed.

I should be with him, I tell myself. How can I expect to bond with my baby if someone else is feeding him, hugging him, soothing him?

In the morning, I tell her.

'It's been so helpful, having you for a couple of nights, helping him get into a routine, giving me some sleep.'

'It's been a pleasure.'

'I think we'll be OK for the rest of the week.'

'Really? Are you sure?' Is she offended, or just surprised? It doesn't matter, I tell myself; it is the right thing to do.

'I'm sure.'

'Well, you have my number, if you need me again.'

'Yes.'

'All right. Good luck with it all, Stevie.' She is putting on her scarf now, gathering her things. 'He's a lovely baby.'

'Thank you.'

She pauses by the door.

'It will get easier,' she says. Then she smiles and closes the door quietly behind her, and we are alone again.

Twelve

Lex and I were standing on the rooftop of the club, waiting for the opening party to begin. It was a warm April evening, and the sun was starting to duck between the high-rises, setting their windows on fire. Far below, a line of black town cars hugged the kerb like dominos. A door opened. A series of flashes illuminated the sidewalk.

Lex looked at his watch. 'Showtime,' he said.

We rode the elevator to the ground floor.

'Are you keeping your cap on?' I asked him.

'Uh-huh,' he said.

I had never seen Lex without a beanie or a baseball cap on his head. I was beginning to wonder if Nathan's theory – that a rapidly thinning crown lay beneath – was correct.

'And those?' I said, pointing at the knitted sneakers he was wearing below his midnight blue suit.

'Yup,' he said.

We reached the ground floor and the doors opened.

'Holy shit,' whispered Lex. Right in front of us, under a sputnik light fixture in the middle of a thicket of men and women dressed entirely in black, was a tall man wearing an outfit identical to Lex's, from the woven sneakers right up to the baseball cap. It was the actor from Jess's dinner.

Lex walked towards him, his right arm outstretched. 'Love your look, buddy,' I heard the actor say. I'd written his name on the invitation's thick cream envelope and thought, *Worth a try*. He'd listened when I'd told him about the club, he'd seemed interested. I'd never thought he'd actually come.

I found Nathan standing at the top of a staircase, cocktail in one hand, mini fish taco in the other. 'Was I right about the dress?' he shouted above the chatter and laughter.

We'd spent the previous Saturday searching Soho for my party outfit – one that would, said Nathan, 'scream co-founder'.

'But I'm not a co-founder,' I'd reminded him.

'Exactly,' he'd replied.

'Yes, you were right about the dress,' I conceded. 'Although I don't know how I'll pay my rent this month and my hair keeps catching in these.' I pulled at the rainbow of faux gemstones that ringed the neckline.

'You look incredible,' said Nathan, flicking his fringe from his eyes.

'Thanks. I can't decide whether I feel more like me or less like me.'

'More!' said Nathan. 'Stevie Stewart has arrived.'

I laughed. We looked out at the shifting swarm of people below, a glossy Mexican wave. 'Can you believe how many of your bold-faced names are here?' I asked.

'Actors to the left of me, politicians to the right . . . Did you see the mayor? I keep having to remind myself I'm at a co-working space for geeks rather than the hottest bar in the city. You know who I met?'

'Who?'

'Your double. I spotted her at the bar.'

'Jess is here?'

'I couldn't believe how alike you are – I mean, she's older,

63

obviously, but the eyebrows, the mouth . . . I literally accosted her and said, "You HAVE to be Stevie's sister."'

'We do share a genetic code.'

'She told me she'd been looking for you all over, but she had to leave soon. That was,' he pulled out his iPhone, 'about half an hour ago.'

'She didn't look very hard.'

'You're not mad, are you? This place is packed. Anyway, she's . . . '

'She's what?'

'She's a chameleon, isn't she? Enigmatic.'

'In what way?'

'Well, she seemed to know everyone, I saw a ton of air-kissing going on before I went up to her; smiling and laughing and *intense* conversations, people leaning right in to talk to her.'

'She speaks really quietly.'

'Yeah, which I *love*, so unexpected in this city. Anyway, as you said, she's clearly a kick-ass in the boardroom. I mean, talk about well-connected. But when I got to her and told her who I was, she kind of retreated; she suddenly seemed sort of wispy and fragile.'

'She's always been a bit odd with my friends. Maybe you intimidated her.'

I couldn't find Jess. But for the next four hours, Google Map's blue dot seemed to hover directly above our building. Nowhere else existed.

When everyone had gone, Lex and I took the elevator back to the top of the building and dived behind the bar. 'The last green bottle,' he said, popping a cork and pouring two glasses.

'I guess we did it,' he said, raising his glass. 'Well done, team.' He passed me a glass.

'Thank you,' I said, and he didn't know, but I was thanking

64

him for all of it: the mosaic of yellow lights that rose towards Midtown and dropped into inky blackness at Central Park; the cabs that skidded and hooted far below. For giving me a foothold here; letting me in.

We held each other's gaze an extra beat over our glasses before we both smiled and looked back down at the traffic below, and that was the first time I wondered whether it would ever become something else.

Thirteen

Why a café with a children's play area was chosen as a meeting place is unclear. The eldest baby materialised only seven weeks ago. Squeezing a finger is its most vigorous action. The wigwam, the miniature kitchen, the rainbow abacus – none of them will receive a second's attention. Still here we are, six women and six babies of assorted shapes and sizes, all born within a month of each other, sitting around a trestle table on reproduction Eames chairs.

I regretted sending the night nanny away, of course I did. I cursed myself for it. I wondered, as Ash and I eyeballed each other in the early hours, what I was thinking, sacrificing three unbroken nights. How could next-to-no sleep help our relationship?

I was too pig-headed to ask the nanny back, but I could take the advice she'd given. Accept every offer of company, she'd said, so I reached through my black mood and broke my silence on the new mums' WhatsApp group. Perhaps, after the agony of seeing Ash with a pro, these amateurs could make me feel better about my parenting. Perhaps they were as lost as me.

I'd attended only half of the antenatal course's eight evening classes, held in a room with thin brown carpets and walls painted municipal white gloss. If a labour occurred prematurely, freckling the walls with afterbirth, they could, I supposed, be wiped clean. Work was the excuse I gave for my erratic presence. Between seven and nine in the evening my phone buzzed with emails from New York that required, I told my prenatal colleagues grandly, an immediate response.

In truth, it was the empty chair next to mine that kept me away. Everyone else came as a pair – or a threesome if you counted the nearly borns who kicked below clasped hands. The attention-deflecting lesbian couple I'd hoped for – anticipated, even – didn't show. A more heteronormative group you couldn't have imagined.

The midwife who led the course did her best, teaming up with me for massage sessions and quizzes about mucus plugs and when to call the midwife, but I'm sure the irony wasn't lost on her. Why bother with an understudy when there was no actor?

So it was a perverse sort of FOMO that made me succumb to the WhatsApp group, to write my number on the sheet as it was passed around the circle. That evening, the push notifications started to ping. I turned them off. But from time to time over the next couple of months, while I was waiting for the baby, I opened the app and dipped back in.

When I scrolled through what I'd missed, I found photos of the first minutes. Two faces, one ruddy with post-natal triumph; the other with existential horror, and something along the lines of 'Ruby Mae was born in time for tea. Family Wright couldn't be happier'. Then came endless conversations about feeding routines and poo colours and red rashes and crocodile smiles. When someone asked a question, everyone felt compelled to answer. It didn't matter that they were all as ignorant as each other.

I continued to lurk on the WhatsApp, contributing nothing. I suppose it was cruel, really, not to answer their queries, not to say, yes, he had arrived, safely; not to drop my own green message among the white ones. It was pure self-interest that made me stay. What if I had my own urgent question in the middle of the night?

When, eventually, I got in touch, the mums received me, the prodigal singleton, with open arms.

'Over here!'

'Here he is, the baby of the babies!'

'He's gorgeous!'

'How *are* you, Stevie?'

'I'm OK, thanks,' I say, unwinding my scarf. 'I'm sorry, I can't remember your name.'

The woman — long black hair, hollow eyes — flushes. Her mouth flatlines. She strokes the nest of auburn hair on top of her baby's head. It looks like a wig.

'We're Stanley and Katie,' she says.

I sit down and survey the group. Heads bow to babies. Sucking intrudes on silence. My own nipples prickle reflexively.

'So, is Ash sleeping?' asks another.

'Only three hours at a time, if I'm lucky.' Unwise to mention the respite Jess had bought me.

'Three hours? Already? That's amazing!'

'Is it? He's a monster during the day. His screams became even screamier this week.'

'He's three weeks now, isn't he?' says one in a pale grey bobble hat, no doubt an attempt to disguise unwashed hair. 'Maybe it's a Wonder Week,' she continues.

'Come again?' I say.

'They're developmental leaps,' she continues. 'Babies become really fussy at that time. Ash was a week late, wasn't he?'

'Yes.' Bobble hat knows my baby better than I do.

'So, he's actually four weeks old. That's a little early for the first Wonder Week, but perhaps he's advanced!'

'Undoubtedly.'

'Ha. Anyway, it's when they start to make sense of their environments.'

'I see,' I say. 'What can I do about it?'

'Nothing, really.' She smiles. 'Just buckle up.'

I pull out Rebecca's hand-me-down nappy bag and extract a baby bottle, thermos flasks of cold and hot water and a dispenser of milk formula. When I place the arsenal on the table, there is a collective intake of breath. *Bottle feeding!* I feel the room's oxygen levels drop. The wigwam in the corner appears to sag slightly.

'I started this week. I wasn't sure Ash was getting enough from me,' I say. Why can't I tell them the truth? 'I thought I was going to burst for the first few days, but it's passed now. Also: no mastitis – I think they just tell you that to put you off.'

The room is silent. Imagine how they'd react if I told them a complete stranger had looked after Ash two nights in a row.

'Right,' says Stanley's mother briskly. 'Anyone for another tea?'

'Yes *please!*' they all chant, as if she has suggested cake, or cocaine. Two-pound coins are proffered – what are we, students? Stanley-and-Katie go to the till to order four chamomiles and an Americano for me.

Another woman – a child, really; I remember thinking in the classes that I was old enough to be her mother – pats my arm. 'We haven't heard your birth story, Stevie!' she says.

Suddenly, I am in the hospital again, on all fours, each contraction a tornado, a staggering urge to push but the midwife has gone, she has left the room. I need her, I am blindfolded without her. How am I supposed to give birth on my own?

I'm terrified, we are going to die, the baby and I, and then another contraction floors me, and I hear a howl as sharp and loud as overhead thunder and I realise it has come from me.

I will the memory away, squash it into its box and slam the lid. It is not public property, my birth, it is not a story to be told to people I barely know.

'I'm going to nip to the loo,' I say to the woman. 'Would you mind keeping an eye on Ash for me?'

The toilets are at the other end of the café – they must be thirty metres away. For the first couple of seconds, I feel as if I've forgotten something – my handbag, perhaps, or a limb. But soon the warm light of relief dawns. A sense of clarity. I sit there long after I've finished peeing, staring at the bloody polka dots on my pad.

By the time I return, Ash is in another woman's arms and they are on to 'the dads'.

'He's *so* great with her.'

'He does all the night feeds.'

'The day after his paternity leave ended was the *worst*.'

'He's completely besotted. I feel quite jealous!'

When they notice me, the plaudits turn sour.

'He keeps pestering me for sex. I couldn't be less interested.'

'He pretends not to hear when she cries in the night.'

'He says *he's* tired all the time.'

'He thinks I'm on holiday. I'd like to see him looking after an infant all day.'

Is it for the benefit of the single mum? Save your breath, I think, my blood pressure rising. You don't need to tell me that a baby bends a relationship out of shape. Look at Mum and Dad, look at Rebecca and David. Ladies, you have barely begun.

You will hiss at each other in the early hours before the dawn, I heckle in my head as I drop six scoops of formula into a plastic bottle and each hits the bottom with a satisfying phut.

70

When he snores and you jab him in the ribs, you will realise it's the first time you've touched in weeks.

And yet.

Try to imagine for just one second what it would be like to do all of this on your own. Never having an extra pair of hands to help. No one to hold him when your dinner is getting cold; to take him when you need a shower or a shit.

I add 100ml of hot water and 100ml of cold water from their respective flasks. Try to imagine being screamed at sixteen hours a day for an entire month. I shake the bottle until the poison has dissolved.

'When's everyone going back to work?' I ask.

As Ash finishes his bottle, I plan my escape. This is not the support system I hoped it would be. My world is not theirs.

But when I start to gather my things – muslins, flasks, nappies, dummies, wipes, spread across the table like the contents of a crashed aeroplane – everyone else does the same. Then, one of them suggests a walk.

Half an hour later, I find myself at the end of a line of box-fresh prams advancing slowly up a hill between oak trees. There was a storm last night and it has littered the path with short, blunt limbs, garish white at either end.

I ran here early in my pregnancy, skipping over dog leads, catching fragments of conversations. The wood isn't far from the centre of the city: you can walk to St Paul's Cathedral in an hour and a half, to the club in about the same, but its elevation means you feel as if you are floating high above it. From time to time, I spy a flash of steel-and-glass tower between the trees like the wing of a kingfisher.

We walk up, passing a lurcher with iron-filing fur and a skiving teenage couple who cover smirks with hands when they see us, six women pushing six buggies in solemn single file. We pause at the top and the woman-child pulls out her phone. Suddenly, the group is all smiles, rearranging woolly hats and scarves, smoothing hair.

She holds the phone at arm's length and flips the screen so that we can see ourselves in the crosshairs: a merry band of mothers and me, in head-to-toe black, my hair in a severe bun. She presses the camera button, then five pairs of eyes leap back to their babies. There is a chorus of pings as the photo lands in the WhatsApp group. What fun I look with my bundle of joy, willing myself somewhere else, while the others fizz with the first hit of motherhood.

I stare at the photo again that evening and think of that moment on the hilltop, of those women, not a bad bone between them, their worlds wrapped in onesies and laid in branded buggies. I look at the member of the funeral party and it's her I feel sorry for, the woman who turns from one face to another to the shining city through the trees. Who looks anywhere except at the baby boy in front of her. Me.

But mostly I feel sorry for Ash.

Fourteen

I loved my place, or my *palace*, as it became known after a mis-spelling in an email to Nathan who never forgot it: 'It *is* a palace, Stevie, three-hundred-square-foot of prime East Village real estate.' It was pocket-sized but it was mine, my crumb of New York, with seventies-movie tenement views, craggy brick walls and herringbone floors, a bathtub so small I had to bend my knees to sit in it, and a minimalist cluster of fridge and two-ring stove between bedroom and bathroom that called itself a kitchen. 'Am I missing something, or is there literally no countertop *at all?*' Nathan had said the first time he visited.

For all its charms, my apartment didn't have a roof terrace or a trash chute or integrated aircon, as Jess's did, so when she went to Miami on a work trip and asked me to look after it, I packed a bag and took a cab downtown. I was delighted that she wanted me in her apartment again, that she had forgiven me sufficiently for moving out of it. And at the same time, I wondered if she was trying to remind me what I was missing.

I slipped my summer dresses, my fruit salad of reds and yellows and purples, on to wooden hangers in the space she had made for me in her walk-in closet – 'use my bedroom,' she'd said – and watched as they swung to a standstill next to her monochrome blouses and sleeveless shifts. They looked garish, my clothes, foolish. Then I noticed a grid of Polaroid pictures stuck to the inside of the closet door that I hadn't seen when I'd stayed, snaps of coordinated outfits that tracked the seasons. Wide-legged jeans with suede pumps and a cashmere rollneck. A black dress, knee-length boots in cracked leather and a biker jacket. Instructions for what to wear.

'Habits of successful people,' said Nathan when I told him; 'take notes.'

I did take notes; I behaved like Jess that week: visiting her nail bar where the manicurist gave me a double-take because we looked so similar; running up and down the river, past the helicopter landing pad, the piers, just as we'd done the weekend I arrived in New York.

I was scrupulously tidy, as she was. I even carried myself differently: I tried to glide like her, an effort not to scuff anything, smash anything. 'Have people over: Nathan, whomever,' she'd said, as if suggesting a playdate, but I didn't. I imagined disorder blooming like mould in a jar of jam. I couldn't risk it.

'That's not your usual direction of travel,' said Lex when he saw me crossing the road to the office one morning. I smiled; I could guess what he was thinking. I let the possibility hang in the air for a moment, then, 'I'm staying at Jess's this week,' I said.

'Back on the best side.'

'I like the east side.'

'Jess's is something else, though. That view.'

'You've been there?'

'My buddy Aaron dated her; we went round for dinner a couple times.'

'Oh.'

'She didn't tell you?'

74

'No.'

'It was, like, five years ago.'

'I take it Aaron cooked?'

'He's a chef, so, yeah.'

'Why did it end?'

'Dunno really, they had some big falling-out over something. Probably for the best. He's a good guy, mostly, big personality, but who'd date a chef? Man, those hours.'

When I got back to Jess's apartment that evening, I imagined her there with Lex and the chef whipping up something in her kitchen. Why hadn't she told me about him?

I realised I was hungry then; I'd order something in. But when I looked for her delivery menus – in the drawers beside the cooker where they'd been before; in the box on the coffee table – I couldn't find them. Perhaps they're in her desk, I thought, walking to the other end of the room. I paused before I lifted the lid. Was I snooping, intruding? No. It wasn't as if I was looking for her journal.

The takeaway menus were there, in a neat pile, and there was something else as well. It wasn't her diary, but it was, in a way, mine.

There were three fat stacks of pale blue airmail letters, each tied with a thick raspberry ribbon, and I recognised my own teenage handwriting and her old East Village address on the top one.

I sat down on the sofa facing the window and wound the blind down – was I shielding my eyes from the glare of the early-evening light or worried that someone would look in? – and pulled one end of the ribbon on the first pack.

I had forgotten the drawings. A pen-and-ink of the house from the bottom of the paddock. A charcoal cartoon of a classmate. A portrait of Jess and Rebecca copied from the photo on the mantelpiece: school uniforms, plaits. I was no art prodigy: the house looked flat; my sisters' features exaggerated; lips collagen-pumped, eyelashes too fluttery, but Jess had encouraged my drawing, complimented me on it, she had given me confidence. Crayons and charcoal arrived in the mail; an easel one birthday, a set of oil paints another. Coffee-table books from New York art museums – the postage must have cost as much as they did. Mum had been tickled by my hobby – 'So unexpected, an artist in the family,' she'd said – but Dad thought it was a waste of time – 'Mickey Mouse', he called it. 'Won't get her into a decent university; won't get her a proper job.' Was Jess's enthusiasm a deliberate effort to needle him from the other side of the Atlantic? Either way, the seed was planted. Drawing was an escape; it shaped the way I looked at things.

Scrawled between the sketches in round, upright handwriting was more evidence of Jess's impact on my childhood. *You were right about Louise*, I had written in one letter. *I was friendly to her in class and it took her by surprise, and she was friendly back, and I think it'll be fine now, so thank you, big sista.*

I cringed at the spelling, the heart over the 'i', but I wished I could remember what she'd written to provoke my gratitude; I wished I still had the letters she had sent me. I'd kept them in a shoebox in my room at home, forgotten about them. Then, a phone call from Mum one evening when I was living in London. 'I've been tidying up,' she'd said, 'that stuff under your bed: you didn't want any of it, did you?'

There was a gap of several months in the dates at the top of the letters I'd sent Jess after that. I remembered it now, how hurt I'd been; I'd tied myself in knots wondering where she'd gone. When they resumed, I could hear my plaintive pre-teen voice.

Are you OK, Jess? I haven't heard from you for ages.
Have you moved apartments? Are you coming home?
Please write. Or if you can't, please call.

After that, she was back, it seemed, as if nothing had happened. I was answering her questions about my birthday, my summer holiday, thanking her for gifts, updating her on friendships. I'd forgiven her, forgotten about it, children do.

I read every letter and tied the ribbons around them and put the bundles carefully back in the drawer.

My ardour for the palace had cooled by the time I left Jess's apartment at the end of the week. I'd miss the West Side light, the feeling of calm and order, not having to Tetris my belongings into every inch of space.

'I enjoyed thinking of you there,' Jess said when she called on the way back from the airport and I told her that everything was fine, the apartment was still standing. 'You know, the guest room will always have your name on it. If you ever feel like a change of scene, whether I'm in town or not, you're always welcome to stay.'

'Thanks, Jess,' I said as I bent down and slid my suitcase under my bed. I was tempted, but I knew I wouldn't take her up on it. For all its flaws, this was where I belonged.

Fifteen

'He's got the ears!'

My mother, pulling at the fingers of her gloves, her woollen hat still on her head, is leaning over the Moses basket.

'Has he?'

'Yes, look. I don't know why I didn't notice before.' I peer into the basket. 'The Stewart pixie ears, pointed at the top, can't you see?'

'Oh yes.' At least he doesn't seem to have the webbed hands Nathan claimed I did. 'Are you *very* good at swimming?' he'd said once, holding one of my hands up to the light, pointing at crescents of skin between my fingers.

My mother's second visit is less fleeting than the first – two days this time. She'd take the train down, she said on the phone the week before; Dad didn't want her driving in the dark, and she'd stay both nights at Rebecca's house. 'It was just so short last time,' she'd said, slightly breathless, 'I barely saw you both, but I know what it's like the first few weeks, visitors can be more trouble than they're worth, so *do tell me* if you'd rather I came just the one day.'

I worry that her excitement is out of proportion with what Ash and I offer – we are two mainly catatonic humans, we are no sold-out West End show – but perhaps I am underestimating the allure of escaping my father.

'Oh, my baby's baby! He's changed so much,' Mum says. *I haven't*, I want to say. *I am exactly the same as I was the last time we met, my heart numb.*

She plucks the hat from her head, exposing white curls. She has had the new hairstyle for more than a year and I'm still not used to it. 'What an angel.' I lean in again and see the bulbous eye sockets, the scaly scalp, breathe its oily smell. 'It knocks the breath out of me every time I look at him,' one of the post-natal mums had said, 'the *love*.' Perhaps it will help, having my own mother here: perhaps spending two days in her company will trigger something maternal in me.

'Stevie?'

'Sorry, Mum, miles away.'

'I'm so pleased for you, my darling.' She has said it every time I've spoken to her since I told her I was pregnant. I know what she is doing, she is atoning for the way she reacted when I first raised the idea of having a baby on my own, for the long pause when I told her I was pregnant. 'That's terrific news, Stevie,' she'd said eventually, but the beat she had missed had hung in the air.

'What can I do?'

'Just . . . take him.'

'Of course. Why don't you go and have a shower?'

It is a relief to be alone. I stand under the water, tracing the mould outlining the bathroom tiles with my finger, anything to avoid running my hands over my unfamiliar body, until the room is opaque with steam and the shower runs cold.

As I dry myself, I look at the poster above the loo, an ad for a gig at the New York club. My mind wanders to my maternity cover, Mike. 'Big shoes to fill,' he said when I left. Is he coping, I wonder? I should check in with him without making it look as if I'm checking up on him. I should schedule a keeping-in-touch day, ask Rebecca to babysit, set up a few meetings, find out about the plans for Christmas, the magazine, the progress on the new clubs. Remind Lex that I'm still here, that I'll be back before he knows it. Yes, that's what I'll do.

When I emerge, Ash looks up and bursts into tears.

'Oh darling, does Mummy look different now she's all clean?' my mother says.

'He's probably hungry,' I say. 'Time for his bottle.'

'And cake-time for you?' she says to me, as if I am six years old. 'I brought you one,' she says, putting Ash in his bouncy chair, a hand-me-down from Mira, and giving me a box. 'I'm afraid I didn't make it.'

'So I see.' My mother has never baked anything in her life. 'Thanks, Mum.'

We eat the supermarket cake and discuss other possible genetic commonalities. Then, 'Recognise this?' she asks, as she takes a rattle from her bag. It is a plastic sunflower with googly eyes and a smiley face that belonged to me.

'Of course.' She waves it at Ash and his eyes widen.

'And this?' My rainbow telephone-on-wheels. I close my eyes as Mum pulls it across the room by its orange string and the clacking sound takes me to the farm kitchen, the lemon-yellow cabinets, the terracotta floor. I open my eyes – I am in danger of falling asleep – and see Ash trying to turn his head towards the toy, Mum cooing encouragingly. Within minutes, he has passed out on his play mat, his tiny brain crisp with stimulation. I should have played with him like that; I thought he was too young. Guilt waves through the window.

'I think we should go out for lunch, Mum,' I say. My stock of frozen soups and stews is dwindling and, reluctant as I am to leave the flat, I feel I must show her something of the neighbourhood.

She looks uncertain. 'Not too far?'

It is a fifteen-minute walk to the High Street, but it takes us twice that long. Mum dawdles behind with the buggy, eyeing up her grey-and-brown surroundings like a newly released convict: people moving behind windows, electric cars plugged into charging points, helicopters overhead.

'Come on, country mouse,' I say, when they finally draw near me.

'Sorry, darling, I'm rather out of puff. Would you mind if we sat for a minute?'

The bench at the end of my road is permanently choked by diesel fumes and has a main-road view; I've never seen anyone use it. Still, there we sit. Mum puts her arm through mine. 'This is nice,' she says, over the noise of a passing bus. 'Precious moments, these.'

When, at last, we make it to the High Street, I scan the shopfronts for a restaurant with a changing table and menu gentle enough for an almost-eighty-year-old, reject the play café and the risk of another encounter with the mums, and settle on a pizza place.

'Very jolly,' says my mother, appraising the exposed brick walls and open-plan kitchen. 'Rather like New York, don't you think?' I nod at the pressed-tin ceiling above us.

'Jess is flying over next week, isn't she?' asks Mum when we've ordered.

'Yes.'

'I'm going to come down again, to see her – and you, obviously.'

'Great. Have you spoken to her recently?'

'We write. I think she's well. Thrilled for you, of course.'

'She didn't seem to be at first.'

'Well, it rather surprised us all.'

'Because I didn't have a man?'

'I know I'm very old-fashioned, darling, and I know things are different now, but yes, a man has *generally* been something of a prerequisite for having a baby.'

'Do you think Jess would have liked to have had one?'

'A baby or a man?' My mother pinches her earlobe, looks over at Ash, asleep in his buggy. 'You'd have to ask her that. And, you know, while *none* of us wanted her to go to New York, she has been very happy there.' In her mind it is an either/or. New York or children and a relationship. She is probably right.

'It's been good for her,' she continues. 'It was good for *you*. But I'm so pleased you came back. I can't tell you. I felt *bereft* without you here, the baby of the family. And I'm so glad I visited before you left. It was great, wasn't it? The three of us together in the Big Apple!'

She is good at evasion; we all are. I let her recall her holiday highlights, the view from the apartment, the Broadway musical she half slept through, while I think about the cloud Jess left under all those years ago.

She had come down from London for the weekend. She seemed tense, she told me she needed to talk to Mum and Dad about something, and on Saturday morning she called them into the living room. I listened at the door.

'It's time,' that's what she said. Then I heard Dad.

'London?' he shouted. 'Over my dead body.'

I didn't hear any more. Anticipating the door opening and Jess bowling out, I fled to the garden. When I saw her tears and asked what had happened, she just looked away.

She wanted us all to visit her in London, I thought. That was it. She was working as a management consultant there, and, unlike her university friends with their scarcely paid creative jobs, renting a flat on her own. 'I can't wait for you to stay, Stevie,' she'd told me, and she wanted Mum and Dad there too, to see what she'd achieved. She wanted them to be proud.

But she had underestimated Dad's antipathy to the city. 'Noisy and dirty, rude people, rubbish on the streets, and buildings blocking out the light,' that's what he always said. Her invitation had angered him, intimidated him. That was why he'd exploded, I thought. Later, I realised how excessive his reaction had been and what it was for Jess: the last straw of a haystack of arguments and indifference.

Rebecca stood at the kitchen door, the sun making a halo of her dark-blonde hair, as I helped Jess wash up after a lunch at which no one spoke. 'I'm sorry, Stevie, I'm going to have to go now,' Jess said, then bent to my height and hugged the breath from me.

She drove to the gate and paused as she checked for traffic. Had she changed her mind? When she turned on to the road, I walked back into the kitchen and saw the wet swirls like the swooshes of an expressionist painting lingering on the table she had wiped.

While none of us wanted her to go.

A few months after that, Jess moved to New York.

The service is slow, the pizzas mediocre, but the restaurant feels warm, the smell of baking carbs and melting mozzarella, the animated chit-chat of lunch-breakers – office politics, weekend synopses – and it is a relief to be among other people, sharing space with adults with jobs and textured lives.

'Who are all these at two o'clock on a Monday afternoon?' Mum asks, and I explain that they probably work nearby, and she says how lucky they are, having pizza for lunch. It makes me ask her about her near-miss with the working world, how I'd thwarted her plans.

'I didn't know you knew that,' she says, as if it is a guilty secret.

'You had to give up when I came along.'

'Yes. You weren't, well, we weren't really expecting you.'

I nod. 'I knew that, too,' I say. As if I could have been anything else, with an eleven-year age gap.

'I'm sorry, Stevie. It doesn't mean you were loved any less.'

'I never felt unloved,' I say. 'But did you resent me for it, for having to give up a career before it had started?'

She twists her wedding ring, bites her lip. Is it cruel of me to ask; have I gone too far? Perhaps I should add, *I would have.*

'I'd be lying if I said I didn't a little, from time to time,' she replies. 'I wanted to have my own life outside the farm – beyond motherhood. Intellectual stimulation. But now, would I have had it any other way? Of course not. The three of you, everything you've done with your own lives, that's achievement enough for me.'

I pass Ash to her. Compensation. She kisses his head, moulds her body to his.

'And, Stevie,' she says, 'your father, he's not good at expressing his emotions,' she pauses, as if giving me an opportunity to inter-ject, to say, *Well, he's always been good at expressing his disapproval,* 'but he's delighted you're back, too.'

'Is he? Is he going to come and see me and Ash? I've been won-dering.' I could hear my voice escalating.

'You know it's difficult with the farm, and it was evensong at the church yesterday, so . . . '

'Right.'

'He really did miss you. I do wish you two could get on. If you gave each other a chance, if you got to know each other again . . . You can't see it, but you're so similar: you, Jess and Dad.'

Where is she going with this? She has never seemed to want to throw us together before, my father and me.

'He'd like to make amends,' she continues, 'I know he would.

84

Will you think about it? I hate the idea . . . ' She stops abruptly, places her knife and fork together on her empty plate.

'Of what?'

'Nothing.'

At home, I put the kettle on, drop teabags into mugs. Mum sits on the sofa, leaning over Ash, tickling his stomach.

'Has he smiled yet?'

'He's only three-and-a-bit weeks, he's not supposed to yet.'

'Of course. You forget when they do things. He will soon. Lovely, that moment, when you finally get something back.'

I place our mugs on the table, open the cupboard and take out the tub of formula, a clean bottle from the steriliser.

'Would you like to give Ash his milk, Mum?' I say. I turn around. 'Mum?'

Her eyes are closed, her chin is on her chest. I take the checked blanket from the back of the sofa and drape it over her lap. I scoop Ash from the floor, sit back in the armchair, put the teat to his lips. *Here we go again.*

As he feeds, I survey my flat. The buggy folded by the door. The brick-red highchair at the kitchen table. A chain of paper-doll Babygros drying on the radiator and a knitted dinosaur on a shelf. None of it looks like mine. 'You chose all this,' I whisper. 'This is what you wanted.'

'I'm *mortified*,' my mother says when she awakes an hour later. She blames the previous night's fitful sleep – 'Don't tell Rebecca this, but the bed in the spare room is *not* comfortable' – she blames the long walk to and from the restaurant. We watch Ash, lying motionless on his play mat and I try not to feel irritated. I remember Rebecca's phone call before she arrived: 'Be gentle with her, Stevie. Don't forget – she's old.'

A ringtone sounds.

'My mobile! It's Dad. Yes, darling, I'm fine. *Fine*. They're well too. Ash? Yes, he's still the sweetest baby. I will. Speak later.' She hangs up. 'He sends his love. He's desperate to meet Ash, he really is. Perhaps you could come to us?'

I give a noncommittal 'hmm' as I fill the kettle again. When I turn around, Mum has lifted Ash from the play mat and they are twirling slowly around the front room together, hand in hand, cheek to cheek, like mismatched ballroom dance partners.

'Do you sing to him?' she asks me, and I don't want to say no so I pretend I don't hear as she begins to hum, then sing. She has a good voice, my mother, and I haven't heard music for weeks. Before Ash arrived, earphones were lodged permanently in my ears, my every move was sound-tracked, a shoebox of gig tickets under my bed, each one a memory. A woman in white sneakers standing on a stage in the dark. A man swigging from a bottle of wine between ballads. But then, the birth, and I don't know why, the music stopped.

When my mother sings, it reminds me of the tapes we played in the car, the same four or five over and over and over again until the ribbon wore thin: Elton John, Stevie Nicks, The Rolling Stones.

'Blue jean baby, LA lady,' she sings as they twirl, and it is so incongruous and so perfect, and I feel a smile lift my lips.

Sixteen

We had made something out of nothing, Lex and I.

The club was eighteen months old. Scores of members pushed open its unmarked door every day. New companies took shape under, and on, our roof: tech start-ups, creative agencies, non-profits. Inside, everyone was high on adrenalin and caffeine and *getting shit done*. It always took me at least an hour to reach the office upstairs, to weave through the laptops spotlighting their owners' faces with Python code and PowerPoint pitches, because everyone wanted to talk to me, to gesture to new friends, to the staff, to the art on the walls, and tell me how pumped they were to be part of it.

I was, too. I'd been sceptical about Lex's community-building mission when we first met. Wasn't making a lot of money his *actual* plan? I'd taken the job because my alternative was a flight back to London. I'd find something else later on.

But over time, my cynicism had faded. Whatever was driving it, it had value, what we'd built. It *was* a community; spend any time at the club and you'd see it: how the members interacted, hatched plans, supported each other – supported me, suggesting new recruits, making introductions. Everyone was talking about it, writing about it, tweeting about it, and I was the co-pilot. How could I not feel excited? I might sigh when Nathan talked about my Kool-Aid consumption – 'Glug, glug, glug!' he'd crow – but he was right: I believed in it.

I believed in Lex, too: his creativity, his work ethic. 'You know, people like to think successful businesses are just born,' he once said, 'but anyone can have a good idea; what it takes to make something is *work*,' and the struggles, the midnight food deliveries, the staring bleary-eyed at spreadsheets, they had threaded us together. 'We're like a club within a club, you and me,' he often said, raising his hand for a high-five. Was it just a natural side-effect of working so closely together, this connection we had? Yes, I'd tell myself firmly. That was all it was.

I was lucky to be inner circle, I knew that. The rest of the team – a handful when I joined, a roomful now – were envious. 'Flavour of the year,' the head of marketing once muttered as I walked past. He was tough, Lex, tyrannical even, but if he gave you a 'well done' it would echo in your head for a week.

I told myself not to become complacent. That was the other thing about Lex – I'd heard it from people who'd worked with him before. If you let him down once, you were out.

'You know, it's so different here,' I said to Lex as we walked down to the grilled cheese truck on Broadway one lunchtime. 'At my office in London people were constantly saying things like, "Is it only Tuesday? It feels like Friday," and, "Can it really be *four* hours until home time?" People seem to thrive on work in New York. It's refreshing.'

'I hope you're including yourself in "people"?'

'You know I am. It's exciting, what we're doing.'

We walked to Madison Square Park, sat down on an empty bench and opened our sandwiches.

'I think I've found someone for the start-up membership role,' I said.

'Fantastic. Who is he – or she?'

'She. She's very experienced, super-excited about the company – she described herself as a "fan-girl", actually.'

'Nice. And she gets it – that the role's about giving a home to businesses that aren't big enough for their own office yet, letting them benefit from our ecosystem – it's not some corporate play?'

'Totally. She had some great ideas; she's so plugged into that scene. I'd learn loads from her, I know I would.'

'Age?'

'Like, mid-to-late thirties?'

'*Hmm*. Married? Kids?'

'I didn't ask her that. I think she was wearing a ring, though. Why?'

'It's just . . . this is a young brand, Stevie.'

'Well, I'm over thirty. You are too, Lex.'

'That's different: we're leadership. We're targeting young Millennials; it makes sense to hire young Millennials. And I just want to make sure everyone we bring on board is a *hundred per cent committed*. You know?'

'I don't know what to say, Lex. I think she'd be committed; I think she'd be great. I don't think we should discriminate against experience – we should *value* it.'

'And I think you should keep looking, Stevie.'

I felt myself stand, smooth the crumples in my linen skirt.

'I'm going to go for a walk,' I said. 'I'll see you back at the office.'

I was fuming. The age question, the ring question, they made me uneasy – would I become less appealing as I aged? If – unlikely as it was – I ever got married? But more than that was the fact that Lex had undermined me, questioned my judgement, something he'd never done before.

I headed uptown, in the opposite direction to the club, on to

Broadway as it zagged across the twenties. The sky had turned granite above the art deco towers and high-rises.

I kept walking for another fifteen minutes until I found myself in Bryant Park and the deluge began. I sheltered under a coffee stand as I waited for it to pass and thought about what our disagreement meant. Was this it, my strike? Was I on my way out, on my way home?

I should ring Jess. She'd know what to do, whether I should show my teeth or back down. I took my phone out of my handbag and scrolled to her number. Jess, who had never put a foot wrong. What if she said I'd screwed up? What if she was on Lex's side? I put my phone back in my bag.

I was relieved when I arrived at the club and Megan, the office manager, told me Lex wasn't there. But when I got home after dinner and opened my laptop, there was a message from him. *yt?* it said.

The first-time Lex pinged me a 'yt?', shortly after I started the job, I answered '???', and he wrote back 'It means "you there?!"' and I felt as if I had learned the first words of a new language. Now, when we talked online, it was rarely in anything but acronyms and abbreviations.

y, I replied. I waited for the animated ellipses to morph into a reply.

lk, S, im sry. An apology?

k . . .

ive been thinkng &. . . yr right. Wow. I resisted the temptation to respond.

if she's the right person for the job u shd hire her.

sure?

sure. see how the trial goes.

k. gd, I replied.

90

I trust u.

k.

so, friends? Friends. So that was what we were.

y.

Seventeen

If a septuagenarian can sit on the floor waving a sunflower rattle, then so can I. I am a different mother the day after my own leaves. I will atone for three-and-a-half weeks of indifference in twelve hours, I tell myself that morning. Like a baking show contestant on her last life, I'll throw every ingredient at it.

First, I lie next to Ash on his play mat, batting the cloth animals hanging above it with an index finger, telling him what each is, offering a cluck or moo. He stares at them, dribbling. Would he turn his head towards me if he could? Would he giggle in appreciation?

Next, I play nursery rhymes and force myself to sing along, jiggling Ash in time to the music. He looks at me, at the goggle-eyed maniac I have become, unsmiling, unmoved. I persevere, through 'Humpty Dumpty', 'Twinkle, Twinkle', 'Hickory Dickory Dock', trying to ignore the absence of feedback. You can't expect approbation from a newborn, I tell myself.

I continue the Fun Mum routine after his nap, shaking the bottle of formula like Tom Cruise – 'The bar is open!' I declare. Finally, I read him a bedtime story, one of the board books Mira gave me, never mind that it will be months before he understands a single word.

I am worn out when we both go to bed, but I feel more positive than I have in days. *I can do this*, I think. The thought of another minute of it might make me shudder, but I *can* do it.

Then, a minor miracle. I give Ash his feed at midnight, and he does not wake again until six.

I have heard of this: it pops up on the WhatsApp group from time to time – *she slept through!!* – along with hands-in-prayer emoticons and multiple theories: a Wonder Week, a monster-feed, an extra half-hour – or in Ash's case, eight – on the play mat.

They never take advantage of their babies' random acts of kindness, though, these women, that's the irony. They lie, eyes open, stiff as boards, hovering their hands over their newborns' mouths to check for breath, whispering in their partners' ears – *Is she all right? Should we wake him?* The next day they are even more exhausted than the one before.

I, on the other hand, sleep for the six hours Ash sleeps, and wake feeling refreshed. My eyelids no longer flicker. I hum while I shower. When I open the shutters, I expect to see wildflowers poking through the paving stones, a double rainbow – I'm surprised to find my street as grey as always.

Still, I will seize this windfall, I think as I drink my coffee, beginning to feel a little wired now, I will do something with it, something that will prolong the high, because it will not come again. That's the other mistake parents make – they think they've cracked it after one good night. But I know it for what it is: an anomaly. I know that, nursery rhymes or not, tonight, Ash will wake at between five and eight minutes past the hour every hour, just as he did the previous six nights, and tomorrow I will find myself googling 'sleep deprivation – fatal?' again.

But what can you do, actually *do*, when you are the single mother of a tiny baby? I tap Instagram for inspiration. I see Nathan on the Westside Highway. He posted the picture only seven minutes earlier, but already it has over five hundred likes. I refresh the page and the likes grow.

'It's *super* superficial,' he'd said the last time I'd talked to him about his social media career. 'I miss the magazine. But no one wants words any more. They want pictures. Pictures pay. And if someone wants to give me a ton of cash for eating pre-shelled pistachios and posting about it, well, why the hell not?'

In his latest post, Nathan is flexing his right thigh while looking dead at the camera, as if about to take off down the Westside Highway. He always ridiculed me for my morning runs – 'I don't know why you bother, Stevie,' he'd say, 'you've got one of those bodies that burns calories by breathing.' Then selfie-induced vanity pushed him into a pair of sneakers. He looks so different now from the pliable specimen I first met it is as if his head has been placed on another man's body.

As I double-tap Nathan's post, I think of all those mornings I sprinted down the East River and my mind unknotted. That's what I need; I need to move, I need to get out, I need it for me and for Ash, for both of us.

I check the time. Eight o'clock. In an hour, I will feed Ash and put him down for his hour-long morning nap. He rarely sleeps at night, but he is a napping champ, and an hour is more than enough.

When he's dozing, I find my running leggings buried at the bottom of a drawer, a sports bra at the back of another and a T-shirt and zip-up hoodie in the laundry basket. I pull on the leggings hurriedly, coaxing the waist panel over my paunch, then accommodate my lopsided breasts in the sports bra.

I look at my reflection in the bathroom mirror. It is not a forgiving outfit. With my distended stomach and jelly thighs I am the 'before' picture in a weight-loss advertisement. How will I ever manage office clothes, clothes with buttons and zips? Even more reason to do this, I think. I extract my neglected trainers from the shoe pool at the bottom of my cupboard, give my teeth a brush, take another quick look at Ash and close the front door gently behind me. I am doing this for him as well as for me, I tell myself again, I am doing this for our mutual sanity.

I power-walk up the road, pumping my arms back and forth in an attempt to dislodge the flab that has appeared since I stopped exercising. I wait for the tick of remorse. It doesn't come. Why haven't I done this before? What possible harm could come to Ash, fast asleep in his Moses basket? He can't sit, let alone get out – he can't even roll. He is perfectly safe.

I yearn to run, but I don't, not this time. Walking briskly is enough to raise my blood pressure. I am puffing as I pass the newsagent at the end of the road, then the pub; I worry that some geriatric curtain-twitcher might notice I am alone, buggy-less, but I keep walking: no red ribbon draws me back.

I've been gone ten minutes by the time I decide to return. As I near the newsagent I remember I've run out of coffee.

'Afternoon,' says the guy behind the counter, 'no baby today?'

'My sister's looking after him,' I reply, 'and she's desperate for caffeine.'

'Right.'

Suddenly, there it is: guilt tugs at my conscience.

'Actually,' I say, 'don't worry about the coffee.' I put the bag back on the shelf and push open the door and the bell sounds, like an old-fashioned fire-truck, a warning.

I bolt the fifty yards back to my flat, pray I won't see anyone in the hallway, march up the stairs two at a time, listen out for a high-pitched wail and turn the key in the lock.

The flat is silent. I tiptoe to my bedroom and search the gloom for the Moses basket. Oh, God. Where is it? I remember I took it off the bed and put it on the floor. I crouch down and peer in. Ash's plump cheek is rosy on the white sheet. His chest rises and falls.

But it is dogged, the memory of pounding along the East River, the city ticking by, the discomfort of the first twenty minutes evaporating as I hit my stride, and my first solo outing only intensifies the desire.

I am right, of course. The night after his sleep-a-thon, Ash remembers that he is a newborn baby rather than a teenager and reverts to his regular schedule. I am tired the next morning, but not on-my-knees tired: I am determined to use what energy I have left.

I will be gone half an hour this time, no more.

It will be enough time to run to the hill where I was last with the mum group, where we stood in a circle and squinted at the camera in the low winter sun, and to run back again.

It will be enough time to feel the wind on my face and the concrete slap-slapping beneath my feet as I run to the top, to leap over labradoodles and cockapoos, eavesdrop on pensioners and buggy-pushers, to feel part of the city rather than shut away from it.

The sky is flat white with hopeful patches of forget-me-not as I close the front door behind me. I attempt to accelerate immediately this time, but for the first ten minutes I am stuck in first gear. Still, it is refreshing to be travelling faster than a walk; surreal to look down and see my thighs stretching my grey leggings taut as I pad along, left, right, my belly wobbling above them. As I pass the gates that lead to the path that snakes up the hill, I feel a burst of energy, and I am amazed when I make it to the top without pausing.

My phone says nine thirty. Enough time to catch my breath. I check off the valley of high-rises like old friends: the fifties tower block in the foreground; the diamond-patterned phallus and blinking pyramid way out east; all the newcomers germinating in the centre, cranes swinging over them like parents helicoptering above first steps.

It is when I start puffing down the hill that I feel something wet between my legs. At first, I have no idea what it is. I don't need to pee. Perhaps my period has returned, or the bloody discharge that gushed, then oozed after the birth.

Maybe I am imagining it, I think, and I try to ignore it, to focus on the spidery trees either side of the path, to enjoy being outdoors. But then I pass two forty-something women with amplified lips and porcelain cheeks and see their eyes sink to my crotch. When I turn back, I see smirks behind jewelled hands.

The toilets at the bottom of the hill smell of stale urine. I look in the mirror and gasp. My pale grey leggings have turned a deep slate around the crotch area. I hear someone enter the building and shut myself hurriedly in a cubicle. Bitter tears spring to my eyes. Thirty-nine and incontinent. What is this – punishment? For leaving a baby asleep, dead to the world, in a crib he can't get out of?

I take off my running top and tie it around my waist, arranging the arms so that they drape over the wet patch. I look in the mirror. It will have to do. I take a different route home and I sprint as best I can.

When I open the front door, I hear voices. The downstairs neighbours. Then I hear a baby crying. It doesn't sound like Ash. It sounds like torture, like terror, like the end of the world.

I tear up the stairs two at a time.

'He's been screaming the house down for at least ten minutes,' says the woman.

'But he was fast asleep when I left.' I fumble for my key, my hands shaking, stab it in the keyhole.

'We heard you slam the door. We were about to call the police,' says the man.

'I just popped out for a pint of milk,' I say desperately, my voice see-sawing. The man and the woman stare at my empty hands. 'I forgot my money,' I say. At last, the door opens.

'We'll be fine now,' I say. 'Thank you for helping.'

'You shouldn't . . . '

'I know. I won't again.'

I race to my bedroom and find Ash in the Moses basket, face screwed tight, eyes spitting tears, mouth a black ululating hole. When he sees me, he screams harder.

I kneel down and pick him up.

'Hush,' I whisper. I hold him so tight I could crush him. 'I'm so sorry, baby,' I whisper between sobs. 'I'll try to be a mother now, a real one. I'll try, I'll try.'

Eighteen

Mira arrived at my apartment with a suitcase the size of a coffin from which she unloaded armfuls of sweets and crisps, teabags and chocolate. I hadn't the heart to tell her that I could buy each packet, box and bar at the grocery store on Union Square.

'What's the plan for tonight?' she asked.

'I thought we could start with sushi at this new place on Second Avenue,' I said, pulling the air bed from under my sofa and plugging it into the wall.

'I don't really feel like sushi this evening,' Mira said, as the bed began to inflate with a whine.

'No problem,' I said, 'Manhattan is your oyster: pick a food, any food. Actually, how about oysters?'

Mira bit her lip.

'Burgers, then? There's that place in the West Village we went to last time?'

'Perfect.' Mira lifted a pile of neatly folded clothes from her suitcase and put them on the bookshelf I had cleared for her.

'After that, I got us on the list at this bar in Chinatown that specialises in absinthe – it's like an old-school apothecary. Nathan and a few others are going to meet us there.'

'Right,' she said.

'And then, depending on how you're coping with the jet lag – I mean, I can always give you a bit of *help* – I thought we could all go to this club nearby.'

'I am feeling pretty tired, actually . . . ' Mira looked longingly at the air bed. It was three o'clock in the afternoon.

'I bet you'll get a second wind,' I said. 'I bet we'll all be back here yacking when the sun rises.'

We were finishing our burgers when I saw that her glass of wine was full. I glanced at the bottle: perhaps she'd refilled it and I hadn't noticed.

'Mira!' I said. 'You're *not?*'

'Not what?' The slightest smile was beginning to colour her face and she was trying to stop it, as if I was a toddler who had done something naughty and she didn't want to laugh.

'You're bloody pregnant, aren't you?'

The smile broke free. Everything smiled: her eyes brightened, her eyebrows and ears lifted.

'Yes!' she said. 'Only a little bit, though; only seven weeks.'

'Why didn't you tell me?' I took a gulp of wine and looked away. I felt hot and faint.

'I was waiting for the right moment. Anyway, we haven't told anyone yet, not even our parents.'

The chatter and the rock music in the packed pub had risen to a deafening pitch. I couldn't focus.

'You're so young,' I said at last.

'Stevie, I'm *thirty-four*. Thirty-four isn't young. You want children one day, don't you?'

'Yes. Not yet, though. It seems so . . . soon.'

'We've been trying for months, since the wedding.'

'But you've just been made features editor!'

'Exactly, it's a good time to take a break. My career hasn't ended, Stevie; I'll take a year off and then I'll go back to exactly the same job I'm doing now, maybe work from home one day a week. Look, it'd be nice if you congratulated me. You're my best friend and I'm pregnant, for God's sake, I haven't slept with your boyfriend or robbed a bank.'

I stood up, reached across the crowded table and put my arms around her narrow shoulders. 'I'm really sorry, Mira. Congratulations. You'll be such a great mum.'

'And one day, so will you,' she said, and it sounded like a threat.

That weekend I saw the city through Mira's eyes.

I saw that there were no children in downtown Manhattan. The city was not built for them. Sidewalks rose and fell like skateboard ramps; subways lay buried at the bottom of endless flights of stairs. This was no place for a buggy; you didn't have to have seen *Battleship Potemkin* to know that. Manhattan's apartments were store-your-shoes-in-the-oven small, the walls so thin you could hear the couple next door arguing and make-up fucking. Where would you put a baby? Who would put up with its shrieking?

There were no gardens; nowhere for sandpits or tricycles, only rooftops covered in asphalt. There was almost no one older than forty or younger than twenty-five. Downtown: it was a playground without any playgrounds. When Mira pointed out what looked like a primary school a few blocks from my apartment on the way to breakfast, I shook my head. I had never seen a single child enter or leave its gates. It was probably a film set.

We arrived at the restaurant I'd booked for breakfast the following morning, a tiny place with blackboard menus and waiters in leather aprons, early for our ten o'clock reservation. I was surprised it was open.

Mira was jet-lagged, or maybe just pregnant, and, having gone to bed and risen so early, I also felt jet-lagged. I drank black coffee and Mira reviewed the embryo-friendly menu options.

'Why is everyone here on their own?' she whispered. In the booths and at the bar overlooking the kitchen were men and women wearing work-out clothes and eating kale and eggs while reading the Sunday papers.

'It's what you do in New York.' I shrugged. 'I often eat by myself.'

'Don't you feel lonely?'

'Not at all. I love it.'

'I can't remember the last time I had a meal alone,' she said.

And now you never will again.

Mira and I met in the student bar the first term of university, history and history of art freshers. We bonded over alcopops, eye-rolled at the boarding-school hurrahs and walked off the early hours through soot-blackened streets. We drifted through the next decade and a half together, sharing damp flats during our first jobs, putting nascent flings and career woes to rights with cheap wine. Each other's plus one at all-night house parties and first-wave weddings; on anti-war marches and budget beach holidays.

We are not the mirror image of each other, quite the opposite. Her upbringing, in a London borough heavy on the chlorophyll, with double-doctor parents, private school and piano lessons, was not mine. I am tall with big everything: mouth, jaw, eyes. 'Striking' is the adjective people use if they're being generous, as if I'm about to land a punch. Mira is a delicate thing, five-foot-nothing with chicken-bone limbs, thick black hair and eyes the colour of honey. My smile is wider; her laugh is louder. We both tread the cracks between introvert and extrovert, take deep breaths before parties and presentations, and, five minutes in, forget to fear.

Moving to New York didn't change our friendship. Mira told me she'd never forgive me if I didn't go. You miss a hundred per cent of the shots you don't take. When she visited the month after I'd arrived, we returned to the red-and-white restaurant Jess had taken us to on the Westside that first time. The neighbourhood was so different now, rooftop bars, rooftop swimming pools, the meat vans and the smell of stale blood gone, the ragged edge gone. But it felt the same between us – we felt exactly the same.

Then her wedding, the following year. I worried, as I followed her up the aisle. But by the time the photos had been slipped into their frames and the veil was stored in the attic, we were back where we had begun.

'There are some things Pete will never understand,' she'd whispered down the phone, her hushed voice bouncing off the bathroom tiles.

But now? Now, a clump of cells had burrowed between us. Mira had something I didn't; something I wanted but had no path towards.

There was a silence after I asked for the check at the restaurant. It was our first-ever proper silence. There had been comfortable, companionable silences, but this one was excruciating. It had been prowling since Mira arrived; I had seen it in the distance as we exhausted our common ground, took wrong turns: back to the baby when I asked about Pete, to a dead-end when she brought up Jess – did we see each other often? Was I getting to know her better?

Desperate for a way out, we both looked up. I heard her exhale. She saw me hear. We looked down.

*

After breakfast, I scrolled through my mental list of 'Things Brits like to do in New York', a game Nathan and I played inspired by the countless times I had hosted friends from home, all of whom requested the same 'only-in-New York' experiences.

The itinerary included a discount shopping spree downtown. Brunches in restaurants where everyone else was a tourist because real New Yorkers ate breakfast and lunch, but the loud music drowned out the foreign accents. A walk on the High Line. Cocktails at every opportunity.

Mira's visit was going to be different. No schedule was necessary. We would amble from block to block, content in each other's company.

But her – our – new predicament had forced me to recall my list and when I remembered the last, illicit, jet-lag-busting entry, I cringed. 'It's so cheap in America! And they deliver in thirty minutes!' Nathan liked to say in his sing-song Dick Van Dyke.

'Let's go to a museum,' I said. We took the subway up to 86th Street and trailed the black railings of a denuded Central Park to the Guggenheim, its snail curves powder-white against the blue sky. Then we walked the winding path to the museum's summit, and Mira leaned, exhausted, against the half-wall and I followed her amber eyes as they corkscrewed to the concrete floor, where a vast, steel sculpture in the shape of a Zeppelin lay, like our friendship, leaden and immobile.

Nineteen

After the run, I retreat. *You left your baby!* I whisper to the ghoul in the mirror. It was an act worthy of a daytime talk show, a tabloid front page. I will ground myself: there will be no more outings, neither with Ash nor without him. Locking the door is the only way to make sure he is safe.

I try to summon the enthusiasm for the jungle gym, to put on music and twirl him to it, but I can't. I'll hold him, I'll keep him alive – that's all I'm capable of today.

My phone vibrates on the sofa beside me. Mira, again. The voicemail icon appears on the screen. Then a text.

U ok, S? I've been calling . . . Call me back? Or I'll try again later. Hope all well.

She calls every other day. I answered at first, tried to sound bright, but I can't keep pretending, not to her, and I can't bear the shame of admitting how I feel, what I've done and haven't done.

'Tectonic plates shifting.' That's how Mira described Beatrice's birth, four years ago, a life remade. How could I possibly understand? Since then, she has managed to balance Beatrice and the big job, she has found it easy, spinning plates like a circus professional, always in one moment or the other, focused, fulfilled – that's the impression she gives.

I thought our paths would coalesce once I had my own baby, once we were on the same plain again, but they have continued to diverge. And so, today, I don't answer.

I think back to the flat we shared before I moved to New York and she moved in with Pete, when things were easy between us. I see the road from the station, shiny with drizzle and red taillights, the smell of chlorine sluiced over fish innards from the market. I think of what happened when we lived there. Of Will. Of Mira's part in that relationship. How it brought me all the way here.

The flat had been advertised as 'shabby chic' in a nod to the interiors trend of the time, but the chic was well-disguised. Still, it had what we needed: a box room for me, subsidised, in the early days, by the Saturdays I spent selling white lies in expensive clothes shops. A bedroom with a window and a cupboard for Mira, whose parents supplemented her reporter salary. And an open-plan living room with a table that sat ten.

Everyone crowded around that table at one time or another: the upstairs neighbours, uni friends, work friends, school friends. We called them dinner parties, though it was too generous a term for the level of hospitality we offered. Mira did the table setting and drinks pouring; I liked standing at the kitchen counter with my back to the party, in it and out of it, as I chopped onions, ladled boiling chicken stock into risotto, grated parmesan.

'You? Cook?' said my New York friends, most of whom never even saw the inside of my East Village apartment, when I talked about my domesticated past. The food was always late, or overdone, or not quite right, or all three, but no one minded.

One night, when Mira said Pete wanted to invite someone, I

didn't think anything of it. Then a tall, unmade man with black hair like a Russian fur hat bellowed in. He held an expensive-looking bottle of wine that everyone said we must open immediately because it didn't look like the kind that should wait until the eighth glass, and I forgot what I was supposed to be doing with the bag of frozen peas in my hand.

He was called Will, he lived in Manchester and he was a surgeon.

'You don't look like a surgeon,' I said. There was an appealing air of chaos about him.

'Next time I'll wear a green cap,' he replied.

Mira sat me next to him and I couldn't work out whether it was a set-up — I would never have agreed to one — but suddenly, I wasn't aware of anyone else. He told me about meeting Pete at medical school; about the stresses and satisfactions of his job, and the hours drifted past in a haze.

After the risotto, I served meringues with whipped cream and defrosted berries, summer fruits in winter, and their juices pooled around the white mounds like bloody moats. He stabbed and splintered the meringue and when he put down his spoon, he brushed his hand against mine as he reached for the wine and I caught my breath.

Later, he talked about his mother, how she'd passed away when he was a teenager, and that was why he'd become a doctor, and his voice softened. Then it was three o'clock and it was just the two of us, everyone else had left.

'Shit, I'd better go,' he said. 'I'm working tomorrow.'

'Where are you staying?' I asked and regretted it because it sounded as if I was inviting him to sleep over and I wasn't.

'My brother's.' He smiled.

As we sat on the sofa waiting for the cab, he asked if he could kiss me, and it sounded so formal, so old-fashioned, and I said,

'You may,' in a silly voice. He tucked my hair behind my ear and leaned towards me and his eyes were the colour of slate and he tasted like blackcurrants and the beginning of something.

'Well?' said Mira, when I opened my box-room door late the next morning. She was sitting in her dressing gown at the kitchen table with a pot of coffee.

'Thanks for telling me,' I said, walking towards the cupboard.

'Look, Stevie, I know you hate the idea of being set up. It's just . . . you're amazing, and the only time you ever go out with anyone they're *children* like Tom and Max. You haven't had a serious boyfriend in all the time I've known you.'

'Come on, Mira, Tom ran a restaurant.'

'For about three months.'

'And Max had his own production company.'

'Funded by the bank of Mum and Dad.'

'That's a bit rich . . . '

'OK, OK. But neither of them had any intention of having a proper girlfriend. Neither of them was in the slightest bit worthy of you.'

'Why are we even talking about them?' I said. 'Anyway, I'm fine being single, you know that. I like it. It's easier.'

'You don't know how you'd feel if you were in a proper relationship. I know you find it difficult opening up but perhaps that's because you've never met anyone worth opening up *to*. Was it really that awful sitting next to Will? He's a proper person with a proper job; he's *hot* and you seemed to be getting on really well.'

I opened the cupboard door. It pivoted awkwardly on its single hinge.

'*Stevie*.' Mira spread her left hand flat against her cheek. 'Please say something.'

I placed a mug on the table and poured coffee to the brim.

'You're smiling!' she said.

My first date with Will, a week later, wasn't like all the other first dates, those reluctant stumbles into relationships in pubs with pints and crisps and other people. He booked a table for two at a tapas restaurant in Soho. I wore heels.

'What would you like to do instead?' he asked, after I admitted I was tiring of working in television.

'I'm not sure,' I said. 'Something with a bit more permanence, maybe. You spend months on a programme, and it finally runs and sixty minutes later it's all over. And the hierarchy, the politics. It's exhausting.'

Spring came and I went up to Manchester, cast an appraising eye over Will's bachelor pad – the heavy pine furniture, the neon street art in white frames – and wondered if I'd ever live there. I nodded when he said all his friends were out of town; it was a shame, they'd been hoping to meet me. A few weeks later, he invited me, at the last minute, to join him in Venice – Venice! – after his conference there finished, and we drank hot chocolates at a baroque café on St Mark's Square and looked up at the cherubs and saints and patrons that gazed from the ceiling frescos until our necks ached.

All the while, the declarations kept coming, extravagant – 'You know I'm crazy about you?' – but never cloying, and, though we were becoming tangled up in each other and I felt everything he said and more, I did my best not to reciprocate. Hush, I said to myself. Not yet.

Then, one night, five months in, after too many beers with the mockneys at the pub, I offered what, I suppose, was a sign of intent.

'I wish we lived in the same city,' I said.

For a second, there was silence down the phone. When he told me about his last operation, how relieved he had been when the patient had woken up, I wondered if I had spoken only to myself.

'My sister, Jess, is in town next weekend,' I told him the following week. 'She doesn't come back from New York very often . . . She'd like to meet you.'

'I'd like to meet her too,' he said, but his voice sounded thin and flat.

'Are you OK?' I asked.

'I'm fine. Just tired. Just your typical tired medic.'

The next day, his shifts changed and his visit to London was aborted.

'You don't suspect foul play, do you?' Jess asked, when she arrived at the flat and I told her Will wouldn't be coming.

'What do you mean, that his shifts haven't actually changed, or that he changed them himself?'

'Well, either.'

'Why should I?'

'No reason. So everything's OK with you two?'

'Of course. It's wonderful – *he's* wonderful.'

'Good.'

But when Will and I spoke on the phone the week after, it was in different keys. I talked about my day in an airy lilt I barely recognised.

'You're being completely neurotic,' Mira said, as she unpacked the shopping later that evening, slamming a tub of protein powder the size of a bucket on the table. Pete's. He had practically moved in.

'Will can't be gushy for ever,' Mira continued. 'No one can.'

That weekend, our half-anniversary, Will and I didn't speak at all. I waited and waited. Checked my phone wasn't on silent.

Flicked through the slings and arrows of outrageous texts he'd sent, the future trips, the flights booked, the multiple 'miss you's. Then the recent messages with no plans, no hearts bursting, no virtual sighs or swoons, their sign-off 'x's, which had once formed battalions, diminishing rapidly: six, five, four, three, two, until only one lonely, capital kiss remained. X.

'It will end,' Mira said, weeks later, when I was past the feather-spitting and the convulsed sobbing and on my way to the quiet pain. 'Trust me, in three years' time you won't even remember his name.'

I would remember his name. His name, his grey eyes, the ripple of his laugh and the weight of his hand. I would remember him because, when I finally raised my head above the swamp, filled my lungs and worked out which day it was, I realised I had missed a period.

But more, way more than that, I remembered him because I didn't let people in often, Mira was right about that, and Will had kicked the door down.

I didn't want people to think I was moving to New York because of Will. I'd remind them that my sister lived there, that was why I was going. That and the sense of possibility – 'What first attracted you to the City of Dreams?' I'd quip. They'd nod and talk about skyscrapers and cocktail bars and cocktail bars in skyscrapers, as if that was what I'd meant, and they'd say they'd come and visit, that they were pleased for me, it was what I needed, a fresh start.

Mira saw me off. When my gate number flicked up on the flight board, we enclosed each other in a long, *so this is it* hug. 'I hope Jess is waiting for you at the other end,' she said, and I left with her tears damp on the shoulder of my parka because she was small and I was tall, we were the awkward couple.

I wasn't running away from Will, but he followed me on to the plane, he stared at me from inside the overhead locker as I wedged my parka into it, from the cup dimple in the folding table as it fell and I pinned it back up. For eight hours, through rustled newspapers and new releases, sweet wine, stale air, I thought about him and tried not to think about him, and I hoped by the time I pushed my luggage past the sniffer dogs and into the city, he would be gone.

Twenty

'Mira's pregnant.' I'd met Jess for a walk on the High Line.

'Wow,' said Jess, 'that's big news. Seems like yesterday you two were here after your finals.'

'I know. It's a bit sudden, isn't it?'

'Is it? She's been with Pete for years, hasn't she? And you are in your thirties.'

'I know,' I said as we sat down on a bench. 'I guess it just feels as if our lives are going in different directions.'

I was hoping for some reassurance from Jess. Friendships see-sawed, she'd tell me, that was just what happened. Or perhaps she'd extol the virtues of a child-free life. But she didn't do either.

'Is that what *you* want?' she said; she couldn't say 'baby', I expect she thought one might appear if she did. Even so, it stunned me, her response: she'd never asked me that before. And how should I reply? A yes would undermine the choices Jess had made; a no would be a lie.

'I haven't thought about it,' I said instead.

She nodded, looked relieved, but then she said, 'Stevie, I . . . '

The sentence lay hanging. Embarrassed for her, I led her back to stable ground: I told her about the argument I'd had with Lex.

I couldn't help wondering what she'd stopped herself saying, though. An admission of regret? A cautionary tale? She'd get there, I told myself. She'd open up another day.

My disagreement with Lex, it turned out, had been a temporary blip. Perhaps he'd just wanted to flex his authority or check I wouldn't buckle. In the months that followed, my responsibilities had grown.

'I want you to be my number two, Stevie,' he'd said. 'I want you to head up marketing as well as membership, and I'd like Ted to report to you on design. You have a great eye, no one gets our aesthetic better than you do, and I need to focus on operations and expansion.'

'What about Hannah? She won't like that. Or Ted.'

'Ted will get used to it, and Hannah's going to be leaving us.'

'Does she know that?'

'Not yet.'

As our relationship had strengthened, the team at the club had begun to fall apart. It wasn't only the people that Lex was picking off like a sniper who were leaving; several had quit, and the restlessness of those who remained was palpable, like the seat-squeaking you hear in a movie that goes on too long.

'It's a couple things,' said Megan, when I asked her, early one morning, what was happening.

'First of all,' she said, 'the club has a great reputation, so people are getting calls.'

'Right,' I said, and wondered why no one had called me.

'Second of all, people don't feel that invested in the company.'

'What do you mean?' I asked.

'I mean, Lex and you run the club, which is fine,' said Megan, 'but the rest of us don't really know what the plan is, what direction the company is taking, if there is a direction *at all*, apart from random firings, and, you know, we want to. We want to feel like we're part of the *bigger picture*.' She paused, ran her right hand over her left arm, which was sheathed from the shoulder to the wrist in butterfly tattoos so realistic that the first time I saw them I expected them to take flight.

'You know, members ask the staff all the time if there's going to be another club, if you're going to put on events here, networking opportunities, extend the opening hours, how business is going,' Megan continued, 'and we want to feel that we know some of the answers, and that it's all of us, not just you and Lex, going off for your secret lunches and talking about whatever you talk about.'

Lex had greeted the Megan revelations with an eye-roll. 'What are we supposed to do, invite twenty-five people to every board meeting?' But when I told him I predicted the haemorrhage would continue without intervention, he accepted that a solution needed to be found. We would have weekly All Hands meetings, even though they would inevitably become, Lex said, 'a platform for people to vent about pay rises and stock options and three-sixty reviews and' – he spat this one – '*flexible working*.'

Before that, I should organise a company outing, he said. 'Kids in their twenties love all that team-bonding shit – sports, free beer, free junk food.'

'You mean a baseball game?'

'Nah, something we can actually *do* together. Choose something you're shit at, Stevie, something that'll make you look fallible, approachable, you know? Like, one of them.'

It wasn't hard to choose: I was shit at all sports. I chose bowling because it offered booze and snacks and silly footwear, and because there was an alley two stops from the club, and the next Thursday after work, that was where we went.

Two hours, a hot dog and a couple of beers in, Lex still hadn't made it. At first, I pulled my phone from my back pocket every ten minutes and looked for a message. Nothing. How dared he? This was his idea, not mine.

But gradually, I forgot about Lex, about Mira, about Jess; I started enjoying myself. It was working, the bonding effort. I was, predictably, a bowling disaster: I must have thrown that ball thirty times and not once had the animated little guy in the Mexican hat leapt on to the screen above our lane to proclaim *STRIKE*.

I went to the bar for another round. Megan was already there.

'So is Lex actually coming?' she asked.

'Of course. He's just finishing up a presentation.'

'Right.' She leaned in, tequila on her breath. 'Is there . . . ?'

'Is there what?'

'Is there anything going on between you and Lex?'

'What?'

'I just . . . I shouldn't have asked.'

'Of course there isn't.'

'Sorry, I . . . Are you mad at me?'

'I'm not mad, only, *dumbfounded*.'

'It's just that you spend a lot of time together . . . '

'We *work* together.'

'Yes, but you've always seemed . . . '

'What?'

'Like, super close. I often catch you laughing about stuff together.'

'I'm pretty funny.'

'And you arrive and leave together fairly often.'

'We often finish work at the same time.'

'I shouldn't have said anything,' she said again.

'Don't worry about it,' I said airily. Quashing the evening's good vibes was the last thing I wanted. 'And please, if you're not the only person to think this, do tell the others there isn't a grain of truth to it.'

'Sure. Sorry again, Stevie. Forget I said anything.'

I tried to make a joke out of it. 'I mean, as if I'd be interested in Lex!' I said, and just then Lex strode into the room, and he smiled and pushed his beanie up slightly so that his widow's peak showed, a tiny arrowhead of brown hair, pointing down.

I had tried, persistently, to quell any fantasies I might have had of an office romance. Every time I thought we might be straying beyond the bounds of regular co-worker interaction – the almond croissant he left beside my laptop, a business book he'd raved about slipped into my bag – I had a word with myself. Lex was a considerate colleague, that was all. He needed me. We got on. We had an intimate *working* relationship.

Anyway, he was the kind of guy who didn't date anyone without a Wikipedia entry; he wouldn't be interested in me. I'd seen him in action. We were at a restaurant in the West Village, Nathan and I, sitting together at the bar, and I went to the bathroom and spotted him. It wasn't until the waiter had come to take our order that he'd seen us, given us a little wave, and then his date had swivelled, and she was perfect: a model, clearly; glossy, with yoga arms and wide eyes and Upper East Side cheekbones, the sort you don't get in England.

'Stunning,' Nathan had muttered, and the next time we looked they were gone. At the club the following morning, I said 'Good evening?' to Lex, because I had to say something, it would have been weird if I hadn't, but my intonation had been off, and it sounded as if I was wishing him a good evening at eight in the morning and he just grinned.

No, Lex was not an option. I must uncouple my work and personal lives, I must devote my attention to the meaningless liaisons that were there to be picked like roadside daisies, enjoyed and then forgotten, zero risk of emotional damage.

I had, in the past few months, discovered both a talent for

117

and an appreciation of casual dating. Nathan had dredged up straight friends for me, and others whose sexuality was not so well-defined but were no less entertaining, and I had begun to think that they suited me, New York's ambiguous mating rituals.

I liked wondering whether they'd text afterwards, and, if they did, deciding whether to answer, and how long to leave it. Two hours? Two days? I liked the lack of expectations. That no one was ever staying for breakfast, that no one was looking further than next week, that the only certainty was that you wouldn't end up together. Lex? Lex, I kept telling myself, was a false lead.

Eventually everyone gravitated to the bar. We were all getting on, and I was beginning to worry about my hangover. Despite my internal monologue's best intentions, I found myself wondering if Lex was looking at me, if it was his gaze I could feel on my neck, on my cheek. *Stop it*, I told myself, and suddenly I felt exhausted, and I hunted for my coat and scarf under a vast pile beside a pin-ball machine, hoping I could slip out undetected. Someone said, 'Hey, Stevie, you're not going already, are you?'

'Afraid so. It's late,' I replied. 'You kids keep going, though.' But then Lex beckoned and said, 'Stevie, over here!' and I hesitated, then walked towards the bar, and he handed me a vodka tonic, and I put down my bag.

Twenty-one

I lay out cotton wool balls and a towel, dip my fingers in the water, then lower Ash gently on to the lounger. I've started to bathe him every evening, even though the internet tells me I only need do it three times a week. Ash seems to like it, or at least he rarely cries, and I enjoy it, too. It is the one predictable part of the day: when Ash feeds and sleeps is up to him, despite my efforts to influence them, but bath time I can control. Bath time, I'd go as far as to say, I'm good at. So now, at seven o'clock every evening, here we are.

As I wipe Ash's tummy with the wet cotton wool, I think of Mira bathing Beatrice the first time I met her. What a risky endeavour it had seemed, how vast the responsibility.

It was Beatrice who lit the torch paper, who put the vague assumption that, somehow, I was meant to be a mother, into focus.

Despite what had happened in New York, the sundering of our friendship, Mira made me an 'oddmother', and I met Beatrice the day before the ceremony.

When she flashed her pale brown eyes at me, I saw Mira. She could belong to no one else.

'She is you,' I said.

'You think? I can't see it.'

'Blinded by love.'

'Well, she loves *you*. I knew she would.'

'Any warm body at this stage, right?'

'God no, she shrieks when Pete's sister comes anywhere near her. It's embarrassing.' I picked up Beatrice's hand. She looked up at me and smiled.

'Look, I'm sorry it's taken me so long.'

'Don't worry, Stevie, I know how it is, how crazy your life out there is. You came for the do, that's what matters.'

'He's not going to be there, is he?' I asked.

'Will? No, of course not; I wouldn't do that to you. It's just family and close friends.'

'But you still see him?'

'Pete does.'

'I heard he got married.'

'Oh God, did you? I'm sorry, I didn't know whether to tell you or not.'

'Don't worry, it's been, what, three years? Anyway, it's my own fault for stalking him on social media.'

At the pub where the naming ceremony was being held, I watched the balloons dance beside the open window, avoiding people I hadn't kept in touch with, overhearing conversations about primary schools and childcare and moving to the country.

Then Mira gave Beatrice to me and she put her chubby little arms around my neck and played with my ears. I pulled faces at her and she laughed, and Pete gave me a glass of champagne and said, 'Cheers, Oddmother,' and I relaxed.

Mira, Pete, two of his friends and I passed Beatrice between us like a parcel, a gift, and promised to guide her, mentor her throughout her life, and I felt the room thinking, *Spare the poor baby. What's Stevie going to teach her? How to use a dating app? How to order takeout?* I shifted my weight from one leg to the other and the second it was over I ran to the bar.

The next morning, as the bus to the station wheezed past identical red-brick Edwardian houses, street after street after street of them, I thought how lofty and important and loud London had seemed when I'd moved here for university. Now, it reminded me of the model village my mother had taken me to for my sixth birthday; a maze of roads with broccoli-floret trees, roads that, apart from the occasional blackbird warble or sparrow chirp, were quiet, as if everyone was permanently asleep.

I was on my way to the farm, and as I boarded the train, the strangest thing happened. I felt a tug, like a jumper catching on a necklace clasp, and as I closed my eyes and leaned my head against the window and toy-town London shuttled by, thoughts of Beatrice filled my head. It was as if there was an endless red ribbon connecting me to her. I swore I could see it spooling behind us through the train window.

My mother met me at the station and drove me down those narrow, familiar lanes. 'The best time of year,' she said, and I nodded, winding down the window and breathing in the lusty scents of wildflowers, nettles and manure.

She had aged. When I was in New York, my mother was the photo in the wooden frame on my bedside table, taken ten years earlier, at Rebecca's wedding. She was wearing a raspberry suit with a matching pillbox hat and standing beside a yurt criss-crossed with bunting. She'd looked utterly out of place, as if Jackie Onassis had put on a few stone and got lost, but I'd never seen such light in her eyes. It wasn't just Rebecca's wedding; it was the fact that Jess had flown over when no one had been certain she would.

Jess had flung her arms around me, run her hands over the length of me. 'I can't believe how big you've gotten, kiddo,' American words in an English accent, and then she had walked over to Mum, looking down at her shoes, and Mum had reached towards her. The rift, it seemed, was repairing.

'You look exhausted, Mum,' I said, and she just shrugged and said it was a busy time of year, what with the lambing and the calving. Her hair was gathered into a messy low bun; an inch of white root glared at the top of her centre parting. Her skin was the colour of putty and taut over her cheekbones.

'I don't understand why you and Dad don't get more help. Are you sure you're OK?'

'Of course I am,' she said, 'I haven't seen you for three years. I expect you think I look *elderly*.'

'I wish you'd get Skype,' I said. 'It's amazing, like being in the same room.'

'You know our internet's not up to it, Stevie – or my internet skills, for that matter – and anyway, I'm not sure I'd like my face being beamed around the world. The phone is more my speed.'

We drove into the yard, sending chickens squawking.

'There,' she said, turning off the engine. 'Home. I suppose you're going to tell me it's changed, too.'

I surveyed the rusty machinery, the feed sacks piled up like pillows. 'It's exactly the same. Dad out, then?'

'Milking. I gave him sandwiches this morning. Lunch?'

'Yes, please.' I sat down at the table and looked over at the pine dresser. Propped against a jar of pasta was a photo I'd sent them, an optical illusion of Jess and me standing with our index fingers on the point of the Empire State Building. She'd probably fished it out of a drawer that morning, I thought, because almost all the photos around the house were childhood snaps of Rebecca and Jess, as if the camera had handed in its notice when I arrived.

There had been cheese sandwiches and pork pies for lunch, a supermarket ploughman's.

'Do tell me about Beatrice's naming ceremony.'

'It was fine,' I said, helping myself to a pie. 'The old crowd. Lots of new babies. Beatrice is . . . '

'What?'

'Wonderful. I wish I could see her all the time.'

'Perhaps you will one day.'

'I don't think Mira and Pete are moving to New York anytime soon.'

'You might come back. I wish you would.'

'Well, you never know.' There was a pause as we ate.

'Do you see me with a child, Mum?' I asked.

'A child of your own? Stevie, I didn't think . . . '

'That I wanted one?'

'Well, it's just that you've never seemed to have much luck, or much *truck*, with relationships.' Another pause.

'You're right,' I said eventually. 'But perhaps I could have a baby on my own.'

Her eyes flitted to the door, as if she was worried my father would walk in.

'Is that what you're thinking of doing?' she asked.

'I don't know, but seeing Beatrice yesterday . . . ' She had done something, that plump little soul, she had awakened something. 'Lots of two-parent families end up as one-parent families, Mum,' I continued. 'At least there wouldn't be any surprises.'

She put down her sandwich and looked out of the window at the hill, its grassy strata and speckles of sheep.

'I think it would be hard,' she said.

Twenty-two

On the first and third Fridays of each summer month, Nathan, Jenna and I left work at noon, wrestled our way on to the train at Penn Station and rattled all the way to the end of the line where the ocean shimmered into view. Jenna was a friend of Nathan's from college, and the three of us had taken a part-share in a decrepit yet cripplingly expensive ranch house at the eastern tip of Long Island.

By five o'clock we were standing with our feet in the sand and beers in our hands. 'To Lex,' I'd say. He allowed the team this perk because he had his own place at the beach.

Jenna was loud and amplified with each glass of white wine she drank. She had, by her own admission, a socialised form of attention deficit disorder: she treated restaurant- and bar-going as a competitive sport, preferring them with the paint still sticky on the walls; never going to the same place twice. Nathan had been amazed, given her issues, when his beach house campaign had succeeded and Jenna had committed to weekends in the third bedroom.

It was not hard to see that Jenna's ravenous appetite for the shiny and new was a distraction from the area of her life in which she craved continuity. Jenna wanted a relationship, one that would, in her words, 'bear fruit'. And as that relationship steadfastly refused to materialise, she preoccupied herself with hits from the experience bong, even though looking for the next thing was exactly what she criticised her suitors for doing. And she clung, like everyone in New York, to her friends.

'What's the lease?' she'd asked when we met at Nathan's birthday drinks and spent the evening laughing through her tales of dating disaster.

'What do you mean?' I'd replied.

'I mean, how long have I got with you? What's the *visa* situation here? Are we talking, what, three years? With an option to renew?' When I continued to look confused, she said, 'I'm wondering how much to *invest*.'

'Ah right, yes,' I'd smiled, 'at least three years. Possibility of a green card after that.'

'A green card? *In perpetuity*, then.'

'I suppose so.'

'In that case,' she'd said, 'I'm in.'

I preferred Jenna by the beach. Her cartoon chestnut eyes adopted an ambrosial glaze when the doors of the LIRR train parted, when we stepped from the air-conditioned carriage into the heat of an early-summer afternoon, the popped collars and their yappy dogs having disembarked a few stops earlier.

I relaxed, too. When Nathan had first suggested the summer rental, I wasn't sure. I'd learned to love the scalding, stinking city in summer, its weekend emptiness, when only the truly committed stuck around.

Then Nathan had taken me to the beach on a freezing February day and we'd slipped off our shoes and socks, dug our toes through the frost and shrieked as the foam had washed around our ankles. I'd said, yes, OK, let's spend the summer here, let's *summer* here. And now, every other weekend, here I was, cycling from barbecues to beach picnics in flip-flops and sundresses over bikinis, pulling on frayed jeans and hooded tops when the temperature crashed after sunset, a different person, more like the childhood me, someone who recognised hedgerow flowers and pointed out constellations.

'You know, Stevie, I'll be thirty-seven in October,' said Jenna. She was watching a child pull a red wagon loaded with plastic beach paraphernalia along the road in front of our house. His mother and father strolled behind him, hand-in-hand.

'I know,' I replied. I knew where this was going.

'I'm just wondering if I should *do* something before it's too late.'

'About babies, you mean?'

'Yes, about babies.'

'Well, first of all, when is too late? Cherie Blair had a baby at forty-six.'

'Who's Cherie Blair?'

'Doesn't matter. What I mean is, thirty-seven is nothing.'

'My mom had me when she was twenty-four. I might already be infertile.'

'Rubbish. The biological clock is a right-wing conspiracy to take women out of the workforce.'

'I've been looking into egg-freezing.'

'You have?'

'It's the same price as Botox.'

'Unfurrowed brow or screaming infant? I'm not sure which is more appealing.'

'Funny.'

'But don't you want to meet someone? What's going on with the architect?'

'Disappeared.' She pushed her cereal bowl to the middle of the table and placed her hands flat in front of her.

'What? Really?'

'Yup. Dating other people, usual story.'

'Agh, sorry.'

'Perhaps he'll reappear when something ends.'

'But how keen on him were you *really*?'

'I don't know, I thought we had chemistry.'

'You like him now he's gone.'

'I guess. I'm just so sick of being part of a smorgasbord, Stevie. I want to be an entrée.'

'Don't you think you'd get bored if you were in a permanent relationship?'

'Not with the right person.'

I leaned back in my chair. 'I don't think I want to be anyone's entrée,' I said.

'You haven't been here long enough. The novelty will wear off. Believe me, you'll get over it – the dating, the multiple dating, being stuck in first gear for ever. Everyone does.'

'There are pros to New York dating, you know.'

'Like what?'

'Spontaneity. This guy stopped me in the street the other day, we had a chat and he took my number. That would never happen in London.'

'Has he called?'

'No, but whatever; it was a fun five minutes.'

'You'll probably hear from him in six months' time when he's exhausted his current options. He'll be scrolling through his phone and he'll see your name and he'll think, *Hang on, what happened to that cute British girl I met on Bleecker* or wherever it was, and he'll call you as if nothing has happened.'

'And I won't answer.'

I poured us glasses of water from the filter jug on the table.

'It's the way their eyes drift around the room, Stevie, the way they look over their shoulders that I can't take, as if they're working out who to hit on next.'

'I don't notice that,' I said.

'Is multiple dating really not a thing in London at *all*?'

'Nope. Dating isn't really a thing either. You meet someone in the pub, wake up on their futon the next morning, and bingo, boyfriend and girlfriend.'

'Do you miss that? The honesty? The lack of agenda?'

'The honesty? No, I don't miss it,' I said. 'I don't miss any of it.'

Jenna was still talking about dating as we neared the beach, even though I hadn't said anything apart from 'hmm', 'no' and 'you're right' for the last ten minutes. *You don't get it, do you?* I thought, as she rummaged in her bag for suncream. *It's a game, dating, nothing more, and as long as you accept that, as long as you don't expect a jackpot ending, then nothing can go wrong, and no one can get hurt. You want honesty? This is honesty.*

'So, you'd do it on your own – you'd have a baby by yourself?' I asked, working cream into her back with the heels of my hands.

'I don't know,' she said. 'I'm beginning to think I might. But I mean, it's not as if single parenthood is something I ever dreamed of. I always hoped I'd end up with someone. My therapist says my parents' divorce is the reason I'm so obsessed with having a forever relationship. What about yours?'

'They're together. My father's a difficult man. I've never really understood what my mother sees in him.'

'Perhaps he's different when you're not there,' said Jenna.

'Maybe. He wasn't around much when I was growing up,' I said. 'He's a farmer and farming's hard work, but it was more than that. He didn't seem interested, not in me. He was only interested in Rebecca.'

'The other sister?'

'Yes.'

Dad and Rebecca, chairs turned to each other at the end of the kitchen table, laughing at something a teacher had said at school, a TV programme they'd watched after I'd gone to bed, that was how it was. Was I ever alone with him? Surely, at some point. That time Mum took Rebecca to a university open day, I must have been six, it was just us then. Dad wanted to go but it was a five-hour drive, they'd need to spend the night and he couldn't leave the farm.

The school gates, home-time, there he was, scanning the crowd for me, frown beneath side-parting, hands in the pockets of his wax jacket, a middle-aged shadow among the young mums flicking yellow perms. 'Is that your dad, Stevie?' a classmate said. Dads didn't do pick-up, and I nodded, proud, and when we found each other, I beamed, thrust my hand into his, looked down, saw he was wearing his brown church shoes instead of wellies. We didn't know what to say to each other in the car. I fastened and refastened the three buckles on my school belt, slipped a sheet from my bag.

'What's that?' he said, glancing left, hands on the wheel.

'Spelling test.'

'Oh, good.' Something to do, something to talk about, and at dinner I sat on Rebecca's chair next to his and he spooned Mum's shepherd's pie on to my plate: grey mince, stiff mash. 'Delicious, this.' Then he tested me, *half, whole, would, could,* and again at breakfast, spreading marmalade on to my toast. At dinner that evening, he said, 'Well?' and I said, 'Ten out of ten,' and he looked delighted, and Mum sat down next to me and Rebecca pulled out her chair and we slipped back to where we had been.

*

'What about Rebecca — she's married, right?'

'Yes, ten years, two kids. He's a solicitor. Deeply into cycling. It seems so boring, their relationship. I bet they never have sex. And Jess, as you know, has always been on her own, or if there's ever been anyone significant, she hasn't told me.'

'Do those two get on?'

'Not really. I think Rebecca's jealous of Jess, in some ways. I mean, they rarely see each other, but when she talks about her there's always some sort of sarcastic comment. They don't exactly have much in common.'

'Well, I can see why she'd be jealous. Jess is a great advertisement for the single life. Her apartment sounds insane. When did she move out here again?'

'Decades ago. I was eleven; she was twenty-five.'

'You must have missed her, growing up.'

'I did. It broke my heart when she moved to New York.'

'So, Jess is why you came here?'

'One of the reasons. She was at boarding school when I was little, but I still felt close to her, and we lost that when she moved away. I wanted to get to know her again.'

'Why did she never have children?' Jenna asked.

'I don't know. It's not something we've ever discussed.'

'Really? That's odd.'

Still, Jess had asked me about my plans when I'd told her Mira was pregnant. And she'd almost said something in return. I'd hoped that that moment might herald a new era of transparency. But we had returned to our regular subjects of conversation and I wondered whether I'd misread her signals entirely.

'What about you?' Jenna asked. 'Marriage? Kids?'

'I don't see a wedding, never have. I'm not even sure I see a long-term relationship.'

'You've been hurt. I get it.' I shrugged. 'But a child?'

'That's different,' I said. I stood up, shook my towel. A child wasn't a line in the sand, waiting to be erased by the next wave. A child was bedrock.

'I've always wanted a baby,' I said.

'So, you'd do it on your own, then?'

'Yes,' I said. 'I would.'

Twenty-three

The wheels of the pram skid through the late-autumn mulch. I've decided to break my confinement, the punishment I assigned myself for leaving Ash alone, with a visit to the supermarket. Staring at each other and the four walls of the flat, brooding on my inadequacies as a mother, is not helping us. I've tried to appreciate the everyday moments with him, to celebrate small wins, as Lex would say – a well-executed bath time, a rapidly drained bottle – and they are not enough.

I don't need to shop, there is another delivery arriving tomorrow, but it is something to do, and I am too full of self-loathing for the greens and browns of the park. I want traffic and noise and strangers' faces, people going about their lives.

In the supermarket, I see a young woman staring at the rows of baby formula boxes. She can't be more than twenty. I surprise myself by asking if I can help; I haven't heard my voice in days.

'There are just so many,' she says.

'That's the one I use,' I say, pointing. As she pushes her pram to the next aisle, I speculate. Was the baby planned? Is the father around? *This is what people wonder about me when they see us alone*, I think; I felt it in the hospital the day Ash was born. They need only get closer, though, to read my mid-life lines and see fertility treatment, last-ditch, eleventh-hour. Then they'll know.

The trouble I went to.

Less trouble than many, granted, but more than most. More than the average skip-the-contraception couple, anyway. More than Mira and Peter and their bonny baby. 'You must have wanted him so much,' said the woman when I registered his birth, leaving the father box blank, and I had.

The four walls of the waiting room were covered in an infant mosaic: identical twins co-sleeping like inverted commas; toddlers with gappy grins. To the right of the reception desk was a photo of a plump child, a scrap of blonde hair rising from its crown like a feather, a girl, probably, though at that age it was hard to tell.

That one, please.

I'd booked the appointment at the fertility clinic two weeks before I'd left New York, and here I was, fresh off the plane, my worldly goods bobbing across the Atlantic, jet lag still pinning the corners of my brain like paperweights. No time to lose.

I was relying on Project Baby to lift me from the slump I'd felt since I'd touched down at Heathrow. Since my pulse had returned to its London rate, as if I'd dismounted a bike at the end of spin class. 'The New York come-down,' Nathan had called it. 'I get it if I leave the city for forty-eight hours, so . . . good luck!'

It will pass, I told myself, as I set the wheels of the new London club in motion, meeting with architects and builders, typing out lists of potential members, my mind permanently elsewhere, not even the dream job – 'It's your gig, Stevie, I'm just checking in,' Lex would say on video conference – able to distract me fully. I'd nod and smile into my computer's cyclops camera, and I'd think, *You have no idea. I'm not just building a club. I'm creating a life.*

In the waiting room, I sipped insipid coffee and observed my potential parent peers. They gave a different impression from the baby collage on the wall, those sad stories of indolent sperm and empty shells, of blood-stained knickers and single lines on pissed-on sticks. The studs looked particularly despondent. Nothing worse for a man than tossing into a pot only to be told it's as potent as a mocktail.

The exceptions were the ones I assumed to be the turkey basters, the bring-your-own-motile-sperm brigade, four of them if you didn't count me – *Just think, nine months from now* – and the two, pregnant middle-agers who couldn't believe their luck but knew not to let it show. Kind eyes. Folded arms. *We sat where you are sitting.*

'Stevie Stewart?'

I stood up too quickly, felt faint. The doctor was a no-nonsense type, her greying hair tied back, navy cardigan buttoned beneath white coat. The sort that wouldn't judge.

'Hi, Stevie, I'm Dr Kimble.' She looked down at her notes. 'So, this is your first visit. Tell me why you're here.' I'd rehearsed my answer a hundred times. Nothing to be ashamed of: she'd seen it all. And yet.

'I'd like to have a baby,' I said.

'*Yes.* That's why most people come here.'

'Sorry, I mean I'd like to have a baby using donated sperm.'

'Good.' *Good?* Not what I was expecting. 'Do you have a partner?'

'Not currently,' I said defensively, impossible not to be.

'Don't worry; it's just for form-filling purposes.'

'I do have sperm, though.'

'You do?'

'I mean, not *with* me.' Obviously. As if I was going to pass it to her under the table. 'It's in New York.'

'Aha. Easier to come by there. An ID release donor, I assume? The sperm won't comply with UK law otherwise.'

'Yes, I made sure of that. I did a ton of research before I chose the clinic and the donor.'

'Good. We screen sperm for inherited diseases and infections anyway.'

'It won't be too hard to bring over here, will it?'

'Shouldn't be, no. We've done it before. Great. So, I'll start with a few questions.' She returned to her checklist.

'Have you ever been pregnant before?' There it was: the killer.

'Once. I had a termination.'

'Can I ask when it was?'

'About six years ago.'

'And you're,' she glanced at her notes, 'thirty-eight.'

'Yes. Thirty-nine in June.'

'On any medication?'

'No.'

'Generally in good health?'

'Very healthy, yes.'

'Do you smoke or drink?'

'I don't smoke; I have a few glasses of wine each week.'

'I'd advise cutting down. Even better, give up. It'll increase your chances significantly.'

'I can do that.'

'Good. So, as you probably know, you have two treatment options: artificial insemination and in vitro fertilisation.'

'Artificial insemination being the official name for the turkey baster method, right?'

'Indeed. IVF is more invasive, more arduous and more

expensive, but it does have much higher success rates. I'd recommend starting with IUI, and then . . . '

'I'd like to go straight to IVF, please. I have the money and I don't want to wait.'

Next came Dr Kimble's step-by-step guide to sexless reproduction, beginning with daily injections to 'switch off' my ovaries and then flick them back on again to produce mature eggs. When she mentioned egg harvesting, my mind skipped to the farm. Plunging my hot little hand into the box, rummaging, circling, wiggling my fingers back and forth, then hitting on two warm eggs lying on the hay. Picking up one and tucking it gently into the left pocket of my corduroy jacket, putting the other in the right. Running back to the house, pushing open the kitchen door and triumphantly laying both eggs on the table beside my father's milky tea. Seeing him look down and his face darken and noticing that both were cracked. My Mum saying brightly, 'Don't worry, Stevie, I was going to scramble them anyway. You've saved me a job.' My father pushing his chair back from the table with a scrape like thunder and walking from the kitchen without a word.

'A few days later, after they've been fertilised, all things being well, the blastocysts – five-day-old embryos – will be checked and graded, and transferred to the uterus via the vagina,' Dr Kimble concluded. 'Some couples – some women – prefer to transfer two; obviously, this carries the risk of twins.'

'I won't be doing that. One is enough for me.' One and done.

She smiled. 'If you have other blastocysts, they'll be frozen in case the cycle isn't successful.'

'And if it isn't? How long would I have to wait until I can try again?'

'If you have blastocysts left you need only wait a month. Any more questions?'

'I'll be forty in eighteen months,' I said. 'I should prepare myself for my fertility to fall off a cliff then, right?'

'Don't fixate on forty,' said Dr Kimble. 'It's not as if your body suddenly downs tools on the stroke of midnight. Look, I probably shouldn't say this but you're in a stronger position than ninety per cent of the couples that walk through my door. You've been pregnant before; you have tried-and-tested sperm. Obviously, there are no guarantees,' she continued, 'but I wouldn't be surprised if, six months from now, you're buying Babygros.'

Twenty-four

'Prat. Plonker. Pillock. Why do all funny British words begin with P?' said Nathan, tracing the letter in the sand.

'They don't,' I said. 'What about brolly, or biscuit, or bloke? You seem to find those highly amusing too.'

'You're right. Bs *and* Ps. Bits and pieces! Another of my favourites.'

It was late afternoon, and we were lying on our stomachs on the beach, flicking through profiles on Nathan's dating app. I'd told him that I thought one guy, whom he had called 'shockingly hot', looked like 'a bit of a prat' in his jacket and pocket square, which had required translation.

'Well, perhaps I like prats,' said Nathan. 'Perhaps prats are my type.'

'Perhaps they are. I wouldn't know – I haven't been allowed to meet any of your hook-ups,' I said.

'Because that's what they are: hook-ups. I barely know most of them myself. I mean, the last guy? I found him bent over the bath. Never saw his face.'

'Really?'

'And I like keeping business and pleasure separate.'

'You probably think I'd put them off – the ones with relation-ship potential, anyway.'

'A real-life Brit? Hardly. You're my best asset – I talk about you constantly. Anyway, I haven't met any of yours.'

'None of my dates has been worth meeting, you know that.'

'Look at us, two New York love stories,' he said. 'I heard you telling Jenna you wanted a baby last time we were here.'

'Eavesdropping again. I do, one day. Not now, not yet. Do you?'

'Christ, no. Well, I don't know. Maybe? What makes you so sure?'

'It's just something I've always known.'

'Known you wanted or known would happen?'

'Known I wanted to make happen.'

The sea had calmed since morning. Surfboards leaned against a wooden fence with slats missing, like a mouth of British teeth, Nathan said.

What had Beatrice done with her Saturday, I wondered, what did ten-month-olds do between purée, afternoon naps and bottles of milk? A visit to the park? A swim in the local pool? Mira had told me she'd taken her since she was two months old; she'd texted me a photo of her in the rainbow swimsuit I'd sent.

Or perhaps it had rained in London and none of them had wanted to leave the flat – why should they, everything they needed was there? They'd sat in the kitchen, drinking tea, watching the rain on the windowpanes, blowing bubbles at Beatrice, singing songs to her, reading books, letting her turn the cardboard pages with her fat little fingers. Happy, whole.

'Stevie?' Nathan was standing over me, folding his towel.

'Sorry, did you say something?'

'Shall we go? It's getting late.'

'What's the plan for tonight?' I asked.

'There's that party, remember? Where's Jenna?'

I pointed down the shore towards town. She was standing where the sea met the sand, hands on hips, long legs shoulder-width apart.

She swivelled and strolled ten or so metres in our direction, then looked through her sunglasses at the bodies on the shore, paused, faced the sea for a few moments, and walked back in the other direction.

'The prowl,' said Nathan, and we laughed.

It was almost nine o'clock and as we arrived, garlands of fairy lights strung between the buildings flickered on and highlighted the tanned limbs and glossy hair of the shifting crowd.

'You got the memo, then,' said Nathan to Jenna. At least half the women were dressed in skinny white jeans like her. No wonder she'd asked, 'Is that what you're wearing?' before we'd left the house. I straightened the halter-neck she'd lent me. 'You look great, Stevie,' Nathan said. 'I mean, you could wear a garbage sack.'

'Do you actually know the person who's having this party?' I asked him.

'I do not,' he replied, pushing his fringe out of his eyes, a note of triumph to his voice.

Jenna spotted a friend and disappeared. Nathan and I found the drinks table; he plunged our bottles of grocery-store wine into a trash can filled with ice and poured champagne into two plastic cups.

'Stevie!'

The voice was so loud half the party turned around.

Lex.

Of course. His summer house was in one of these towns: Amagansett or Bridgehampton, I couldn't remember which, just that he'd frowned when I'd told him that ours was in Montauk. 'All the way east,' he'd said. 'That surf, though.' Suddenly, here he was, barrelling over, arms outstretched.

'Hey, Lex,' I said. 'Fancy seeing you here. This is Nathan.'

'Sure, I remember Nathan.'

'Hey,' he said.

'Are the hosts friends of yours?' I asked.

'Yeah, Bill's an old college pal,' he said. 'What about you guys?'

'Yeah,' said Nathan vaguely.

'Friends of friends.' I blushed.

'Party crashers!' said Lex. 'Right, anyone need a refill?'

'Someone seems *super* happy to see you,' said Nathan when he was gone.

'You think?'

'Uh-huh. And that someone is looking *super* hot tonight. Why have we never discussed the relationship potential here?'

'Nathan, I'm not looking for a relationship, and even if I were, there isn't any.'

'For you or for him?'

'He's my boss.'

'So?'

'And I'm not his type.'

'But he's your type, right?'

'He's a good-looking, successful guy. He's everyone's type. I don't want a relationship and a fling would be a total disaster.'

Lex returned, clasping three plastic cups, a grin spread across his face like jam.

'Shame,' whispered Nathan. 'Because he's into you.'

Twenty-five

'Tarot Card Reader Open' proclaims the blackboard sign in my path. I smile, think of Jess, then push the pram on.

We've walked for miles this week, through street markets, over bridges, down roads screaming with six-lane traffic. It is a relief to leave my pinprick of London, and moving feels like progress, like purpose. Ash often sleeps as I push and if he doesn't his cries are easier to ignore.

Today, I am heading west. America is out there somewhere in the distance, Jess, Nathan and my old life.

I feel, instinctively, for my necklace, the one Nathan gave me, my leaving present, an antique gold chain with a hand clasp and a tiny emerald stone on one finger that he pressed on me as we said goodbye. The necklace that has disappeared.

I can't shake the habit of patting my collarbone, where it used to be, in case I only dreamed of losing it, in case it has been there all along. When I find it is naked, as usual, I relive the moment of panic the morning of my first transfer, when I realised it had gone and where it was most likely to be. That I wasn't going to get it back. I miss that necklace every day.

*

My first transfer took place two months after I had moved back to London.

I was, as always, the last person in the office at five past six on the evening before; the British team was fastidious about leaving on time, and I pulled up my jumper and imagined my flat stomach as a bump.

For the first time, I thought how strange it was to be doing it on my own, that there was no one else whose life this seedling would change, and I did what I usually did when I felt alone: I called Nathan.

'It's happening,' I said as soon as he picked up.

'The embryo transfer?'

'The *blastocyst* transfer.'

'Well, excuse me. Only the best for Stevie Stewart. What *is* that?'

'It just means the embryo's a little older.'

'Like its mom.'

'Thanks. It's supposed to help its implantation chances. Anyway, it's tomorrow, ten o'clock.'

'Fuck. That baby is going *in*. Are you excited?'

'Shit scared, to be honest. I just hope it works and I don't have to extract any more blood or inject any more gunk for a while. I'm looking forward to not feeling like a hormonal, headachy pin cushion.'

'Well, good luck with that. Doesn't all that stuff continue when you're actually pregnant, bar the pricking?'

'I guess. I hope I find out.'

'Where are you, anyway?'

'Shopping for dinner.'

'Could be your penultimate meal as a childless woman.'

'God, I hope so.'

'Does Lex know anything?'

'Nothing. Just one of the advantages of working three and a half thousand miles from your boss. I'll be back online by the time he gets to work.'

'Watch a few cute YouTube baby videos tonight to get you in the mood and call me if you get bored. We can go through our parenting strategies again.'

'Nathan, you do know it's not *your* sperm that made the embryo, don't you?'

'I keep forgetting that detail. Kind of feels like it, though, right?'

London had begun its winter hibernation; the streets were empty except for the odd after-work drinker sashaying drunkenly to the tube. I took a long breath of chilly, damp air and felt more positive than I had in weeks. *I am doing something*, I thought, *I am moving forward.*

My first instinct was to walk straight past him, hugging my handbag close as if he were a thief. Then I thought, *Perhaps it's not him after all.* You didn't bump into people in London, particularly people who weren't even supposed to live there; it wasn't like New York, where everyone worked in midtown and lived within a ten-block radius. People disappeared into the ancient roads and squares and underground stations like butter into toast.

Then a tap on my shoulder. 'Stevie?'

'Will.'

'Hi.'

'I was just . . . I'm on my way home . . . '

'Right,' he said. 'Look, I'd really like to talk.'

I don't know exactly why I did it, but the drugs I'd been injecting can't have helped. Perhaps it was revenge. Did I think that I might, after all these years, find out why he had ended it? Or maybe it was my heart, quiet for so long, which started beating out of my chest the second I saw him.

Ten minutes later we were sitting opposite each other in a tapas restaurant.

'Do you remember our second date?' he asked, pouring me a glass of red wine.

'No,' I lied.

'Another tapas restaurant.'

'Was it?'

'Look, Stevie . . . '

'How's married life?'

'It's over.'

'What? Why?'

'You'd have to ask her. Look, Stevie,' he began again.

'I think I'd better go.'

'Don't, please,' he said. 'Are you married?'

'I'm really not the type.'

'I still think about you, you know.'

'I doubt it.'

'About what happened, and how we rushed in.'

'How *you* rushed in. How *you* rushed out.'

'I think I know now why it didn't work.'

Here it comes, I thought. 'And why was that, Will?' I speared a chorizo disc with a cocktail stick.

'I was scared.'

'Scared?'

'My mum died when I was young.'

'You told me.'

'And I think it made me frightened of committing because I thought it would happen again.'

'You mean you were worried that I'd *die*?'

'Subconsciously, yes.'

'Sounds like a bad case of post-rationalisation to me,' I said. 'Like something a shrink would say.' He blushed. 'And even if it were true, you got over it, didn't you? You got married less than three years later.'

'And it didn't work out. I wasn't emotionally available.'

'Will,' I raised my head, 'this might not sound very empathetic, but we've all got our shit – I've got mine; you've got yours, that guy making the sangria at the bar has his.' The barman looked up and I lowered my voice. 'What you *do* with your shit is up to you.'

He swilled wine around the bottom of his glass. 'New York has made you hard,' he said.

I should have left then. But I allowed him to refill my glass, put his case again, and then, when I didn't answer, lean towards me and tuck my hair behind my ear. Lips brushed lips, once, twice. Stayed.

The next moment we were standing on the street. A bus whooshed past. He waved down a black cab; its yellow eye winked shut and the taxi trembled north, I don't know where, I didn't ask, perhaps we were going all the way to Manchester, where he'd lived when we'd been together.

Sometime later, a key in the lock, up creaky stairs, coats flung on the floor. The same street art. A clothes airer dense with black socks and white T-shirts and grey pants. A coffee table piled high with weeks-old weekend papers.

Afterwards, we lay there in silence, until he said, 'That was amazing. It always was.' And I smiled behind closed eyes, because it hadn't been amazing, not until tonight. Perhaps he was more comfortable in his skin now, his slackening skin. Or I was. I suppose, when you know for sure it's the last time, when you'd bet your life on it, there's nothing to hold back.

'Stay?' he said.

His alarm went at 6 a.m., just as I shut the door behind me.

Later, it wasn't the sex but the tap on the shoulder that stayed with me. I thought of the hollow sound he would have made if I had tapped him back.

Twenty-six

The club was going well. Lex had raised another round of cash with a view to rolling out more; he ended every All Hands meeting by shouting: 'SCALE!', and, to my surprise, the team repeated the mantra after him. I'd been promoted to chief-of-staff, though I wasn't entirely sure what it meant, and the company's lawyer had been in touch about my green card paperwork.

Tonight, Friday night, Lex was taking me out to his favourite fish restaurant in Soho to celebrate. *A work dinner, a work dinner.* I recited it like a mantra. *Don't expect anything more*, though it was a hard sell when he could have chosen breakfast or lunch. When the restaurant was in his neighbourhood, a night-cap mere moments away.

The reservation was at nine and I arrived an acceptable ten minutes late. Lex was already there, in a beige leather booth that looked as if it belonged on a yacht, stirring a drink.

'Hey!' he said when he saw me.

'Sorry I'm late,' I said, suddenly nervous. I leaned in for a double kiss, he for a hug; we ended up rubbing cheekbones. I was as tall as he was; I wished I'd worn different shoes.

'You come here a lot?' I said, idiotically, as I sat down.

'Yeah,' he said. 'I mean, it's two blocks from my apartment and the food's great. You?'

'I've been here before. But I sat over there.' I smiled, pointing to a cramped area beside the bathroom. I noticed a couple of girl-friends. One of them mouthed 'Hi, Stevie,' and raised an eyebrow when she saw who I was with.

'Well, they know me, so . . . drink?'

'Sure, a vodka and tonic, please.'

He ordered. 'Good day?'

'We got a ton of enquiries about San Francisco.'

'I'm headed out there next week – you should come.'

'I'd love . . . I mean, I think that would be really useful,' I said. Our drinks arrived.

'Cheers, Stevie. Congratulations on the promotion. You were doing the job already, but I wanted to make it official.'

'Thanks, Lex, I appreciate it. And the pay rise, obviously.'

'Thank *you*. For your hard work. For calling me out on stuff.'

'For keeping you real?' I smiled.

'Well, yeah, I guess so, in a way.' He fiddled with his watch.

Three women sitting in a row at the bar turned in formation and stared at Lex.

'Spotted,' I said.

'Perhaps I dated one of their friends or something.'

'Rubbish,' I laughed. 'You're a business TV pin-up.'

A half-smile colouring his face, Lex studied the menu as if he didn't come here every week, then looked up for a waiter. After he had ordered for us, he draped an arm over the booth and looked towards the door. Then the conversation began again, about Los Angeles, the third club, *the pivot*, he called it.

In meetings, adrenalin stretched Lex drum-tight; at the club, he was the perpetual host, meandering through the velvet arm-chairs, a motivational poster come to life, thwacking backs and saying, 'How's that balance sheet? You're killing it, aren't you? Kill-ing-it!' Tonight, despite the tumult of the restaurant, the as-per New York decibel level, he seemed dialled down, quietened by the low light of the lamps.

It felt different, being far from the Flatiron District after dark, not a co-worker in sight, no Megan and her coven to X-ray every sleeve brush, laugh or low whisper – to come to the conclusion that, because we had both ordered avocado on toast for breakfast, we must be having sex. It was a rubber stamp on our relationship: we could operate beyond the confines of the club; we got on. Perhaps this was what the best sibling relationships were like, I thought, as I studied the last piece of sushi and hoisted it between my chopsticks, this ease; perhaps that was what this was.

When I took a bite, I was tongue-stung by wasabi and my eyes pricked, and I saw Lex's profile through a glaze of tears as he asked the server for two more glasses of wine. His aquiline nose, hooded eyes, the widow's peak beneath the beanie. Something else burned and I thought: *Siblings? No.*

As I chewed, trying not to splutter, I wondered why he hadn't mentioned his girlfriend, the one I'd seen him with; whether he still had a girlfriend, and what he'd tell his friends about me after this evening. If he'd say, 'She's not really my type, but I don't know, I think there's chemistry,' or if the occasion would pass unremarked. Did he want children, I found myself wondering, or was the business the only baby he needed?

'Look,' Lex said, after two large glasses were placed in front of us, 'my pal Sam's having a party – it's Brooklyn, but not far – just over the bridge. After these, shall we go?'

The taxi crossed Williamsburg Bridge, its ironwork red in the headlights. I texted the friends I'd planned to join if my dinner with Lex hadn't had a second act and then I called Jess. It was Lex's suggestion. 'Friends in common,' he'd mumbled. 'You should ask her to the party.'

'Everything OK, kiddo?' Jess said. We rarely spoke on the phone.

'Thank you, *both* of you, for the invitation,' she said when I told her about it, 'but I'm about to go to bed – I'm meeting a friend for a run at seven.' I felt guilty, remembered our morning runs when we lived together, how I'd sworn we'd keep them up.

'Stevie?' Her voice sounded faint, was she about to say something she didn't want Lex to hear?

'Yes?'

'Just be . . . '

'What?'

'Oh, nothing. Still on for dinner next Sunday?'

'Of course, looking forward to it. Sleep well, Jess.'

I felt both disappointed and relieved.

The taxi stopped beneath a black iron subway bridge that shuddered visibly with the weight of a passing train. We crossed the street and Lex bashed on a dimpled metal door. When we were buzzed in, I followed him up a narrow flight of stairs between flaky primrose-coloured walls. A tall man opened the door and threw his arms around Lex.

'Buddy!' he shouted above the music and turned to me. 'You must be Stevie.'

'Hey, Sam,' I said, 'thanks for having us.'

'Lex and I were roommates,' said Sam, as he took my coat, waved it vaguely at a heaving row of pegs, then laid it on a radiator.

'One of us took a more creative route,' said Lex. 'Sam's an actor.'

'An out-of-work actor,' said Sam.

'Come on, you've had some great parts. Stevie used to work in TV.'

'Until Lex saved me,' I said.

Sam shook his head. 'I mean, I love this guy, but I can't imagine working with him.' Sam excused himself to answer the door again and Lex and I pushed past the other guests to a galley kitchen where he unscrewed a bottle of red wine, found two tumblers in the cupboard and filled them.

'This reminds me of my last flat in London,' I said.

'It does?' said Lex. 'You didn't have wine glasses either?'

'Ha. Not many.'

'Do you miss London?'

'Not much,' I said. 'Actually, not at all. Weird, right?'

'Not really. The day I moved here I knew I'd never leave. The things that had happened here, the things that would happen. That was twenty years ago. Fuck,' he took a swig of wine, 'I'm ancient.'

'You know, every morning, when I open the door of my apartment block and step outside, I feel excited.'

'It never gets old. The city sheds and regrows its skin and everyone who lives here does too. There's always something else around the corner, something to keep you here. I often think that, even if it were possible, leaving New York would seem like a step back. A failure. Like giving up.'

Before I had a chance to agree, someone smothered Lex in a bear hug and shouted, 'Lexi!'

'Rafa!' he replied.

'Where you been, man?' Rafa said to Lex, and then, 'Running the world, I guess.'

Lex introduced me and I hovered, looking around the party, while the two of them talked. All the women were wearing jeans and ankle boots; I felt self-conscious in my dress and pumps; too polished, too corporate. I watched them as they leaned into each other, leaned out and jabbed the air, talking intensely all the while. One of them collapsed into hysterics, spilling her drink on the whitewashed wooden floor. Sam appeared. 'So, Stevie,' he said, 'tell me more about your time in TV.'

I told him about the mockneys and the programmes we'd made and he talked about his understudy role in a Turgenev play and the unfailing good health of the lead actor.

'Send him to the club,' I said, 'we'll put something in his coffee.'

Lex looked over and he and Sam smiled slightly at each other, a coded smile twenty years old that reminded me of what I used to have with Mira, and I told myself I'd call her the next day and I knew I wouldn't.

'Anyway,' said Sam, 'I guess if he had been ill this evening, I wouldn't have met you.'

The next day, I traced the route to the bathroom via a trail of discarded clothes. I peeled back the sheets of alcoholic gauze in search of inappropriate things I might have said to Lex, to Sam, to Rafa. I recalled the taxi ride over the rattling bridge, an empty seat on my left. Lex saying, 'I think it's home-time for me,' me replying, 'And for me,' and the gut-kick I'd felt when he hailed a yellow cab and said, 'You take this.'

All weekend, sitting in the park with the papers, running beside the river, watching my cell phone, refreshing my email, Lex was in my head.

'That was fun, Stevie,' he said on Monday morning. 'Thanks for putting up with me all night,' and I said, 'Of course, anytime,' and a name flashed up on his cell-phone screen, and his eyes darted to mine and he pressed reject.

Twenty-seven

Fake it till you make it. Nathan's advice is echoing again. I hold Ash under his armpits, look into his impassive eyes and force myself to smile, for my expression to say, *I am happy to be here with you.* I feel the corners of my own eyes tilt.

Ash stares back at me. I wonder if I have convinced him. I wonder if I can trick myself into feeling what I should by telling us both that I already do.

I will practise this all day, I tell myself. I will try it for a week.

But really, the faking started way before the birth. I felt like an imposter the morning of the embryo transfer, sitting in the surgery with my four hours' sleep and my hangover next to all those bereft couples. Ten thousand pounds up in flames; a uterine bonfire. The baby mosaic was no consolation that time – the squishy faces seemed to gloat, to taunt, *We are what you sacrificed last night.*

I sensed someone's gaze. A brave smile. I smiled back. Another single? Her skin glowed, the result of a protein-and-vegetable-rich, alcohol-free diet, no doubt. Light gym workouts and early nights. I, meanwhile, could still taste the wine on my tongue. I rummaged in my bag for gum, popped a piece into my mouth, looked at the label. HYDROGENATE STARCH

HYDROLYSATE, ASPARTAME, MANNITOL, ASPARTAME-
ACESULFAME, SOY LECITHIN, ACESULFAME K—I spat it
into my hand and stared back at my lap.

Any minute now, I would enter Dr Kimble's office and she
would poke a catheter up my vagina where less than twelve hours
before . . . 'You are still on the pill?' Will had asked me, and my
response had been a moan, an open-to-interpretation moan, and
he had carried on.

'Stevie Stewart?' the receptionist said. I stood up, wobbled like
a sapling in a high wind.

'Oh,' Dr Kimble said.

'Oh?'

'You don't look yourself today, Stevie.' It had not been my plan
to confess, but . . .

'Dr Kimble, I . . . I had a few drinks last night.'

'Ah. And you're wondering whether you should go through
with the procedure?'

'Yes.'

'Look, Stevie, drinking the night before is far from ideal – I
advised you to give up alcohol altogether while you're going
through IVF . . . '

'I know, and I *had*, it was just, last night . . . '

'I don't need to know what happened last night,' there was an
outline to her voice, 'but the answer is *yes*, you should still go
through with the procedure today.'

'Really?'

'I said it during your first appointment: you're in a different
position from many of the women in this surgery. You haven't
experienced the fertility challenges they have – not yet, anyway.
And we all know how many people conceive by mistake when
they're drunk.'

'Well, I'm not drunk, but . . . '

'You're tired, you're hungover, your uterus isn't quite the perfectly ploughed field we practitioners like to transfer an embryo into, but this is the most fertile point of your cycle, and, as you know, the blastocyst that made the grade is ready and waiting. Otherwise, we'll freeze it.'

'Right. Yes.'

'So we'll go ahead?'

'Yes. Thank you for making me feel better about it.'

'Forget last night, Stevie. Your chances of success are still good. Just try to relax and hope for the best.'

'I will. Thank you.'

The second half of the confession remained, thank God, lodged in my throat. I swallowed it as soon as the nurse gave me a hospital nightie and took me to the theatre, which had the same baby wallpaper as the waiting room, as if visualisation were part of the process.

The blastocyst transfer was a midge bite. Perhaps it was the anaesthetic effect of the previous night's alcohol, and the fact that, after all the intrusive procedures, legs akimbo, stirrup splayed had more or less become my resting position.

Soothing music played and ten minutes later it was all over. The arid alchemy of sexless reproduction. Now you're not pregnant, now you are.

'Right. That's it,' Dr Kimble said. 'Relax here for half an hour, then go home.'

'Thank you, I will. And then?'

'Take it easy for the next couple of weeks. No vigorous exercise, no sex.' I must have blushed then. 'Continue to eat a balanced diet of fruits and vegetables, protein and fibre, avoid soft cheeses and mercury-rich fish, just as you would if you were pregnant.'

The singleton was on the narrow stairs down to the street. I thought about avoiding her by answering a phantom mobile call, but she turned and saw me.

'Oh, hi,' she said. 'How was your appointment?'

'Fine, thanks,' I replied, 'and yours?'

'OK. Transfer. Third time.'

'Oh, right. Me too. My first. I'd ask if it gets easier, but I think I know . . .'

'It gets harder. I'm on my own, so . . .'

'Me too.'

'Really?' As if she hadn't guessed. 'Don't suppose you fancy a quick decaf?'

'Oh, I've got to head back to work now, but . . .'

'Let's swap numbers, then? I might need a shoulder to cry on in a couple of weeks, someone in the same boat. You might, too. Although it's the waiting that's the worst.'

We took out our phones.

'I'm _____, by the way,' she said.

Leah? Carrie? Claire? Whatever it was, I forgot it instantly. I should have asked again, but my mind, my one-track womb mind, was elsewhere.

'I'm Stevie,' I said.

'Great to meet you, Stevie. Are you on WhatsApp?'

'Yes.' She tapped in my number. A message from @prgal777 appeared below the Chrysler building on my screen. 'Hey, Stevie!' it said, a hatching chick emoji after the exclamation mark.

'Got it!' I said, and we went our separate ways.

As I walked to the station, I imagined catching my pregnancy metamorphosis reflected in shop windows when I returned for appointments, transitory versions of the smug #bumpwatch snaps on my Instagram feed: inflating women, photographed in profile, hands gently cupping tums.

On the tube, I stood at the end of a bank of seats and looked through the smeared partition at a man with a blurry black-and-white photo of a foetus on his phone. I watched him move his fingers apart on the screen to enlarge the image and stare intently at its tadpole body parts: the head, the black dot heart, until I felt as if I were intruding and looked above his head at the adverts for internet dating and hair-thickening products.

I took the man with the scan as a sign. I took many things as signs after the transfer. The three magpies I spotted on a Saturday-morning walk up the hill. The metallic taste in my mouth on day five. My tender, inflating breasts. The streaming cold on day eleven, because my body had thrown everything into baby-making.

The wait for the results was, as @prgal777 had predicted, excruciating, but it was not unhappy. I was high on hope: nothing had been disproved, no dreams had been shattered, I was waiting for the present I was sure I'd be given.

I compensated for my train-wreck conception eve by going into full nesting mode. I made sure I had nine hours' sleep every night; jogged gently each morning before work; turned down drinks and dinner offers, old friends wanting to catch up: I hadn't been back in London long. Every evening, when I sat on the sofa with a plate of something grilled and something steamed, a home improvement programme on the television, my mind would wander to a baby lying solidly in a Moses basket, blinking her green eyes.

Occasionally, the record would stick, and I would see Will looming over the basket, and think, *How could I have been so reckless?*

I googled the shit out of that little issue, of course I did. Was it possible that I could have released an egg so soon after a dozen had been plucked? And if it were possible, could Will have fertilised it? In other words, did it all add up to a baby?

My research had been inconclusive. The answer: maybe. But gradually, I worried less. The father or not the father, I made my peace. Plenty of people fall pregnant on one-night stands, I thought – some even do it deliberately. Will deserved far less – anyway, he would never know, and nor would she.

Towards the end of the week, I felt bloated. Moody. With child.

'And that's different from your normal state of mind *how*?' Nathan joked. He was the only person, other than @prgal777, I had told. The idea of fecund Rebecca cooing and coming around with ready meals was too much to bear, the thought of confiding in Jess too weird.

By the time the nine days were up, I knew. I didn't need to piss on a stick to know. I had the Stewart fertility genes. I had slipped from one room to another.

Twenty-eight

On Tuesday morning when my alarm went at six, I opened my emails and saw one from Lex, sent at 02:24. There was no text, just a photo of the exterior of our building in the Mission, caged in scaffolding, with 'FUCK OFF BACK TO NYC, YUPPIES' sprayed on a brick wall in large, pink letters.

My San Francisco trip was cancelled. 'I'm still going out tomorrow, but I think you should stay here,' Lex told me when I met him at the club a couple of hours later. 'Don't be put off, Stevie. Shit like this happens all the time when you're disrupting.'

'Do you think it's the neighbourhood?' I asked. 'Do you think it's because the Mission is gentrifying so rapidly, because property prices are way up?'

'Look, property prices are going up everywhere in San Francisco – have been for decades. We're only there because Silicon Valley is there. And I mean, we're creating scores of jobs for unskilled workers that won't be getting on a Google bus anytime soon. *And* we're building communities and supporting early-stage businesses that will go on to create a ton of jobs themselves. We're contributing to the city of San Francisco in *myriad* ways. I don't want you to lose faith.'

'OK,' I said.

'We'll get the PR agency on to it – set up an interview with one of our non-profit founders, get it in the local press, turn the tide.' He flung the strap of his weekend bag over his shoulder, pushed down the peak of his cap and headed to JFK.

I was still feeling the blow of the aborted trip on Sunday when I met Jess at the bar of a new Italian restaurant a block from her apartment.

'Even Nathan can't get a table here,' I said, as we were guided through the crowd to a two-top by the window. 'How did you score this at such short notice?'

'You know, connections,' she said with a half-smile. 'We invested.'

We sat down and looked at our menus. I thought of the meals I had with my girlfriends, with Nathan, never a pause in conversation, the server returning again and again to ask if we'd decided – *Sorry*, we'd say, *we've been chatting, we haven't even looked, can you give us five minutes?* Shouldn't it be like that with sisters; shouldn't it be *more* like that with sisters?

It was the years we'd spent apart. After all the time I'd been in New York, they still gaped, they gulped our words. It was my fault. If I'd stayed at Jess's apartment a few more months at the beginning, we'd be closer now.

Before we'd had a chance to choose our food, a cloud of ricotta sprinkled with sea salt and herbs arrived. 'Compliments of the chef,' said the server.

'So, how was the party on Friday?' asked Jess, tucking her hair behind her ears.

'Good. You should have come,' I said.

'I'm not a big party person,' said Jess. 'You know that.'

'Come on, I bet you went out every night when you first moved to New York.'

161

'Well, yes, but that was a long time ago. I'm more of a dinner type now. I like this.' She gestured at me and the menu.

'You mean you don't like crowds, or you don't like drinking to excess?'

'Both, probably. So, go on – the party?'

What would it take, I wondered, to find the armour chink, the dropped stitch?

'It was fun to hang out with Lex away from the office.'

'Just fun?'

'Jess . . .'

'I know what you're about to say.'

'About Lex?'

'Yes.'

'So?'

'Don't, Stevie.'

'Why not?'

'Lex is a great guy. He has energy, drive . . . he's fun. I knew you'd get on when I introduced you and I can see the allure. It's the power thing, partly.'

'It has nothing to do with *power*.'

'But he's not the kind of guy you should be dating.'

'Why not?' I could feel tears coming.

'He's your boss. And he's so focused on the company – everything else is peripheral. Guys like Lex treat dating the same way they treat business deals. You're a prospect, they go in for the kill, they move on. Honestly, he's just never going to be . . . *available*.'

'Maybe that's what I want.' I stabbed a slice of sourdough in the ricotta. 'Maybe I don't want a relationship,' I said.

'Well . . . Fine. But not with Lex,' said Jess. 'I just . . . I just can't bear to see you hurt, Stevie.'

'You talk as if you've experienced this yourself, Jess.'

'I gave up on dating a long time ago.'

'Why? Why was that?'

'Well, I . . . ' She spread her hands on the marble table and stared at her fawn-coloured nails. I waited. 'I had a serious relationship a while ago, something that meant something, to me, anyway.' Something she had never thought to tell me about.

'The chef. Lex's friend.'

'He told you.'

'He mentioned it. How long did it last?'

'A year.' A *year*.

'And what happened?'

'We wanted different things in the end. He got scared. Or I scared him off. I told him something he couldn't deal with. And that was that.'

What was it? I was desperate to know. Had she told him she loved him? That she wanted them to be *exclusive* – that bizarre New York relationship rite of passage – surely, they had reached that stage after a year? But I sensed Jess had revealed as much as she was prepared to. Something – was it shame? – quietened her.

'I'm going to the bathroom,' she said.

'You know, I've been thinking,' she said when she returned. 'We should get Mum over here for a visit.'

'Woah, do you think?' It seemed an extreme way to change the subject.

'It'd blow her mind, wouldn't it?' Jess said.

'It'd blow *my* mind. Worlds colliding. She'd love it, though, seeing where we live, her eldest and youngest.'

'She would. Shall we wait for her seventy-fifth?'

'No, let's do it soon. We can celebrate your fiftieth when she's here, considering you refused to do anything for it. Let's start planning now.'

I pulled my phone from my handbag to find a date. There was a message from a number I didn't recognise.

Hey Stevie, this is Sam. Hope you don't mind me texting – Lex gave me your number. Great to meet you Friday. How about dinner Thursday?

'You were right,' I said to Jess.

'About what?'

'Lex isn't interested in me.'

'I didn't say that.'

'He gave his friend my number.'

'Which friend?'

'Sam – the one who had the party.'

'An actor, right? I think I've met him. I'm sorry, Stevie. I know you're disappointed.'

'He's asked me out on Thursday.'

'You should go.'

'Actors aren't my type.'

'Perhaps that's a good thing?'

Twenty-nine

An oat milk latte; a café I haven't been to before. 'I'll have the same,' I found myself saying when the woman at the next table ordered one.

'We think he might be lactose intolerant,' she explains, nodding at the baby beside her. She could have given up breastfeeding rather than dairy. Still, I say 'poor both of you,' ask how it's been, the feeding, the sleeping. Find common ground.

We have ventured into society again, swapped our solo walks for human contact, been friendly to other mat-leave mums – there is, I've discovered, an epidemic of them in my neighbourhood – engaged in lengthy conversations about tummy time.

My face aches from the smiles I have forced it into, but it is working, this impersonation. I come across, I'm fairly sure, as tired but content with my lot – your average late-in-life mum. You wouldn't pick me out in a bad mother line-up, you wouldn't point at me and say, *She's the one who doesn't love her baby.* And they help, these encounters; they shorten the days. I feel hopeful as I leave them.

It never lasts. Back at the flat, there is always a melt-down, he is hungry, I can't get the formula into the bottle quickly enough. *I* am hungry and he won't let me eat. The switch trips and I am in the dark again.

I find myself wishing I were at work. When he's calmer, I check my messages, hoping for a text from Lex, from Mike, even, *So sorry to bother you, Stevie, but you're the only person that can help with this.* There is never one there.

The farm's number appears on my phone. If only I could talk to my own mother about this move, one life to another, the discomfort of it, but she wouldn't understand, she never experienced it, her career was ended before it began.

I imagine her looking through the window at the sheep on the hillside, wondering if I'll pick up. I set my face in the cheery expression I have been perfecting. 'Shall we say hello to Grandma?' I ask Ash.

'Hi, Mum,' I say.

'Stevie.' It's Dad.

'Is everything OK?' There's some kind of crisis, it's the only reason he'd call.

'Yes, everything's fine.' He sounds nervous. 'I was just ringing to find out how you were.'

'Oh, right.' Ash is waving his arms at the wooden flowers on his bouncy chair. I move to the bathroom, shut the door. 'I'm OK.'

'And Ash?'

'He's fine, too. Five weeks, now.' I doubt myself even as I say it. *Five weeks?* Is that all? 'How are you and Mum?'

'We're well. Mum enjoyed her visit the other week.'

'It was great having her here.'

'Any plans to come up?' I stare at my reflection in the bathroom mirror, the pallid skin and zombie eyes. Why can't he come here? The idea of taking a train, of summoning the energy to make any kind of journey, is so far from the realms of possibility it is almost comical.

'Maybe when there's a bit more of a routine.'

166

'Good. Well, that's it, really. Just wanted to check in.'

'Oh, OK, Dad. Thanks for calling.'

'OK. Bye.'

I remain dumbfounded. It must have been Mum's suggestion. She seems to have had an urge, since the baby arrived, to force us together. It is strange: she never seemed to care whether or not Dad and I had a relationship before. Perhaps it is because Ash is a boy. The first grandson from a trio of daughters.

'Come on, dear, this has gone on too long,' I imagine her saying. 'She's back, she has a child, a son, you're her father, if you won't go and see them at least act like a grown-up and *call* her.'

Did she sit at the table nodding encouragingly as Dad stood with the receiver against his ear, mouthing questions for him to ask? *Well done, love, it'll be easier next time.* And me? Am I supposed to reprise my devoted daughter role now, the one that failed in childhood?

I wonder how much Mum has told Dad about his grandson's conception. Do fertilised animals take pregnancy tests? Perhaps, with his experience of breeding farm animals, he understands the process more than most.

I think back to my own test.

Have you done it? @prgal777 had messaged the morning we were due to take them.

I had considered not replying, but the temptation to hear her result was too great.

Nope, I typed. *You?*

Can I call you came the instant reply. Bad news.

About to start a meeting . . . R U OK?

Test was negative. Third time unlucky.

Oh God, I wrote, *I'm so sorry.* I wished I could remember her name then. *I can't imagine how that feels. I'll call you later. Don't give up!*

I decided to wait until midday to relieve myself on my own stick, for reasons – no doubt justified by a magpie or black cat sighting – I don't remember. But as twelve ticked closer, doubt cast its shadow and I wanted to do it less and less. Finally, I felt a womb jab followed by an internal rumble – an irrefutable sign. There she was.

I closed the door of the cubicle and turned the lock. My hands shook as I tore at the foil; my thighs trembled as I crouched above the seat. I snatched loo paper from the roll, wiped the stick dry and slipped it into my handbag.

'Everything all right, Stevie?' Mollie called from the front desk as I walked past.

'All fine – won't be long,' I replied as I left.

I walked to a leafy square a few minutes from the office and sat on a bench, my heart baying. I took a deep breath, fished the plastic stick from my bag and turned it over to see the window at the thicker end. Sunlight obscured it, so I tilted the stick into the shade and felt my mouth open in a silent scream.

In the window was a single blue line: *Not pregnant*.

The clinic confirmed the result and offered counselling. I declined. I'd survived five years in New York without the therapy sessions on which almost everyone I knew depended and I wasn't going to start now. 'My shrink thinks I need to come three times a week,' Jenna had sighed one summer at the house by the beach. 'Your shrink thinks you're a mug,' I'd replied.

I blamed myself, of course. It hung around, the guilt, waking me up before dawn like a phony form of consolation for the baby I'd been promised, waking me up to remind me that I'd failed.

It had been my fault, of course, my *bad*. The spontaneous booze-and-shag session – I knew, whatever Dr Kimble had said, that it had lowered the odds, while my unreliable narrator of a reproductive system had been the willing accessory, convincing me it had happened, that one blastocyst was all it took. There was, of course, a glimmer of consolation: that Will's baby was not going to be mine. But it wasn't enough.

The remedy? There was only one: to do it all over again. Another cycle, and, as @prgal777 kept telling me, no superior odds, because your chances never improved, no matter how many times you tried and how bloated with false hope your belly became.

I didn't call @prgal777 the night of our twin negative tests, but she called me. I listened to the voicemail. Her name was Olivia, it turned out, and she was thinking about me. She'd be delighted if the test result was positive; she'd be there for me if it wasn't. Platitudes, all of them, but I recognised sincerity when I heard it. And I thought, *You deserve this far more than me. You are a better woman with a bigger heart.*

Thirty

Sam was standing by the entrance to the noodle bar, a wide smile narrowing his dark eyes.

'What happened?' I asked, wondering why he seemed so elated. 'Did the lead actor die?'

'No such luck.' He pushed his hand through his cropped hair. He was taller than I remembered, better looking. 'Waiting in the wings, as usual. Guess I'm just pleased to see you. I wondered if you'd come.'

'I'm so sorry I'm late, I . . . '

'Don't worry. I'm always late when the restaurant's half a block from my apartment, too.' He gave my shoulder a gentle fist-bump, held open the door for me. I squeezed past him, smelled sandalwood and fig.

I ate alone at my local ramen place at least once a week. I didn't usually wait for a table – being seated immediately was one of the many benefits of solo dining – and when Sam and I finally got to the front of the line and the manager saw me with someone she did a double-take. 'Two?' she said, with a conspiratorial smile, and directed us to chairs next to a pale wooden bar, behind which three chefs in white hats were chopping and frying.

'I love sitting at the bar,' Sam and I said at the same time, then laughed.

'So, Thursdays are your nights off?' I asked.

'Yeah,' he said. 'Got to let another understudy have a go. Or not have a go. So, what's good here?'

'I always have the pork ramen,' I said. 'I'm a noodle-eater of habit.'

'Sounds good, I'll have the same. So, how was your day?'

'Not bad, thanks. I'm supposed to be in San Francisco this week.'

'I heard.'

'But it's good to catch up with stuff at the club. You've been there, right?'

'Yeah, and you know, Lex is always telling me I should come down more often. I was at the opening party and I've been in once or twice when I've had auditions nearby, but I guess it's not really my scene. I'm rarely in the city these days, actually. I'm a confirmed Brooklynite.'

'Well, I'm flattered you came tonight. It's so different, the energy over there.'

'I did my time in Manhattan, but I couldn't live here now. And not just because I couldn't afford the rent. I felt as if I was on speed when I lived in the Village.'

'I kind of like that.'

'It's addicting. But I'm from Queens, so I'm more comfortable with a river between me and the bright lights.'

'I expect I'll tire of being in the thick of it someday.'

'Most people do. Lex won't. You know, it took me a few days to prise your number off of him. I would have gotten in touch earlier otherwise.'

What did he mean? Lex *was* interested in me, after all? 'He's a busy guy,' I said.

'When he wants to be.' He smiled. 'Busier than me, I'll give him that much.'

I didn't think about Lex again that evening. The next two hours passed easily and when our bowls and bottles had been cleared away, Sam and I were the last people in the restaurant.

'So now what?' he said. 'You've got work tomorrow and I haven't – unless Jonas takes a turn for the worse, which, as we know, is unlikely.'

I wanted to take his hand, to lead him to the bar on the park with the bottles of warm beer and the walls dripping with graffiti and condensation; to take turns putting quarters in the jukebox; to find tunes we both liked and tell each other what they meant.

No. I killed the thought like my mother clapping a clothes moth between her palms. Too risky. Too soon.

'I really should go to bed,' I said. Sam's eyebrows lifted a fraction.

'No problem,' he said evenly. 'I'll walk you home.'

I couldn't sleep that night, and as I listened to the sirens on Avenue A, I held the evening like a prism and examined every face. I looked for what I knew about Sam, for the résumé of his life so far and his plan for what was ahead, the brag-filled fuel of first New York dates, but I couldn't see it. His questions were different, too: he'd asked about things I thought and felt and not about things I'd done.

Sleep came late and I woke early. I walked to the coffee shop and prepared myself for the day ahead. I'd text Sam to thank him for dinner, I thought, and many hours or even days later, he would reply. He'd reply at the speed of a carrier pigeon, because that was the way here, it was what we did. It was possible, when he replied, that he would suggest meeting again, but likely that he would not.

What was more likely was that he would send a response that would, quite deliberately, require no response.

However atypical his behaviour the previous night, whatever texture it had added, I was surely not the only one he was dating, and we must take our turns. And still I found myself sighing when there was no message. *This isn't what you want*, I reminded myself. *You are better off on your own.*

When I pushed open my door, the sky was an impeccable blue. I allowed myself to slip back ten hours and remember how Sam had said, 'Talk me through your day, what time do you get up? What time do you go to work?'

I heard two full refrains of a cell phone before I realised it was mine, and I thought, *It's eight o'clock, it must be someone in England; it must be Mira, or Mum*, but I saw Sam's number.

'Hey!' he said. 'Are you on your way to work?'

'I am.'

'Look, I just wanted to say I had a great night last night,' he said.

'Thank you. I did, too.'

'And I wondered if you were free Sunday afternoon? There's this thing I go to – there are DJs, tacos, sangria – I think you'd like it. Come?'

'Sure,' I said, surprised at how certain I felt. I hoped it wouldn't put him off, and that Jess would forgive me for missing our dinner. 'I'd like that.'

Thirty-one

I bump into a mum from the antenatal group on the corner of my street. She lives close by; I have seen her before and pretended not to, but this time there is no escape. After we peer into each other's prams and offer the usual inanities, there is a pause.

'You know, if you ever need a break, I'd be happy to take Ash for a couple of hours,' she says. 'You could drop him off at my flat, have a walk, or just go home and sleep.'

She is concerned because I look mad, I think, mad and ravaged and desperate. I thought I was playing the role convincingly, but the mask has slipped; she can see me for the fraud I am.

I feel as if I should try to reassure her, I *am* a fit mother, he *is* safe with me. And at the same time, I want to cry. It is kind of her: she barely knows me.

'That's so thoughtful,' I say, wondering whether to accept.

'Not at all, I just, well . . . it's hardcore, isn't it, all this? I don't know how you do it on your own.'

I *wanted* to do it on my own, I remind myself. I had IVF so that I could do it on my own. It was a calculated decision, solo parenting; it was *my choice*. Why should she suffer for it?

'You know, I'm fine for the moment,' I say. 'My sister lives fairly near and friends have offered, so . . . '

'Of course,' she says. She looks embarrassed, she has over-stepped. We push off, both of us, back to our cells.

I waited two months after my first failed round of IVF before trying again. I had neglected my day job during the first cycle, but this time the London club would be my priority. The baby-making experiment would be relegated to side-hustle; it would never be my first thought of the day or my last. 'You're treating IVF the way you treat dating,' Nathan said, and I supposed he was right.

It didn't stop me living the requisite monastic life. It was January, and a life of privation was easy in London in January. I fed my ageing body vitamin pills and curly kale. Not a unit of alcohol passed my lips. As for the injections of fertility cocktail, this time I relished every stab. No more eye-scrunching or pillow-biting: I lined up my equipment after my morning coffee, gasped as the needle punctured my skin and delighted in the bubble of blood it produced, because there was proof in pain.

The London club was a jumble of concrete floors and plaster walls, the ceilings hung with wires like Spanish moss, and yet, in eight weeks' time, there would be tap-tapping beneath the motivational posters, tranquillised to suit the locals' sensibilities. There was so much to do, and though we had been here before – there were clubs in New York, San Francisco and Los Angeles now – this time, I was in charge. This time, as Lex kept reminding everyone – and I was never sure whether to take it as a shout-out or a threat – it was 'Stevie's show'.

At weekends, in an effort to trick my mind from the petri dish, I attempted a social life. I reconnected with old friends from university, people I had ghosted during the first IVF cycle. Their repertoire of questions was small.

'Do you miss New York?'

'Not yet.'

'What's different?' This, I'd come to understand, didn't mean what are the differences between New York and London, to which the answer would have been 'everything', but what about the city had changed since I'd left.

What *had* changed in five years? If there had been a shift in mood it was too subtle to detect. A vigorous strain of optimism had infected London during the Olympics, I'd been told. 'You should have come back last year,' everyone said, 'London was on a high.'

It certainly looked different. Tall, pointy buildings had sprouted haphazardly about the City and beside the river – fleshy masses of steel and glinting glass that caught the low winter light and in summer, I'd heard, set cars on fire.

'Wasn't this a fishmonger when we lived here?' I asked Mira when I met her at the café she'd suggested one Saturday afternoon.

'It was. The source of many a fish pie.' The floor, once slimy with guts and chlorine, was laid with tasteful ceramic tiles in geometric blues and greens. 'I bring Bea here,' she continued. 'The cupcakes are delicious – I mean, not New York delicious, but not far off.'

It was good to see Mira. But it was sad to be so close to where our relationship had reached its acme and to feel so far apart. Her lusty laugh, too big for her body, I didn't hear it that day. I wished Bea had come: we could have walked to the park together, the three of us, hand-in-hand. I felt the drug-induced bulge in my belly and hoped it would eventually bring us back together.

We ate cake and drank Earl Grey, and then she took me across the road to a hive of independent restaurants in the shell of an old market. Mira was proud of the city London had become. She was showing it to me because she wanted me to feel I'd done the right thing.

No one ever asks you why you move to New York. But they do ask you why you move back. 'It didn't feel real any more,' I offered as we walked to the tube and travelled two stops together before Mira took the over-ground to the semi with the garden and the pond, way out wherever, far from the sprawling city.

'I'm so glad you're here,' she said as she stepped out of the train, 'I've missed you,' and I knew what she meant by it, she'd missed the pre-New York me, and as the doors closed, I wished I'd told her about the IVF. I'd been embarrassed, doing it on my own, I worried she wouldn't understand. You're going to be on the same page again, I told myself, as I waved. That's what matters.

I considered flinging Olivia aside for round two, but after a couple of her missed calls, I answered. Trying to be ambivalent about my treatment all the time was exhausting, and, as the drugs ravished my reproductive and psychological systems, impossible. Thirty tearful minutes of 'what ifs' with Olivia allowed me to squish the issue to the back of the bottom drawer and get on with my real-life life.

That time – my second cycle; her fourth – she was ahead of me: her twin blastocysts, because they often double-up for the over-forties, inserted three days earlier.

On the eve of her transfer, my phone vibrated and I saw @prgal777. It would have been cruel to reject her, so I picked up.

'How are you feeling?' I asked.

'Anxious. Jittery. You know, Stevie, I think this is it. I can't go through it again.'

'Don't think of it that way. Think of tomorrow as the day the egg hatches.'

'I'm not in the right mindset for tomorrow.'

'That's bullshit, Olivia, the blastocysts don't care. You're super healthy. Your uterus is a perfectly ploughed field. There's every chance that this is – or these are – the one.'

'Thanks, Stevie. I don't know if I could have got through the last two months without you.'

'Just think, a year from now we'll probably be bouncing babies on our laps.'

Would we? Would I? This time, it happened, for both of us. Blue crosses, positive blood tests and six-week scans. The journey, as I'd found myself calling it, because New York habits die hard – the journey had begun.

Thirty-two

'You and Sam are meeting on a Sunday *afternoon*?' said Jenna. 'You mean, you're dating in the *daytime*?' We were having burgers at the club before I took the subway to Brooklyn. 'Wow, that's just so . . . intimate.'

'I agree, it's unusual,' I said. 'He's unusual. I was surprised when he asked.'

'Perhaps it's because he lives in Brooklyn,' said Jenna.

'Perhaps it's because he's really into her,' said Nathan.

'But are you into *him*, Stevie?'

'I don't know yet,' I said.

Nathan wanted to come with me. 'I think it's time I diversified my portfolio,' he said.

'When was the last time you brought a friend on a second date – or any date, for that matter?'

'Perhaps that's where we're both going wrong.'

Eventually, I shook him off and took the subway over the river. Sam was beyond the turnstile, and I was surprised to find my hands were shaking when I swiped my MetroCard. The walk from the station took us past red- and beige-brick two-storeys that looked film-set flimsy, with plastic tricycles in front yards and stars-and-stripes flags fluttering beside porches. 'Where are we?' I said and Sam laughed.

By the time we arrived, the ankle straps of my sandals were rubbing and sweat was sticking my dress to my stomach. I glanced at the crowd. 'Are you OK?' asked Sam, and when I nodded, he looked down at my sandals. 'Why don't you take them off?' he said, and I did. He held out his rucksack and I slipped them in.

Sam knew everyone: the DJ, the girl pouring the sangria into plastic cups, the guy serving the tacos; at least half of the people swaying gently to the music in a glade of trees. 'They're my crew,' he shrugged when I remarked upon it, 'but don't worry, Lex isn't here. It's not really his vibe.' I turned away in case he saw me blush, and noticed a woman sitting cross-legged on a picnic blanket beside the canal, breastfeeding her baby, stroking its head.

'This is my friend, Stevie,' Sam kept saying, which was what guys did here on dates when they bumped into people, even when you'd been seeing them for months. But this time it didn't feel like a brush-off; it felt like an accolade. Whenever he told me about the person he'd just introduced me to, or someone he'd just waved at in the line for sangria, superlatives poured from his mouth. 'Couldn't like him more,' he said. 'Sean is the nicest guy you'll ever meet.' I wondered what he'd say about me.

We moved away, from the edge of the canal to the taco stand. 'Come on, one more, we'll split it.'

'You know, you don't seem like an actor,' I said as we waited. 'Why?'

'I don't know,' I said, 'I guess I've always thought of actors as a bit self-obsessed.'

'And I'm not like that? Perhaps it's just a part I'm playing.' He smiled. 'Also, I haven't exactly made it. Just ask my parents. Not much to be egotistical about.'

We were dancing in the birch tree glade in front of the DJ booth and the sun had dipped, and a giant glitter ball suspended from one of the trees sprinkled the crowd with light when I put my arms around his neck and kissed him. I felt my stomach knot, and when the kiss ended, the embrace went on. It was a hug that meant something.

Thirty-three

She was right, the woman with the pram on the corner of my street. I do need a break from Ash. I can pretend all I like, but I'm not coping, not really; I'm waving at the window as the flames lick my back. I need a way out. After I see her, I become obsessed with finding one.

I think about contacting the night nanny: I go so far as to pluck her card from the fridge and start to stab out the numbers before I stop myself. *A hundred and fifty pounds a night!* Who do I think I am? I have twelve weeks' maternity pay to last me twice that long, and I can't bear to ask Jess for the money, she has been generous enough already.

I consider and promptly dismiss Rebecca's suggestion of her taking him for the afternoon. I can see her I-told-you-so smile.

I could call the woman with the pram, of course, but it wouldn't feel right, offloading my problems on to her – and, by association, everyone else in the mum group. Even though I have nothing in common with them, even though I will probably never see them again, I don't want them to know the state I'm in.

No, none of these is a solution. They would come and they would go, these helpers, and I would be on my own again.

I scroll to the last message I received from Olivia, who

wanted what I have so much. Perhaps she can shake me out of my ingratitude.

Although it wasn't meant to be, I'll always be glad I was pregnant. I was a mother for eight weeks. Nothing can take that away.

I didn't see Olivia again after her miscarriage. I understood why. I couldn't have stomached the sight of her pregnant, had her uterus – her fate – been mine and mine hers. There is only so much heartbreak a person can take.

Still, I felt her absence. Her loss was, in a sense, my loss. Our friendship had budded in the six weeks that followed our positive pregnancy tests; it had begun to mean something. How novel, I'd thought, to found a relationship on decaf and ginger tea rather than cocktails and wine. How honest.

We had swapped nutrition tips; enrolled in prenatal yoga; shared pregnancy books. We had talked about what it would be like when they arrived, just us: two families of two, about the prejudice we would experience. That day, those weeks, as our new realities were dawning, we told each other important things, dark things, things we didn't tell other people.

Will. Lex. Sam. Jess. Dad.

Her brother. Chris. Mark. Her mum.

'You know, after everything that's happened,' she said, 'I still believe in relationships. I don't think everyone always leaves.'

When she messaged to tell me she'd miscarried in the toilets at work the following week, I called and she didn't answer. I texted offering to come and see her and she said no. I sent lilies and a note that said, *I'm so sorry.*

After that, I was on my own. It was too early to tell anyone I was pregnant, apart from Nathan, and he was as useful as a sushi takeaway at that stage. 'This is all sounding a little too *Alien* for my liking,' he'd said. 'Can we talk about it when it's a real baby?'

Naturally, I wondered if I, too, would miscarry. I did a test every few days and, despite the cross or second line looking darker every time, I found it hard to believe there was a ball of cells multiplying inside me. I was tired but not sick. I didn't gag at the smell of coffee or curry. My jeans zipped all the way up.

'You dreamed it,' the sonographer will say, I thought, as the hospital's double doors swung open and I walked through.

The maternity wing was large and chaotic like a hellish game of Pac-Man: everywhere there were pregnant people shuffling in sliders and hospital gowns; murderous roars penetrated shut doors. I walked down one corridor, past a presentation case of knitted booties and hats, came to a locked door, turned around, came to another, pressed a buzzer and was told to go to a different floor. A woman leaned against the handrail of the staircase, head down, panting, and then let out a desperate, strangled howl.

'Can I help?' I asked, and she looked up and her eyes were wild. But then the baying stopped, the tormentor, for now, appeased, and she shook her head.

When I finally found the screening area, I sat in a blue plastic chair and waited, next to a couple in cashmere who stared straight ahead, acrimony freezing the air around them, even in this overheated room.

'Is anyone joining you?' the sonographer said as I lay on the bed, belly out.

'Why?'

'I was going to wait.'

'No one's joining me.'

He squeezed cold gunk on my stomach and jabbed the probe into my skin.

'There,' he said.

I gasped. On the screen, a grey broad bean trembled in a black cocoon, head as round as a coin, leg cocked like a broken matchstick.

'Would you like to hear the heartbeat?'

The deafening clatter of a locomotive filled the room.

'Is that normal?' I asked.

'Perfectly.' He smiled, and that was the moment I knew she was real. The moment I felt a detonation in my heart.

Ash is opening his mouth and fixing me with his anime eyes as he warms up for his next wail, and I wonder, for the millionth time, why my heart has been still since he was born.

Olivia. Yes, Olivia was far more worthy of a baby than me.

I could give her my baby.

I could pick up his Moses basket, order a taxi, drive to her flat, put the basket on the doorstep, ring the bell, leave before she answered and fly back to the life I have left.

You're mad, Stevie!

Instead, I think of another way to help Olivia, to comfort her. I start to write her a message.

It is not everything you hoped it would be.

It is not easy, but not for the reasons you imagined.

The green dot beside her name tells me she is online and my fingers hover, but I can't send it. I don't.

I think of the photo my mother took of Ash and me in hospital, the first and last photo I ever posted of him. Tired eyes. Obligatory smile.

Olivia must have seen that photo – she was always posting, peering, double-tapping. I hope she saw through the smile. That was the message I wanted to give her.

Would she have accepted it? I doubt it. People always think they need to have experienced things for themselves in order to know, really to know. Dear Olivia. She'll be forty-five soon. I hear it becomes easier after forty-five, when you know there's no hope left.

I pick up the night nanny's card again, bend it between my fingers. I am the lucky one. I must do what I can to keep what I have. One night will make all the difference. I dial.

When the nanny arrives that evening, the flat is in disarray. In the kitchen, the microwave door yawns open, spilled soup burned on to its glass plate. Toast crumbs dot the floor, coffee mugs list in the half-filled sink, and I am still wearing my pyjamas.

'One of those days?' she asks, and I nod. 'How have you both been, the last couple of weeks?' I wipe my eyes. It is the kindness in her voice.

'Can I make you a cup of tea, dear?' she continues. 'A herbal, if you have one, so you'll sleep?'

'Yes, please.' I had planned to slink into my bedroom the moment she arrived, but something is stopping me.

'Tell me, then,' she says when she has set the cup in front of me.

There is concern in her eyes; she is a good person, this woman, she doesn't know me, but she cares, and something unblocks.

'I just . . . I'm just not good at this,' I say. 'I can't do it.'

'Not good at what? What can't you do?'

'At being a mother to him, I don't feel . . . what I *should*, what other mothers feel.' In the pause that she doesn't fill, relief and regret jostle. I've said enough; I should stop now, but I don't.

'I thought I'd feel this overwhelming rush of love, of joy, when I had him, but I just felt numb. Then I thought I just needed to wait, it would come, and it hasn't. I see other women with their babies, I see *you* with Ash, and there's so much affection, there's a sort of mutual understanding. There isn't between him and me. There isn't anything.'

'I can see affection,' she says evenly. *It's an act,* I whisper to myself, *surely you recognise that.* 'But, Stevie, you're not the only woman I've helped who's said they don't feel as they think they should.'

'Really?'

'They're not always instantaneous, these feelings. They can take time.'

I can't tell if she means it; I don't know her well enough. 'I've tried, you know, I really have,' I say. I sound like a student offering a poor excuse for a bad grade. 'I've tried telling myself I care about him; I've tried everything I can think of to feel something and nothing's worked.'

She passes Ash to me. I'm surprised she trusts me with him, after what I've just admitted. He grips my thumb.

'Stevie, look at him: he's a healthy, contented baby. He's perfect. You may not feel it, but you're doing a great job.'

'He'd be better off without me,' I say. 'He'd be happier with someone else. I know he would. I can't give him what he needs.'

'That's not true, Stevie. You're his mother, he needs *you*.'

When I feel Ash, rigid in my arms, it hits me, what I've told this stranger. I've betrayed him. She is talking a good game, but the moment she leaves, she will call someone, and they will take him away. It would be better for him. But would it be better for me?

'I'm sorry,' I say, 'I didn't ask you to come this evening so that I could say all this . . . '

'I know you didn't,' she says, 'but I'm glad you have. Look, everyone gets the baby blues in some form – a day, a week, more. I know I did.'

'I've just had a run of bad nights, that's all it is. Most of the time I feel perfectly fine.'

'I'm sure you do, but I still think you should see someone. A counsellor. Someone who helps women like you all the time.'

'I don't need that, honestly. I'm just tired. I really shouldn't have said anything.'

'There's no shame to this, dear, and I do think it would help to keep talking about it. Your sister in America, the one who got in touch with me, have you told her?'

'I wouldn't want to worry Jess . . . '

'Or your mum, or a friend, someone you're in regular contact with?'

'Yes, there's a friend in New York, I talked to him a couple of weeks ago.'

'Good. I'll give you some numbers in the morning, some professionals. In the meantime, what you need most of all is a decent night's sleep. So, bedtime?'

'OK,' I say weakly, standing up, giving Ash to her. It is out there now, my confession, I can feel it deadening the air, and I can't take it back.

Thirty-four

Mum shuffled through arrivals, pulling a suitcase with a red-and-green strap buckled around it, carrying the cracked grey handbag she had had since I was at school.

'She looks so old,' I whispered. It had happened, the shift people talked about, when you became responsible for your parents. I wasn't ready for it. It was all right when you were old too, when you were fifty, as Jess was, but it didn't seem fair when you hadn't hit forty.

We waved and shouted, 'Mum! Over here!' and I wondered but did not ask, *When was the last time you saw her, Jess? When was the last time you saw your mother?* They wrote to each other, Jess told me, they spoke on the phone, but she never went back to England; it must have been years.

'Are you going to introduce her to Sam?' Jess asked, and I shook my head.

'Definitely not,' I said, 'it's far too new.'

Soon, we were speeding over Brooklyn Bridge and Mum had wound down her window and she was running her fingers through her white crop. She'd had it cut six months earlier: 'So much easier like this, I didn't even have to pack a hairdryer.' At that moment, her mouth open in wonder, she looked like a child.

'Oh, girls, I don't know whether to talk or to look out of the window or both. This is so thrilling!'

The best times of the week were the quiet times, when we were all together in the apartment, when, apart from the view, we could have been anywhere. I regretted all the dinner reservations I'd made; it was stupid of me when Mum was exhausted by four o'clock, when she wasn't impressed by the provenance of the chicken or the maritime décor. When she was constantly shocked by the menu prices – 'Twenty-five dollars for a cheese-and-ham pancake?'

Then there was the noise. I'd researched the restaurants' acoustics, but now I realised that they were not the problem, it was the people, who did not possess what Mum called 'indoor voices'. When I listened to them as she asked, 'What's branzino? What's brisket?' I realised that they were not talking about the mid-terms or the new museum on the Westside; they were all shouting, bellowing, barking, all of them, about themselves. Was that what I did? Was that what I did with my friends?

Three days in, I cancelled the remaining reservations and took her to breakfast at the diner at the end of my street. I had never been there before – why would I have? There was no chalkboard menu, the patrons were not in athleisurewear. Mum ordered silver dollar pancakes with bacon and maple syrup and I had corned beef hash and bottomless coffee ('Why don't they do bottomless tea?'). As she slouched comfortably in her orange chair, she said the diner reminded her of the movies, and when she snatched the bill from my hand and delved in her bag for her dollars, I didn't stop her.

That afternoon, we went to the grocery store on East Houston, and spent hours walking up and down the aisles with our plastic basket. When we got back to Jess's apartment, she told the doormen how dear everything was, even the milk, even the pasta; how did anyone make ends meet in this city? As we ate the passable Bolognese she'd made, she asked Jess when she had last used the oven in her pristine kitchen, and we all laughed when Jess refused to say.

I noticed that week that Mum teased Jess, but she didn't tease me. She could be short with her, but she was not with me. When I was exasperated one afternoon because Mum couldn't find her glasses, she became inconsolable, as if she were the child, desperate for my approval. Had she always been like this? It had been years since we'd all been together; years since I'd spent so long with her, that must be why I couldn't remember.

'She adores you, kiddo,' Jess said, when I mentioned it. 'She always has.'

'Because I'm the baby?'

'Yes,' she said.

As for Jess, she seemed to shrink a little that week. Perhaps it was the responsibility of having a seventy-something to stay, or the stress of taking time off work. Still, we got on, all three of us. Better than I had expected.

On the fourth evening, we went to a Broadway show. Mum fell asleep even though it was hard to imagine a more invigorating production, and as her head lolled on my shoulder, I tried to forget that I'd paid over a hundred dollars for each ticket and that I hated musicals. We went back to Jess's apartment afterwards and when we got upstairs, Mum didn't want to go to bed: her nap had revived her. She wanted to have a cup of herbal tea and for Jess to open the birthday present she'd brought: a silver hand mirror that had been her mother's.

As I was coming out of the bathroom, I heard something that made me stop.

'I think it would be a good opportunity, Mum, while you're here, while all three of us are here. I think it would be a good time to tell her.'

I shut the door noiselessly and wondered what it could mean.

'What have I missed?' I said when I came out again, and they looked at each other and Mum said, 'Oh, we were just talking about the musical,' and I didn't hear anything else on the subject, whatever it was, that week.

'It went well, didn't it?' said Jess, when we had chaperoned Mum to the airport, put her on the little cart that would whizz her to the gate; she'd had me laughing, just as the tears were springing, by saying that she was glad they didn't weigh her as well as her suitcase because she would have to have paid extra. All that pizza, all those pancakes, all those briskets!

'She seemed much happier than she is at home,' I said.

'Dad. It's a difficult dynamic, when we're there. I'm not sure Mum helps it much, to be honest.'

'Was it always like that?'

'Not always. I have some fond memories of him from when I was a child.'

'Such as?'

'There was one New Year's Eve,' she began. 'I was twelve. Dad said I was old enough to stay up until midnight. "We'll go out," he said, so we left the house at half past eleven, cut through the fields and walked towards the hill. It was a beautiful night; we didn't need the torches we'd brought: the moon was full; you could smell the new year in the air. It was exciting, being out there with Dad, it felt as if we were on some sort of secret mission.'

'Where did you go?'

'Not far. You know that oak tree, at the top of the hill?'

'Yes.'

'We got there just before midnight. "Why don't you climb it?" Dad said. I'd never been a big tree-climber, but I didn't want to disappoint him. He helped me on to the first bough, and I kept going. I was almost at the top when the bells in town started to ring and Dad smiled at me and cupped his hands so I could hear him and he said, "Well done, Jessie, what a place to see in 1974!"'

The warmth, the levity – it was so unlike any memory I had of my father I wondered if she'd made it up. I was about to ask her why they fell out, when did it first happen, that one of them always left a room when the other one entered, when she got out her phone and passed it to me. 'Look at my new screensaver.'

The photo was of the three of us on a bench in Central Park. Jess and Mum were smiling and my mouth was wide open in horror because the guy who took it had said, 'Three generations?' before he pressed the shutter and I'd said, 'Excuse me!' I'd felt terrible for Jess. I kept telling her, afterwards, that she looked years younger than fifty.

Thirty-five

The night nanny calls twice the day she leaves. I listen to the voicemail.

'I've found the numbers of a few people I think it would be helpful for you to talk to,' she says. 'Do call me back.' Before I delete her number, I send her a text.

Thank you so much for last night. Sorry for bothering you about baby blues. No need to worry any more — feel like a different person today!

After a day or so, I stop worrying about a knock on the door; if they were going to come, they would have by now. But my betrayal? Now that I have said it aloud, what I don't feel for Ash, the wasps in my head have taken flight. They are out there, wherever I look, on the fruit bowl, the windowsill, nesting in the tree outside. Visible to Ash and to everyone else.

I need to return to the things that give me comfort, the things I can do. I'll give Ash a bath, even though it is three in the afternoon. I'll drown the wasps.

I turn on the taps, go to collect him from his bouncy chair. I can't meet his gaze. I want to tell him I'm sorry, but I have done that so many times before.

I focus on the task in hand. I put the baby lounger in the bath, then undo the poppers of Ash's onesie – pop, pop, pop. I peel back the tabs of his nappy. Willy! Balls! Surprise! It still gets me every time, ten times a day, whenever I change his nappy. Not what I expected.

Is this why it's so hard? Is it because it wasn't a child I longed for; it wasn't a daughter? A daughter like Bea?

Perhaps things would have been different if I'd known I was expecting a boy, if I'd said, 'Yes, please do tell me,' at the scan, instead of smiling and shaking my head. Perhaps Ash would have seemed less unfamiliar, less other. Perhaps he would have felt more like mine.

By fourteen weeks, I'd had everything the internet associated with a girl pregnancy: the mood swings; the swelling around the trunk; the oestrogen overload that slicked my skin and hair with oil; the sugar cravings that made me slip bars of chocolate into my shopping basket like a hopeful Charlie Bucket. And there had been the rapid, girl-baby heartbeat. I had played the audio file from the twelve-week scan a dozen times a day and every time it had seemed faster and louder and she had seemed closer.

Nathan, across the Atlantic, was unconvinced.

'I mean, I know even less than you do about this,' he said on the phone one evening, 'but all this "her", "she" business? You haven't actually had the gender confirmed, have you?'

'No, that happens at twenty weeks.'

'So confusing, all these weeks. Can't we just work in months?'

'OK, five months. That's when I'll find out. Or maybe I won't. I've met people who told me they just knew. I have all – well, almost all – the girl symptoms.'

'You've been collecting them.'

'But it's more than that; it's a conviction, in my womb.'

'Your womb is telling you you're having a girl? I mean, I'd expect this kind of unscientific nonsense from Jenna . . . '

'How is Jenna?' I said, grateful for a subject change.

'The same. She met a cute guy on St Mark's a couple weeks ago. He was carrying a chair.'

'What kind of chair?'

'I don't know. They talked for like thirty minutes. He asked for her number.'

'Sounds promising.'

'He hasn't called.'

'Oh.'

'Do you meet guys in the street in London?'

'Never.' Through the window, the road was empty, silent. A woman in the flat opposite saw me and drew the curtains.

'So, do you have a baby belly? Can I see it? Let's Skype and you can show me.'

'What about *Alien*?'

'I'm over it.'

'Yes, I do have a slight bump. I'm disguising it with baggy jumpers.'

'Look, Stevie, obviously I'm enormously flattered to be the only person you've told, but I'm feeling the pressure of this information. Don't you think it's time to spill the beans, or the avocado, or whatever she – FUCK, I can't believe I said that – is now? To tell Mira? Jess? Rebecca? Your *mom*, for God's sake?'

I liked Nathan and me being the only people who knew. I hadn't wanted to expose her, to expose either of us.

'You know I ran into Jess the other night?' Nathan said. 'She was super friendly. She asked if I'd spoken to you and I pretended I hadn't, and she said she kept missing you.'

'Story of our lives.'

'Perhaps she's psychic, perhaps she already knows. But you need to call her back. Come on, Stevie; you need to tell her. Do it this week, OK?'

*

After I'd told Jess about my baby-making plans that summer evening, a few weeks before I'd left New York, the issue had been swept away, along with the jagged fragments of the glass she had dropped.

When I returned to London and we spoke, I never said I was puncturing my thighs with ovum-inducing drugs. I don't know exactly why I couldn't talk to Jess about it, only that she wouldn't want me to.

Her face leaped on to the screen. 'Jess!' A luminous day in New York.

'This is a nice surprise,' she said. Behind her, Corinthian columns rose. 'I'm about to meet Mickey.'

'How is she?'

'She's good. We're going to go look at colleges in a couple of weeks.'

'That's amazing. Tell her I say hi.'

'You can tell her yourself. She just got here. We were going to call you, actually, she wants to study History of Art, so she needs your advice.'

The last time I'd seen Mickey she had been marooned in acne and angst. This time, her skin and her voice were clear; she stood up straight, only a couple of inches shorter than Jess, and met my gaze.

'Jess,' I said, when Mickey and I had finished talking, 'there's something I want to tell you.'

Jess didn't call back when they left the museum as she'd said she would. The next day, I texted and she didn't answer. I tried her again that night. *So sorry, S*, she wrote, *Call me tomorrow. Really want to hear your news.*

Perhaps she thought that if she kept rejecting my calls, the baby would cease to exist, that it would retreat into my ovaries like a time-lapse nature video in reverse. Because surely she had guessed by now.

I couldn't tell my boss before my sister; even I knew that, and Lex was coming to London later that week. I tried Jess once more and, again, she didn't answer, so I messaged her. There was no alternative.

I've tried so hard to get hold of you, Jess. I wanted to tell you that I'm pregnant. Due end of October. Call me when you can.

A second tick appeared below the message, and I watched both ticks turn blue.

Thirty-six

Nathan took a key from his pocket, dipped it in a plastic pouch and snorted.

'Really, Nathan?' I said.

He shrugged. 'The line for the bathroom's way too long.'

I looked around the crowded dancefloor. No one had noticed. He passed the bag and the key to me.

'It's Tuesday,' I said.

'What was that you told me about not settling down?'

I sighed. 'OK.'

In an effort to convince Nathan that I had not fled permanently to the outer boroughs, I'd agreed to meet him at a club in the Lower East Side where one of his favourite DJs was playing.

'I have news,' he said, when I'd finished. 'I met someone.'

'You did? Who?'

'He's called Brice, he's a showrunner, he has two dogs.'

'You hate dogs.'

'I like dogs in costumes.'

'Tell me you didn't meet at the Halloween dog parade.'

'We met at the Halloween dog parade. It's a great event – I thought you were coming?'

'What are his dogs like?'

'Sort of medium-sized? They were dressed as Michael and Janet Jackson.'

'Did they like you?'

'They were a little snarly, actually.'

'I'm not surprised, in those costumes.'

'He calls them his barriers to intimacy.'

'Well, that should suit you down to the ground, seeing as you don't like intimacy.'

'What about you? How's the long-term relationship?'

'Is five months long-term?'

'In this city it is.'

'He met Jess last weekend.'

'Sam came to one of your Sunday dinners? That's huge. Shame he didn't meet your mom when she was over.'

'No chance of that. He invited himself to dinner with Jess, booked the restaurant – a place in Williamsburg, he does shifts there sometimes.'

'Of course. I forget he's a struggling artist.'

We went to the bar. 'How's work?' I asked. 'Are the consultants still circling?'

'Yup. I'm a little worried, actually. At least I'm cheap. I have that on my side.'

'You could always come and work for us.'

'And do what? Take coats? Make poached eggs?'

'Content.'

'*Content*. God help us. Can you buy that by the yard?' He picked up his beer. 'You love it there, don't you?'

'Yeah. It's, I don't know, satisfying, having so much of a say in things, seeing my ideas come to life. It's doing well: it feels as if it's going places. And it's like a family, kind of. I know how lame that sounds, but we look out for each other, the team and the members.'

'How?'

'All sorts of ways. Like, if I'm not in the club one day I get calls, people check up on me, make sure I'm OK.'

'Every living-alone New Yorker's dream. Christ, you really have been gulping Lex's Kool-Aid.'

'I always thought when I worked in TV that if I didn't show up for work one day, they'd just replace me. You know, I've been thinking, Nathan: the other thing *you* need to do with your career is build your own brand. You need to stand out from all the other writers.'

'You think I don't? Aren't my caustic wit and impeccable taste enough?'

'Have you opened an Instagram account yet?'

'Hell, no.'

'You look great; you take great photos – it's made for you. You need to evolve. Let's set one up right now.' I get out my phone, tap the app, type in his name. 'Damn, Nathan Walker's gone. Walker underscore Nathan. Gone, too.'

'Lord Nathan?'

'Let's try Nathan underscore Walking. Bingo. There. Done. It's yours.'

'What am I supposed to do – post photos of myself *walking*?'

'Why not? It can be your USP!'

'My what? Anyway, you were telling me about Jess and Sam, the intro.'

'He seemed super nervous – his hands were shaking when Jess and I arrived. And he'd dressed up: white shirt, chinos.'

'He *is* keen. Did they get on?'

'It took a couple of drinks for him to loosen up, but yes, they liked each other. They'd met a couple of times before, years ago, through Lex. Jess approved.' *What a lovely guy!* she'd texted me afterwards.

'And how is Jess?'

'I don't know. I think I'm getting somewhere with her one moment – like when she mentioned the chef she dated for a year, did I tell you that?'

'The one you already knew about from Lex? Well, that's progress, I guess.'

'Except she didn't really *tell* me anything: we were talking about why they broke up and she got all defensive and changed the subject. Still, it was good when Mum was here. Well, Jess seemed a little out of sorts, but I think that was Mum rather than me.'

'You know what you two need?'

'What?'

He flicked his hair, leaned back in his chair. 'Couples' therapy.'

'Funny.'

'Do you think it's her boarding-school education?'

'What do you mean? She's emotionally repressed?'

'Yeah.'

'She was only there a few years.'

'Well, she's clearly been hurt – the chef, others, probably – I bet she dated like a mofo when she moved here, what else are you going to do in your mid-twenties when you don't know anyone in New York? Perhaps she just doesn't trust people any more. Look, why don't you take her away for a few days? I know it's months away, but you could have the first weekend of next season at the beach house.'

'Memorial Day? Are you sure?'

'Yes. Jenna had more than her fair share of solo weekends this year and I'll take Brice later on if we're still together.'

'OK,' I said. 'Thanks, Nathan. I will.'

Thirty-seven

While Ash naps, I scribble down ideas. A crèche for the club. A mentoring programme. Annual awards. I email Lisa, the membership manager with the wedding ring that Lex had objected to my hiring, for her thoughts. Seconds later, a bounce-back: *Lisa Owens is no longer at this address.* Has she left? How sad; how strange of her not to have told me she was going.

It's always there at the back of my mind, work, it's a dripping tap, and some days the faucet is on full. I know it stands between Ash and me, my very own barrier to intimacy, but since the night nanny I have let it flow, because it's solace, the thing I haven't failed at. It helps to push the treacherous thoughts away.

I pick up the magazine that arrived in yesterday's post. I'd drafted Nathan in to help and it was ready to go to press when I left, Lex's signature on every page proof. 'You don't have to do anything,' I'd told Mike, who'd nodded meekly: he wasn't the type to have an opinion on content strategy or art direction. That didn't matter, the magazine was bi-annual, the second issue had been commissioned, I would be back before it was published.

When I wrestle it from its plastic sleeve something has changed. It takes me a second to realise that the font is different, bigger and black instead of crimson. My hands shaking, I flick to the contents page. Two articles are missing. In their place is something called 'The Collector', and when I turn to it, I see a full-page photograph of Lex standing outside his apartment building holding a skateboard, then a collage of his boards by contemporary artists and an account of his 'collecting strategy'.

Lex must have suggested it, I think: Mike is malleable and I was not. Still, I'm annoyed I didn't come up with it myself. Perhaps this is an opportunity to contact Lex, I think; perhaps I should call him and tell him how great he looks in it.

I place the magazine face-down on the table and try, for now, to forget about it, to return to my current day-to-day, to my spiralling to-do list.

I think about clearing the fridge of its on-the-turn items. Filtering Ash's drawer of the onesies he has already grown out of. Denuding the mantelpiece of its baby cards. I pick up Nathan's 'IT'S A GIRL!' card. *Oops! No it's not!* he had written inside, along with a poem discrediting my psychic powers. My thoughts return to work and to Lex when I think about the card that isn't there.

Lex had sent, or signed, a card when I had left for maternity leave, but there had been nothing since. No flowers, no soft toy or personalised story book or dressing gown embroidered with Ash's initials. Not even a reply to my email announcing his birth. Lex was busy, of course, but that wasn't it.

Even before I had begun IVF, I'd dreaded the moment I'd have to tell him I was with child, which, considering my chosen method, felt like the correct way to describe my condition. A phone call or video conference wouldn't do; it had to be in person, so I waited for Lex to visit the half-formed London club in May, by which time I'd be four months pregnant.

Apart from the two staffers I had lured from the New York club, none of my London colleagues had met Lex, and they prepared for his arrival with a mixture of relish and apprehension.

Their impressions of him derived from his single-letter email responses – 'y', 'n', 'k' – the All Hands meetings we video-conferenced into on Monday afternoons and the breakfast TV segments they'd watched, in which he pontificated about the rise and fall of start-ups, adjusting the peak of his baseball cap very slightly as he did, a trademark tic that soon became an internet meme.

From afar Lex was, I suppose, impressive. Intimidating, even. The team, a European hotchpotch I'd plucked from competing members' clubs and co-working spaces that, in some cases, lacked the chutzpah of their American counterparts, seemed to regard his upcoming visit as an episode of *The Apprentice*. Their work on the new club, they'd assumed, would be appraised, and if it was found to be wanting, heads would roll.

I had done my best to reassure them that Lex wasn't a micro-manager: he trusted us to get it right, by which I meant he trusted me. Lex had barely been involved with the project: he seemed, as Nathan had predicted, to regard the London club as a sort of minor colonial outpost, an amusing diversion. When he called me, which he did at least twice a day, it was generally about America. I never told the team that, though. And I certainly didn't tell them what was preoccupying me as Lex's plane landed and his emails began to ping in.

By then, my work wardrobe consisted entirely of tunic dresses, flat boots and long scarves that hung distractedly about my mid-riff. It had been three months since Lex's last visit, but I hoped his visual image of me – if he had one at all – was from my leaving party when I'd been at my running acme, arms sinewy, stomach flat. I'd worn a silk, sleeveless dress the colour of mango flesh and spindly sandals that had elevated me to six foot. 'Has anyone seen Stevie?' Nathan's refrain had been that evening, the joke being that I was hard to miss.

I didn't expect to have to tell Lex anything about my altered state – one glimpse would do it.

But I was wrong. 'Have you shrunk?' he asked as he hugged me. 'Or is this just London's casual, no-heel vibe?'

'The latter, I hope,' I laughed, and cursed myself for missing my opportunity, felt my pulse racing – was it the tip-of-the-tongue confession or the effect of seeing Lex in real life after three months?

I passed him a hardhat and a pair of the blue plastic overshoes, then put on my own. 'The design team are on their way. You're going to love what they've done.'

'Good. Can't wait. There,' he said when he was ready, shower caps covering his sneakers. 'My favourite look.'

'That was great work,' Lex said, as we walked to the café I'd booked after the walk-through, an old favourite that served kidneys-on-toast and tea in red enamel pots. 'You've evolved what we've done in the US; you've given it a sense of place. It's a little more old school, but this is London, London *is* old school. And you've integrated all the stuff our community needs. I love it.'

As we sat down opposite each other, I rehearsed my lines in my head again and tried to quell the excitement of being close to him. *Old habits*, I chided myself. 'What's good?' Lex asked.

'I like the chicken-and-leek pie.'

'So British. I'll join you. I'm looking forward to meeting the rest of the team this afternoon.'

'They're crapping themselves about meeting you.'

'Ha! Anyway, what's going on? How are you finding London – for real?'

'I've been meaning to talk to you about that, actually, Lex.'

'You hate it? I knew it! Just stay until the opening, then we'll book you on the first plane back. I only ever wanted you here for a few months; I told you that, you were the one who insisted on moving. I miss you. We all miss you.'

I'd forgotten how much New Yorkers miss people. Acquaintances, people I'd met only a handful of times would say it: 'I miss you, Stevie, when are we going to hang?' when you both knew that even if you did make a plan, one of you would cancel and you'd see each other at the next birthday or holiday party and say the same thing all over again.

Had Lex missed me? I'd missed the energy that pinged off him and on to everyone around him – his avatar on the video conference screen was a poor substitute; the tinny audio didn't do his Midwest foghorn justice. But had I missed *him*? When you've built a company together, when you're always in each other's eyeline, it's impossible to filter one emotion from another. That was what I told myself as I smoothed the raised hairs on my arm.

'It's been good being back in London, actually,' I said. 'Well, I mean, it's been a mixed bag. There's a lot I miss. But, you know, reconnecting with old friends, family . . . And working on the club has been super exciting. I've appreciated the autonomy.'

'You've earned it.'

'Thank you. It's . . . There's something else.'

'What's that?'

'I'm pregnant.'

'You're *what*?'

'I'm having a baby.'

'But . . . I didn't even know there was someone.'

'There isn't.'

'So, who? Was it a mistake?'

'I'm using a sperm donor.'

'A *sperm donor*? Nathan?'

'No, not Nathan.'

Lex tapped his fork rapidly on the table: tap-tap-tap.

'Well, it is what it is,' he said as he cut the pie open and it spilled its innards on to the white plate. Then, his human resources training must have kicked in because he said, 'Congratulations,' just loudly enough for me to hear.

'God, Stevie,' Lex continued, 'this has really thrown me. I'm wondering . . . '

'How much time I'll take off?'

'Well, yeah.'

'You're not really supposed to ask me that. I mean, legally.'

'I keep forgetting we're in the UK. OK, don't answer.'

'I'm due in October and I don't think I'll be off longer than six months.'

'Six *months*?'

'That's pretty standard here. Most of my friends take a year.'

'And when you come back . . . ?'

'It'll be exactly the same as it is now. Full time.'

'I guess I just thought . . . I thought you were *in* this.'

'I am in this, Lex.'

'I didn't think you were into *that*. I need you to be a hundred per cent focused on the job.'

'I am and I will be. Have you found my attitude or my work any different the last four months?' He looked out of the window, as if mentally reviewing my performance. 'You gave me a great review and my entire bonus,' I said.

'I did.'

'I mean it, Lex. Nothing will change.'

'That's good to hear. I just hope you know what you're doing, Stevie.'

'I do.'

'It's going to take some adjustment.'

'For you, maybe. For the next five months, nothing will change. I'll help to hire my cover; then, when I come back, I'll have a nanny and, again, nothing will change. The only difference is I'm going to want to stay in London. For the next year or so, anyway. That's all.'

We had drinks with the team that night.

'Do they know?' Lex asked as we walked ahead of them to the bar.

'Of course not; I wanted to tell you first.'

'I appreciate that.'

'But I guess I should tell them tonight.'

'I guess so.'

It had been hard work pretending not to be pregnant; it was a relief for it to be out in the open, not to have to bolt to the loo and flush a decoy glass of wine. My colleagues seemed delighted. It was normal here for women to be pregnant; it was what we did. The gender was speculated upon; names were suggested. No one asked about the father.

But something woke me at three that night and I felt a sense of rising panic, as if I'd flicked a switch and the light hadn't gone on, and I wondered if it was a mistake, after all – not the telling Lex, I had to do that before someone else did – but all of it.

Just then, deep in my stomach, I felt a punch.

Thirty-eight

'I've been to Montauk before, have I told you?' Jess asked. We were off the motorway now, beyond the Hamptons; soon we'd be roller-coastering through parkland and the ocean would appear. I'd worried we wouldn't have enough to say to each other during the drive, that the weekend would falter before it began, but I needn't have. Jess seemed far more relaxed than usual; chatty, even.

'Who did you come with?' I asked.

'Oh, an old boyfriend.'

'The chef?'

'No, years before him. A finance guy who fancied himself a surfer. It was more motel than boutique hotel, then, the town. Dive bars and pancake houses. Not the hotspot I've heard it is now.'

'Always ahead of the curve, my sister.'

'Hardly. I loved it, though. I don't know why I haven't been back. Those beaches.'

'Did you ever think about getting your own place outside the city?'

'Not really. I prefer to sponge off other people.'

'Ha.'

'I wouldn't want to be tied to one place for weekends, holidays.

I like being able to hop all over: Upstate, the North Fork – my friends there. Shelter, Amagansett. And further afield, obviously. I wouldn't want to feel guilty for booking a plane ticket. Plus, I'm a city person now. Being too far from a subway station for any length of time makes me anxious.'

'Right.'

'What's the plan for tonight?'

'I thought we'd have beers on the beach, watch the sun set, then I'll cook. I brought barbecue stuff – nothing fancy.'

'Perfect,' she said. 'Leave the restaurants to Manhattan. So much nicer to eat at home. Stevie?'

'Yes?'

'Thank you for all this.'

We ate charred chicken and under-baked potatoes on the terrace.

'I'm sorry, Jess,' I said, 'I've forgotten how to cook since I moved to New York, did that happen to you?'

'Oh, I never learned.' She smiled, looking up at the sky. The stars were beginning to show. 'This is heaven,' she said.

'Ready for a glass of wine?' I asked. She hadn't wanted a drink since our beers on the beach.

'I'm fine,' she said. 'You know what, it's been a long week, and this has been the most perfect evening . . . I'm going to crash; save myself for tomorrow.'

'Really? It's only ten.'

'I know. Serves me right for getting up so early.'

'OK, sleep well,' I said. I thought she'd wanted us to spend time together; why did she always pull away? Why was she always leaving?

When we'd said goodnight, I poured myself a glass and sat outside, listening to the inhale and exhale of the waves, telling myself that relationships weren't linear, people ebbed and flowed.

In the morning I found Jess in the kitchen, wringing out a cloth.

'How long have you been up?' I asked.

'Oh, I always wake at six,' she said. 'But it's fine, I like cleaning, it's meditative.'

I took the cloth from her hand. 'Let's go for a hike.'

As we walked down to the beach and along the bluff, the tide was out, flat, and the path rose up and down, grass rippling on either side.

'I remember this,' she said. 'I must have run along this path.'

'Did you surf, when you came?' I asked.

'I tried. Borrowed a board as big as a dinghy and floated on it for a while. Then I got whacked on the head a couple of times trying to catch a wave and decided I was better suited to sitting on the beach with a book.'

'Sounds like my experience. I love the idea of surfing; the reality turned out to be less appealing.'

Suddenly, there was a flash of tan ahead of us and we both gasped and she grabbed my arm as we watched a deer bound into the scrub. We looked at each other and laughed.

'That really gave me a shock,' said Jess.

'Me too. I've seen deer a few times out here but it's always a surprise – a wild animal so close to the city.'

Perhaps it was the intimacy of that moment: at home, stepping on the backs of my sneakers, squeezing out one foot and then the other, watching Jess bend down and unlace hers, I found myself asking her when she'd last spoken to Rebecca.

'And is she always asking you about your love life?' I asked when she didn't reply. Perhaps it would lead us back to babies, to the talk we'd almost had when Mira was pregnant with Bea. 'That's what she does with me,' I continued, 'she's one-track-minded, Rebecca, it's as if she needs everyone to mate for life to justify her own choices.'

'I haven't spoken to Rebecca for a while,' Jess said finally. 'But no, she doesn't ask me about that.'

'What do you talk about? When you do talk.'

'I don't know . . . the kids?'

'And Mum and Dad?'

'Yes, of course.'

'Did you ever get on well?'

'Rebecca and me?'

'Yes.'

'We did, when we were young. We squabbled as well, though; sisters do.'

'What about?'

'Who got the bigger slice of cake, whose turn it was to do the washing-up . . . '

'It's always seemed fractious between you, I mean, from my perspective.'

I was thinking of a Christmas holiday; I must have been four. I wanted someone to help me write a letter to Father Christmas and Jess was doing homework, so I'd gone to Rebecca's room and found her lying on the bed, stonewashed jeans, velour sweatshirt, mist of hairspray, stereo blaring. She'd been livid when she'd seen me.

'Get out!' she'd shouted, and when I stood there, pleading, she'd screamed, 'Mum, Jess, Stevie is *not* my responsibility, come and get her *now*!'

The music was too loud, they didn't hear, and after what seemed like forever, Rebecca screaming, me standing there, shocked to the spot, Jess walked in and the two of them glared at each other and Jess took me by the hand.

The sting of rejection I felt soon passed, but the animosity between them stuck. Or perhaps it had always been there. I couldn't remember them getting on after that.

'Stevie?' Jess's voice was ascending.

'Yes?'

'I don't want to talk about Rebecca.' She raised her hands as she said it, pushed them towards me like a mime artist with her invisible wall.

'OK . . . ' I wasn't used to this; she was always so mild-mannered with me. I didn't want conflict, that wasn't what this weekend was for.

'I don't want to talk about Rebecca or Mum and Dad. I just . . . I don't want to go there. Not this weekend.'

After that, she mumbled something about air and walked down the road back to the beach. What nerve had I touched?

I stayed where I was; let Jess have her space, I told myself, watching her slim silhouette recede, wanting to follow, wondering why I wanted to, where did it come from, this impulse to be closer to each other? Was it the holes in her life I wanted to fill, or holes in my own?

I thought about having a child, how it would change the dynamics. If it would make things more complicated. Then I pulled on my trainers and ran after her. 'Jess!' I called, and she turned around, her face bright with the midday sun, and I knew I'd done the right thing.

The afternoon was different. The lines had been drawn and I knew not to cross them. We talked about Sam, because she beamed when I mentioned him, and about our mutual history. Sharpening colouring pencils together on the kitchen table, lining them up in a rainbow. Camping on the outskirts of a seaside town with ice-cream-coloured houses. We left Rebecca and our parents in the wings. Some of her stories I recalled, some I didn't. Myths or truths, I allowed Jess her memories.

*

That evening, we cycled to the Mexican place and I asked her what she'd like to drink. We always had margaritas here, I said, and she shook her head.

'Just a soda, please, anything they have, but don't let me stop you.' When I returned with the drinks I sat down and took a sip, and I felt her watch me.

'Are you sure you don't want one?'

She knitted her fingers together then said, 'You know, Stevie, I don't actually drink any more.'

I put down my plastic cup.

'Really?' I was astonished. 'I knew you didn't drink *much*; I knew you didn't drink at home, or on Sundays, at our dinners, but not at all?'

I waited for her to say that it wasn't that much of a thing in New York, it wasn't like London, that she needed a clear head for her job, that it was funny, she'd lost the taste after a while. But she didn't.

'I gave up because there was a time when I drank too much,' she said.

I couldn't believe what I was hearing. Jess, my successful, shit-together sister, had had a drinking problem?

'Do you want to talk about it?' I asked. 'You don't have to.'

'It's the last thing I want to do,' she said. 'The last thing I want you to know about me. But I think I should.'

'Jess,' I said, as gently as I could, 'whatever happened, I won't think any less of you,' and she nodded, but she didn't look convinced.

'It was soon after I moved to New York,' she said. 'It was supposed to be my big chance, a new life, but the city was dark and full of shadows. I was lonely. I missed my friends in London and I missed you. I felt awful for leaving you.'

'Oh, Jess,' I said. 'I was heartbroken when you went. You were

215

my favourite person, the only one who really understood me. But you shouldn't have felt guilty. You were twenty-five, you'd been given this incredible opportunity to move abroad, make your own life. An eleven-year-old sister was no reason for you to stay in England.'

I knew this; intellectually, I knew this. My hurt at her leaving was irrational. But it was still there, that scar of sadness, like a faded tattoo. I wondered if she could see it.

'It woke me up in the night, the guilt,' she continued, 'it prised open my eyelids, told me I shouldn't have come. But it was too late: I knew I couldn't go back. Gradually, I made friends at work and they led to other friends, the sorts of people I'd never met before, people like Celia.'

'The one who recommended the tarot hairdresser?'

She laughed. 'Yes. A waitress with a sideline in magical thinking who could smell a party three blocks away.'

'She sounds fun.'

'She was – they all were. I don't know what they saw in me, that crowd. Perhaps they found me amusing, corruptible, this straight Brit, far from home in every sense. But it made me feel better, going out every night, wine bars and dive bars and clubs where I danced on the stage.' I imagined a strobe flashing across her face. 'I forgot about the past. For the first time in my life, I let go.'

'And that was when it became a problem, your drinking?'

'Not really, not then. I was just doing what every other twenty-something in New York did – it wasn't as if I was necking neat vodka. I worked hard, through the hangovers, through the weekends. I told myself I could stop any time I wanted. I didn't need it, I liked it.'

It passed, the take-it-or-leave-it phase. She'd wake up wanting a drink and ignore the nagging until lunchtime; then she'd go to a restaurant a safe distance from the office and drink a bottle of wine while she picked at a salad.

'I was irritable, tired all the time,' she said. 'I fell asleep in a meeting. A guy I was seeing stayed over, and when I was in the bathroom vomiting that morning, I heard him slam the front door. I never saw him again.'

'Did you think of giving up then?'

'No, not then. It was a reason to keep going. An anaesthetic.'

'What about your friends, didn't any of them say anything?'

'I don't think they thought I had a problem,' she said, and I wondered if I would have. Alcohol was so woven into my social life I couldn't imagine myself without it.

'So, what happened? Why did you quit?'

It was one evening in July, a little more than a year after she'd moved to New York, she said. She'd come home to shower and change and have a vodka, just enough to lift her mood, it had been another tough day.

'On the way to the elevator, I decided to check my mailbox. I'd been neglecting it; I couldn't remember the last time I'd put the little key in the lock, and it was so full it took me a couple of moments to open the door.

'Among the avalanche of unpaid bills and pizza menus and health plan statements, there were three airmail letters. I picked them up, there's something miraculous about airmail letters, light as air and bursting with life, and I saw your round handwriting and the bubbles above the "i"s, and something snapped.'

She'd promised to write to me when she moved to New York and at first she'd written every week. But for those last few months, her mind had been so clouded by the drink she'd just had or the one she was planning there wasn't room for anything else.

'I hadn't written once, not one letter,' she said. 'I'd let you down and I couldn't forgive myself. Then I remembered the date and I realised I'd forgotten your birthday – and that was it. I gave up drinking that day.'

She looked up for the first time since she'd started her story; her eyes, green like grape halves, held mine. 'So, there you go, Stevie. You saved me.'

I tried to reconcile the woman opposite me with the one she'd described. What was she like when she was drunk? I wondered. Was she loud? Did she shout and swear and laugh?

'Are you in touch with your friends from that time?' I asked.

'No. I moved on, I had to. I changed jobs, met other people. I met Lex and his group a couple of years later. People come and go in New York; you can become someone else so easily.'

Still, the city did its best to pull her back: whenever she wandered around the East Village or the Lower East Side or Soho, she'd see the winking neon signs of the places where she used to drink, their wide-open windows and the warmth inside. Gradually, one after the other, they turned into something else too. A dive bar made way for an apartment block; a club became a clothes store.

I asked her if she was ever tempted to have a drink now – hadn't she had a beer last night? No, she said, she'd poured it into the sand when I wasn't looking. But she did want one, from time to time. Addiction was like grief, it crouched in the gloom of a bad day and the glare of a good one; you just learned to live with it. She had coping strategies: yoga helped, work helped, and if the itch became unbearable, she'd go to a meeting.

'I hated them at first, that ragtag group of lost souls on orange plastic chairs, the ignominy of saying my issues aloud, as if carrying them inside wasn't punishment enough, but they did the job. They still do.'

'I don't understand why you didn't tell me before, Jess. Why didn't you tell me when I moved here?'

'I was ashamed,' she said. 'This isn't who I want you to think I am.'

'But you've done everything you've done *despite* this. I'll respect you even more now, can't you see that?' She shook her head.

'How can I help you, Jess?' I asked. 'What are your triggers?'

'My triggers? Oh, too many to mention,' she said, smiling. She had told me enough.

We didn't talk much on Sunday, we cycled to a yoga class, bought quesadillas from the truck on the beach, pulled them apart, cheese lacing the segments, stared at the ocean as we ate them. For now, silence seemed the best support.

When I got home, I called Nathan and told him the news.

'Christ,' he said, 'well, there you go, mystery solved. That's why she's been so distant. That's why she's been so hard to reach. All this time, she's been keeping it from you. All this time, she's been scared of telling you.'

But I knew there was more to it than what Jess had confessed; there were things she was holding back. The shadows that followed her to New York. What it really was that led to her drinking, opening her post-box one evening and three months of mail falling out. I knew there was more.

I didn't say that to Nathan, though. I didn't tell him about the fissures in her story, in her many lives.

'Yes,' I replied, 'that must be it.'

Thirty-nine

'I saw Sam,' Nathan says. He's used FaceTime to call me; he must want to see my reaction.

'Did you?' I say, trying to look unmoved. 'Where?'

'We went to this play at the Cherry Lane – Brice booked it, I didn't know Sam was in it – and you know he was *good*, Stevie, *really* good.'

'That doesn't surprise me.'

'I hung around afterwards like some kind of superfan and I told him about Ash. I hope you don't mind?'

'Why would I?'

'He knew, right, that you were expecting?'

'Yes.'

Sam had been in touch soon after I'd told Lex I was pregnant. *I heard your news, Stevie,* he'd written. *Congratulations. You'll make a great mom.*

'Stevie?'

'I'm still here.'

'Do you ever miss Sam? Do you think about him?'

'Of course not.'

It wasn't true. I'd scrolled back to that message many times since Ash was born. *A great mom.* He hadn't needed to send it

220

after everything that had happened, and I'd wondered why he'd thought that; what evidence he'd had. Had he meant it? He wasn't the kind of person who said things because he thought he should. And yet, when we were together, he'd often complained that I worked too late; he'd joked about my priorities. Had he seen nurturing qualities in me, too? The capacity for love?

That morning, I'd been playing with Ash, waving the sunflower rattle as he bounced in his chair, and he'd reached, jerkily, for it. He'd never done that before, and I'd found myself wanting to tell someone. I'd wondered how Sam would have reacted if he'd been there, if things had turned out differently. What a fuss he would have made. How proud he'd have been.

'Well,' Nathan continues, 'he said he was pleased for you and he sent his best wishes. He said he hoped you'd be able to switch off and take some proper time with Ash – despite having Lex for a boss.'

Lex. Contrary to Sam's concerns, I still haven't heard a word from him.

As I walk, I think of the way he responded when I told him I was pregnant. I hadn't expected unbridled enthusiasm, or a Sam-style endorsement. But horror? I hadn't expected horror.

Was Lex jealous? Had I been in his long-term plans after all: make a business, then a baby – had there still been a chance, which I had thwarted? Because what was the alternative? That he, a progressive, liberal-minded entrepreneur with a woman as his right-hand, honestly thought a child and a career were incompatible?

My first theory might have been more appealing, but as time wore on, the second seemed more likely. 'I thought you were *in* this,' he'd said, as if I were being disloyal by having a baby, pulling the cord on our joint endeavour and lifting off on my own, because in his eyes, there couldn't possibly be time, headspace, energy for both. It was devastating, that realisation, and not just because of what it said about Lex's prejudices. It meant that our friendship – after all that time, after what we'd built – had been an illusion. I had been a fool to believe in it.

I'll show him how hard a pregnant woman can work, I thought, as he fixed his eyes on my belly, as he talked to it, rather than to me. The fug of the first twelve weeks had passed and I found I felt braver than I had before. Perhaps the progesterone coursing from my placenta was firing up my synapses, too, because I was more efficient than I'd ever been, feeding back on design and marketing ideas in double-quick time, cracking the whip with member and influencer outreach.

And still, Lex stared at my bump whenever he came to the London office, his visits more frequent now, stared at the bottom of the video conference screen as if trying to catch a glimpse of it. He started every meeting the same way – 'How are you feeling today, Stevie?' – as if I had been given a terminal diagnosis rather than a child I'd longed for. It always startled me, because generally, at work, I forgot I was pregnant. I was too busy doing my job. After he said it, I would remember and keep on remembering. That, I suppose, was the whole point.

His attitude affected the way I felt about him, too, of course it did. And that's where a silver lining glimmered. I no longer felt attraction, or admiration, or intrigue. I felt repulsed. Impossible to respect a man who had cast my pregnancy as an inconvenience beyond his control, who couldn't conceive of a woman leading a company while raising a child. And as for lusting after him?

The torch that had flickered, confusingly, an uninterpretable Morse code, a distraction and an impediment to other relationships, went, quite suddenly, out.

After one of those video calls, I found myself sprinting to the loo; I found myself pushing up the seat – *quick, quick* – vomiting whatever comfort food I'd had for lunch: tuna melt, cheeseburger, BLT, into the bowl, and three days later I did it again. 'There she is,' I said, wiping my mouth with the back of my hand, 'there she is at last,' because morning sickness topped every 'signs of a baby girl' list; it was cast-iron gender evidence. Even though I knew, deep down, that it wasn't her that was making me sick. It was him.

'He's probably never been around pregnant women before,' Rebecca said when she came over to the flat, hauling a bin bag up the stairs, one Saturday afternoon. 'He probably thinks he's being considerate.' When I didn't reply, she said, 'Stevie?'

'Sorry. Nearly finished.'

She walked over and shut my laptop.

'Rebecca!'

'You've got to take a break now and again,' she said. 'It's not good for the baby, or for you. Seriously, you and Jess, you're workaholics.'

'I don't think updating a spreadsheet ever killed a baby, or her mother.'

'How long are you thinking of taking off work?'

'You're not supposed to ask me that.'

'I'm your sister, for God's sake, not your boss.'

'OK, OK. I don't know. About six months? Depends how long Lex will pay me.'

'He hasn't said?'

'Not yet. I expect it'll be the minimum he can get away with.'

'Really? But you've been there – what – five years?'

'Nearly six. I think he sees my pregnancy as a betrayal.'

'Honestly.' She put her finger on the bridge of her tortoiseshell glasses, shook her head and her salt-and-pepper hair swished from side to side. 'How does he think he came into the world? Doesn't the club need babies to grow into members?'

'He doesn't think like that.'

'Still, he's given you the means, hasn't he? He's allowed you to do it on your own.'

'Given me the means?' I asked.

'Well, he gave you a great job . . . '

'You make it sound like some sort of *present*. As if he's my benefactor. I've given him and the club – the company we built *together* – years of my life. Blood, sweat and tears.'

'You've loved it, though.'

'Mostly, yes. But I've worked bloody hard. The club wouldn't be what it is without me.' She is jealous, Rebecca, she is jealous of my independence, of my success, a flat of my own, she can't resist attributing it to someone else.

'OK, OK, Stevie,' she says, hands on her hips, thinking of a way to reassert herself. 'My advice?' The advice, always presented as a question, as if I had actually asked for it, has been coming thicker and faster since I had told her I was pregnant. 'My advice is, *see how you go*. You might want to take six months; you might want to take two *years* . . . '

'Well, I can't take two years, because the legal allowance is one, and anyway, I couldn't possibly afford it . . . '

'The most important thing is to enjoy it.'

'Of course.'

'To be in the moment.'

'Right. How long did you take again?'

'A year, the first time.'

'When you were working at the ad agency?'

'Yes.'

'And how was it when you went back?'

'Difficult. You know, the hours. David away a lot.'

'Is that why you didn't go back after Penny?'

'Not really.'

'What was it, then?'

Rebecca took a deep breath and whistled it out.

'I didn't go back because they didn't want me back.'

'What?'

'They made me redundant.'

'I don't think you've ever told me that.'

'No. I was embarrassed. And then I tried to forget about it. Brushed it under the carpet.'

'I always assumed you didn't want to go back.'

'That's what you were supposed to think. And I didn't, after that. I didn't have the confidence. And I left it too long.'

She sat back down and stroked the sofa's coffee-cup-stained arm with her left hand.

'How do you feel about it now?'

'It took me a long time to adjust, to shift my perception of what I had been to what I had become. I suppose I coped with it by becoming the archetypal stay-at-home mum.'

It had been a part she'd played so convincingly that later I would almost forget we'd had this conversation. 'But yes,' she continued, 'I am happy. I like my job at the gallery.'

'And happy with David?'

'Stevie, what is this? Yes! *We even have sex.* After all these years. I know that was what you were wondering. Shocking, isn't it? And no, I'm not going to tell you how regularly.'

I wasn't sure I believed her. I'd imagined David lying on the sofa in his cycling gear, reading the news on his phone, creeping up to bed while she continued to chirrup away downstairs, oblivious to his absence. Showering, putting on his plaid pyjamas and pulling the duvet up to his chin.

'Look,' Rebecca continued, 'if you're gathering evidence to

225

support your choice to be a single mother, I'm sorry, you've come to the wrong place.'

'That's not what—'

'David and I have had our ups and downs, but we're happy, we're together. He's a great dad. I respect your decision and I'm going to be there for you, and it would be nice if you respected my decisions, too. And, you know, me being around for Mum and for Dad, well, it's allowed you and Jess not to be – and why isn't *she* here, helping you with all this?' Her raised voice wobbled.

'She offered, I told her to come after the birth . . . '

'Well, good, but she should be here now as well.'

'I don't mind; she's got a lot going on.' I passed her a tissue. Perhaps Jess should be here. She might not be much help with the nest-building, but she would understand the conflicts of work. 'I'm really sorry, Rebecca.'

'It's OK. Oh dear, I don't know what came over me. *I'm* sorry. I shouldn't have shouted. I expect the baby heard and it'll hate me for it.'

'Don't be idiotic, she can't hear you.'

'It's a well-known fact that babies can hear voices in the womb. Anyway, I brought a whole load of Penny and Lily's newborn clothes with me. Some are a bit feminine – I know you think you're having a girl, but if it does turn out to be a boy . . . '

'You know I'm not due until October?'

'Yes, but I wanted you to see what I had before you started buying things. OK, what have we got in here . . . ? Be honest, if you don't like something just say. Here we go, a pram suit. Bit pink?'

'I remember Lily in that, and Penny. I can't believe how tiny it is.'

'You forget how small they are at the beginning, although when you first see them, they seem so big you can't believe they were curled up in there. Right, Babygros, you need way more than you think. Muslins, a couple of these are a bit ratty but I just couldn't bring myself to throw them away.'

'I'll take the ones without the shit stains, thank you.'

'Oh, and shoes. Look at these.'

'Adorable.'

'Completely unnecessary, I mean, they can't actually walk at that age, but still . . . Oh, and the changing bag. I'm not sure it's quite your style . . . '

'Wow,' I said. It was pink and hideous, but I couldn't afford to upset her again. 'I'd love it.'

'There.' She squished the black bin bag into a ball. 'Handover complete.'

'Quite the haul. Thank you.'

'I really am sorry, Rebecca,' I said, as she stood at the kettle, waiting for it to boil, 'About all the questions. I'm not judging you, really I'm not. I know motherhood comes in all sorts of guises.'

'It certainly does.'

'I'm just figuring things out. I'm halfway to being a mum and I'm still deep in work and I need to convince Lex that pregnancy doesn't go hand in hand with a lobotomy.'

'For goodness' sake.'

'And I can't imagine *not* checking emails and scheduling meetings and I'm going to be doing the whole baby thing on my own and it feels like, I don't know, going from limbo land to uncharted territory.'

'I understand, Stevie, honestly. I'm glad we had that talk, even if it did get a bit heated. And now you know it hasn't been all that straightforward for me, either. And as for doing it alone . . . '

'Yes?'

'You know, I've never asked you. Is the father not going to be involved *at all*?'

'The father's a sperm donor, Rebecca.'

'Yes, but I just thought . . . '

'I don't know him – I haven't actually ever *met* him – you did know that, didn't you?'

'Well, I wasn't sure, and I didn't want to ask.'

'You do know how these things work, don't you?'

'Not really.'

'He donates the sperm. That's his only role.'

'Oh, right. It's just that . . . '

'Babies need fathers, is that what you mean?'

'Well, maybe a father *figure* . . . '

'I didn't really have a father, did I, Rebecca? Dad had no interest in me – he didn't want to be anywhere near me. I've barely spoken to him since I moved back – not even since I told Mum I was pregnant. But – you may disagree – I think I turned out all right.'

'I'm sorry, I should never have . . . I'd better go.'

'Yes, Rebecca. I think you had.'

After she left, I opened my laptop and refreshed my email. Right at the top was a message about a meeting the next afternoon.

CANCELLED: Stevie & Lex one-to-one

Forty

It was October and another hurricane had been forecast. The last one had been the definition of a storm in a teacup, the snapped branches I hurdled on my run the morning after the only evidence of the devastation that had been predicted. I was sure this would be the same: the hullabaloo was just hype to spur TV ratings. But Sam disagreed, and he arrived at my apartment that afternoon with two flashlights, candles, a pen-knife and a week's worth of non-perishable food zipped into his backpack.

'It won't be the most gourmet experience,' he said, unloading bottles of water, crackers, corned beef, baked beans, sweetcorn, chocolate, 'but we'll survive.'

When we went to bed everything was eerily quiet, but in the middle of the night, we were woken by an almighty boom. The building shuddered, wobbled uncertainly – would it? Wouldn't it? We heard a crackle like a metal sheet being waved, then a crash, and another. Sam tried the bedside light: the power was off.

'Blackout,' he said.

We drifted back to sleep, faces turned to each other, limbs woven. The next morning, the booming had ceased but the electricity was still dead and the taps were dry.

Our phones had wi-fi, so we checked the news and saw entire trees lifted from the ground, avenues turned into rivers, playgrounds drowned. It didn't feel right, looking at the world upturned.

'I need to speak to Jess,' I said, but I couldn't get through.

'She'll be fine, Stevie,' said Sam, 'she's on the third floor.'

But it wasn't her apartment's susceptibility to flooding I was worried about; it was what she'd told me five months earlier.

We hadn't talked about her drinking again and I was no closer to discovering what provoked the relapses she'd alluded to, the AA meetings she'd said she attended. Would this storm, this literal shaking of foundations, topple her?

I wanted to speak to Sam about it, but he didn't know what Jess had revealed that Memorial Day weekend. I hadn't told anyone but Nathan. I had taken her secret and made it mine.

At noon, we woke again, and I tried Jess again. The phones were down.

We decided to walk to Sam's apartment because we'd heard there was power in his part of Brooklyn. We nodded grimly at the people we passed on Brooklyn Bridge, united in our status as storm survivors, and from time to time we stopped to stare back at the beaten-up city.

Over the river in Dumbo, crowds surrounded the trees that lay like felled buffalo, their tattered, blood-drained flesh bright white.

That evening, when the phone lines were up again and I had retrieved six messages from Jess and called her back and spoken to Mum and reassured her that yes, we were both fine, Jess came over to Sam's apartment.

She'd been terrified, she said, when she couldn't get hold of me. 'Come on,' I said, 'you knew I'd be all right. I was with Sam,' and she smiled.

'Are you sure it's OK if I sleep on the sofa?' she asked. 'I really don't want to intrude. A few friends uptown have offered.'

'We'd love you to stay – right, Sam?'

'Of course. You're so welcome here, Jess.'

For six days, the three of us lived together, taking turns to buy groceries and cook, visiting Sam's parents in Queens, helping out with the club's relief effort, volunteering in the shelters. Whenever we crossed from Brooklyn to Manhattan after sunset, we saw the island bisected: Lower Manhattan to midtown was black and everything above was illuminated.

I kept a close eye on Jess at first, but I soon stopped worrying. She seemed to enjoy staying with us, she liked Sam's cooking – soups and spicy stews his grandmother had taught him – and we liked her being there: she was an elf in rubber gloves, scrubbing surfaces, tucking stray books on to shelves, returning clothes to cupboards.

'I'm just so grateful to you for putting me up – and putting up with me,' she said when I thanked her, but now I knew more about her past, I wondered if it was the reason for her tidiness, a way of carving order from disarray.

A couple of evenings in, Jess said she was beginning to miss her yoga classes.

'It's not the physical effect so much,' she said, 'It's taking a pause, being *present*.' We both laughed; she sounded so American.

'Can you imagine saying that at home?' I said. 'Can you imagine yoga at all where we grew up? Look how far we've come, discussing the psychological benefits of ashtanga in a Brooklyn loft. What would Mum have thought?'

'Well, why don't we go the whole way and *do* ashtanga in a Brooklyn loft?' Jess said, and we pushed the sofa and the coffee table to the wall and there was just enough room for the three of us, it would have been easier if we hadn't all been so tall, Jess instructing from her mat at one end, Sam and me on towels on the wooden floor.

'You know, you're good, Sam,' Jess said at the end, and Sam admitted that he had, at one point, done 'quite a bit' of yoga. 'I bet you dated a yoga teacher,' Jess said, and winked. Sam looked embarrassed.

'Don't worry, I know I'm not your first,' I said, but I felt the whip of jealousy; feelings, evidence, and a reminder that nothing is permanent; you shouldn't kid yourself for one moment that it is. *That's not what you want*, I told myself.

That evening, when Jess had gone to bed and I'd opened a bottle of wine, he started talking about exes.

'You know, we've never really spoken about our past relationships,' he said.

I shrugged. 'I don't see the point of bringing all that stuff up.'

'OK. I get that. But I want you to know that if there's anything you'd like to hear about mine, I'm happy to tell you.'

'Thanks, Sam. Same with me.'

He was right: it was strange that we hadn't shared that part of our lives. I took a deep breath. Why shouldn't he know? It was ancient history. 'I was pretty hurt at one point,' I said. 'Let down by someone I thought cared about me. Lied to, I suppose.'

'Oh, Stevie. I'm sorry.' He put his arms around me. 'I'd never do that to you; I hope you know that.'

You shouldn't make those sorts of promises, I thought to myself.

I wondered, when we went to bed, whether I'd done the right thing, telling Sam about my past, exposing myself. I wasn't lovable enough – wasn't that what I'd said? And he had offered nothing of his own life in return. When he put out his hand to touch me, I pretended I was already asleep.

*

On the seventh day, the lights went on in Lower Manhattan. Jess and I walked back over the bridge to our apartments, talking about silver linings, time together, parting at the foot of the Lower East Side. I drained the bath Sam had filled before the storm and put the candles in the kitchen cupboard. 'I miss you,' he said when he called, and I missed him too, but something stopped me saying it.

Forty-one

I buzz Jess in, open my door and wait for her to walk up the stairs. Ash is in my arms, wrapped in a muslin. I am suddenly conscious of the effort I haven't made: my make-up-free face; oily, scraped-back hair; sweatshirt with sick marks; of the crash-site front room behind me. The preparing-for-Jess time I had earmarked had been swept into the keeping-Ash-alive vortex, as everything is, every day.

'I'm sorry,' I say when she appears. 'I feel as if this should be a Kate Middleton outside the Lindo Wing moment, but, well . . . I – *we* – went for the natural look in the end.'

I am struck by how relieved I feel when I see Jess. Perhaps it's because, for so long, I wasn't sure we'd make it to this point at all. The early signs – Jess's reaction when I broke the news about my maternal aspirations; her elusiveness when I wanted to tell her it was happening – were not good.

But in the end, the silence after I messaged her to announce my pregnancy had lasted as long as an intake of breath, that was all. Then the congratulations came. I was glad I had relayed the information digitally; that I was spared the wobble in her voice. 'Come over a couple of months after the due date,' I'd said.

'That'll give me a bit of time to get into some sort of routine.' It seemed laughable now.

When she sees Ash in my arms at the top of the stairs, Jess stares, her arms folded. Then her lips part. Her green eyes widen, and her hand shields them like a salute because she doesn't want me to see her cry.

'God, look at me, I didn't even think I liked babies!' she says.

'You're probably just tired from the flight,' I say. 'Would you like to hold him?' She nods, and I pass Ash to her, see her hands tremble, the gold bracelets on her right wrist clink. Perhaps she is worried she might drop him; God knows when she last held a baby. But she takes him, cradles him stiffly, then seems to relax.

'I can't believe you made him,' she says.

'Immaculate conception.'

'How are you feeling?'

'Oh, you know.'

She doesn't, though, does she? She doesn't know one thing about having a baby. Is that why part of me wants to tell her how I'm really feeling, what I'm not feeling? Because she won't be judgemental, she won't offer unwanted advice. And she has just cried, Jess, she has shown vulnerability, just as she did that weekend away. Her cheeks are still wet with it. '*Talk* to her,' Nathan had advised on the phone the night before. 'Take advantage of her being there.' Was he right – he and the night nanny? I'd blurted it out to a complete stranger – why was it so hard to tell her?

But she has come all this way. She doesn't need to know I've failed; she doesn't deserve that. She wants to go home thinking her little sister is nailing motherhood, she is *killing* it. It might be, it might very well be, that what I have is what she's wanted all along. She doesn't need to know how ungrateful I am.

So when I take Ash from her, I hold him closer than I usually would. I kiss his cheek when ordinarily I wouldn't. When he cries, I whisper, 'Come here, darling; hush now, *hush*.' I stick to the script.

And when she leans forward, because she *really* wants to know how I'm feeling, she isn't going to accept a casual brush-off, I give her the only criticism of early motherhood that is acceptable. 'I'm mainly fucking tired,' I say.

'Of course you are.' She looks relieved; I am being honest.

'He basically never sleeps – well, not at night, when it actually matters. Did you bring Ambien?'

'Um, no, but . . . '

'Kidding. I wouldn't.'

'Is the internet a good resource? I mean, for advice on getting him to sleep. I can imagine myself googling constantly . . . '

'Yes and no. It's all so conflicting. Soothe your baby; get them to self-soothe. Swaddle; don't swaddle. Establish a strict schedule; let your baby sleep when it wants to sleep. And my personal favourite: ask your partner to do the night feed.'

'Ah. Annoying. I'm sorry the nanny didn't help.'

'Don't be sorry – she did. In fact she came round again the other night.'

'Really? Good.'

'Anyway, enough of my moaning. Other than the sleep, well, it's brilliant. I'm very lucky.'

'You are lucky. Just look at him, he's perfect. And – *other than the sleep* – it's OK, I mean, doing it solo?'

'It's fine. I mean – compared to what you do, running a company of what, a hundred people? Compared to that, managing, or being managed by, a baby – how hard can it be?'

'Well, it's a different kind of pressure. What can I do, while I'm here? I want to help you, Stevie.'

I pass Ash back to her, pick up the kettle, walk two steps to the sink. It feels heavy in my hand as I turn on the tap. I wonder how many times I do this every day, fill it to the mark, flick the switch, wait for the hiss – eight? Ten? I blink tears away.

'Just do what you're doing, sit on the sofa with him while I make the tea,' I say, steadying my voice.

'It must be hard, not having anyone to talk to, Stevie. You have Ash, of course, but adult company.'

'I'm not sure I'm really capable of grown-up conversation at the moment, to be honest, Jess. Apologies in advance . . . '

'Don't be silly, of course you are. But, you know, let it all hang out while I'm here, OK? Whatever you're feeling.'

'OK.' Does she know? Can she tell how awful I've been? Would she forgive me, if I told her?

She sits down and turns towards me. 'Oh look, you've set up the highchair,' she says.

'I wanted to give you something you might not buy yourself,' she'd said when I'd called to thank her. 'Well, I knew you'd buy a highchair, but a really nice one, one that'll last. And I thought about all the meals we had together, so . . . '

I struggled to see the connection between a toddler throwing food and two grown women having dinner at a Manhattan restaurant, but I said 'mmm' down the phone all the same. I understood what she was doing, trying to make room in my present, to thread the past and the future together like a daisy chain.

The highchair was red, like a warning. And there was no question of it not lasting. It was made of sturdy Norwegian beech and when I opened its giant box a leaflet slipped from inside, a concertina of evolving children perching on its zigzag frame: babies, toddlers, primary schoolers; long-haired, guitar-strumming teenagers, a boast of longevity, and a reminder: *This child, swaddled in his Moses basket, is here to stay. He will never not be in your life.*

How I managed to piece it together, to slot and screw between feeding and burping and changing and cursing – had Jess *ever* made a flatpack herself? – I don't know, but even though it would be months before Ash was capable of sitting in it, of smearing it with carrot purée, slicking it with spilled milk, it was the one thing I had done in preparation for her visit.

The chair protruded from the table, stubbed toes, snared bag straps; stood out like a flare, offending the flat's muted tones. *We have history*, the pink velvet sofa, the gig poster above the table, the dented Anglepoise from Mira ('Happy twenty-fifth, light of my life!') seemed to whisper. *What are* you *doing here?*

At midday, we leave for lunch at Rebecca's house. We take a black cab, Ash's car seat strapped between us, his pupils shifting back and forth like a metronome. Jess looks out of the window. She hardly knows London; she's barely been here since she was twenty-five. Then she fishes her phone from her bag and scrolls through emails, even though it is Sunday and early in New York.

'How's work?' I ask.

'Good, actually. I've been promoted.'

'To what? I thought you already ran the show?'

'Well, not quite. I was managing director; I'm chief exec now.'

'Wow, Jess!'

'Thanks. Not all that different in reality but it's nice, the recognition. I thought the board would get someone else in after Damian left. Someone younger. You know, you worry about being less relevant when you get to my age.'

'That's great.' I think about my own career, in stasis. I count the months until my return – one, two, three, three and a half . . . I must fall asleep then, because Jess has to wake me when we arrive.

*

I always feel a mixture of disdain and envy when I visit Rebecca's house. It is a detached, red-brick colossus with stucco pillars either side of the front door in that far north-London belt where the neighbourhoods all have park or green or wood in their name. My flat would fit into the double-living room, the garden is almost as big as the playing field at the end of my road, and it cost Rebecca and David the same, fifteen years earlier, as my one-bed cost me.

Jess and Rebecca hug awkwardly at the door.

'It's been—'

'Too long,' says Jess. 'You look great. This is for you – a few things from New York.' She hands Rebecca a large white deli bag.

Rebecca does look good: she's brushed her silvery hair to a shine, crowned it with a leopard-print hairband, put on make-up, tucked skinny jeans into high-heeled boots. An attempt, I suppose, to compete with Jess, with the yoga body that makes anything she wears look as if it has been tailored for her; with the double-cream skin, which I'm never sure is the result of Botox or self-discipline.

'How's my favourite nephew?' Rebecca says, putting the bag on the floor and peering inside the car seat. 'He's changed so much since I last saw him.' She squeezes my arm. Now I'm here, I understand why she asked about the donor, the *father*, when I was pregnant. This is her world – the detached house, the solicitor husband, the indulged children, the job that isn't a career. My world is too far from the heavy door with the stained-glass window and the triple Chubb lock for her to fathom.

Jess and I add our sneakers to the pile in the hallway. Rebecca takes our jackets, wonders where to put them and drapes both over the banister. The house feels cluttered, despite its size, as if more than four people live there: coat pegs crowded, threatening to surrender; kitchen surfaces dense with cooking oil and half-full wine bottles; photos three-deep on the fridge.

Mum is already here, sitting on the sofa by the sliding doors with a tangle of knitting on her lap. 'Darlings!' she says, and struggles to her feet, her crucifix swinging over her pink jumper, her face dull and drawn above it. 'Where is he?'

'In the hall. Asleep.'

'Jess, dear, you must be exhausted, what time did you get here?'

'About seven,' she said. 'But I slept on the plane.'

Rebecca, pouring tea at the kitchen island, leans in, raises an eyebrow. *Business class.* 'Lily! Penny!' she shouts. 'Table!'

'You've lost weight, Mum,' says Jess. I feel terrible for not noticing when she visited. Other things to worry about, I tell myself.

'Well, I needed to,' Mum replies. 'Can I see him?'

'Stay there. I'll bring him to you,' I say.

'No David?' I hear Jess ask as I go to Ash.

'Triathlon training camp,' says Rebecca. 'He's so sad to miss you but it's been in the diary for months. I'm a race widow most weekends these days.' I remember the 'Ha!' with which David had greeted the 'RATHER BE RIDING' T-shirt Lily had given him the previous Christmas.

'And no Dad?'

'He sends his love, darling,' says Mum. 'It's a difficult time on the farm and you know he doesn't like to miss church on Sundays. He's dying to meet Ash, of course.' A split-second smile colours Jess's face.

'Yes,' I say. 'He called me.' Jess raises her eyebrows.

'Come here, dear baby, let me look at you.' I put Ash on Mum's lap. He opens his eyes. *Damn.* I should have left him in his car seat. Sometimes, he naps for two hours at lunchtime. Stupid of me, scuppering what little routine he had.

Mum looks from him to me. 'Our little girl. I still can't believe it.' She pulls a paisley handkerchief from her pocket.

'This little girl is forty next birthday, Mum,' I remind her.

'I know. But still. It takes me right back. It doesn't seem that long ago that *you* were this size. I'm so pleased for you, Stevie. He's just a delight. Look.' She lifts a striped scrap between knitting needles from the coffee table beside her. 'I've started on a cardigan.'

'It's beautiful. Thank you, Mum, I love the colours.'

'Do you? High praise from the artist of the family.'

'How are you feeling? You were exhausted when you came to see us.'

'Oh, I'm *fine*, Stevie. Absolutely *fine*.' Rebecca, stirring something, looks over, her mouth a straight line. 'Seeing you all is such a tonic.' Lily and Penny appear. Crop tops and tracksuit bottoms, braces and bare feet.

'Oh my *God*, he's so cute!'

'He's *grown*!' Phones are produced, photos posted.

We sit at the glass dining table with a view of the garden, the sky pavement grey, the wind making the bare trees dance. I wish I could creep up to Rebecca's spare room, stretch out on the double bed and stare at the sprigged wallpaper until I fall asleep, but I can imagine what she would say. *Is Stevie coping, do you think? I'm worried. I'm not sure she is.*

Rebecca fusses around, pouring me lime cordial when I want wine, offering Jess wine when she wants lime cordial – 'Did you drive here?' she asks. 'Did you hire a car?' and Jess says, 'No, but, you know, alcohol doesn't help with jet lag.' She checks on Ash. 'Could he be cold? I see he's not wearing socks.'

'He's fine,' I reply.

Penny passes Jess a plate with a slab of salmon on it – 'Lily's turned us all pescatarian!' says Rebecca – and she takes it and attempts to engage the teens on exams and university courses, to turn one-word replies into conversation. Their mother fills the gaps: 'She's doing *brilliantly* in chemistry, I don't know where she gets it . . . They do sports scholarships, so . . . '

'Becca, that was wonderful,' Mum gushes as we finish. 'You really are a fantastic hostess. Isn't she, Jess, Stevie? How *do* you do it all?' I stand up to collect the plates, Ash in one arm.

'Can I take him?' Jess says, and I feel Rebecca's eyes on us. Mum asks Jess about work, and I know she's not going to tell her about the promotion, so even though speaking is a struggle – I feel drugged, my eyelids flicker; 'Was it a bad night, Stevie?' Mum asks. 'It's always a bad night,' I reply – I tell them that we have a CEO in the family.

'Oh, darling!' I wonder if Mum understands the acronym.

Rebecca looks up from stacking the dishwasher. 'That's *great*,' she says, drawing out the vowels with the fake enthusiasm of the speaking clock. After Jess has offered to help with the washing-up and Rebecca has waved her away, she slides open the door to the garden and closes it behind her. We watch her walk to the wall at the end and take a packet of cigarettes from her back pocket.

'I didn't know Jess smoked,' says Rebecca.

'I thought you were the only smoker in the family, Becca,' smiles Mum.

'Thirty-five years ago, maybe.' Rebecca pours herself a glass of wine. 'While Jess rebelled in *other* ways.' She raises the glass to her mouth. Mum looks up from her knitting.

I open the garden door.

'Shall we go?' I ask Jess as I approach her. 'I think Rebecca's had a couple too many.'

'Yes.' She stubs out her cigarette. 'Let's go back to yours.'

*

'When did you start smoking?' I ask Jess later that afternoon.

'I haven't, well, I used to, but I haven't properly for years.'

'So why today?'

'They caught my eye at the airport.' She smiles. 'I knew lunch was going to be *challenging*. Better cigarettes than the alternative.' She winks, takes out the packet and looks at it. 'Quite fun shocking Rebecca, too.' I laugh as she throws the packet in my kitchen bin. 'There. Gone. One thing, though, Stevie.'

'What?'

'Do take advantage of Rebecca. I know how annoying she can be, but she does care about you and she wants to help with Ash, she really does. She's desperate to be involved. Don't be too proud to let her.'

I nod, grudgingly. *I don't want Rebecca's help*, I think. *I'd rather have yours.*

I make tea while Jess plays with Ash. She seems so natural with him, laying him on her lap, tickling his tummy, scooping him up to take him for a nappy change without my asking. 'It's not rocket science, is it?' she'd said when I'd asked her if she knew what to do.

When Jess flies back to New York, I see the red highchair sitting awkwardly at the end of the table and regret sideswipes me.

I should have told her while she was here. I should have confessed.

Not because she could offer any useful advice: how could someone who had never had a baby tell a new mother how to bond with hers? Not because she would offer any sin or foible in return: she has done that already. But a sympathetic ear? She would have been that. She would have listened, and my spirits would have lifted.

Forty-two

'I didn't know you wore glasses,' I said to Lex as the doors to his apartment opened. He had invited Sam and me for Thanksgiving – *Friendsgiving*, he called it – and when I had told him I usually spent it with Nathan and Jess, he had asked them too.

'I don't, ordinarily,' Lex said. 'These are wearable tech. Prototype from a club member. You like?'

'I *love*,' said Nathan, whose crush had not faded in the years he had known Lex. 'What exactly do they do?'

'What *don't* they do, Nathan,' said Lex. He nodded rapidly. 'How do you cook a perfect Thanksgiving turkey?' His irises moved up and left. 'It's given me a bunch of recipes,' he said. He nodded again, twice. 'OK, let's go with Rachael Ray. How to deep-fry a turkey. OK.' He nodded. 'I'm playing the video. Hey, Rachael, looking good!'

'Oh my God, that is super cool,' said Nathan.

'Do your glasses turn the oven on and pour the wine, too?' I asked.

'They do not. Yet! You've reminded me. Champagne?'

As Lex continued to scroll through recipes and Nathan continued to offer superlative responses, I wandered around the apartment.

It was the first time I'd been there – in real life, anyway: I had spent hours examining the photos Lex posted on social media, enlarging them with my fingertips so that the minutiae of his life were visible, the liquor brands on his vintage drinks trolley; the art on the walls. I'd imagined sprawling on the L-shaped sofa below the spot painting, spinning the collection of vintage globes together, closing our eyes and sticking out our fingers – 'Where next? Patagonia? Portugal?' I didn't do that any more, of course. I hadn't since I'd met Sam. But now I was here, curiosity returned.

I checked that Lex and Nathan were still deep in wearable tech in the kitchen and peered into his bedroom. A grey-and-black striped blanket spread over a king-size bed. Three monochrome cushions arranged, corners up, in a neat row.

'Hi!' said a voice. I stepped back. A small woman with a bleach-blonde bob emerged from the en suite bathroom.

'I'm Kristin,' she said. 'You must be Stevie.'

'Yes, I'm sorry . . . '

'Happy Thanksgiving! I was just changing. I went to Pilates this morning.'

'They have Pilates classes on Thanksgiving?'

'I have an instructor. I bribed him with cookies.'

'Right.'

'I've heard all about you,' said Kristin. 'I'm so glad we're doing this. My parents are pretty mad I'm in the city for the holiday, but I'm going home for Christmas. Trying to persuade Lex to come too. Will you get back to England?'

'Not this year,' I said, and then – I didn't know what else to say, I was so taken aback by her presence, by her very existence – 'Sorry, do you mind if I use the bathroom?'

My face loomed in the mirror, each feature an exclamation mark. 'You're stunning, Stevie,' Sam often said, 'every time I see you,

I think it,' but I was a caricature compared to Kristin. I opened the cabinet. Birth control tablets. I slammed it shut and hoped no one heard.

I tried to remind myself that everything had been better since Lex had introduced me to Sam; it was as if the preceding three years in New York had been a prelude to this, as if, after running beside the East River all this time, I had finally hit my stride. Everything was better. I even slept better, I reminded myself, without the mosquito nagging at my ear – *How can you have a baby if you don't have a boyfriend?*

'I guess you two met,' said Lex, as Kristin and I approached the kitchen area.

'We did,' I said enthusiastically. 'Nathan, this is Kristin, Lex's girlfriend.' Nathan's jaw dropped. The intercom buzzed.

'Hey, buddy,' said Lex down the line.

'Why didn't you bring your guy?' said Lex to Nathan. 'Is that still on?'

'It is,' said Nathan. 'But, you know, Thanksgiving . . . I don't want to give him the wrong idea.'

'I get it,' said Lex, who was still wearing his glasses. He nodded his head twice, rapidly. It wasn't clear whether he was agreeing with Nathan or scrolling the internet.

'Just finding out which wine goes best with turkey,' he explained. 'I'm telling you: these glasses are changing my life.'

The elevator doors opened. 'Look who I found on the doorstep,' said Sam.

'Hey, everyone,' said Jess.

Sam came over and put his arms around my neck. 'Happy Thanksgiving, babe,' he said.

'Jess is my date tonight, right, Jess?' said Nathan.

'Lucky me,' said Jess.

'So, how long have you two been together?' asked Nathan, gesturing to Lex and Kristin with his champagne glass. For once, I approved of his line of questioning.

'Six months?' said Kristin, looking at Lex.

'And how did you meet? Interweb?'

'I don't do online dating,' said Lex.

'Celebs don't Tinder,' I said.

'Ha!'

'We have a couple of mutual friends from grad school,' said Kristin.

'Jess knows them, actually,' said Lex. 'Mart and Wendy?'

'Oh yes,' said Jess, submerging a tortilla chip in the artichoke-and-spinach dip. Kristin filled my glass with champagne, and I stiffened as she walked towards Jess. I thought about putting my hand over her glass, but then she said, 'Not for me, thank you,' and the conversation moved on.

'OK, I think we're nearly ready, right, Krist?' said Lex. Kristin opened the oven and peered inside.

'Tell me you didn't cook all this yourself, Lex,' said Jess.

'I wish I could take credit,' said Lex. 'I reheated. The restaurant at the end of the block did it all.'

'Ahem?' says Kristin.

'Oh, Kristin made the pie,' said Lex.

'And?'

'She also did the table decorations.'

'It looks beautiful, Kristin,' said Jess, sitting down beside a mini pumpkin with her name drawn on it in gold pen, looking around the room. 'All my favourite people.'

'I've always thought Thanksgiving was so much more civilised than Christmas,' I said.

'Helps if you don't have any parents to factor into the equation,' said Lex. '*Friendsgiving* is certainly more civilised.'

'Yeah, I don't know how I got away with it,' said Sam, pushing his hand through his hair, beaming at me.

'You loved Christmas when you were a child, Stevie,' said Jess. 'You used to get so excited . . . Have you seen pictures of her, Sam, when she was little?' She placed her hand on his.

'I haven't. Stevie doesn't talk much about growing up, actually.'

'Well, she was the cutest kid,' she said. 'Big green eyes. Curly blonde hair. Butter wouldn't melt. I used to long to see her when I was away at school.'

It wasn't like Jess, laying out the past like this. It was almost as if she was staking a claim, marking territory.

'Every time I came home,' she continued, 'Stevie would run into the yard in her red welly boots. "Jeth! Jeth!" Mum used to say she was like a cat, waiting in the window. She knew I was coming home, even if they didn't tell her.'

And then you moved away. You left me. There it was again, my emotional knee-jerk. It winded me, Jess's departure, whenever I thought of it.

Kristin placed a vast tart, orange and radioactive looking, on the table.

'Now *that* is a pie,' said Nathan, as we all cooed dutifully.

'Straight out of central pie casting.'

'OK, Thanksgiving tradition,' said Nathan, when we each had a triangle.

'Here we go,' I said.

'Says the cynical Brit in the room,' said Nathan.

'Not cynical, we just have an aversion to gush, right, Jess?' I said. I had hated the chorus of Thanksgiving gratitude ever since my first Holiday.

'Right,' smiled Jess. 'But I'm going to make an exception tonight. I'll go first. This year, I've had a ton of adventures at work, I've done a ton of great travel, and I'm thankful that my job allows me to. But above all, I'm thankful for you guys. To Stevie, my family . . . ' She raised her water glass. 'Our weekend in Montauk, the home you and Sam gave me during the hurricane – they've been the highlights for me.' Was she going to cry? 'The time we spend together, it means the world. And you guys: Lex, Nathan, Sam, I know you play different roles in Stevie's life,' there was a collective laugh, 'but I'm so glad she found all of you. Knowing she has you to look after her – and you have her – it's such a relief to me.'

Nathan's fingers flashed across his phone screen, then my phone vibrated. *What is she ON today?*

I tapped back: *I know!*

'Finally,' Jess continued, raising her water glass again, 'Kristin, it's truly been a pleasure to meet you.'

'Well, that was *lovely*,' said Lex, in a British accent, 'Krist, you're up.'

'OK, well, I'm not even going to try to top that,' said Kristin. She turned to Lex. 'Lex. I'm thankful for . . . ' Lex cocked his head, as if he knew what she was thinking. I didn't think I wanted to hear this. I didn't think I *could* hear this. I thought about excusing myself and going to the loo. 'I'm thankful for your glasses, which are entertaining me – and, dare I say it, everyone else here – more than I thought possible.'

'What?'

'Oh, come on, babe, the head-bobbing. It's hilarious.'

The four of us left Lex's building, pulling our coats close. 'Christ, the wind in this part of town,' said Nathan.

'You take this one,' said Sam to Jess as a cab drew up.

'Bye, kiddo,' said Jess, pulling me tight.

'I thought she was great,' said Sam in the taxi.

'Who, Kristin?'

'Yes, didn't you? Smart, interesting, funny.'

'Yes. Beautiful, too.' She and Lex had danced around each other in the kitchen, taking trays out of the oven, putting vegetables in dishes, spooning sweet potato – their movements so fluid, so practised, so easy.

'Not half as beautiful as you,' said Sam. 'Anyway, they seem to get on really well. Like, *genuine* chemistry. She's really got the measure of him.'

Did we have that, Sam and I? Could we feel that, with our different continents, accents, industries, a river and an ocean between us? We didn't spar as they did, even though I was British and being rude to people was in my genes: a sign of affection. Was that a mark of inequality, of inauthenticity?

It was easy with us, Sam and me; it was comfortable, it had been since the beginning, 'Since the get-go,' he always said. But was it too easy? Didn't there need to be friction, something to rub against? Were we being polite – were we being ourselves? 'The youngest partner in her firm,' Lex had said, proudly, and Kristin had turned her face to his, and lifted her chin, and a pout had pushed up her cheekbones so that her eyes wrinkled gently around the edges.

'Stevie?'

'Sorry. Yes, I'm pleased for him too. He deserves someone great.'

Sam rolled the window down and cool air rushed in.

'Also, your sister.'

'What about her?'

'She was on such good form tonight . . . '

'I guess we all got to know each other after the hurricane. She's been more relaxed since then.'

'I really like her.'

'You really like everyone.'

'Not everyone,' he said softly. He turned to me. 'Look. There's something I've been meaning to say for a really long time, Stevie. The only reason I haven't before is that I wasn't sure you were . . . '

The taxi pulled over so that an ambulance could squeal past, and for a moment, the sound was so deafening it precluded conversation.

'What?' I asked.

'I love you.'

I felt hot then, and I opened my window, and a second ambulance howled by, and, again, mercifully, it prevented any response. When it passed, the moment and the words went stale in the air.

'I feel sick,' I said. I sounded as if I was underwater.

'Not the response I was hoping for,' said Sam.

'I'm sorry, I . . . '

'Don't worry, babe.' He shuffled to the middle of the seat and put his arm around me. 'We all ate and drank too much. We'll get you to bed; you'll feel better in the morning.'

I woke early and watched him sleeping, his lips slightly apart; black stubble for a new theatre role pixelating his chin and upper lip; the bold arches of his eyebrows and his dense lashes framing his closed eyes. When he opened them, he smiled, and pulled me to him, and I said, 'I'm sorry, Sam, I'm really sorry. I can't do this any more.'

Forty-three

Rebecca offers to babysit before I've persuaded myself to ask her.

'It's not as if you're breastfeeding now,' she says, she can't help herself. 'Take the night off, go out, have some adult conversation, have some *fun*. And don't hurry back!'

I congratulate myself for involving my sister while only having to spend half an hour with her as she bustles and chatters, checks nappy numbers and formula ratios and how to use the steriliser – 'You know I haven't had to do this since *you* were a baby – although in those days we put a pan on the hob – Lily and Penny refused anything but the boob' – and have my second shower without a Moses basket balanced on the loo seat.

As I turban my head in a towel, I stare at my naked torso in the mirror. No wonder only one per cent of women are breastfeeding exclusively by the time their babies are six months old. The bloody scabs that clung to my nipples eventually fell off, but the nicks that his steel-trap gums made are still there. Their shape has not recovered, either: they look down, dejectedly down, my breasts, like the deflated balloons tied to a gate long after the party has ended.

I put on and take off four pairs of pre-baby jeans, then, defeated by flab, fish a black maternity pair from the laundry basket, roll the elasticated waist panel over my paunch, pull a long, silky black V-neck jumper over my head and zip a pair of suede, heeled boots on to my feet. I blow-dry my hair and layer foundation and blusher, eye shadow, eyeliner and mascara on my face. Apart from the deep troughs that no amount of concealer seems able to fill, I can almost see myself.

'Well, hello, yummy mummy!' says Rebecca when I emerge. 'You OK? You seem a little flat.' I shrug. 'A good night out is exactly what you need.'

My arms feel strange by my sides as I walk to the tube, no pram to push. *You haven't left him,* I remind myself, *Rebecca is babysitting; he is in good hands.*

I hover beside the bank of blue-and-green seats on the tube to Soho, no one standing up as they did when I rode with my beach-ball bump, then walk to the bar Mira booked, worrying that I won't have enough to say to her, we won't find our way back to each other.

When I sit down, I check the time on my phone and the view from the rooftop of the New York club that always makes my stomach lurch flashes up.

'No Ash pic?' Mira asks over my shoulder.

'Mira.' I slip off my stool and we hug. She is tiny and taut; I feel every inch of my flab. 'It's been too long. I've been rubbish, I'm sorry.'

'That's baby-rearing for you,' she says.

'Margarita?'

'Please.'

'They're strong, by the way, and my tolerance is on the floor.'

'I'm sure. You're pumping and dumping tonight, then?'

'No, actually; I've given up, gone full-formula.'

'Oh. Right. That makes things easier. Who's looking after that sweet baby?'

'Rebecca. She's been itching to since he arrived. He won't miss me at all.'

'But you'll miss him.'

'Well . . . it's a relief to be out, to be honest. First time I've left the flat after dark.'

'I'm honoured to be your inaugural away-from-baby date.'

'As if I'd ask anyone else.'

'So, how are you finding it?'

'Well, I mean, obviously he's amazing.'

'Of course.'

'But, Mira, it's . . . '

'Tough. It's difficult enough with someone else to share the responsibility, the sleepless nights.'

'You warned me. But it's harder than I expected.'

'Doing it all by yourself – the nappies, the night feeds – I can't imagine . . . '

'It just seems . . . endless. Thankless. The monotony.'

'It gets better. Has he smiled yet?'

'I don't think so.'

'You don't . . . He's six weeks – he will soon. It's a real watershed moment, when you finally get something back. It's like . . . feedback. You really need it by then.'

'Yes.'

'And after that . . . They change so quickly. The days are long, but the years are short. Honestly, you blink and they're four, like Bea, *four*, and their feet make you cry because they're so big. Enjoy it while you can, that's my advice. Savour *every* moment.'

'I just, I find myself wondering if . . . '

'What?'

I take a sip of my drink. 'How were the first weeks with Beatrice?'

'Hard, but I had Pete. He was a huge help. Although we drove each other nuts at first. For the first few years, actually.'

'Why?'

'I don't know, different ideas about parenting, partly. He's always been a total pushover. Pure exhaustion, mainly. He was the only person – the only grown-up – there, so I threw every black thought at him. At least you won't have that. And it does change things, when you've lived with each other for years, when you've been everything to each other – present company excepted, of course – and then, suddenly, there's someone else. It changes the dynamic.'

'How did you deal with it all?'

'Screamed and shouted. Left her with him and went for a walk.'

'But you never thought of actually *leaving*?'

'You mean leaving Pete?'

'Just . . . leaving.'

'I fantasised about escaping with Beatrice. I'd look on the internet for flats with little gardens and dream about the two of us living there. God, Pete would never forgive me if he knew that. But then I'd have a better night's sleep, or I'd get another hit of oxytocin – it came in waves, do you find that?'

The oxytocin myth; the old lie. I suck noisily at my straw, pretend I haven't heard.

'And then I'd completely forget about escaping. Honestly, thank God for those happy hormones, I don't know what I would have done without them.'

I need to eat. I can feel the alcohol tugging at my tongue when I speak and I am enjoying it, but the conversation is making me feel weary. I have come out for a break from Ash, and he is inveigling his way into every sentence. I wish Mira and I could go back to our twenties, slumped on the sofa with hangovers and cups of tea. 'We just pick up where we left off,' people always say of old friends, as if they are in a perpetual relay race, but sometimes history is not enough. Not even our new shared present – mothers, now, both of us – is enough. I still feel as I did when Mira visited me in New York all those years ago, and the crack that appeared then has widened, like subsidence in a Victorian terrace. A gap you could stick your finger in.

I order tacos and burrow in my handbag for my wallet. My fingers find dollar bills, my passport – I needed it when I registered Ash's birth – then a small, square plastic pouch I had forgotten was ever there.

'Don't worry, you got the drinks, I'll get this,' says Mira.

'Really? Thanks. Might just dash to the loo, then,' I say.

Mira would be appalled, I think, as I extract my green card from my wallet, tap the white powder in the baggie on to the toilet seat and carve it into two fat, stubby lines. So would Jess. *It's a one-off*, I tell myself as I roll up one of the dollar bills, bend down and snort. I stand up, sniff again sharply and it hits the back of my throat like a memory. I lower my head again and inhale the second line. Then I tidy away my kit and check my nostrils in the mirror.

When I get back, there is a train timetable unfolded on the bar.

'Do you remember when we lived on the tenth floor of that scary tower block?', I said. 'We must have been twenty-five. You were going out with that loser lawyer . . . '

'You were single.'

'As usual.'

'And the flat had bars on the front door, a family of pigeons on the balcony and a handwritten sign that said, "If you shite on the stairwell I will kill you."'

'Hard to forget. And do you remember that party we went to one summer night, in the empty warehouse with the illegal roof deck?'

'I think so. Didn't we have to climb through the window to get up to it?'

'Yes,' I say. 'There was an amazing view of Hackney Marshes from the top.' We sat there all night, the two of us, while the party below reached a pounding climax and then tapered, until the sun rose behind the domino skyline, a sliver of moon still visible high above, and mist hung over the marshes.

'Yes, I remember,' says Mira. 'I remember the heron.'

A grey heron picked its way across the grass on long, bony legs and tripod feet. We'd been talking about what we wanted from life, Mira and I, what we would become, and then the heron appeared: first an apparition, then a sign. We swore we could hear its footsteps as it strolled delicately but deliberately through the marshland.

'I keep thinking about that night,' I say. 'When I'm feeding Ash, trying to get him to sleep, trying to get him to stop crying. I keep trying to remember what we said to each other – the plans we made. But I can't.'

'I don't think we looked further than next Friday night at that age,' laughs Mira, 'did we?'

'Come on, of course we did. *You* did. You wanted to be a section editor on a national newspaper by the time you were thirty-five and you were. But what did I say that night? What did I want?'

'Oh, Stevie.' Mira folds up the timetable, takes a long sip of her drink. 'I wish I could remember what we said that night.' A waiter places bowls of tacos and guacamole on the bar. 'But I remember who you were then,' she says, 'if that's what you're asking. You were frustrated with your job. You wanted more from it; you hadn't found the right thing. You were single because you were never *obsessed* with relationships the way the rest of us were. And there was always the idea of a baby,' she waves her hand vaguely in the air, 'somewhere on the horizon. I'm not sure where that came from, although I have a few ideas. There was no nuclear family in your plans, but you knew you wanted a baby one day, someone you'd belong to, who would belong to you.

'So, if you're asking if this is what you wanted,' Mira continues, 'and I think you are – then, yes.' She lifts her glass to her lips and turns her eyes to me. 'I think the girl on the roof would be pleased with the way things have turned out. I think she'd think she'd done OK,' she says. 'What you have is what she wanted.'

Forty-four

On the Saturday morning after Thanksgiving weekend, I opened my bottom drawer and found Sam's clothes underneath mine like the bruised strawberries at the bottom of a plastic punnet. I extracted them and piled them neatly on my desk next to his books and scripts with their highlighted lines, then opened the bathroom cabinet and took a tin of hair product and a razor from the middle shelf. My iPhone buzzed.

'Hey, Nathan.'

'What's going on?' asked Nathan.

'Oh, you know, just putzing around.'

'Just putzing around in your lonely little apartment, loving the single life.'

'Something like that. Are you pleased to have your wing-woman back? Want to meet for coffee?'

'Are you kidding? I preferred my wing-woman when she was getting some.'

'Give me a break, Nathan.'

'Sam is great. You were great together. Stevie and Sam – you had it all, even alliteration.'

'*Nathan . . .*'

'You still want kids, don't you?'

'A kid, yes . . . '

'Sam would have been a great dad. I mean, I honestly don't know why you've done this.'

'Come on, we've been through this. It was just too . . . '

'Good?'

'Nathan.'

'Easy?'

'Maybe.'

'Two years – no, *ten* years from now, you will look back on this as the biggest mistake of your life. You will *beg* for easy.'

'Don't be such a drama queen. I didn't think you even liked him.'

'I did like him. Maybe I was a tiny bit jealous.'

'Of him?'

'You got on so well.'

'Did we? Well, it's over. And it feels right. So, coffee?'

'I need to get his stuff back to him,' I said when we were sitting in the window of the coffee shop, looking out at the dogs and their owners parading through the park in matching coats.

'I thought you didn't want to talk about Sam?'

'I don't. That's why I want to give his stuff back. Draw a line under it. How do you think I should do that?'

'Well, I don't think you should give it to Lex, if that's what you're asking. What did he leave at your place?'

'T-shirts. A sweater. Books. That kind of thing.'

'Not super urgent, then. Why don't you wait for the dust to settle?'

'I guess.'

'If I didn't know you better, I'd think you wanted to see him again.'

'Well, I don't.'

'What did Lex say, anyway?'

'He said it was a bad move. That Sam was a really great guy and he'd never seen him so happy, and he'd thought I'd been pretty jazz hands about the situation, too.'

'He said "jazz hands"?'

'Yes.'

'Funny, that all your friends could see it and you couldn't. You know, Stevie, I feel like there's more to this than you're letting on.'

'Like what?'

'I think you were shit-scared.'

'Of what?'

'Of falling for Sam and being hurt. Hurt like you were by that London douche, Bill.'

'Will.'

'Right. You were worried it'd happen again, that he'd get cold feet, so you chucked Sam before he chucked you – which, by the way, he wouldn't have – and you made up a load of crap about not being suited to each other. Self-sabotage, basically. Am I right?'

I took a sip of coffee and it scalded my tongue.

'I just hope it doesn't have anything to do with Lex,' Nathan continued, 'because, you know, that ship – and I may be wrong about this, but I *did* think there was a ship – that ship has sailed.'

'You'd make a great therapist, Nathan,' I said. 'Shame this town has so many already.'

'Look, I'm just trying to help. You know, *everyone* gets hurt at some point. Sometimes it's worth taking the risk. Anyway. I'm here if you want to talk about it.'

'How's the dog whisperer?'

'Good, actually.'

'And his barriers?'

'I'm taming them. We're reviewing a dog-friendly hotel upstate next weekend.'

'It's getting serious.'

'I know a good guy when I see one.' Nathan's phone rang. 'And here he is. Hey, honey, you coming over? Fifteen minutes? See you there.'

'Oh,' I said. 'You're off, then.'

'Sorry, girl. Dinner next week maybe?'

That evening, I reclaimed my solo seat at the noodle bar. 'How's Sam?' asked the server, and I smiled weakly and shook my head, and she put down the empty bowls she was carrying and gave me a hug. 'Honestly, it's fine, it was my idea,' I said, and she looked at me as if doubting this information.

The next morning, I walked to the farm-to-table restaurant with the servers with leather aprons, ordered kale and eggs and spread my Sunday newspaper across the marble bar. I ignored the phone messages from friends wondering if I wanted to meet; the only interruption I allowed, as I read all five sections, was the server collecting and refilling my coffee cup. I left feeling whole, somehow, like a clementine that had been segmented and put back together again.

Later, I went to the movie theatre on East Houston early enough to see all the commercials before the film. Then I crossed the pockmarked street and walked back to my apartment via the wine shop, my thoughts unencumbered by conversation. I bought three splits of Rioja, and when I got home, I opened one and I took a packet of tortilla chips from the cupboard and plugged my phone into the speaker and lay on the sofa.

Jess called and I let it ring. We had talked the day before; I'd tried to explain why I had ended it with Sam, and she'd sounded distraught. I'd made light of it, joked about the two of us and relationships: neither of us seemed able to do them, neither of us seemed to *want* to do them, what did Rebecca have that we didn't?

I'd heard sighing, sniffing, down the line, and I told her I was going to go. I wondered why on earth Jess was wallowing in *my* loss, *my* ending.

The music shuffled to a song by a band that Sam and I saw one sticky summer evening; he'd said they sounded like a pack of wolves howling melodically at the moon. I checked myself for regret, but I didn't find any; I felt glad that we were together and glad that we were apart, because I felt more like myself on my own. *It is easier like this,* I thought, *it is safer. This is what I need; the city is all I need.*

Forty-five

I open my front door with the methodical movements of a killer — no lock-fumbling, no dropped keys — and find Rebecca dozing on the sofa, the remote control in one hand. I close the door and she opens her eyes.

'Gosh, sorry, Stevie, I must have fallen asleep. How was it?'

'Good. Thank you so much, Rebecca. I hope he's behaved himself.'

'He's been an angel. I haven't heard a peep since his last feed. I think you'll have an easy night.'

I tiptoe over to my bedroom and peer into the basket. His eyes are closed, his arms raised above his head, a beatific look glazes his face.

Rebecca gathers her things and leaves, pausing to look at a photo of Jess, Ash and me propped on the cooker hood, and I sit in the divot she has made on the sofa.

The flat is silent, but my head is a hive of discordant buzz and clatter. I try to remember when I snorted the other half of the little white stowaway in my handbag and I can't: the baby has hollowed out my memory like a pumpkin.

I take off my boots, lie down, cover my legs with a blanket, close my eyes. My mind continues to whirr, my teeth to grind.

I push away the recurring nightmare of late-stage labour, on my back, the midwife gone, and turn on to my side. I turn over my mobile and press an app and there is a photo of Lex, standing outside the San Francisco club, arms folded, beanie low. *Hey, SF*, says the caption. I check the date. Yes, today was the opening. I should have been there.

A gentle snoring continues to emanate from the bedroom. Unbelievable. What tincture did Rebecca pour into his ear, mix into his milk?

Olivia would never have gone out and taken drugs – drugs! – if she'd been fortunate to have had a living, breathing six-week-old to take care of. Never! She would be appalled by what I have done. Incensed. Incredulous. The IVF roulette got it badly wrong.

I roll on to my front, a feat impossible three weeks before. How much I wanted him, how much I yearned for a baby's hot little hand to clasp, how I chose to have him, went out of my way to get him, stabbed a needle in my thigh for him, how I made him happen. How lucky I have been, how lucky I *am*. How can I have everything and feel nothing?

I open the living-room shutters and the sky is pale pink behind the plane tree. I look at my phone, gasp. A calendar notification: Ash's six-week appointment is at the surgery at nine o'clock, in three hours' time.

I sink into my armchair and think about running beside the East River, the rhythmic pounding of trainers on tarmac; left, right, left, right, left, right; metres of Manhattan passing under my feet. Just as sleep finds me, he wakes.

The doctor cocks her head to one side.

'And how are *you*?' she asks, Ash's health record with its graphs of ascending biro dots on her desk, her voice as slow and thick as condensed milk. I take a deep breath and exhale the urge to tell the truth. 'Are you coping?' she continues, straightening her head. 'I mean, *on your own?*'

'I'm surviving,' I say. 'I'm tired, of course, but then who isn't at this stage?'

'How's baby sleeping?'

'He slept through for the second time last night, actually, and the first was weeks ago. I couldn't believe it.'

'And you didn't, I'm guessing?' Her head tilts thirty degrees. I shake mine. 'Always the way.' She smiles, pats my knee. 'You were worried, weren't you, that he wouldn't wake up?' I nod – it is a plausible explanation.

'There's really no need to be concerned, Stevie,' she continues. 'Baby's eating well; he's putting on weight – some do start sleeping through the night at this stage. Just don't tell the rest of my mums! Is he smiling yet?'

'No.' I feel as if I should offer a reason, but I don't know what. We both look at the baby on my lap.

'Can I have a cuddle?' she says. I pass Ash over.

'Ooooh,' she says. 'You are *so* squidgy!' He looks up at her with his dinner-plate eyes. 'Lovely baby!'

The smile, when it comes – because it comes then, of course it does – isn't for me, it is for the doctor and it is for Rebecca, who cared for him when I was out, who made him feel cosy and coddled and safe.

Ash knows what I am, what I am not.

He is looking at me from the GP's lap when he smiles for the first time, but the smile is not for me.

Forty-six

I held on to the lie for two weeks, maybe three.

The city was once all I needed, and it is no longer. It has come back, the three-in-the-morning yearning. A jab in the ribs.

Sam had quietened it. His presence wasn't just a distraction; it was a promise, smoke whispering from a chimney: *it could happen, it might happen*, even though I kept telling myself, or fear kept telling me, that it would never happen with him.

The baby was missing, there was a hole where it should be. And now Sam was gone, a flashlight was pointing straight at the hole.

Jess kept asking about Sam. 'Have you seen him?' she said, hopefully, when we met at a new pizzeria in Nolita. 'Have you had second thoughts?' I shook my head once, then twice, and she looked pained. The crease that appeared between her eyebrows when she frowned deepened to a fissure, and she shook her head and said, 'I'm sorry, Stevie, I just don't understand; he was so *nice*, he seemed so *right*.'

The fourth time she mentioned him, I said, 'You know, you have Sam's number, Jess. If you'd like to see him you should just give him a call,' and after that she didn't ask again.

*

I met Lex at the club at eight the Monday morning he flew in from London. He had been there with Kristin and he leaped to his feet when he saw me and clapped me on the back as if he'd been away far longer than a week.

'You don't look as if you've just stepped off a red-eye,' I said. 'How was it?'

'Such a great city, don't know why you left.'

'Thanks. I'll try not to be offended.'

'It's just so *multicultural*, you know, way more than here, and the food has improved a ton in the last five years. The first time I went I basically didn't eat for a week. And East London? Cooler than Brooklyn – *way* cooler. The energy there. I mean, Brits *smile* now. When did that start happening?'

'You're not thinking of moving there, are you?'

'Hell, no, NY till I die. But I do have some news.'

He's engaged, I think. He took her up the Shard or to Columbia Road Flower Market or the Millennium Bridge or somewhere an American would think was romantic and he got down on one knee with a diamond the size of the Ritz and he popped the question. In London, my London.

'I found a building.'

'What?'

'For a club!'

'I didn't even know you were looking.' We'd talked vaguely about international expansion, but London? Why hadn't he told me?

'I wasn't looking, not seriously, and I didn't mention it before because, you know, it's where you're from, and I knew you'd be *invested*.'

'It's not where I'm from, actually.'

'But I found one, and it's perfect.'

'Really? Where is it?'

'Old Street. You know it?'

'Of course. Shoreditch. Silicon Roundabout.'

'Right. Super hipster; super techie. It's a complete rebuild – it's going to take months and months to get it ready, you know how this goes – but I want you to open it when the time comes, and I figured, what with Sam . . . '

'You do?'

'London's your city. You know the lay of the land. You know the scene. You probably already know the members. This is your project.'

'That's a really big deal, Lex.'

'Yes, and you're ready for it. But then you come back. Ultimately, I need you here. But I'll need you *there* for, like, six months through the opening.'

'Wow.'

'You like?'

'I'm just getting my head around it. Last I heard the next opening was Portland. But yes, I like.'

'Portland can wait. London's where it's at. This is it, Stevie. This is going to be your club. You've proved yourself – *more than* proved yourself. It's time for you to get your own train set.'

The next morning, on my run, as I watched the wind rippling the East River, a plan formed in my head. The knot that bound me to New York began to loosen.

Forty-seven

I know from the rat-a-tat that it is Rebecca. It has been harder to shake, this slump since my night out with Mira, and company is the last thing I want. But when I open the door and Rebecca reaches for Ash, I feel my body lift and I am glad she has come.

I run myself a bath, as Rebecca suggests, sink deep into the water, close my eyes.

I try to wash away the rage I felt in the black hours after midnight.

I try to forget that when he screamed, I found myself screaming back – *STOP CRYING, FOR GOD'S SAKE, STOP!* – that I put my hand over his mouth and his eyes widened in shock and it had been such a relief to hear nothing. That when I took my hand away his crying transposed to a more melancholic key.

'I thought you could do with a few hours on your own,' Rebecca says brightly, when I am dressed. 'And – ulterior motive – I'd like to see my nephew with his eyes open, unlike when I babysat the other night. Maybe catch one of those smiles.'

'Are you saying I should go out?'

'Yes. Go for a walk. Go into town, have lunch on your own – I remember you telling me you did that all the time in New York.'

'It's lovely of you to offer, Rebecca, but I'm just so tired . . . '

'You'll feel different when you're out. It'll give you a new lease of life, a change of scene. And you'll be doing me a favour. Honestly.'

A chance to escape the coop for an afternoon. Exhausted or not, I should seize it. 'OK – if you're sure?'

'I am. I know where everything is; just tell me when he needs to be fed. We'll be fine, won't we, Ash? We'll have *fun*. The girls get home from school at five on Fridays, and I like to give them something to eat before they disappear out with their friends, so if you're back by four-thirty . . . '

There's no time to think about where to go, so when I leave the flat, I click into autopilot. Into the lift at the underground station, one tube, across the platform to another, up the escalator and out of the second exit, straight, then right, then left.

There it is, the unmarked door to the club, shutting behind a member as she walks in.

I haven't seen it in its full glory: I left just as the final touches were being made; I gave birth the day of the opening party. I want to follow her, to see what it looks like now, pictures hung, armchairs occupied. I want to see Dean, the receptionist I brought over from New York, for him to throw his arms around me, hear him sigh when I mention my maternity cover. I have missed work; I have missed myself in it. But I'm rooted to the pavement as if it is wet concrete. I just need to psych myself up, I think. It's been so long.

There is a greasy spoon diagonally opposite, where I used to have lunch, jacket potatoes with tuna mayonnaise, delighting in their Englishness, so I go there, I order that. I sit at a table by the window and whenever I see a colleague come in or out of the building, I turn my head.

The café's lunch crowd soon disperses. Before long, I am the only customer. I ask for a cup of tea and continue to watch. The light is fading now; rain has started to freckle the windowpanes.

'Anything else I can get you, love?' says the man behind the counter.

'No, thanks,' I say, and gather my things. I walk towards the club, my heart pounding.

But again, I am a horse refusing a jump. Instead of pushing open the door, I walk past it and keep going. Into a furniture store where I pretend to be fascinated by a wall of clocks and shake my head when someone offers to help. On to a fashion boutique, a shoe shop. I touch things, look at labels, move on.

I keep walking east. I don't know what time it is, but I know I don't want to go home. I walk into a bar, order a gin and tonic. Then I think of Jess, drinking alone. When the bartender's back is turned, I put down ten pounds and slip out.

I see a coffee shop I once went to with Olivia, halfway between the club and her flat. Perhaps she is there, I think, and as I peer through the window, scanning faces lit by laptops, I remember the idea I had.

The idea of giving Ash to Olivia.

When I turn it over in my mind now it doesn't seem as mad as it did then. And I am out in the world, rather than confined to my flat: I am able to think rationally. Now, giving Ash to Olivia seems like a compassionate solution to two – no, three – people's problems. Redemption for what I have done and not done. An injustice settled.

I won't leave him on her doorstep as I had thought I might, though. That wouldn't be fair on either of them. I will go and see Olivia and suggest it; I will float it, as Lex would say. We will discuss it, calmly, and come to an agreement. An informal adoption, a sort of delayed surrogacy. Ash need never know, and he will certainly never guess. He even looks like Olivia with his black eyes. He looks more like her than me.

I can't be more than fifteen minutes' walk from Olivia's flat now. My pace quickens, I can taste the relief on the other side. When my phone vibrates in my pocket, I ignore it. It is only when it happens for the fifth time that I take it out. Rebecca. I change the settings so that it won't distract me again.

There is light flickering in the front room of Olivia's flat. She is in, watching television. I take a deep breath, then ring the bell.

I think how ecstatic she will be when I make my offer.

I try to mask the sudden terror I am feeling with that thought.

The light goes off. I hear footsteps on the stairs. I set my lips in a small, empathic smile.

But the person who opens the door is not Olivia. It is a man, about the same age as she is. Tall, silver hair, bare feet.

'Oh,' I say. 'Has Olivia moved?'

'No, she's just out for the evening. Can I help?'

'Um, I . . . ' Tears blur my eyes.

'Are you OK?' asks the man.

'I'm sorry,' I say, wiping them with my sleeve. 'It's . . . it's been a long day.'

'Would you like me to phone Olivia?' he says. 'Would you like to come in, out of the rain?'

'No, don't worry, I shouldn't be here. I'm sorry.'

'I'll give her a message, then. When she gets back.'

'No,' I say. 'There's really no need. I'm sorry to have bothered you.'

I scurry away, back down the street, back towards the club, swerving the streetlights, as if I am fleeing a crime scene. I walk until I see a black taxi.

When the roads narrow and the streets of my neighbourhood appear, row upon row of identical terraces, I feel like a bird trapped in a house, hurling itself at a windowpane.

'Stevie, I've been worried sick,' says Rebecca when she hears me on the stairs and opens the door. She is holding Ash, eyes wide like a bushbaby. 'Thank God you're OK.'

'Why?' I say. 'Am I very late?'

'I thought you were going to be back by four thirty. I kept calling, didn't you hear?'

'What time is it now?'

'*Eight* thirty.'

'I'm sorry, Rebecca. I had no idea – it gets dark so early.'

'Where have you been?'

'I don't know, wandering. I went to see a friend, but she wasn't there.'

'Why didn't you answer your phone? Why didn't you call me?'

'It was on silent.'

'*Honestly*, Stevie.'

'I'm sorry. How is he?'

'He's been fine, but he won't settle.' She passes him to me. Is that a smile? It is hard to tell. Rebecca puts her arms around us both. She's probably worried I'll drop him; she probably thinks I'm drunk. But her tone is gentle when she speaks again.

'Stevie,' she says, 'are you OK?'

'I'm fine,' I say, trying my best to keep my voice even. 'Thank you for looking after him. You were right: it was good to be out on my own. I just lost track of time.'

She doesn't look convinced. 'I'm going to stay the night.'

'What? Why?'

'I've told David and the girls. I'll sleep on the sofa.'

*

The next morning, Rebecca asks again. 'Stevie, *talk* to me. Tell me how you're feeling.'

'What do you mean?'

'You didn't seem yourself when I babysat the other day, and then, last night, when you didn't come back . . . '

'I was only a few hours late.'

'You've seemed, I don't know, *detached* since you had Ash. Distant. I've been meaning to say something for weeks.'

'I'm just exhausted, Rebecca. It does funny things to you, sleep deprivation.' I stare through the window at the bare tree outside. He woke every hour last night.

'I know you're shattered. You're on your own, there's no respite. And it's a big change, from your previous life. It's just . . . '

'What?'

'Are you *enjoying* him? I mean, overall? I'd hate to think, I don't know, that you *regretted* it.'

For the time it takes for the postman to walk the three steps to my door, I consider telling her.

'Stevie?'

I hear the mail smack on to the mat. Where would I start? How could she possibly understand? Mothering came so easily to her.

'Of course I'm enjoying him, of course I'm glad I have him, how could I not be?'

'Well, good. But still . . . I'm worried. Is there anything else I can do?'

Ash sits in his bouncy chair, staring at the wooden flower.

I imagine Olivia taking him out of the chair, her hands under his armpits, careful but firm, taking him away. I gasp.

'Stevie, are you OK?'

'Yes.'

You didn't do it, I tell myself.

It was a moment of madness, that was all. Even if Olivia had been there, I would have come to my senses. I would still have walked away.

'Please, Stevie, I want to help. You know, when Lily and Penny were tiny, Ash's sort of age, they were in our bed. David hated it; I liked it: it was cosy. And their sleep definitely improved. The advice has probably changed since they were babies, but I don't know, you might both get a better night if you tried it. And it might help with . . . '

'What?'

'Oh, nothing. Just give it a go, will you?'

'You're going to hate me for saying this, Stevie,' Nathan says down the phone. A car door slams. 'Forty-seventh and eighth,' he says to the driver. 'But I really think you should get in touch with those mom pals of yours again.'

'I hate you for saying that.'

'Look, you won't admit it but you're lonely, you're bored, you're tearing your hair out, you need *people*. I mean, I get cabin fever after a day in my apartment, so God only knows what weeks with my screaming godson are like.' In the bedroom, Ash begins his post-nap drone. I shut the door.

'And I know they're never going to be your BFFs – you can only have one of those and *hello* – but I'm here and they're there and Mira doesn't seem to be much help at the moment . . . '

'We went for drinks the other night, I told you.'

'But you didn't *talk* to her, did you? You need to see people during the day when you're with Ash, and Jess and your mom have been and gone and Rebecca drives you crazy . . . '

'She came around the other afternoon, unannounced. Told me to go out.'

'Well, good for her, I've always liked your sister.'

'You've never met her.'

'Anyway,' he continued, 'the moms. There must be something to be said for being in *exactly the same position* in life as them right now.'

'But I'm not. They've got partners.'

'OK, well, apart from that . . . wasn't it OK, when you met up last time, when *I told you* to meet up with them last time? I mean, they might actually have some advice about getting him to sleep, about getting you to feel less mad, because I've got to tell you, you're sounding kinda mad lately, Stevie, and I've been googling London shrinks, but what I actually think you need is *company*.'

I realise my cheeks are wet. I wipe them with my sleeve. 'I'm going to fuck up his life for ever, I know I am,' I say. 'The things I've done . . . '

'Seriously? Come on, Stevie. I don't even speak to my parents and look how great I turned out. It's all going to be fine, you and Ash. You'll get there, I promise. You know, I bet motherhood's like Instagram: it's blood, sweat, tears and a million hashtags for every one of your first ten thousand followers, and after that you're cruising; it's easy.'

'You think becoming a mother's like becoming an Instagram influencer?'

'OK, it was a terrible analogy, I'm sorry. Forget I said it.'

'Don't worry, it was funny.'

'Well, I'm glad I made you smile. So, are you going to message them?'

'I'm not sure I've got the energy.'

'Look, I bet their babies aren't sleeping through the night either. I bet they're fucking knackered too.'

'I suppose.'

'You'll do it, then?'

'Maybe.'

'Good.'

'Thanks, Nathan. I bet you didn't expect all this when I told you I was pregnant.'

'What, to become your baby camp counsellor? No, I guess not. But I expected to be your friend, so . . . '

'My sister suggested co-sleeping,' I say to Bobble Hat; does she ever wash her hair, I wonder?

We are sitting on the fake Eames chairs at the long table in the play café, our babies on our laps, and sleep is, again, on our waning lips.

Someone had asked me how Ash and I were, how they were sorry they hadn't seen me, and I'd said, 'It's completely gone to shit,' and I'd felt the room stiffen with the swear word. 'I thought babies were supposed to get better at stuff,' I'd continued, 'I thought it was all a gradual process of *evolution*,' and the young mums had shaken their heads in unison, back and forth, like choreographed owls.

'When you say . . . '

'Gone to shit?'

'Yes.'

'I mean, he's waking up every hour – every two hours, if I'm really lucky. I thought I was exhausted six weeks ago, but now . . . '

'Sleep regression.'

'Stanley's doing it, too.'

It was then that I mentioned co-sleeping. It had been on my mind since Rebecca raised it, but still, the term filled me with dread. It was from the same family as reusable nappies and home-schooling and breastfeeding until their children could say 'done'.

'Well, you're not really supposed to,' says Bobble Hat, 'not when they're tiny.'

'Midwives hate it. *Sudden Infant Death Syndrome*,' someone whispered.

'But . . . we do it. From time to time.'

'It's our guilty secret.'

'We're really careful – we'd *never* drink before.'

'It's just easier than yo-yoing to and from the Moses.'

'And I have to say . . . '

'We really like it.'

'It's better for everyone. And after all, they'll never be this age again.'

I turn Ash to face me. Shadows smudge his wide, black eyes like morning-after mascara.

'That's what my sister said,' I say.

'She's got kids, has she?' says Bobble Hat.

'Teenagers. She said she did it with them. They survived.'

Bobble Hat winks. 'And are they sleeping in her bed now?' She rearranges the hairband on her baby's hairless head, then looks up.

'Not as far as I know.'

'Well, there you go.'

That night, I place Ash's Moses basket on the left side of my bed. He is fast asleep, but I know it won't last long, and, sure enough, by the time I've brushed my teeth, his eyes are open. I wait for the wail, but he lies there, his mouth parted slightly, a black felt-tip-pen line, looking up at the light that hangs from the ceiling, a new view.

I get into bed and turn off my bedside lamp. The wailing begins. Does he know what I almost did? I pick him up. 'Hush,' I say, as softly and repentantly as I can.

I put him back in the basket. He continues to cry. I pick him up again and push the basket to the floor. I lie on my back in the centre of the bed, my hair spread on the pillow like a Pre-Raphaelite corpse and rest him face-up on my chest. His tiny arms flop over my sides. He turns his face so that his left cheek rests on my pyjama pocket. He stops crying.

My alarm clock says ten thirty-five. An hour until he will wake again. I close my eyes; open them immediately. What if I fall asleep and roll over and squash him beneath me?

The thought and the uncomfortable weight and warmth of him keep me awake. My arms are a safety belt around his tummy; his breathing the second hand of a clock: in, out; tick, tock. I keep my eyes open and stare at the lampshade that captivated him an hour before and my thoughts drift to New York.

It is Friday evening, time for the weekly wash-up meeting, then beers in the bar. What successes will they be celebrating today? I try to blink the thought away, to return to where I am. How ironic to co-sleep only to stay wide awake.

I think of Olivia. Is she out with her boyfriend, or sitting on the sofa, hand in hand, a movie on the TV?

When he wakes and I wake, the room is no longer black but not yet light. He turns his head, he is wondering where he is, and I lift him up and he looks at me with terror in his dark eyes. Who is that? Then, recognition. His mouth opens into a smile.

'Good morning, baby,' I say.

I lean over to see the neon green hologram on my bedside table. It is nearly six.

Forty-eight

'Jess, I'm . . . ' I stopped myself before the next word. *Hungover.* Should you tell a recovering alcoholic you've had too much to drink? 'I was over-served last night,' I said instead. It was a phrase Nathan used.

'I used to hate when that happened,' Jess said, sounding amused. 'Rain check, then?'

'No, no, I'd still love to see you, but I don't think I can face a restaurant. Do you want to come round here instead? We could get a delivery.'

'Sure,' she said, 'and I promise I won't say one word about Sam.'

Jess had been to my apartment before, of course, but she'd never stayed for dinner. If we ordered in, it was always at hers. She had a table, after all.

'What are we eating?' she asked when she arrived.

'Sichuan? I feel like something spicy.'

'Is this the place you told me has given you food poisoning?'

'*Suspected* food poisoning, and that was ages ago. I've been back since. I'm addicted.'

'OK, I guess I'll roll the dice if it's really that good.' She looked around the room, smiled when she saw a photo of us from our weekend away. 'It's a great space, this,' she said.

'Well, there are no mod cons and it's tiny. But yes, it's served me well.'

'When's your lease up?'

'Six months, I think.'

'Will you stay here? Or try somewhere else, a new neighbourhood?'

'No reason to,' I said. I wasn't ready to tell her I was leaving New York. Not yet. 'I like it here.'

'And what about work? What's next?' She was always looking for an upgrade, Jess, stretching higher, closer to the sun. How would she react when I told her I wanted a different kind of life?

'It's going well,' I said. 'Lex is looking at new sites, and the bigger the company gets, the more responsibility I get.'

'That's *great*.'

When the delivery arrived, we sat cross-legged on the floor in our sweatpants and I spooned noodles on to our plates. 'Your turn on the iPod,' I said, and she played a song I recognised from the night before.

'How was the party?'

'Fun,' I said. It was at a bar I'd often been to when it first opened, when for months, years even – far longer than the usual New York minute – it was the hottest place in town. I'd caught up with friends I hadn't seen for a while, bought and accepted round after round, had a line, stayed late. Still, it felt different. There was something stagnant about the place, like the smell of a vase of flowers left too long.

'Any cute guys?' Jess asked.

'For you or for me?'

'For you, of course.'

'I'm not looking, Jess. I've enjoyed being single the last few months. Honestly, I wish *you'd* do some dating instead of taking such a keen interest in mine. You're as bad as Rebecca.'

Jess laughed. 'Maybe I should.' She helped herself to more food. 'This is a bit of a change from our usual Sunday dinners,' she said.

'I know,' I said. 'I'm sorry. I'll drink less the night before next time. Or at least borrow a chair for you to sit on.'

'What are you talking about?' she said. 'I was just thinking how nice this is. I might even prefer it.'

Forty-nine

An ordinary afternoon, a Thursday, I think, a Friday, perhaps; the days of the week do not distinguish themselves. We are where we always are. I am sitting on the velvet sofa, Ash gurgling on my lap. Mum is looking out of the kitchen window, but rather than standing, winding the phone cable around her fingers, she is sitting, she tells me. Dad has moved her armchair there, so that she can watch the lambs bolt across the brow of the hill, their long tails dancing behind them, and, along with the weight loss, the cropped hair, the grey skin, it is another hint I do not take.

We must have been speaking for ten minutes by the time she says, 'Stevie, I have something to tell you.'

I stand up with Ash in my arms.

My mother says things like 'treatment' and 'prognosis', and I don't understand why I can see a magpie dive-bombing from a branch and a schoolboy pushing open a gate, why these things are still happening when she is telling me she is dying. 'I'm sorry, Stevie, to have to tell you this, I'm sorry,' not years left, or months. She might have a week. *A week.*

Something is missing. The middle part is missing.

'Stevie?'

'Stevie?'

Eventually the typhoon in my head, my heart, lands on anger. Even as it happens I am not proud of it but I cannot stop it.

'How could you keep it from us?' I scream. 'Why didn't you tell us when you got the diagnosis?'

'Darling,' she says in a reedy voice that isn't hers – how long has she sounded like this? How long have I been deaf to it? 'The last thing we wanted was for you and Jess to fly back from New York when it wasn't serious.'

'You've known for years, then?'

'It came, and then it went, and I was fine – I had that wonderful week with you and Jess – and then it returned, and you had Ash to worry about.'

'So, when did you find out it had come back?'

'Shortly after Ash was born. I decided not to have any more treatment.'

'I don't understand – why not?'

'I didn't want to go through it all over again when there was no guarantee it would work. I'm old, Stevie.'

'What – and you've had a good innings? I need you, Mum! We all do!'

I don't remember how it ends, the conversation about all conversations ending; all I remember is sitting on the sofa, my breathing quick, Ash in the bouncy chair, his head tilted – *What's happened?* – then reaching out his arms to me, one word in my head: No, no, no.

Rebecca calls as I am packing to go to Mum.

'Did you know?' I ask, and there is a pause.

'Yes,' she says.

'When did she tell you?'

'When she got the diagnosis. Look – I was here; you and Jess weren't – she wanted to protect you, that was all.'

Mother superior. Florence Nightingale. I wish I could shake her.

'Then *you* should have told us,' I say, just as I am putting down the phone.

Rebecca picks us up at the station the next morning and we drive in silence to the farm. We turn into the yard and see Dad coming out of the house.

'Do you really think I wanted to keep this to myself?' she says as she turns off the ignition. 'To deal with it on my own? I didn't have a choice. I had to respect her wishes.'

'They've always treated you differently,' I say.

Jess arrives the next morning and there is something different about her, she seems distracted, we are not the comfort to each other I thought we would be. I want her to share my anger towards Rebecca, I want us to wallow in it together, but she refuses. It has been hard for her, Jess says, we should be gentle with her.

Rebecca tells us everything then, she plots the waxing and waning of our mother's cancer like an electrocardiogram, she spares no details, the bruised arms and parched skin, the crushing exhaustion and lost hair, clumps like sheep's wool on barbed wire.

'Rebecca,' Jess says when she finishes, 'thank you for looking after her for us, for doing all this. Thank you.' The air feels heavy. Rebecca says she was glad to have been the one of the three of us who was with her, with Mum and Dad, the dutiful daughter. And it is wrong to say this, it is not the time – she knows that – but she'd felt resentful, too.

'One Monday morning, not long after Mum's diagnosis,' she says, 'I was sitting in the hospital waiting room, flicking through my phone, and I saw a picture Stevie had posted. It was the two of you, a selfie, some fancy restaurant, you both looked so happy. I stared at that photo for ages, trying to be pleased for you, pleased that you were spending time together – it was what you both wanted – but I couldn't help feeling you were laughing at me.

'There I was, ping-ponging to the farm every other weekend, filling the freezer, checking Mum's medication, sitting in front of the nightly news with Dad, wishing away his tears, while there you were, living it up, completely oblivious to all of it. I felt like a mug.'

'Rebecca, we didn't *know* . . . ' Jess started.

'You should have. If you'd just been in touch more regularly, if you'd been *in our lives*, you would have known. And Stevie, I know you've had Ash; you've been on your own . . . '

'And you've been such a support, Rebecca, I'm so grateful to you . . . '

'But still. You could have been here. You chose not to know, both of you.'

We leave Rebecca on her own, Jess and I, we give her space, and offer to help Dad with the calving, but he doesn't want it. 'I have help,' he says, gesturing to the farmhands standing in the yard with their hands in their pockets and their eyes on the ground. 'Be with your mother.'

We take it in turns and when it is mine, I walk past the window at the top of the stairs on the way to her room, Ash in my arms, and I see Rebecca and Jess outside in the paddock. Jess's arms are folded, she is talking. Rebecca nods and steps towards Jess, but Jess shakes her head and walks back towards the house, arms still crossed tight. Rebecca stays where she is.

We are all there when Mum dies. We are sitting on wooden chairs around the brass bed, the hospice nurse hovering discreetly in the background, giving her morphine, making sure she is comfortable, telling us that it is possible she can hear us and that we should say goodbye before she sets off, into the underworld, alone.

And at the same time, we are not there, not really, we can't be, because it can't be happening, I won't believe it, none of it makes any sense. I feel as if I am watching her, watching us all spread around the bed, from above, from the wicker lampshade that hangs from the ceiling rose. I wonder why we are sitting there in silence when we should be shaking her shoulders, shaking her alive, we should be screaming, *Stop! STOP! Don't let her go! There has been a mistake!*

But I don't say anything, I try but I can't, and when the nurse says it is time, I hold one hand and it is cool because life is already leaving her, invisible blood pouring from her fingers, pooling on to the quilt, and Dad holds the other hand and Rebecca strokes her hair, white and tight and curled, and Jess, next to me, stares at the faded patchwork quilt that covers Mum's motionless body – sprigs and stars and stripes in beiges and browns, blues and pinks – while the afternoon sun and the voices of the cousins minding Ash on the lawn below streak through the half-open window. We let it happen.

The yellow curtains billow briefly as if moving aside to let her through, and then, we are told, she is gone.

A flat-iron passes over her face then, smoothing the pain, erasing the life; making her look young again. I remember what she said to me the day before: 'You are more than I deserved.' How she paused, her lips a pencil-width apart as if she were about to say something else, before they closed.

Fifty

'Four and a half years you've been here?' Nathan said. 'That's a decent chunk of time.'

'An eighth of my life.'

'And what do you have to show for it?'

'Thanks, Nathan.' I took a sip of my Americano and wiped the condensation from the window. The tulips below the trees in Tompkins Square Park were preparing to burst open, but grey, grit-speckled snow hung doggedly to the edges of the sidewalks and another storm had been forecast.

'Plenty, it turns out,' Nathan continued, pushing his hand through his hair. 'A fabulous shoe collection.'

'Ha. A passable friend collection.'

'A great career. Money in the bank.'

'Not as much as there should be.'

'There never is. Experiences.'

'A ton of those. I've had a blast, as your people say.'

'I'd never say that. Have you ever heard me say *blast?*'

'Maybe not.'

'So many memorable times. The Miracle on the Hudson.'

'The week we met, that was. A highlight, for sure.'

'The election.'

'My second month in New York. *Before* we met.'

'A high point, nonetheless. Dancing on the sidewalks, on the fire escapes, on car hoods. The night the 9/11 gloom lifted. You can't leave, Stevie. You're here now, you're settled. You're a New Yorker. Tell me one thing that's better about London, about England.'

'About London-England?'

'I never say that, either.'

Nathan was right. I would miss all of it. I would miss New York's perpetual roar, its urban tinnitus. Its bright-sky optimism and earthquake-uneven streets. The fact that every day was a fight, that living here was like loving here: completely, utterly unrequited, and that made you want to do it even more. I could be here another five years; another fifteen years. I could stay here for ever, surfing the career wave, having weekends away, dinners out, dates where we looked at the drinks menu and then at each other and thought, *You're cute, you're smart, you're funny, and this will never work.* All this would continue. The city would freewheel forward and I would move with it. And yet I would stay exactly where I was.

Would that be so bad? It wouldn't if there wasn't a baby hovering at the edges of my mind like a shadow puppet, jolting me awake in the middle of the night.

'Don't you think you'll go back to London and it'll be grey and quiet, and you'll be like, "What the hell have I done?"' Nathan continued.

'I don't, no.'

'You don't know?'

'I think I feel sort of rootless here.'

'Isn't Jess a root?'

'Yes, and you know, when you asked me what I had to show for my four and a half years, she was my first thought.'

'A sister.'

'Yes.'

'A sister not a spectre.'

'Well, sort of. I get her now. Parts of her, at least. I mean, she was pretty annoying about Sam after we split up, but perhaps she felt she could do that *because* we're closer now, because we've spent more time together. So apart from the experiences and the great job and the great *friends* . . . '

'I was waiting for that . . . '

'She's what I've got.'

'But isn't that another reason *not* to leave?'

'It makes leaving possible. Jess and I are in each other's lives now. She'll come to London, I'll come back here. It's never going to be the easiest sibling relationship, whether I stay or go. She'll never open up entirely. But we have something that we didn't have before. We had our Sunday dinner in my apartment, on the floor, the other week. It was so chilled. We never would have done that a year ago.'

Nathan shook his head. 'I just hope you know what you're doing, Stevie, having a baby on your own, leaving Jess, leaving a job you love.'

'Does anyone ever know what they're doing? And I'm not leaving my job, Nathan, I'm taking a *bigger* job in the same company.'

'Come on, you know you won't have as much influence in London as you do in New York. Lex may love a London vacation, but he thinks the city's a backwater. Anyway, why can't you have a baby here?'

'Do you know *anyone* who has a baby in New York?'

Nathan drained his coffee. 'OK, no I don't,' he says at last. 'So why don't you be the first? Or move to Brooklyn – they have them there.'

'Everyone has babies in London. All my friends have children.'

'Are they still your friends? Will you actually have anything in common with them, apart from reproduction?'

'Of course I will. And there's Rebecca and her teenagers, I'll need some support if I'm going to do it on my own and they're ready-made babysitters. Anyway, I've got to go back; Lex has made the decision for me, and I don't have much time if I want a baby – I'm thirty-seven. If I'm going to do it, I've got to do it in London. It makes sense. Honestly, I'm happy about it.'

A fresh start. A new life. Two new lives. It was what I needed. I thought about pushing a buggy through a park. Birdsong, blossom, children's voices. It felt right.

Nathan screwed up his empty sugar sachet and put it and the wooden stirrer into his cup. 'I'll try not to be offended,' he said. 'Look, girl, despite my obvious vested interest, I want the best for you. If you really are going, you know I'll be right behind you.'

'Thanks, Nathan.'

'I mean, not literally.'

'Funny.'

'But I'll support you. I'll be on your team. Whatever you need.'

'Thanks.'

'Will you promise me one thing, though?'

'Depends what it is.'

'Investigate the having-a-baby thing here first, right? Before you make any sudden moves and, like, snare a British mail-order dad or something. I mean, you might find our American jizz is of a superior quality. Then you can tell Lex you're staying and he can get someone else to do London. Imagine how overjoyed Jess would be – she'd probably pay for childcare.'

'OK,' I said. No reason not to start educating myself while I was in New York.

'And I'm more than happy to interview any potential daddies.'

'Seriously? I don't think that's how it works, and anyway, aren't you supposed to be attached?'

'Details, Stevie. *Details.*'

For the next couple of months, I was a student of assisted reproduction. I acquired a new, acronym-laden vocabulary that, with its blastocysts and retrievals and tubal ligations, made me think of bomb disposal units and space travel. Terrified that Lex would rake through my internet search history and discover what I was plotting, I bought a new laptop and studied in secret in my apartment. I reclaimed my evenings by postponing dinners and deleting dating apps and speckled the walls above my desk with a neon Post-it note timeline, which ran from the 'suppression of the menstrual cycle' right up to 'birth'.

When I was confident that I would ace an IVF exam, I began my search for the supporting actor. I chose a sperm bank based in California because it shipped to the UK and represented 153 Ivy League donors, fifty-two of whom were over six feet tall. The 'client success story' I found right at the bottom of the web page, below the heart-warming testimonials from love-at-first-sight lesbians and reformed Peter Pans with past-its-sell-by-date sperm, helped.

The successful woman, photographed in profile, embracing a dribbling, rubber-band-wristed baby, was a single mother called Lola. Independent by nature, she wrote, she had always planned to have children on her own because of the benefits solo parenting would bring. She would be spared the inevitable emotional, financial and legal costs when it didn't work out with the father. She would be absolved of all co-parenting compromises, including names, schools, bedtimes and candy consumption. The sperm bank had granted her wishes and given her a no-strings baby. Who, I wondered, would choose to reproduce any other way?

As I flicked through donor profiles, it was impossible not to think of the online dating in which I had dabbled since splitting up with Sam. There were, of course, differences. Apart from baby and toddler snaps, there were no photos, although a looka-like tab compared each donor's appearance to a celebrity. While I was aware that this was pure fantasy, the namedropping (Ryan Gosling three times; Idris Elba four) coupled with the unabashed listing of qualifications – 'Harvard grad; Stanford postgrad' – defining characteristics – 'humble, compassionate, easy-going, laughs at anything' – and favourite pastimes – 'fencing and fal-conry', 'building things out of wood' – made the candidates seem infinitely more attractive than the kind the dating algorithms had thrown me.

The rules of engagement were also more appealing. This time, only I was doing the choosing. Our connection would last for the rest of our lives, even though, unless our offspring tracked him down and, say, invited him to her wedding, we would never meet. There would be no rejection. At first, I found myself drawn to the rakes, the players. 'The Cat's Meow'. 'Rugged Intelligence'. I didn't need to see their faces: I could hear the Lothario in their voice recordings. What was I after? Vindication? To attain the unattainable with my cold, hard cash?

I had a word with myself. This was not who I wanted for my unborn child. This was not who I wanted *in* my unborn child. I stepped away.

A couple of days later, I logged on again, and within seconds, I found him.

'The History Boy' was from Connecticut, six foot with green eyes like mine. He had graduated *cum laude* from Harvard and worked as a public-school history teacher. While his fellow alumni, I imagined, spanked their Silicon Valley cash on cars and casinos and Michelin-starred meals, The History Boy spent his spare time serving at a local soup kitchen, playing chess and reading historical fiction.

I wondered if his complete lack of sporting achievements, or the fact that he was masturbating furiously in order to make ends meet, accounted for his 'high vial availability'. Was he *too* available? But I knew I had found my sperm when I listened to the gravelly audio. He sounded gentle, dependable, kind, qualities that more than compensated for not being a state roller hockey champion or a high school football captain, and when I clicked on the toddler photo: rust-red boiler suit, bowl cut, big eyes looking apprehensively at the camera, the deal was clinched.

Fifty-one

The month after Mum dies, we sleep together every night. Gradually the discomfort I'd felt drips away. Ash's strange new baby smell seems to fade. Or perhaps, as our pheromones mingle, his smell becomes my smell, or mine his.

A routine establishes itself and I surrender to it, a lighthouse flashing through the gale of loss. At nine o'clock every night Ash screams for precisely forty minutes. Before, I left him to 'cry it out' – that term my new mum colleagues associated with fili-cide – but now I pick him up and hold him, and although it does not abbreviate the wailing, it seems, somehow, to reduce his rage, and it reduces mine, too. I can comfort him: I know that now; I have some influence over his well-being.

Do I begin to feel closer to him, now that we share a bed? Yes. Gradually, his tiny embrace feels less like something to resist; it feels warm, consoling. I am not sure he feels any more part of me than he did before, but he begins to feel less other. And when he looks at me and smiles, I find myself smiling back.

One night, as his chest rises and falls on mine and I wait for sleep to find me, Rebecca's question rings out. 'Are you *enjoying* him?'

I cross my arms over his back and consider my answer. His

breaths are fast and shallow, two for every one of mine. A motor-
bike zooms past the window. I lock my arms tighter, protectively;
stroke his head. His fuzzy scalp reminds me of kitten fur.

Am I enjoying him?

I could not have said yes before. Now, though I wonder what
part of it is actually him and how much is what he is compensating
for, what is Mum, her absence – now, I could say yes.

During the day, I bury myself in domesticity. Death has made
my mind a blur. Tasks that were tedious are challenging: dropping
the correct number of scoops into the bottle, marrying onesie
poppers. But they also offer comfort. Previously, I considered
myself an abhorrer of habit: I yearned for the struggles, satisfactions and surprises of every New York day. Now I begin to find
pleasure in repetition, in knowing exactly what the next minute,
hour or day will hold.

I didn't cry when Mum was dying – how could I when I didn't
believe it? – but I do now. I cry all the time, like a tap left on.
I am surprised not to see saltwater pooling on the floorboards,
creeping up the skirting. Ash notices: he puts his chubby hands
to my wet face and a new sound like a jackdaw's questioning caw
issues from his mouth. Caw, caw, caw.

She has left mementos for me, my mother. The receipt for
the pizza lunch she insisted on paying for appears in my handbag, folded carefully in two. Her woollen hat, smelling of her
perfume: I breathe it in hungrily before it fades. I find a ball of
tissue under the sofa; it must have escaped from her sleeve when
she was playing with Ash. I remember her sitting on the carpet
with him, even though she was weary, even though she must have
been in pain.

I put the tissue in my pocket and crouch beside Ash and start
spinning the wooden flowers on his bouncy chair faster and faster
and faster until they are a whirr of yellow and green. He leans

forward and lunges at them, one hand, then the other, his eyes locked to mine, and his mouth opens in a toothless grin.

The unexpected side effect of co-sleeping is that Ash's daytime napping also improves. I had thought having more at night would mean he'd need less during the day, but he dozes soundlessly for two hours each morning, and the same in the afternoon. I have time on my hands – time that needs to be filled. I worry, if it is not, that my mother, hovering permanently at the edges of my mind, will turn memories into recriminations: *Why didn't you guess I was ill? Why did you stay away so long?*

I message Lex. I need to schedule one of my 'keeping-in-touch days' – I had planned to months ago, but the weeks have oozed into each other and it hasn't happened, I haven't *made* it happen, and now I must. There will be no more hanging outside the club like a ghost as I did that dark day. I will make an appointment, push open the door, stride on to the polished concrete floor, watch heads turn, smiles break, 'Stevie! You're back!'

I suggest coming in one afternoon, meeting a few heads of department, video conferencing with Lex in New York, and I hover over my laptop after I press send. There is a reply within seconds and my hands shake when I click on it but all it says is '+ Mike' and I see that Mike, my maternity cover, has been added at the top beside my name. Then a message from him pops up.

Hey Stevie! Hope you and the baby are keeping well! Lex is super busy rn but I can meet . . . U around next week?

I don't reply; I won't waste my time. Instead, I message Jess. *Hey, just checking you're OK?*

I have missed her. The few bright moments of that week with Mum were the ones Ash and I spent with Jess. She had seemed enchanted with him.

'You look so good together,' she'd said, taking a photo, Ash on my lap, then, 'Sorry, that sounds strange,' but I knew what she meant. We hadn't the last time she'd seen us. We'd looked thrust together, a mismatch, an internet date. It was better now.

Lovely to hear from you, kiddo, she replied. *Coming over again next month, just booked. Going to help you and R sort everything out. Can't wait to see you.*

Fifty-two

That Memorial Day weekend, two months after I found my donor, Nathan raised the issue. Our routine at the beach house was well established by then. Jenna was still single and still, from time to time, annoying, but then so, I'm sure, was I, with my in-jokes with Nathan and my inability to load the dishwasher properly. And we had things in common now, Jenna and I: she shared my longing for a child, she was someone to talk to about it, to plot with.

'You're the pioneer, Stevie,' she'd say, 'I'll follow in your footsteps.'

Jenna wasn't at the house that weekend – she had had a better offer: a weekend in the Caribbean with a new romantic recruit. We were on our second jug of coffee on Sunday morning when he brought it up, taking me completely by surprise.

'Babies,' he said.

'What about them?'

'Cute, aren't they?'

'Some of them. Why?'

'Your baby journey—'

'Which hasn't actually started yet.'

'Oh, come on, girl, it's been an idea, a seed, if you will, for years at this point.'

'I'm sorry, Nathan, I'm a baby bore.'

'Only in your head. Not to me.'

'Well, that's a relief, because some days, some nights, it's all I think about. When I wake up and can't get back to sleep and I imagine being kept awake by a baby's cries instead of the worry of not having one . . . '

On those nights, I often asked myself where it had come from, the clarion call, sharper and louder every day.

The idea that some sort of biological clock was involved made me seethe. I hated the term, hated to think that my cells were anticipating the chimes of an outdated gender stereotype; that social convention might be playing a part, that I wanted to do it because it was *what women did*. No, that couldn't be it: the route I'd decided on wasn't exactly conventional. Society wasn't keen on single mothers.

Perhaps it was Mira and my friends at home, lobbing their announcement emails and Instagram posts across the Atlantic, that had turned a desire into an obsession; the New Yorkers who had begun to shuffle over the river in pairs and rent apartments with second bedrooms.

As I rearranged my pillows and hunted for my earplugs and rolled over and back again, I'd think of Jess, who had shown me in the broad avenues of the city a different way to live, and I'd imagine, for the hundredth time, what she'd say when I told her, if she would think I was betraying her.

'I mean, I get it, Stevie,' said Nathan. 'It's a big deal; it's the biggest deal of all.' He paused long enough to push his fringe from his eyes, which he narrowed.

'Where are you with the *sperm*?' he asked conspiratorially.

'Oh, that. I've found someone I like.'

'Huh. Tall, dark and handsome or tall, blond and handsome?'

'It's mainly about qualifications and personality, actually,

301

much as that will disappoint you. Did you know you can listen to donors' voices and see their baby photos?'

'So weird.'

'*So* weird. And so handy.'

'I guess.' There was another hair flick, a pressing together of palms, fingers. 'OK, so . . . so it probably hasn't crossed your mind, because I'm kind of an idiot and I'm sure I don't check any of your boxes, apart from handsome, of course, and you wouldn't pick my voice from a line-up, and I was a fucking strange-looking baby, and it looks as if I've missed the cum boat in any case, but—'

'I know what you're going to say, Nathan.'

'Shit, I feel as if I'm about to ask you to marry me or something.'

'You're going to offer to be the father.'

'That sounds even worse!'

'Thanks.'

'Sorry. I mean, well, I'm not there yet – but yes, I'd like to talk about it.'

I didn't say anything for a while.

'Are you tearing up?' Nathan asked. 'No way! I don't think I've ever seen you do that!' He sounded delighted. I walked over to his side of the table and gave him a hug.

'I haven't done anything,' he said, 'apart from make you cry.'

'You've thought about it.'

'I have.'

'Thank you. For even considering me worthy of knocking up.'

'Well, I don't think we'd actually . . . '

'I'm kidding. I just want your sperm.'

'Thank God. Anyway, it's not entirely selfless, you know.'

'You mean you do want a baby after all?'

'Yeah, I think I do. And I know you're the best mama I'm going to find.'

*

We spent the weekend with our imaginary baby, our baby girl, because ever since I decided to have a baby, a little girl had been in my head. We imagined what she'd look like: fair hair like fine nylon thread, like Nathan's when he was a baby; green eyes that will gradually dim to hazel, like mine. We gave her names: flower names, tree names, Daisy if she was born in spring or summer, Holly if it was winter.

'I like Willow, too,' I said.

'What if she's fat?' asked Nathan.

We talked about where she'd live: at the new two-bed I'd rent, with an elevator and a washing machine, and, every other weekend, at Nathan's, just around the block.

'Maybe I'll move in for the first month,' said Nathan. 'Help out.'

'You'd do that?'

'Sure.'

'What about Brice?'

'What about him?'

'No guys at all for a whole month?'

'No. At least, not when I'm on the nightshift.'

'How will your parents take all this?'

'What, me being a papa? Would I need to tell them? We're not exactly in regular contact and I don't think they'd react all that well to it.'

'Well, if you're sure. I guess that would make things easier.'

'Our secret. You'd tell yours, then?'

'I already have – I told my mum I was thinking of having a baby on my own years ago. As for my dad, well, I can't fall any further in his estimations.'

I said goodbye to The History Boy. It stung. I had invested time in this relationship. I had pictured our child lifting her

303

eyes from her book, pinching her ear when she was thinking. I would miss her.

Still, it felt right to be embarking on the baby-making journey with Nathan, a human being rather than an avatar. It was the perfect arrangement: together yet not together; it would give me all the autonomy I needed. When we went to the clinic for tests and observed the unhappy hetero couples, we thought how stressful it must be to be romantically attached and engaging in the least romantic activity, *trying* for a baby; the blame and resentment it must engender. How lucky we were to have none of it.

And the London club? The timings were unpredictable, but if the first or second try was successful, I'd still be able to open it. I'd waddle through the site in stretchy jeans and sneakers, hardhat and bulbous belly, a role model to aspiring mothers, and then, instead of staying in London after the opening, I'd return. That, Lex would understand. *Leaving New York would seem like a step back.* Hadn't he said that once?

And now that Nathan was involved, it made sense to make the city our home.

I looked at it through the eyes of an expectant mother, as I had when Mira visited, but this time the mother was me. And though the child-rearing deficiencies remained – the concrete monotone; the craggy sidewalks; the reek of rat – I saw that there were advantages to living on an island twenty-three miles square, where a global buffet could be delivered to your door and taxis would pick you up and take you wherever you wanted to go.

I no longer thought children were a species the island could not support; now they were everywhere. A toddler pointing as a police car shrieked down the street. Twins scooting through Tompkins Square Park. A basketball court of junior schoolers in Soho. I wouldn't be a pioneer; I would simply join a different tribe, a tribe I hadn't known.

When his test results came back, Nathan was delighted. 'I told you it'd be whole milk,' he said. 'None of this half-and-half garbage. Top quality, high-speed cum.' Nathan bought a 'Made in New York' Babygro. We discussed when to tell Jess.

Then, one late-July day, after a weekend upstate with Brice, he changed his mind.

Fifty-three

It is time to be honest with each other. That is the thought that ricochets as I drive to see Dad on his birthday, the coordinates of the posh pub where Rebecca had her wedding rehearsal dinner on the satellite navigation, Ash blowing raspberries in his car seat behind me.

The occasion was billed as a family gathering – Rebecca, David and the teenagers; Ash and me. But then David fell off his bike and broke his leg and Rebecca had to take him to hospital, so we are borrowing their car and going alone, Ash and I, even though I am sure Dad will be appalled by the idea. Why on earth would he want to spend his birthday with the two of us?

'You know we don't have that kind of relationship, Rebecca,' I'd said. 'You know we don't do one-on-one.'

'Yes,' she'd replied, 'and I think it's about time you did. Don't you want Ash to have *someone* of the older generation in his life? Look at this as an opportunity to get to know each other. Do it for Mum, OK, Stevie? And for me.'

'OK,' I'd replied. I got it, it was my turn, but I'd thought and hadn't said: *There is a conversation that needs to happen first*, despite the circumstances, because of the circumstances. A death is a stripping away, a time for truth. And as I'd gripped the steering wheel, Rebecca's yellow 'DRIVE ON THE LEFT' Post-it note in the centre, I'd rehearsed my talking points.

Why have I always disappointed you, Dad?

Why did you never want me there?

Why did you keep Mum's cancer from us?

We must sweep away the fallen leaves, I think as I turn into the car park, expose the soil. If Dad and I are to have a relationship, this will be its foundation.

My resolve takes a knock as soon as I see him, waiting for us by the door to the pub, his hands in the pockets of his cord trousers. His face is mottled by a life outside; his hair lies in stripes across his crown. He is wearing a tie – the one he wore to Mum's funeral – and a tweed jacket. He smiles a thin smile, takes a step towards us.

'Stevie.'

'Happy birthday, Dad.'

We lean into each other. A polite kiss on the cheek as if we are meeting for the first time, the smell of aftershave and the outdoors.

'I don't know why you came all this way,' he says as he pushes open the door and I wheel Ash's pram through. 'I told Rebecca it was a ridiculous idea, you and the baby driving hours just for lunch – it'll probably be dark by the time you get home.'

OK, there he is, I think, *the same old spiky Dad.* I must do it: I must have the conversation.

'We wanted to see you,' I say, biding time, and his brow knits – is it disbelief or irritation? Ash is in his pram, shielded by its hood, oblivious to the atmosphere; I feel protective of him.

Dad's pale eyes shift around the pub restaurant. Dressed-up people, people with money, people resting manicured hands on white tablecloths. Not his people. He looks diminished; he clasps his hands and looks at the flagstone floor. A man marooned in a field of grief.

My heart crumples. My will is felled. I have no business wallowing in the past; it is not relevant now. I tear up my talking points. What was I thinking? I've come to give my father comfort; I must put everything else aside.

'This room's a bit stuffy, isn't it?' I say. 'Rebecca booked it, it's her kind of thing, but I think there's a bar next door that's more relaxed. Do you mind if we go in there? Less stressful if he screams.'

'If you like,' Dad says.

In the next room, he takes off his jacket and drapes it over his chair. I unzip the pram's bassinet and take Ash out. He beams. Freedom.

'A smiler, I see,' says Dad. He reaches out a hand, freckled with liver spots, then draws it back.

'Would you like to hold him, Dad?'

'Oh, no, he looks happy with you. Don't want to scare him. I'll go to the bar. What'll you have?'

I hold Ash close, stroke the back of his head. The fuzz is growing into baby hair as dark as his eyes.

Dad returns with a pint of bitter and a lime and soda, and sits down.

'Thank you,' I say. It is better in here. Low beams, a fireplace in the corner, a family with a child in a highchair, the yeasty smell of spilled beer from the bar. Ash gurgles and Dad picks up a supermarket bag from beneath the table.

'Your mum was going through some old baby things before she passed away,' he says, taking out two boxes. 'She thought you might want these jigsaws.' One of the boxes has three cheery firemen on the lid.

'I remember doing the fire engine one with you,' he says. 'All

308

the pieces are there. We did them together, your mum and me, on a tray on her bed, just to make sure.'

'Did you?' I open the box, pick up a couple of thick cardboard pieces, half a yellow helmet, a fireman's grin.

'It took us a while, if I'm honest. We must have looked a sight, two geriatrics grappling with puzzles meant for three-year-olds.'

We are crying and laughing now. We wipe our eyes. Dad takes a sip of his beer, places the glass back on the circle of water it has made on the table, leans back in his chair.

'What would you like to eat?' I say. 'My treat.'

He takes a deep breath, sits up straight. 'Well, if you insist.' He hates other people paying for him, doing anything for him, years of struggling to make ends meet in the early days of the farm, worrying about the rap at the door, Mum always said; he hates to feel he owes anyone anything. 'I've heard the steak's good,' Dad continues. 'If it's not too dear.'

'I'll have the same. Would you mind watching Ash while I order?'

'All right.' I put Ash back in the pram and Dad shifts his chair slightly so he can see into it.

'Hello, little lad,' he says. *It's OK*, I tell myself. *He's his grandfather; it's fine.*

'Are you coping OK, Dad, at home?' I ask when I get back. He takes a deep breath, as if wondering how to respond. Sunlight shafting through the window makes his eyes shine. 'It must be so strange,' I say, 'the house without her.'

'Well, I had time to, you know . . . '

'Get used to the idea.'

'I told her she was making a mistake, not telling you. She wouldn't listen.'

'Oh, I assumed . . . '

'That it was my idea? No. Not at all. And then Ash came along, and she said she couldn't stand the illness taking over, *dominating*, that was her word. She couldn't stand the idea of you looking at her and only seeing that.'

'It would have been better.'

'Better than not knowing?'

'Yes.'

'Yes,' he agrees. Our meals appear.

'I keep thinking she's going to walk into the room,' he says, his voice see-sawing.

'Oh, Dad.' I put my arm around his neck. I do it instinctively and it surprises me and for a moment I wonder if it is too much: we don't do this, my father and I, but then I feel his shoulders drop.

'It's just as hard for you.'

'I miss her so much,' I say, and suddenly I feel worn out, I want to curl up in the armchair in the corner of the room and close my eyes.

'Of course you do.' We look over at Ash, asleep in the pram. Dad takes a handkerchief from his jacket pocket, passes it to me.

'Your mum doted on him, you know,' he says. 'She was desperate to see him walk, hear him talk . . . We were worried at first, but she was full of admiration for you, doing it all on your own.'

'It's been . . . Well, it's getting easier,' I say.

'Must have been odd, being off work. I mean, I know you *are* working, being a mother's the hardest job there is, but . . . '

'It is hard,' I say. 'You know, Dad, I'd never have told Mum this, or anyone, really . . . ' His brow softens. A secret. 'But being away from work has been one of the most difficult things about having Ash. My job's always been such a big part of who I am.'

He nods. 'I can understand that. You and Jessie got the workaholic genes. My fault, that. Nothing wrong with enjoying your work, don't let anyone tell you different.' He takes a sip of his beer. 'It's a shame it ended up taking you so far away, though.'

'I think you might have to take some responsibility for that, Dad.'

'And why's that?' He stiffens.

'You wanted us to do well, go to university, get good jobs.'

'Ah, yes, you're right about that.' It was not the accusation he was fearing. 'You want for your children what you didn't have yourself.' He looks into his pint. 'You try, but sometimes things don't go the way you plan.'

I tell him I tried to come and visit when I moved back, but Mum said I shouldn't. 'It was because she was sick, wasn't it? She didn't want me to see her like that.' He nods grimly.

We sit there together, a comfortable silence. Then Ash begins to fuss. I check my phone. Two thirty. Less than three hours ago I was on my way here, stirring the soup of resentment, willing myself to have it out with Dad, to rake over all of it, right back to the beginning. *What did I do to disappoint you?*

None of it seems to matter now. The three of us are here and she is not, that is all. Those thoughts are road signs in the rear-view mirror.

'I do want to come up here more often, Dad,' I say. 'I want Ash to get to know the countryside.'

'Perhaps we'll get him on a tractor one day. It'll be nice to have a boy around.'

Boys on tractors; sons – he would have found that easier. I watch as he pushes the last piece of steak around his plate, spreads a neat layer of mustard on it as if it were butter, closes his blue eyes and puts it into his mouth.

'You can help him with his spellings, like you did with me,' I say.

'Oh yes,' he says. 'I remember.'

I think of the storybook baddie I drew for so many years, hooked nose, fleshy ears, hands at right angles as if dislocated from his body. It is not him. I am beginning to see that now.

'Back to London, then?' Dad asks as I pay the bill, digging his nails into his palms as I punch in the number.

'Yes,' I say. 'Ash'll nap in the car. Will you be OK?'

'Course. I knew how to boil an egg before I met your mum and I know how to boil one now.' He pauses. 'You know, she'd have loved to be a fly on the wall today.'

'I bet,' I say, and we both smile. He watches as I clip Ash into his car seat, as I kiss his cheek before I shut the door.

'Bye, little lad,' he says.

I wind down the window as I start the engine. 'It was good to see you, Dad,' I say. 'You'll have to come to London next time!'

'Yes,' he replies, and before I can say I'm joking, of course I don't expect him to come to London, he is as likely to take a rocket to the moon, 'I will,' he says.

Fifty-four

Nathan was waiting at a table by the window at the Ethiopian place on Fifth Street and he stood up when I came in. I draped my handbag over my chair, sat down and said, 'What?' and he didn't reply. The restaurant was bright and smelled of cardamom coffee, but it was chilly, as if the air-conditioning was on full.

He cleared his throat. 'I'm not ready, Stevie,' he said.

For a moment, I wondered if this was one of his jokes and he was about to pull the particulars to adjoining apartments in an elevator building from under the table. 'Kidding, Stevie, *totally* kidding – I found this, what do you think?'

But he didn't, he just looked at me expectantly as the server placed two bottles of beer in front of us and I thought, *I didn't order beer*, and when I spoke my voice was sharp and I sounded like someone else.

'A weekend away with the dogs made you realise what a commitment a real-life human might be? I'm not expecting you to be a dad, Nathan, just involved.'

'I talked to Brice about it.'

'He didn't know?'

'I didn't think there was any point in telling him before.'

'And there is now?'

'I don't know, I guess I'm kind of into him now. He's worn me down.'

'And he's not into this.'

'Not right now. He says he wants kids of his own someday, and . . . '

'Our kid would get in the way.'

'Look, it's not like that, Stevie. I'm so sorry. I feel terrible letting you down.'

I stood up and put on my coat and wound my scarf around my neck.

'Better to find out now, I guess,' I said, and, ignoring Nathan's protestations, I left the restaurant.

But when I got to my building, I paused beside the fake topiary trees, which had arrived at the same time as a hallway paint job and a rent hike, because I didn't want to go inside. I didn't want to nod at the neighbour I always bumped into on my way to the seventh floor; I didn't want to see her or her new girlfriend, their sneakers sitting side by side outside her apartment, laces still tied, eyelets gawking. I didn't want to be alone.

It was early: twenty to seven. I walked on, towards the park. Suddenly, fifty feet in front of me, the double doors of an apartment building swung open and children swarmed out. One carried a pink helium balloon in the shape of a number five. They started to run and when they were almost level with me, the first tripped on a buckled paving stone and I clapped my hand to my open mouth because she appeared to somersault in slow-motion, limbs shooting in every direction like pick-up-sticks. She landed on her knees and they made a scraping sound on the sidewalk and there was a high-pitched scream that went on and on.

The adults, if there were any, must have been dawdling at the back, so I crouched beside the child. 'Are you OK?' I said, but all she said was, 'Mommy! Mommy!' more and more urgently. The knees of her jeans were torn and wet and red with blood, but no bones or bulges showed.

I remembered when Bea had fallen over and grazed her knees badly and what Mira had done. 'Can you sit up?' I asked, rummaging in my bag with one hand for a tissue, trying to coax her into a sitting position with the other. 'Mommy! Mommy!' she said again, and when she sat up, I lassoed her shoulders gently with my arms and told her that her mom would be here soon. Suddenly, there was a woman hovering above us with terror in her eyes, and she said, 'Is she all right?' and I said, 'Yes, she'll be fine, just bad grazes,' and she thanked me for looking after her.

I walked away – there was nothing else I could do. I walked to the coffee shop on the park, even though I wanted to lift the child from the sidewalk and cradle her home and spray her knees with antiseptic and cover them with Band-Aids and make sure she was OK.

When I pulled money from my purse to pay for my coffee, my hands were shaking. The café was closing so I sat on the bench outside and I thought about the time I fell off my bike on the hill at home.

I knew every jut and dent of the hill, but that summer afternoon there was an interloper, a rock the size of a Frisbee, and I noticed it a half-second too late. I slammed on my brakes and skidded and catapulted and landed on an arm and the snap was like the noise an apple tree branch made when my father split it over his knee.

Jess was back from university and soon after Mum had run to my screams and rocked me as I whimpered, Jess had materialised.

'Is she OK?' she said, and her voice sounded panicky, and her eyes were wide and white.

*

By the time I finished my coffee and walked back to my apartment, the rage I'd felt towards Nathan an hour before had defused. It was a rejection and it stung but I had had worse and it was not the end; it would never be the end with Nathan. I could forgive him. I would.

I'd phone him tomorrow, I thought, and say, *Let's forget the donor thing ever happened, let's move on, let's move back to being pure, platonic friends*, and then I'd close the covers of Plan B and put it gently back on the shelf.

I would slide out Plan A and find the toddler with the bowl-cut and the rust-red boiler suit on the first page and I would move back to London and the big, backwater job, and before long it would be me and her and no one else. We would weave ourselves together, move forward together, mark time together, evolve together, and when she tripped in the street or fell from her bike, I would run to her and bury my face in her hair.

Fifty-five

Suddenly, Ash is almost six months old. He can sit up, cover himself in carrot purée, drink from a sippy cup, roll over. The tiny baby phase is over. In a few weeks' time I will be back at work, peeing with the door shut, eating lunch with both hands, making decisions, calling shots. Away from him. Me again.

'You have longed for this moment,' I say to myself in the bathroom mirror, examining the new lines across my forehead, battle scars. But it is a strange stew, what I'm feeling: the flutter of freedom and the sting of regret.

'They get way more interesting just as you go back to work, that's the irony,' Mira said on the phone when I called her for nanny advice, and I said 'Mmm,' but I wanted to say, 'No, it's not that'; it's more than that and different from that. It burrows into my subconscious, this feeling, and I wake at three in the clench of a nightmare: my finals, an art movement I've forgotten to revise, see-through pencil cases on desks, *Turn over your papers please.*

Because I wish I could rewind the last six months, I wish I could start at the beginning with Ash, I wish I could do it all over again, do it better, be there, actually *be* there. And, simultaneously, I'm relieved it's behind me, the horror, the discombobulating horror of it all.

*

The first nanny I meet is a granny-nanny, 'a spry old bird, thanks to the new hip', she said on the application, and she looks like a blackbird, brittle and skinny, with bright eyes and dark, dyed hair pulled tight in a bun.

It is obvious, I suppose, why I am drawn to her, except she isn't my mother, she is the opposite of my mother, filling my calm flat with chatter from the moment she arrives until the second she leaves, until I can feel my pulse quickening. Most of it is harmless, inconsequential babble, but there are barbs, there are judgements that graze like nails on a blackboard: the bottle-feeding and – in her opinion – my "premature" return to work – stupid that one, considering it is why she is there. And, of course, she asks about him. She can't help herself.

'I take it the father's not around, then?'

'He never was,' I say, and it confuses her and shuts her up, and she leaves soon after.

The next is a lifer, a thickset woman in her mid-thirties who comes dressed as a toddler: a jumper with a cat on it, rainbow tights, Lego figure earrings. Despite the get-up, her enthusiasm for her previous charges and the years of Mary Poppins-peppered references she pulls from her rainbow-coloured file, I detect a sadness somewhere, a sense of a life gone awry, a dream buried too deep to unearth. Her answers to my questions sound over-rehearsed, her eyes keep darting to the window, and when she finally picks him up, Ash wriggles uneasily in her arms.

But Jonna, number three? When she refuses the sofa, folds her long legs and sits down on the floor beside him, he stops swatting the jungle gym giraffe above his head and stares. When she takes his hand and gives it a little shake, 'Pleased to meet you, Mr Ash,' and he grins and she incy-wincy-spiders up to his armpit and tickles him and there are giggles like church bells, I wonder if I should look away, *there were three of us in this marriage*. She is a complete natural, he is falling in love, and I feel an ache, a burn, and then I remind myself that this is exactly what I wanted.

I tell Mira about Jonna on the phone that evening.

'I can't understand why she's been out of work for six months – she's perfect: warm, fun, experienced . . . Perhaps it's because she's a vegan. She says she'll cook him meat and fish, but I suppose she won't actually be able to *taste* it . . .'

'You said she was Danish?'

'Yes, but she speaks better English than I do.'

'Blonde? Tall?'

'Yes.'

'Stevie, she hasn't been out of work because she's a *vegan*.'

'Hasn't she?'

'No.'

'Wait – are you suggesting it's because she's *attractive*?'

'Yes.'

'Would that put you off?'

'Great looks? Yes.'

'That's discrimination!'

'I suppose so. But I can't think of any other professions where you have better career prospects if you're *not* easy on the eye. And why on earth would I hire someone with ogling potential if I didn't need to? It's different for you – you're single, make the most of it. It'll be nice for Ash to have someone pretty to look at and she'll probably help your dating prospects no end.'

'Mira!'

'Seriously. Snap up the hot nanny; I would if I were you.'

There has, meanwhile, been no thaw in my relationship with Lex. The reply to my email announcing Ash's birth, the thoughtful gift, they never came. I just need to get back to work, I tell myself: he will forget all about it when there is no expanding belly to gawp at.

I will never mention Ash. I will never work from home or arrive late or leave early. I will work – if it is possible – harder than I have ever done before. By the end of the summer, I will be back in the bosom of the company, the belly of the beast, re-established as Lex's right hand and confidante, my respect for him reawakened, my maternity cover a foggy memory – *You know that guy who took Stevie's role while she was off? No, I can't remember his name, either* – as if none of it has ever happened.

I check Lex will be in town, then book a trip to New York the week after my return to work. I consider taking Ash with Jonna for back-up, but I'm on a budget now with a mouth to feed and getting my feet back under my stand-up desk is my priority. I will only be gone three days and Rebecca will be on hand just in case. Anyway, there is week one in London to contend with first.

I leave home at quarter-past seven on the last Monday in April, Jonna having arrived fifteen minutes earlier. I am dressed in a cream blouse with a ruffle neck, trousers that I bought in a sale and are no longer two sizes too big, and oxblood brogues. It feels as if I am wearing a costume. When I look in the mirror, paint on eyeliner, brush my lashes with mascara, swipe plum-coloured gloss across my lips, I am surprised not to see epaulettes. At the same time, it feels familiar, what I'm wearing; it feels comfortable.

There had been a long pause when I told Rebecca on the phone that, no, there would be no 'handover' or 'settling-in' period, because Ash and Jonna had bonded instantaneously and, really, what had she to learn about baby craft that she didn't already know? It wasn't as if Ash was a picky eater with his purée and his formula. Anyway, I had left a timetable on the fridge with nap and feed and tummy times and a list of phone numbers. What could go wrong?

Ash looks confused as I put on my jacket and kiss him goodbye.

I take a deep breath and try to ignore the splintering inside me. When I close the door behind me and pause at the top of the stairs, I hear no howl.

When I get to the bench at the end of my road where I sat with Mum and she put her arm through mine I find I can't walk any further; it is as if the pavement is barricaded.

For a minute, maybe two, I submit. I sit on the bench's cold, damp slats and think of her. The early-morning traffic trickles by; a woman on a bus turns her head and looks – have I been up all night? Are those yesterday's clothes?

What would Mum have thought of my going back to work; would she have said, 'It's early days, Stevie, are you sure?'

No, I think, she would understand; she had wanted a career and she hadn't had one, she had wondered what might have been. She had been there and not there when I was young; there had been a gap, something missing. She would think I was doing the right thing.

I remember the card Dad sent me, a teddy clutching a four-leaf clover. He understood what work meant, too. I start walking.

The tube is jammed despite the hour and since I have forgotten to pack my commuting kit – headphones, book, the New York weekly with the restaurant and bar listings that I had studied my first months back in London, drooling with FOMO, 'Neptune is the latest from the chef who brought cod roe soldiers to the East Village; she continues the Lilliputian theme in the form of thumb-sized crab rolls and matchstick goose fat fries' – I stand beside the doors, gaze into the tar-stained tunnel and tune my ear, like a long-absent visitor to a far-off land, to the metallic rumble between stations.

I join the black-clad horde that flows up one escalator, along a tunnel, up another escalator and through the ticket barriers, before being ejected into the pale city, blinking itself awake.

In the coffee shop, the barista nods with recognition – 'Weren't you pregnant the last time I saw you? Americano?'

'You'll probably spend the first couple of days trying to remember what your job is,' Mira said, but I had never forgotten it. I open my laptop, turn off my 'out of office' settings and glance at my most recent emails. Design plans for Lisbon, where a club will open at the end of the year. The all-company meeting in San Francisco next month, where I will present my ideas for a mentoring programme and member awards. I feel a prickle of excitement like the ting of a triangle.

I delve in my handbag for my new notebook and I wonder what Ash is doing. My fingers slide across the cool surface of my phone and I pull it out. There is a message from Jonna – *All fine here! Hope the first day back is going well* – and a picture of Ash looking as if he's just been told a hilarious joke.

'My boy,' I say under my breath, and I put the phone back, open the notebook at the first page and write 'Monday'.

Grace from marketing is the first through the door.

'Oh my God! Stevie! I can't believe you're back!'

'I missed you all.'

'And, obviously, we missed you! We've been quite the rudderless ship without you.'

'Ha! I doubt it.'

'How's everything? How's Ash?'

I'd decided not to mention my mother to anyone – easier to talk about a birth than a death – but still, I resent Grace for not asking, for not knowing to ask, can't she sense it, isn't it written on my face? *My mother died, Grace, she passed away, and it comes in waves, calm and then crushing like labour pains.*

'He's good, growing fast. I found a great nanny, so . . . '

'I can't wait to meet him. Are you going to bring him in?'

322

'Maybe. So, what's going on? How's Mike been?'

'Mike? Well, the launch went well – such a shame you couldn't come – that was the week you gave birth, right?'

'The day, actually.'

'And after that? You had everything so well set up, Stevie, such a great team here, he hasn't been that involved in the day-to-day in London. He's been working on the new European projects, that's been his focus, and in New York quite a bit.'

'Oh, right. He must have been sad to leave the company.'

'Yeah . . . Shit, is that the time? I've got an appointment at the club. We have a one-to-one this afternoon, right?'

'Yes.'

I spend the morning in catch-up meetings, all of which seem to be cut short by a sudden emergency. 'I'll try not to take it personally,' I joke, as each arrives with a tale of a member complaint, a burst pipe or, ironic, this one, a sick relative – something that has to be dealt with urgently. I take out my phone and find the latest missives from Jonna: Ash beaming beside my old telephone-on-wheels, his black eyes bright; Ash asleep under his patchwork blanket. Along with the tick of guilt – I am not there, should I be there? – comes a burst of calm, a whoosh of pride.

Things improve when I walk the three minutes down the road to the club for lunch and Dean embraces and double kisses me – 'I'm so European these days' – and guides me through the club like a visiting dignitary. 'This is the boss lady. She just had a baby, but you'd never know; I mean, *look* at her.' I talk to members who wax about the place; the connections they make here; the ideas they have – 'Yes,' I say, 'Yes,' because I can feel them popping in the air like bubbles – and Dean says, 'Stevie, I've missed you so much,' and, 'I love working here, you have no idea.'

It reminds me of the months after the first club opened, or a matt version of that time, because New York is glossy and peppy and the people are like racehorses straining with shiny hair and big eyes and clear skin. At least that's how I remember them; it seems so long ago now. London isn't like that, Londoners don't glisten like that and they don't get animated like that, you can't talk too loudly or seem too enthusiastic here, it isn't done, people will think there's something wrong with you.

Still, it makes me feel better, being back here. It is where I belong, it reminds me what I have achieved, and it makes me excited for – *about*, in British English, I must remember, relearn that – it makes me excited about my trip to New York in a week's time.

'I asked Mike to join, Stevie.'

When I scheduled a video call with Lex for two o'clock that afternoon, I didn't expect anyone else to be on it. I certainly didn't expect my maternity cover to be sitting next to Lex in the Madison Square Park office with morning light flooding through the window and a look on his face that is somewhere between sheepish and self-satisfied.

'Of course,' I say. 'Hi, Mike.'

'Hey, Stevie.' *Hey*. In the six months he's spent working for an American company, the man from the Midlands has turned his 'hi' to 'hey'. What will he say next, *Let's grab lunch*, or, *It is what it is*?

'So, first things first,' continues Lex, 'welcome back! How's re-entry? How's the baby?' He can't even be bothered to remember Ash's name.

'All good, thanks, Lex, it's great to be here. How are you? How's Kristin?'

'We split.'

'Really? I thought you guys were . . . '

'Rock solid? No. We wanted different things.'

324

'I'm sorry.'

'Don't be. Look, Stevie, it's great to have you back, we all missed you, six months is a long time. Mike's over here because he's really got stuck into the business and he's been taking a lead on the app – bringing the community online – and on content generally, so we're going to have him stick around. He'll be working out of the New York office the next couple weeks.'

Mike smiles and nods. I wonder what phrase will best camouflage my wobbly voice, will replace the trepidation in my heart.

I don't have a mother any more. They are the words I want to say.

'Right,' I murmur instead.

Fifty-six

The day after I told Jess I was leaving New York, that I was angling my life away from hers, I told Lex.

If I was going to open the London club, I said, I wouldn't go there for six months, as he had suggested: I would go there to live.

He shook his head. 'I don't buy it, Stevie. You'll be back here; I know you will. So, if you want to ship your stuff over there, I'm sorry but you'll have to pay for it yourself.'

I didn't mention the baby, of course. Lex was my boss first, a friend second, and it was a figment at that stage. That was the way he'd interpret it, anyway.

But Jess, I had told Jess. That evening, she called.

'Look, the other night ... I think I'd lulled myself into thinking you were here for ever,' she said. 'I was in shock, that's why ... '

I saw the glass fall from her hand, the shards on the floor.

'It's fine, Jess, honestly.'

'I get it, though, Stevie; you have good reasons for leaving.'

You want to have a child. She still couldn't say it, my other desertion. *OK*, I thought. *I won't either.*

'I also don't really have a choice,' I said instead. 'Not in the short term, anyway. Lex needs me in London.'

'Never think you don't have a choice, Stevie. Never think that. You could find another job in a heartbeat if you wanted. Don't go back to London unless it's the right thing for you. OK?'

'It is the right thing. But I'll miss you, Jess.'

'And I'll miss you. I'll look back on these five years as . . . '

'As what?' I couldn't help myself. Needy to the end, I was.

'It's been such a happy time. Hanging out with you. It's been wonderful.'

I was glad I'd be seeing Jess that weekend. We were holding the first of a series of rooftop concerts at the club, a plan I'd devised to get members coming by on Saturday evenings. 'It'll be like when the Beatles played on the roof in London in sixty-nine, but with fireworks,' I'd told Lex, and that was all the convincing he'd needed. 'You're brilliant, Stevie,' he'd said in his attempt at an English accent, '*brill-i-ant*.'

Nathan arrived soon after I did, and we watched the team set up the stage.

'Did you invite Jess?'

'Yes,' I said, 'she said she'd be here. Are Jenna and the Brit coming?'

'Well, Jenna is.'

We'd met Jenna's latest beau the previous weekend at the beach. 'He was no more attractive in the flesh than he was in that photo she showed us, right?' Nathan said. 'I'd give Jenna, what, a nine? And there's no way this dude is more than a four and a half.'

'Supply and demand,' I said, remembering what she'd told me when I was new in the city: 'There are, like, *no* men in New York. Straight men are like unicorns. Straight men who want relationships are like *rainbow* unicorns. And worst of all, they know it.'

'I mean, is that guy even really British?' Nathan said. 'He

looked British. But he didn't *seem* British. There was nothing irreverent about him. Although I guess he did have that uptight thing.'

'Am I uptight?' I said.

'Very.'

'Thanks.'

Jenna arrived looking drawn and deflated.

'Oh, Jenna,' I said, giving her a hug. 'What's happened?'

'*Nothing* is what's happened.'

'She's been ghosted,' said Nathan.

'Ghosted?'

'We drove back to the city on Sunday,' Jenna said, 'and I stayed over at his apartment, we watched a movie, and everything seemed, like, *totally* normal, you know? I felt closer to him than ever before because we'd all spent the entire weekend together out east. And it was great, wasn't it?'

'I mean, I had a great time,' said Nathan.

'And then in the morning we kissed goodbye on the corner of the street, and I walked uptown, and he walked downtown.'

'Cute,' said Nathan.

'And I haven't heard from him since.'

'What?' I said. 'And that was Monday?'

'That was Monday.'

'Has he done this before?'

'Not a whole week, no.'

'I expect he'll message you this evening, Jen.'

'You think?'

'Yeah. Right, Nathan?'

'I mean, maybe?'

'I just don't get it,' Jenna continued. 'We were dating, *seriously* dating – you don't just get to *disappear* after a weekend away.'

'Did you have the exclusive conversation?' I asked.

'We danced around it,' Jenna said. 'Obviously, I've been ana-lysing every single word he said.'

'That can't have taken long,' said Nathan.

'I like quiet guys.'

'I guess you do talk more than enough for two people,' said Nathan.

'And I suppose, on reflection, he *was* a bit evasive about where the relationship was going.'

'And now he's gone.'

'Nathan!' I said. 'I bet he'll be back.'

'If he does come back,' said Nathan, 'you should tell him to fuck off.'

Just then I was called away because the talent – a rising star most of the audience had never heard of with wavy red hair like a cartoon Rapunzel and bare feet peeping from a floor-length dress – was about to begin.

There were no more than fifty people standing in a semicircle around her, so close they could touch her, and she closed her eyes while she waited for quiet, and when she opened her mouth and started to sing, I saw goggle eyes and parted lips and Lex mouth, 'Woah, who *is* this girl?'

Jenna smiled and Jess waved from the back and gave me a thumbs-up, because her voice was an exquisite, throaty, haunting roar.

Afterwards, at least a third of the audience told me it was the best gig they'd ever been to – the backdrop, being among friends, everyone shaking their heads at the magnificence of *that voice, those pipes!*

'Proud of you, kiddo,' said Jess. 'That was exceptional, a real coup.'

Lex joked that that was the night he decided to double the

membership fees. People still asked me about it when I came back to New York years later. She'd sold a million records by then. 'Did you work at the club then, Stevie? Were you there?' and I'd say, 'Was I there? The whole thing was my idea.'

Fifty-seven

I don't go to New York the week after I return from maternity leave in the end. I don't go back to New York for a long time.

After the conference call with Lex and Mike I manage to get through the afternoon's dregs without crying – in front of my team, anyway. Was it even my team now, with my maternity cover still in place? It sounded as if it was just my second-in-command position that he'd swiped, but nothing is clear.

I do a lot of heavy breathing that afternoon, *in through the nose, out through the mouth*, it's like having contractions all over again, but this time the pain is in my head.

I email Lex about the team meeting in San Francisco, about my plans for the London events series, then text him when he doesn't reply. I see that he's read the messages, but I don't hear back.

Jonna is in no hurry to leave when I get home and I am glad when she offers me a cup of tea and has one herself, talks me through Ash's day, his moods and meals and nappy changes. It feels strange hearing what he's done, who he's been without me there. When she's gone, I fill the bath and test the water and put Ash in it. I soap his hair into a tiny black mohawk and show him his reflection, take a photo and send it to Nathan. I try to forget about Lex, about work.

Late that night, when Ash is asleep, I text Lex again, aware that what I am asking isn't particularly urgent, that I am like the desperate guy in the movie who calls and calls and calls. That I am behaving like Jenna, who never gives up, even when the writing is on the wall.

Jenna. I miss her singsong voice, her American optimism. *It will turn out OK in the end*, she used to say. *It always does.*

When Lex finally replies to my text with, *Sounds good, talk to Mike about it tomorrow*, I wonder who to call. I don't want to hear the concern in Jess's voice, and I know what Nathan will think, even if he's too kind to say it: *You should never have left New York.*

I decide to call Jenna, because she'll tell me it's going to be fine, and if she doesn't? Well, she's a lawyer. She'll know what to do.

'Jenna, it's Stevie.'

'Oh. My. God. Stevie! I miss you!'

'Yeah, me too. How are things?'

'The same, I guess. Well, except I'm dating someone.'

'And?'

'I don't know, it feels different this time, somehow. It feels *easy*.'

'That's great.'

'Yes. My therapist is . . . Well, she said she was *quietly confident*.'

'That's huge. What's he like?'

'Tall, dark. Kind of preppy. Not stop-in-the-street handsome, but cute.'

'Sounds great.'

'Yeah. He doesn't want kids, though. He's very clear about that.'

'And that's not a deal-breaker?'

'It's weird, but you know, *no*, I don't think so. I would have said yes six months ago. But I think I've realised that a forever relationship is the most important thing for me. And there's freedom to not having kids. He's an experience junkie, basically, super sporty, obsessed with travelling, loves checking out new places . . . '

'Like you.'

'Yeah, and we wouldn't be able to do that if we had children. Maybe I'm just trying to make myself feel better about the whole no-kid thing, but I feel like, well, there are compromises, there's a lot you give up. God, I'm sorry, Stevie, that's probably *exactly* the wrong thing to say to a new mom.'

'Don't be silly. You're right.'

'Anyway, what about you? Your life has changed and mine is basically the same. I hear the odd thing from Nathan . . . I emailed you a while back, did you get it?'

My lips quiver. 'I did, and the beautiful outfit you sent. Sorry, Jenna, it's been . . . hard. It's as if, I don't know. Everything's changed. And then my mum . . . '

'Your mom?'

'She passed away.'

'Oh my God, Stevie, I can't believe you didn't tell me. I'm so sorry. I can't imagine. You were close, right?'

'Yes and no. Sometimes I almost forget it's happened, and other times I just . . . burst into tears without any warning. So many questions, so many *things* . . . '

'You wish you'd asked her. Gosh, Stevie . . . '

'Just – call your mum, get it all out. Now. That's my advice. But look, that's not why I phoned. I phoned because I need your help – I'm back at work, and I thought it was going to be, I don't know, a distraction, and it's all going to shit.'

'Wait – why? What's happened? Is it Lex?'

'That guy I hired as my maternity cover – I told you about him, right?'

'Yes, I remember, you said on email that he seemed a bit inex-perienced, a bit timid, but super respectful of everything you'd done, and you thought he'd do a good job of holding the fort for a few months until you got back. Did he screw things up?'

'Not exactly. He's still here, well, he's in New York. Lex has kept him on, and he seems to want me to report to him.'

'Wait – are you sure?'

'He's been taking the lead on some of the European operations and when I asked Lex about something to do with the club here, he told me to ask Mike about it.'

'You're fucking kidding me! You're totally being sidelined. Where's this Mike staying in the city? Do you want me to go kill him?'

'It doesn't sound good, does it?'

'I'm going to give you the name of a shit-hot employment lawyer I know, she's in London, hang on . . . '

'You think I need to go that route? I was hoping you'd tell me I was being paranoid . . . '

'I'm sorry, Stevie, I think you need to go that route.'

I don't speak to Jenna's lawyer before it happens, there isn't time. I'm not sure it would have made any difference anyway. That Friday afternoon, my first Friday back, the Friday before I was due to fly to New York, I walk into the meeting room I've booked for another video conference with Lex, an invitation he accepted, to my surprise, and I find Cindy, the head of human resources, and a man I've never seen before, and they tell me that, regret-fully, *regretfully*, my role at the club is being eliminated.

I feel as if a giant eraser is hovering over my head then, and when I walk to my desk and put the hyacinth plant and my note-book and my pencil case into the cardboard box that someone has put there, and Dean escorts me out of the building – 'I'm so sorry, Stevie, this is totally fucked up' – the eraser starts rubbing me out. Rubbing out the six-and-a-half years I have worked at the club, rubbing out my life in New York, ejecting me from the community that I helped create, making a mockery of the feelings I have had for Lex. Until all there is left is a blank page.

Sunset, I say under my breath as I walk to the tube, carrying my box. It is the word, the euphemism Lex uses for pulling projects, for cancelling them, killing them. 'Sunset,' he says, chopping his neck with his hand. *That's it, we're out, it's over.* I wonder if that's what he said about me when he was discussing it with Cindy, with Mike, his sneakers on the desk. 'Let's sunset it. Let's do it now.'

Lex wasn't in the meeting: he didn't make a surprise trip over with Cindy and they didn't dial him into the little room with the frosted windows. I'll call him when I get home, I tell myself. I'm not going to let him get away with it. I can't.

On the tube going home people stare at my face, at my box. Do they know what I have lost, what I am not any more? Has it disfigured me, like the man I once saw on the subway with a scar from his temple to his chin and a ruby nose that had been sliced off and sewn back on?

Jonna and Ash are out at the park and the flat seems emptier and quieter than I've ever known it. It is strange to be there on my own. It reminds me of Sundays in New York when Nathan was with Brice and Jenna was with her latest flame and Jess was at yoga.

In my London street, the sky is turning from blue to pink, and even though we are forty miles from the sea, gulls caw noisily overhead. I imagine Lex putting on his wax jacket, the one he wore when it wasn't quite spring, adjusting his beanie and walking out of the building and over to the park where he'll call me back and explain everything. It has all been a misunderstanding: he has another job for me – a *better* job. He is starting a new company and he wants me to be managing director and he'll give me a ton of equity and we'll smash it, the two of us, together.

Or perhaps he'll say it has all been a big joke, a prank: 'I really had you there, didn't I, Stevie?'

But he never calls; he never emails. There is no reprieve. 'I expect it's some kind of legal thing,' Nathan says, 'he's probably not allowed to speak to you until the ink's dry,' and maybe he's right. But even after I've signed the documents saying I'll never breathe a word about it, even after the hush money has hit my bank account – 'We'll look after you; Lex said *very specifically* that he wanted you to be looked after' – even after my lawyers have been paid and the case has been closed, I never hear from Lex. Our relationship, our partnership, our friendship, has vanished altogether. Our club within a club. Gone.

On my phone, I see a reply to the one-line email I sent Jess explaining what has happened. She is telling me not to worry about money, she will help. Downstairs, the front door opens, and I hear Jonna take Ash out of the buggy. I hear him cooing and I remember what Mira said at the weekend when we visited her at her new house by the sea.

'Before I forget, I've got something for you,' she'd said as she placed a pot of tea and a jug of milk on the old oak table that had followed us around half our lives. She scooped something from the mantelpiece. 'Is this yours?' she said, laying a gold chain with a clasp in the shape of a hand gently on the table.

I gasped. 'My leaving present from Nathan.'

'Will gave it to Pete. He said he found it in his flat. I won't ask how it got there.' She smiled. We're closer, Mira and I, we have come back to one another. Our friendship will never be the same as it was in our twenties. The places we once occupied in each other's lives have been taken by other people. But that's OK, that's the way it should be.

'I can't believe it,' I said, fastening the necklace around my neck, rolling the hand between my thumb and forefinger, feeling for its tiny emerald ring. 'I didn't think I'd see it again.'

Mira poured the tea into two cups and placed a sippy cup for Ash next to the biscuits. 'So, how's he getting on?'

'Good. Want to see some tricks?'

'Of course. What have you got for me, Ash?'

I put him on the carpet on his front and he immediately rolled on to his back.

'Wow, nice move,' said Mira.

Delighted with the reaction, he beamed and waved his arms and legs like an upturned beetle. Mira had gone to the kitchen for a vase for the roses I had brought, and I watched him wail and thrash his limbs from side to side, desperate to flip over. He was fine, I told myself; he could come to no harm where he was. I could leave him there; I *should* leave him there: it was good for him to have a kick around, tire himself out.

Then – a new tactic – he stopped crying and looked at me imploringly with his bottomless black eyes; he reached out his arms to me: *Please, Mama.* He wanted me; he needed me. I was the only person who could help him. I kneeled on the floor and picked him up. I held him close. Then I sat him down in front of me and we looked at each other and his mouth opened into a crescent moon and he blinked and for a moment his eyes – perhaps it was the seaside light streaming through the window – I was sure his inky eyes were stained with green.

'God, he looks like you,' said Mira when she returned.

'You think?'

'You can't see it? I never could with Beatrice. It's his smile. It's yours.'

My heart lifts at the memory. I stop thinking about work, about Lex. I wait at the top of the stairs with tears in my eyes as Jonna carries Ash up.

Fifty-eight

'I'd like us to do something before you go,' Jess said. 'Another weekend away, perhaps. I mean, if you're up for it. I don't want to monopolise you; I know you'll have lots of people you want to see.'

'That's what leaving parties are for,' I said. 'I'd love to. What were you thinking?'

'Somewhere like the Turks or the Bahamas? A quick flight? My treat, of course.'

'Wow, Jess, I mean . . . that'd be amazing. It's just I'm not sure I can spare the time before I leave; I've got a ton to organise, and—'

'Forget it – I should have planned it earlier. Let's save that for another time. Your fortieth, maybe.'

'*Forty*,' I said. 'God, don't remind me.'

What about the baby? She'd be there by the time I turned forty – was she invited? It probably hasn't crossed Jess's mind, I thought. They don't factor in children, the childless, they forget them, that's what Mira always said. I expect I'd been guilty of it myself.

'How about a day trip sometime this month, then?'

'Yes, let's just do something low-key.'

She smiled. 'Leave it with me,' she said.

*

We met at Grand Central early on a Sunday morning, found seats on the left-hand side of the train carriage and traced the grey-green river upstate. We were on our way to an art museum a couple of hours north of New York, one we'd visited the year before I moved to the city.

'Do you remember the last time we came? It was the end of your vacation, one of those unbearably sticky days when you just have to get out of town.'

'I do,' I said.

'I thought it'd be nice to go again; it was such a special place.'

'I loved it: I've been meaning to go back. Thanks for organising this, Jess, it's just what I feel like doing.'

'Do you remember the wall drawings?' she asked.

'Sol LeWitt? Of course.'

'You got me into him. That's why I bought my paintings.'

As we reached the museum and found the line for pre-booked tickets, I thought back to our previous visit.

As usual, Jess had been well-informed about the collection. I'd always suspected she regarded art as an asset, like property or vintage cars; it wasn't something she had a natural affinity for. Whenever we'd been to an exhibition together, I could tell she'd been reading up on it – she probably had a wad of scribbled Post-it notes in her handbag that she fished out when I wasn't looking.

'Michael Heizer's work is all about the power of absence,' she'd said, as we'd stared into a series of deep cavities punched into the concrete floor.

I'd always found it gauche and rather irritating, her commentary, but I wondered now if that had been unfair. She had been attempting to appeal to the child she'd posted art materials to decades before, whose hobby she had nourished, that was why she'd done it.

And Jess wasn't like that this time. As we wandered around

the museum, marvelling at the light casting through the checker-board windows, no theories about conceptual art were posited, no potted biographies offered.

'You know,' she said as we approached that same exhibit, those neat black voids, a square, a circle, a rectangle, dug into the ground, 'there's something about these holes that makes me want to throw myself right in.'

I laughed. 'That's exactly what I was thinking,' I said. 'Shall we?'

'I'm not sure we'd get out,' she said. 'But how about a game of hide-and-seek? Remember those dark rooms downstairs? And those huge, rusty sculptures, like mini-mazes?'

'You're right, it's a great spot for it,' I said. She was wearing black skinny jeans, a black sleeveless blouse. 'But you'll probably be mistaken for art if you hide.'

'I'd better count, then.'

I hurried down the metal stairs to the basement rooms, gig-gling to myself, a child again, remembering all the times Jess and I had played hide-and-seek when I was little. As I folded myself behind a concrete pillar, I thought about the misses and misunderstandings of my first years in New York. We'd been like a couple learning to waltz, Jess and I, stepping on each other's toes. How far we'd come since then, the inhibitions we'd shed. Was that why she'd wanted to return to the museum? To set the present next to the past?

When she'd found me and then I'd found her, in the room with a giant spider crouching in a corner, we looked for the wall drawings we'd seen on our first visit. Cube after cube of gentle grids in graphite and sun-faded rainbow crayon, they were, lines and waves, some as faint as the sea meeting the sky, suggesting and then frustrating any expectation of pattern and order. But the drawings were gone.

*

340

Two weeks after our final outing, our last Sunday dinner. We were at the Italian near her apartment that Jess called 'our restaurant' because we'd eaten there together more than at any other. She placed a square parcel wrapped in brown paper, tied with a raspberry ribbon, on the table.

'Here you go,' she said. 'Sort of a leaving present.' Her three gold bracelets jangled on her right wrist.

'Jess, you didn't need to . . . ' My voice faltered; I wasn't expecting her to give me anything. It made my going real.

'Go on. Open it.'

I slid my finger under the paper. I took a deep breath and rehearsed my reaction in my head in case I didn't like it as I pulled out a frame.

Oh.

It was a print, a mess of dark squiggly lines in green, brown and blue with brighter colours – pink, red, yellow – snaking below and snatches of light in between. I recognised the style immediately.

'Oh, Jess.'

'I was looking for one of his drawings to give you, like the ones in the museum,' she said. 'That was when I had the idea of going back there. Then I saw that print and I knew you liked the pair I have. You don't have to keep it if you don't like it.'

It was colourful and loud, my picture; chaotic, not muted and ordered like the wall drawings. A song instead of a whisper.

'It's perfect,' I said.

Fifty-nine

Letters wait for stamps on her desk, a to-do list is pinned to the noticeboard, coats and jackets hang on the pegs by the door, her shoes stand still in the cupboard. Of course Dad expected Mum to walk through the door at any moment.

'He wants rid of everything and at the same time he can't bear the thought of it not being there,' Rebecca says.

'We'll be careful, won't we, Stevie?' says Jess. 'We'll keep the things that matter.'

Spring has become summer; the anemones are flowering in the bed beside the house; white agapanthus stand regally by the door.

'So,' I say, when we're drinking tea in the garden, side by side on the grey teak bench, shielding our eyes from the sun, Ash on a blanket on the lawn, 'what do you want to do – sort out Mum's clothes or go through her papers?'

Jess takes a deep breath and says, 'I'll start on the clothes. You go through her papers.'

'Sure?' I say, because the clothes are the harder task, the clothes still hold her. The papers are just descriptions of things in black and white.

'Sure,' she says.

'I'll make two piles,' I say. 'Stuff to throw – bank statements, that kind of thing – and stuff to keep.'

'Yes,' she says. 'Good idea.'

Slipped into plastic envelopes, filed between pastel dividers in three lever-arch folders in a metal box at the bottom of a wardrobe in Jess's poster-papered bedroom – 'The last place a burglar would look,' my mother had always said – are birth certificates and graduation certificates, electronic appliance warranties and government bond certificates.

Ash is sitting on the floor below the window with a pile of wooden bricks, picking one up, examining it, putting it down. 'Good boy,' I say, and he smiles, showing two white teeth.

I turn back to the folder. My fingers glide over the plastic sleeves. I wonder, if I look closely enough, whether I'll be able to see Mum's fingerprints.

The first folder is easy enough. Bank statements thirty years old. Warranties for fridges and microwaves long-since departed. Aged invoices for animal feed. Nothing worth keeping. The next is organised into three sections: Jessica, Rebecca, Stevie. I resist the urge to flick straight to my section and turn instead to Jess's.

Her birth certificate is first. I imagine my parents sitting opposite the registrar of some anonymous country town hall, baby Jess wide-eyed on my mother's lap, my father pinking with pride as he says, then spells out, her name. J-E-S-S-I-C-A M-A-Y S-T-E-W-A-R-T.'

Baby photos. Toddler photos. Photos of Jess in her school uniform and sports kit. Piano exam certificates. School reports. *Jessica should be proud of her progress this term. She is a diligent student and finishes the year second in the class.*

I turn the page, to a small, square photograph with rounded edges, floating in its transparent plastic pouch, like a sailing boat at sea. Jess in a spotted, sleeveless dress, standing in the doorway of the farmhouse. I wonder why her eyes are downcast, her spindly arms limp by her sides. I take the photo out of its sleeve, walk to the window and turn it to the light. Even though it must be forty years old, it is crisp and Technicolor bright, as if it has never been exposed to sun until now.

Just then, I feel Ash's hands around my ankles; he has crawled from his perch below the window. I pick him up and for a second, I wonder if the photo has slipped into the wrong section of the folder and that the girl in the picture is in fact me. We look so alike, Jess and I, people say it all the time – Lex said it, Nathan said it, Sam said it. But I'd remember the picture being taken, there are so few photos of me. And I'd never had a dress like that.

Then I see it.

The button-through dress should fall flat over her stomach, but it doesn't. Below the waistband is an unmistakable bump.

I hold the photo close to my face and study it. Perhaps the bump is a pillow, I think; perhaps Jess has been playing some kind of childish game. But she is a teenager in the photo, almost as tall as the doorframe, far too old for Mummies and Daddies. Perhaps there was a fat phase I hadn't known about – too many chips in town over the summer holidays. But her thighs and her arms are poker thin, her belly is like a football stuffed into a Christmas stocking.

When I examine the girl's expression again, I see shame in her eyes and on her lips and I know the bump is a baby.

'Ma-ma!' Ash says. I know better than to think he is calling my name; he is just trying out sounds, but it pulls me anyway. I close the folder and place it on Jess's single bed, below the black-and-white poster of Stevie Nicks. Slipping the photo into my back pocket, I carry Ash down to the kitchen to get his milk.

As he grabs the bottle with his chubby fingers and sucks, I wonder what happened to my sister's baby. Whatever it was must have been unspeakably sad, otherwise I would have been told about it. Did she give it away? Did she give it to the father, whoever he was? Perhaps it didn't survive the birth. Jess must have been, what? Fifteen? Sixteen? It was summer, she was back from boarding school for the holidays. I would have been one or two, far too young to remember.

I take the photo from my pocket and look at it again. No, that can't be right. Jess's boarding school was Catholic, nun-run, prayers every night, chapel every morning – they would never have tolerated a teenage pregnancy – and, besides, there wouldn't have been easy access to boys. No, it can't have happened while she was there. But then, she couldn't have been younger, surely? Surely she couldn't have been fourteen? That was the summer we moved, after the tenancy ended, that was the summer I was born.

The summer I was born.

I drop the photo and it drifts to the floor like a paper aeroplane.

Jess!

I would have shouted out her name had Ash not been on my lap, but there he is, blinking his big, black eyes at me as he finishes his bottle – *Please, mama, more* – so we stay sitting there in the cane chair and I try to tell myself I am being ridiculous while the photograph lies on the floor, an unsolved mystery.

Back in Jess's bedroom, I put Ash down with his bottle and open the folder again. After the teenage photo, the panoply of pre-adult life resumes: A-level results, degree diplomas. There is no record of a baby's birth, no immunisation logs, no adoption papers. Jess's section gives way to Rebecca's and I flick impatiently through her substandard reports and exam results and remember how excessively proud our father was of them, before turning the page to my own.

There it is: my birth certificate. I must have seen it a dozen times – when I applied for a passport, a green card, a bank account. I must have handed it over without looking; I didn't know then what there was to see.

I look, really look at it now, my throat tightening. There is my name, my date of birth, there are the names of my parents, and in the 'Place of Birth' box, rather than the local general hospital, where both Jess and Rebecca were born, the name of our farm has been typed.

'Stevie?' Jess is standing in the doorway. 'I thought I'd make us a cup of tea,' she says.

She is about to turn around when she sees the photo on the bed. She must have known I'd find it, that or some other form of evidence. She must have hoped for it. Jess bends to pick it up, the pregnant girl in the spotted dress, arms hanging leaden by her sides, and tears stripe her cheeks.

Sixty

I arrived with two suitcases and left with half a shipping container. Three men came to my apartment and mummified my belongings in bubble-wrap and boxes — the gig posters in white frames, the stolen hotel bar ashtrays, East River running shoes, first-date jeans and the pink velvet sofa.

As I signed the documents on the street outside and waved the truck away, it occurred to me that I could have bought everything new for what I am paying for it to bob across the Atlantic, but I would miss it. All that stuff is evidence, it is memories, and when it arrives three months from now and I unpack it, I'll look around the fraying London flat I have rented for the first two months, sight unseen, and that stuff will make me smile. I wore that when. I saw that with. It did happen.

'And this is where you'd like to spend your last night ever in New York?' Nathan had asked when I'd told him, two months earlier, that I'd booked the tickets. 'You want to see a washed-up movie director playing a wind instrument while we sip thirty-dollar drinks the evening before you fly back to London, never to return?'

'Yup,' I said.

'Perhaps it really is time for you to go.'

We were hungover from my leaving party the night before, which was lucky, since the cocktails really did cost thirty dollars. As Nathan murmured appreciatively about the dim lighting, how it really set off his Botox, I recalled Jess asking, a tremor to her voice, how I'd be spending tonight. She'd said she liked jazz when I told her and asked, tentatively, if she could join us.

'I don't want to crash, though. We've had our last night together.'

'You wouldn't be. Come. I should have told you earlier,' and I meant it. I was disappointed when she said she'd tried to buy a ticket and it had sold out.

'You're head-bobbing,' I said to Nathan as the second oompah-pah tune began.

'I mean, it's catchy, I'll give you that.'

'What am I going to do without you?'

'Have a baby? Become a grown-up? You'll forget about me. You'll see me on social media, and you'll remember all those fun times we had and then you'll go back to arse-wiping and bottle-sterilising and nursery-rhyme singing or whatever it is you old mums do.'

'I thought you said I'd regret it.'

'That was when I thought I had a chance of keeping you here.'

'You need to take some responsibility for my departure; you know that, don't you?'

'Yeah, I know. Spermgate. I still feel I've been short-changed, though. So does Jenna. She says you promised her *in perpetuity* when you met.'

'She's not upset I didn't invite her tonight, is she?'

'No. She gets it. Our special relationship.'

'You know, I'm not giving up my green card. I may return.'

'You won't.'

'You'd better visit me.'

'You'd better start scouting shoot locations. The content beast needs feeding.'

'Will you be able to prise yourself away from Brice and the dogs, that's the question.'

'I've become so conventional with my little New York family, haven't I? He wants to swing by later, say goodbye – is that OK?'

'I guess,' I said. I wasn't sure Brice and I were close enough to warrant marking my exit. We'd only met a few times; Nathan didn't like to mix us. 'I know too much, don't I?' I'd said once, and he'd grinned.

The cab stopped outside my apartment. 'Here we are. The palace,' said Nathan, and there was Brice beside the topiary trees, taking his hands out of his pockets, stepping towards me, adjusting his scarf, nervous.

'I just wanted to wish you well in your next adventure,' he said.

'Thanks, Brice. Take care of him for me, won't you?'

We gave each other a half-hearted hug. When I stepped back, he had a look that said, *I know I've hurt you and I'm sorry.*

'No hard feelings, right?' I said.

'Thanks, Stevie,' he said.

After he left, Nathan offered to ride up to my empty apartment with me, but I told him I didn't like lingering, it was sad enough already. He passed me a small leather box. 'Now look after this, it cost me *a ton* of money.' After we'd hugged goodbye, he walked south and he didn't look back.

Sixty-one

'Can we go outside?' Jess says. She feels hot, and I do too, a string of lights pinprick my sight, the murmurings of a migraine.

'Yes,' I say, fresh air will help, 'let's go outside.'

I pick up Ash, his gaze shifting from Jess to me and back again. Something has happened, he can sense it. I stand up; the room is swaying.

'Are you OK?' Jess asks, and I take a deep breath, hold Ash tight, arm over arm across his back.

'I think so.'

We pad silently down the stairs in our socks, past the embroidery commemorating the hurricane's fallen trees, past the faded aerial photo of the first farm, out through the back door.

We sit side by side on the grey teak bench, and Jess reaches in her denim jacket pocket for cigarettes, thinks better of it. 'Have one,' I say.

'No, not near Ash.'

I spread my jumper on the bench between us, sit Ash on it. Say something, Jess.

When she finally speaks, it is like the tide broaching a sandcastle's moat, filling it until the whole thing surrenders to the sea.

'I've wanted to tell you all your life,' she says.

'Then why didn't you?'

'Because keeping the secret was the only way I could keep you.'

Mum was devastated when she found out she was pregnant, Jess says. She thought she was throwing it all away, the straight As, a place at a good university, but it was the worst thing that had ever happened to Dad: the betrayal, the shame, everyone staring as her bump grew.

'Did he want you to have an abortion?' I hear myself ask, amazed I am able to form the words, and she says no, God saved your life, and I know what she means, they were churchgoers, Mum and Dad, and you can't read a lesson one Sunday and take your daughter for an abortion the next.

'Adoption, that's what he wanted,' she says. 'When I refused, Mum said we would move from the farm and the village where everyone knew their business and they would bring you up as their own. Dad agreed, he had to: he was scared Mum would leave if he didn't. And that was it.'

'But you named me?'

'Yes, they let me do that.' Stevie Nicks, the poster on her bedroom wall. I'd always wondered why my name had been Jess's choice. 'I was allowed to hold you occasionally and to give you your bottle, but I didn't breastfeed you, not once, and you slept in their room.'

She'd hear me crying in the middle of the night and creep down the passage and sit outside their door, her nightie over her knees, her own face damp with tears.

At least she was near me then, she says. When I was ten weeks old, she was sent to boarding school. She protested, of course, threatened to tell the school. But the full scholarship, the academic potential, a cap and a gown, the father who came from nothing and didn't want his daughter to go back to nothing, despite everything, because of everything – they won. I picture

Jess looking through the rear window of the car, the farmhouse receding, a red ribbon pulling her back.

'Perhaps they were right,' I say. 'You were a child. Finishing your education was important.'

'Was it? It didn't feel like that.' Her voice falters, her bracelets jangle, Ash looks up, eyes the glinting gold. 'It was confusing,' Jess says. She didn't know me: she hadn't cared for me, and babies that age, they're barely formed. It felt abstract, somehow, the hurt. Guilt seeping under her eyelids like blood when she closed them at night. Her knuckles white from squeezing the secret in her palm, from lying about her baby sister to the girls at school. Sometimes she wondered if she'd made the whole thing up.

I ask her if it got easier, it must have got easier, and she shakes her head. She looks through the apple trees in the field to the paddock beyond where the ash trees dance in the breeze, and she says the older we both became the more she understood what she'd missed. The more she worried about the effect it had had on me.

'I still worry,' she says, turning to me. 'They say those first few months of bonding are so important. I've always wondered if that's the reason you isolate yourself, Stevie, why you push people away.'

'Do I?'

'You avoid relationships, you avoid intimacy.'

'I have friends. Good friends.'

'But romantic relationships? Look what happened with Sam.'

'You're one to talk.'

'Now you know why. I don't want you to make the mistakes I did.'

We look at Ash, sitting on my jumper, playing with his rubber giraffe.

'You really liked Sam, didn't you?' I say.

'He reminded me of your father.'

My father was a boy called Jacob and they'd been friends since primary school. Legs stretched out under cut-off shorts, pink marshmallows catching fire – *They taste better burned, like caramel* – silent skies and stars so bright you could see your way home. It was always easy with Jacob, she says, and they knew what they were doing but still, they were horrified when it happened, they were just school kids – *and yet. And yet.* Did he meet me? A few times, in secret, and he said I was the most beautiful thing he'd ever seen.

And then she shrugs and looks away, she looks serious and sad, the fourteen-year-old in the picture, and she says, 'If we met now, we'd have nothing in common,' and she tosses the words into the air so carelessly, like salt over a shoulder, that she doesn't fool me for a minute.

'Where is he?' I ask.

'I don't know. We lost touch. It wasn't just Dad, it was my fault, too. I went off to university; he wrote, and I didn't reply. It was impossible to keep you believing we were sisters and to keep up with him. Rebecca said she saw him once, parked on the green opposite the gate. You know, Stevie, if you wanted to find him, I'm sure you could.'

'What did he look like?' I ask.

He was six foot, she says, even at fifteen, and he had hair like raven feathers and kind, black eyes like the night sky, and I imagine her telling him that, it's the sort of thing teenagers say to each other.

Ash has black eyes. I smile, and then questions crowd in.

Why didn't she come and get me? When she was older, why didn't she persuade them to let me live with her?

'I tried,' she says.

'When?'

She asks if I remember the weekend she drove here, made

353

tea, called them to the living room. The row. 'Yes,' I say, 'I was listening at the door, you were inviting them to London, to see your life there.'

'That isn't what happened,' she says. She was telling them it was time for me to live with her; for the truth to come out. I have been playing the wrong tune in my head.

'"Over my dead body," that's what Dad said. He couldn't stand the idea of you being taken away, of moving to London with me.'

'I didn't think he cared about me,' I say.

'He's always cared. In his own way, he's always cared.'

'And Mum?'

'She said I had made a deal. She didn't want to give you up,' she says. 'Even when you moved to New York, she said, "Don't tell her yet, Jess; she's happy as she is. You'll see her all the time anyway, she doesn't need to know." I toed the line. I owed Mum for looking after you. She had a right to call herself your mother. I didn't.'

I think about scanning the arrivals hall at JFK, circling it once, twice, how remote Jess had often seemed, even when I was close to her. Staying at her apartment. Elbow to elbow at restaurant bars, watching her study the menu, rotate a fork in her hand, refuse to meet my eye. I think about our weekend away, when she told me about her drinking, about the airmail letters she didn't answer and how they broke her fall.

Now I understand. Unspoken words spool silently like tape from a cassette.

I put my forefinger in Ash's mouth, our latest game, and he bites it with his new teeth, chews it like a puppy.

'You know,' she says, 'when you told me you were moving back to London, I thought about how you'd given me a second chance by coming to New York, and I'd blown it, and I thought about what an amazing mother you'd be, and how I hadn't been a mother at all.'

354

'I haven't been an amazing mother, Jess.'

'What do you mean? Look at the two of you.'

'I've found it so hard. I didn't feel the way I should about him, not for a long time. I missed work; I missed my career. I forgot who I was. It sounds awful, so awful, but I was *bored* at home on my own with him, and I wondered – I feel dreadful telling you this after what you went through with me – but I wondered, a hundred times, whether I'd made a terrible mistake.'

Those early months, alone in my flat, staring at a screaming thing, my whole being bent out of shape. I had expected to become a mother in the blink of an eye, the crowning of a head, and it had happened slowly, slowly, like labour, through formula feeds and soiled nappies and sleepless nights, hours and hours and days and months. Until, finally, perhaps it had been there all along and I hadn't seen it, hadn't known how to see it, hadn't wanted to see it because it might leave – finally, it revealed itself. Not with a fanfare, but like a door swinging slowly open. Love.

'Kiddo, I'm sorry.' We are both crying. 'I'm so sorry. I had no idea you felt like that. Why didn't you tell me?'

'I wanted to, when you came to visit . . . '

'I wish you had.' She leans over and puts her arms around me, around Ash and me. We fold into each other.

'You know, I haven't cried about Mum,' she says. 'Not once. I've felt so mixed up. I thought I'd got over it. By the time you left New York, I thought I was OK about it. But it's all come back. Sometimes I hate her. She looked after you; you are who you are because of her. I wouldn't have the life I've had if she hadn't brought you up. But she didn't let me be your mother, and that was what mattered most of all. I'm not sure I'll ever be able to forgive her for that.'

'But, Jess,' I sit back, forcing her to look at me, 'you made me what I am too. I didn't just move to New York because you were there, I went because you showed me the way. My drive, my aspirations. They're you.'

She fixes me with her tourmaline eyes; she wants to believe me. She asks if she can take Ash. You don't need to ask, I say, and she picks him up and his mouth drops open in a grin.

'Come on, Stevie, let's show Ash the sheep.'

When I join her, she is smiling, her face looks different, her skin is bright, a portrait restored, centuries stripped from it.

'I remember doing exactly this with you, you know. "Seeps!" you'd say, pointing at them, jabbing your finger, you must have been about one and a half.' I laugh. 'How do you feel, Stevie?' she asks. 'Are you all right? It's so much to take in.'

It is so much, it is too much. I am probably in shock. And yet, the flickering lights have gone. I shift my weight from one leg to the other, feel the grass underneath my feet, the earth firm beneath it. My son is in Jess's arms, content. I place my fingers on the underside of my wrist, feel my pulse. Even. Slow. I must have known, a part of me must have remembered, all this time, and that is the part that is making me feel calm. What was shaky is stable.

Dad is walking through the paddock towards us, the sheep behind him, a feed bucket in his hand.

'Does it make it easier or harder?' Jess says quietly.

'What do you mean?'

'Knowing why Dad is the way he is. You know, when he heard you were pregnant, I expect he thought history was repeating itself.'

'Except you were fourteen and I was almost forty.' I smile. 'And the circumstances were a little different.'

'We're both his girls.'

*

356

When I find Dad in the kitchen, he is filling the kettle.

'Dad,' I say. 'I know about Jess. I know what happened.'

At first, I can't look at his face; I can't meet his eyes. When I do, he is small and frightened and sad.

'I'm sorry,' he says, and I take a step forward and then another and I put my arms around him.

Sixty-two

Years after he lets me go, I see Lex in New York.

I am there to follow up some business leads. I like saying that: it makes me sound like somebody again, as if the consultancy I have recently set up is a bona fide entity. It has taken a long time to get here. It toppled me, the redundancy, my confidence tumbled like a toy brick tower. Fortunately, my settlement was, loath as I am to use the word, *generous*, and the contacts I made at the club kept me busy with work until I felt brave enough to start my own thing.

Mainly, though, I am in the city to see Jess. Our relationship changed after I found out, of course it did. Not overnight, but little by little – 'in increments,' Jess, who always has one foot in the boardroom, says. We make sure we meet every six months: she comes to London; I go to New York.

Occasionally, I go on my own. We have a lot to talk about, Jess and I, a lifetime. It is easier without distractions and Rebecca is always delighted to have Ash to stay for a few days. But more often I take him, we brave the eight-hour flight and the jet lag, and I am always pleased we have. I miss him otherwise; I ache for him.

While I work, Jess looks after Ash, she *cares for him*, they say in America. 'What's the point of running a company if you can't set your own schedule, take time off?' she says.

They develop their own rituals: hours at the playground with the green train beside the West Side Highway; sundaes at the ice-cream parlour a few blocks from my old apartment. Despite discovering that people do, in fact, have children in New York – they and the things they need do exist – it always feels as if I've smuggled an exotic animal into the city. I am sure I see double-takes as I wrestle his buggy up and down the craggy sidewalks – a baby, then a toddler; later a small, strolling child, in Manhattan – and I wonder if I should buy him ear defenders to shield him from the noise, a mask to protect him from the pollution and the drifts of marijuana smoke. Sometimes I wonder if it would be better if Jess and I kept him indoors, quarantined.

But we never do, because Ash thrives on it, he is as electrified by the city as I have always been, by the sirens' strange wails and the yellow cabs, by the primary-coloured carnations outside the bodegas, by the well-dressed dogs and the twenty-foot inflatable sidewalk rats. The first time I took him here he looked up at me, eyes wide, palms upturned as if to say, *What is this place?* And I smiled and said, 'We're in New York, Ash. It's crazy, isn't it? How on earth did I live here so long?'

I often wonder that. New York seems like a more pronounced version of the city I used to know, as if its lines have been drawn with a Sharpie. We stay at Jess's apartment and when she and I have put Ash to bed, we sit on the beige sofa facing the window. It is a useful reminder, as we talk about all that we missed and wonder whether any of it could have been different, that whatever happens, whatever has happened, the sun sets, the moon rises.

Jess changes, too. Am I projecting what I now know on to her? I don't think so. I am sure that every time we speak her voice sounds stronger, louder, more assured. Her posture is different, too. People used to ask her whether she'd studied the Alexander Technique because she carried herself upright like a ballerina, moved with such precision, such control; she never slouched, as I did. But now, she casts her arms around freely, her chin drops, her shoulders fall. It makes her look older, but also relaxed. Happy.

Mum – her mother, not my mother – is gone. My feelings towards her are complicated, conflicted, like a mass of electrical leads stuffed into a drawer, never to be untangled. She loved and defended and guarded me jealously, and at the same time she loved me differently and never quite passionately or permanently enough, because she wasn't my mother.

We debate it for hours, Jess and I; we wonder who was protecting whom. But then we remember things about Mum, a favourite aphorism, the way she pinched her earlobe when she was thinking, and I remind Jess how fond she was of Ash. I tell her how she danced around my flat with him that afternoon; I tell her again and again because I have so few memories of Mum and Ash, I cling to and replay the ones I do have. Then we think of things we want answers to, small but important things like whether I ever had chicken pox and how old Jess was when she started to walk, things Mum would have known, and we cry and hold each other and forgive her, and the cycle begins again.

The only other person I ever plan to see on those visits is Nathan. I know I'll bump into people: in Manhattan someone is always thrown in your path. Occasionally it is a friend I am pleased to see and they'll scold me for not getting in touch and we'll grab a drink or dinner. More often it is someone to cross the street to avoid or to look past in a shop: an ex-date, an old co-worker, someone I've deliberately lost touch with.

This time, it is Lex.

When I get to the restaurant it is obvious why Nathan has chosen it. It is a minimalist, Nordic-style place that looks good in the summer light, the sun still high enough to wash its white walls yellow, the plates issuing from the kitchen mini masterpieces – a nest full of tiny speckled blue eggs; a mossy hillock laid with a single spare rib. There is an empty round table in the corner with a reserved sign, and I find myself wondering about the best angle to photograph Nathan from, even though I'll have no say in the matter. He is late, as always, and I am trying to decide whether to have a drink or go outside – it is still warm and soon I'll be returning to London and never leave home without a jacket – when I see Lex sitting at the bar.

There are a handful of people you've spent so much of your life looking at, thinking about, that a split-second glance is all you need to tell you it's them. A profile, a silhouette, the swing of an arm will do it, even if it's been a decade since you last met. Their image is burned on your retina like a black dot from looking too long at the sun.

He is alone. He isn't waiting for anyone; he can't be because the seats either side of him are occupied by people talking to their neighbours. He is wearing ear pods, picking at a salad and scrolling through his mobile.

I remember how much I liked doing that when I lived in New York.

Did I? Really?

If I walk up to him, there might be grey flecking his sideburns or the strands of hair that fell on the nape of his neck below his beanie. But from where I am standing, he looks exactly the same as the last time I saw him, four years ago.

Lex.

For a moment, I think about calling his name; I think what Mum would have said about water under the bridge and how short life is and how you shouldn't hold a grudge. I think what Rebecca said after I lost my job: 'It'll probably be the best thing that ever happened to you,' and how she was right.

No.

I say to the host, 'You know what, we're going to go somewhere else tonight.' Before she can reply I push open the door and take my phone out of my handbag and type, *Meet you at the wine bar on tenth*, and press send.

Sixty-three

The fridge has been buzzing for days. I should ask Rebecca if she knows someone who could repair it; I should add 'fix fridge' to the list of things to do, below 'book haircut' and 'collect dry cleaning'; the list that only gets longer because there is never enough time.

Next door, in the bedroom, Ash wakes from his nap and I go to him. He has recently graduated to Lily's and Penny's hand-me-down toddler bed. Before, Ash and I slept side by side, my double bed shunted against the window, his cot inches from the door, like orphans in a dormitory. Now, I sleep on a sofa bed in the living room.

'You'll have to move,' Rebecca said when she delivered the bed, peeling unicorn stickers from the headboard, 'you need your own room.' She's right: I'll start looking for another flat soon, when my finances are more secure, when I've taken on a few more clients. For now, I'm happy to unfold the sofa bed each night; I'm happy that my room has become Ash's, with bookshelves on the wall, a doll's house in the fireplace and a wooden garage on the floor with a car lift he raises and lowers. I feel I have done something right, giving him his own space.

*

Last weekend, Nathan came to London. Ash and he have met several times: Nathan flew over for my fortieth; he insists on a 'playdate' whenever I bring Ash to New York, but he was surprised at how much he had changed since he saw him last.

'Does he ever stop talking?' he asked.

'Not really. He's a chatterbox, just like his godfather.'

'I can't keep up. Do you think he might be a genius? He asked me how many people there were "in di world" when we were at the play park – that's advanced, right? For three?'

'Very. He takes after his mum.'

We were sitting on a tangerine sofa in Nathan's hotel suite, below a triptych of bulldog portraits in neon frames.

'Honestly, it's like the magazine fifteen years ago,' he said, taking a bottle of champagne from the ice bucket, refilling my glass. 'The hotel company paid for my flight, they're giving me this room for free, all my food's comped . . . all I have to do is post. And I mean, as if any of my followers can afford to pay fifteen hundred dollars a night for a hotel room. Not that I'm complaining.' He raised his glass. 'Anyway, what's the latest with Jess? Are you still refusing to call her Mom?'

'Nathan. You know I call her Jess.'

'But does she feel more like your mom?'

'No, not really. We feel close though.'

'Well, I guess it's evolving. A watching brief. That necklace looks so good on you, by the way. I do have excellent taste, don't I?'

'You do,' I said, rolling the gold hand clasp between my thumb and forefinger, feeling for its tiny emerald ring, feeling relief again. 'Nathan,' I said, turning to him, 'did you ever suspect?'

'About Jess?'

'You saw us together more than anyone else.'

He sighed, flicked his hair. 'I don't know, Stevie, I guess

there was always something a little off. The way you talked about her, the age gap . . . It was strange. She blew so hot and cold. There was something brittle about her, something so contrary to the ass-kicking boss lady. And the way she looked at you. I suppose it was sort of feral, in retrospect. So yes, I guess I did wonder.'

'Why didn't you say anything?'

'It would have sounded crazy, and this may surprise you, I didn't think it was my place.'

'Why could you see that stuff and I couldn't?'

'I think you could. You knew, deep down, that something wasn't right.'

There had been a humming somewhere, a whisper that I couldn't quite hear. 'Yes,' I said.

'My shrink would have a field day with all of this. And I mean, it's got me thinking. Big family, significant age gap . . . '

'Nathan!'

'Yeah, you're right. I should be so lucky. My mom is definitely my mom, though she'd probably rather she wasn't. So, are you seeing your dad – your *granddad* – more now?'

'Every couple of months. He and Ash get on really well. Ash is fascinated by men, as you know, he's fascinated by *you*. But he looks at my dad and he just beams.'

At first, I told myself I should visit Dad because he was lonely and it was what Mum would have wanted. Increasingly, I find myself looking forward to seeing him, to being in the countryside; often, when I'm in London, I miss the deep green of everything, the perpetual murmur of birds and insects and things growing, the night-time silence and the stars. Perhaps I am just missing Mum.

I have not forgiven Dad entirely for his part in the secret and the way he treated Jess, for his indifference to me, but I see texture now, like a tissue through a microscope. Anger can come from fear, it can be shot through with love; I understand that now. And lately, I wonder – I try not to, but the thought keeps sprouting like bindweed – whether something else might account for the distance between Dad and me. Something other than where I came from, a baby in a teenager's belly.

'She wanted you for herself,' Jess had said about Mum, and I wonder whether she hadn't just kept Jess from me, she had kept Dad and me apart deliberately too when I was young. If, denied a career, she had denied us a relationship. We were so seldom alone, Dad and I.

'Don't bother him, Stevie,' Mum would say, because it was milking time, or feeding time, or he'd had a hard day and he just wanted a rest. Reluctantly, I'd comply, until eventually, I didn't ask any more.

I shudder when I think that. I rip it from the soil, lead my mind back to the phone call Mum insisted Dad make when she was dying, the attempt to solder us. I console myself with that; *that* was her. And I think, here we are, Dad and I, stitching something together from shared cells, from memories and time, unearthing mutual interests like buried treasure.

We are both making an effort. Last week, Dad came to London and looked after Ash for a day when Jonna was ill. 'He was very well behaved,' he said when I got home. 'It was me who wasn't.' Ash had wanted to ride his balance bike to the park and when Dad had fastened his helmet, he had caught Ash's skin in the clasp. 'The poor lad howled for a full five minutes,' Dad said, showing me a tiny mark under Ash's chin, wincing at the memory. I felt awful, not for Ash, but for him. 'Honestly, Dad, don't worry,' I said, 'It'll have vanished by next week,' but he wouldn't let it go. 'It was my *fault*,' he said, and I put my arm around him and said, 'Shh, I do that kind of thing all the time.' I was taken aback by how much it bothered him, how much he cared.

In the end, Nathan and I decided to eat out, to step into the narrow streets of Soho.

I led him to a dark, decades-old townhouse restaurant with candles in wine bottles, then to a scruffy basement bar. When I came back with the second round, he asked me about meeting my biological father as I knew he would. I told him we were writing to each other, he had been easy to find, happy to be found; it would happen, but not yet.

At midnight I said, 'Walk me to the tube?' because I remembered Ash tugging at my jumper that morning. 'Don't go to work, Mummy, no!' and I wanted to be back in my flat, peering into the quiet of his room, bending over his bed, inhaling his sleepy breath, moving a truant leg back under the duvet. I could have run all the way to him with my eyes closed.

I kick the fridge again. Ash is sitting on the floor now, drawing, and he looks up.

'Mummy, you hurt it!' The buzzing stops.

'See?' I say.

Then it starts again. *Ugh!* I throw my arms in the air and Ash starts to giggle his high-pitched tee-hee-hee. I raise my arms again with the force of a tennis pro tossing a ball and say *UGH!* again, more aggressively this time. Ash laughs as if he's never known anything so funny; he laughs and laughs until he is doubled up with laughter, until his cheeks are pink. 'Funny Mummy!' he says when he is able to draw breath.

When he turns back to his drawing, I pick up my phone. There's a work email I'm expecting and I should call Rebecca about the fridge – it's Friday it'll be impossible to find anyone over the weekend.

Through the window, a triangle of blue is widening in the grey sky. I put my phone back on the kitchen counter. Those things can wait. Those things don't matter.

I walk to the hooks by the door, take down my parka and Ash's duffel coat, crouch beside him on the floor and put my hands on his shoulders. We smile at each other and I lift him up and he wraps his arms around my neck and his legs around my waist, he's heavy now, a proper boy, and I put my cheek against his cheek, warm and soft like washed silk.

'Come on, kiddo,' I say. 'Let's go to the park.'

Acknowledgements

Thank you to my agent, Anna Power, for believing in my writing, your guidance and editorial expertise, and for finding my book the best possible home. To my brilliant editor, Sarah Savitt, for bringing *Hush* to life in every sense and making the entire experience so enjoyable. I hit the jackpot with you two.

Huge thanks to the rest of the team at Virago, including Nithya Rae, who has been so patient with my fiddling, Grace Vincent, Jane Pickett, Emily Moran, Alison Tulett, Rachel Cross, and Sophie Harris for the beautiful cover.

I began *Hush* on a Faber Academy course, and am grateful to the wonderful Joanna Briscoe, for teaching me the novel-writing ropes and my fellow students for their helpful feedback. A special shout-out to Martha Alexander and Jennifer Coles for your ideas. To all at the Bridport Prize: being shortlisted for the novel award gave me the confidence I needed to continue, as well as introductions to Aki Schilz and Anna South, whose suggestions were invaluable.

Thank you to all the friends and colleagues in London and New York who have supported my writing over the years and given convincing impressions of being interested in my novel whenever I've banged on about it.

Among them, my editors at *Condé Nast Traveller* UK and US, including Sarah Miller, Klara Glowczewska, Clive Irving and Deborah Dunn. Eloise Smith, first-rate writing companion and a role model of courage, and side-hustling. Hanya Yanagihara, for the laughs and wisdom during our jaunts, and for being the ultimate inspo. Rebecca Ley, for showing me the way and replying to my panicky WhatsApps – I forgive you for writing three books in the time I've written one. Liza Marshall, for the generous introductions and encouragement. Leila Woodington and Berit Block, the most considerate bosses. Hilary Beaty and Suzy Ross, for your thoughts and input. And Colin Walsh, publishing sage.

To Helen Down, Luisa Metcalfe, Eimear Lynch, Neena Paul, Florencia Panizza, Henrie Clarke, Zoe Norridge, Anna Thomas and Jenny Mathieson for the bolstering, book-related or otherwise. Alina Mindedal, for your help and kindness. To my brothers, Nick and Ed, a grateful high-five. And to all the women who have shared their stories, thank you for trusting me with them.

Hush is dedicated to my parents, who taught me that books are magic and have helped so much with this one. Thank you, Mum, for your enthusiasm, for reading – and re-reading – every chapter first and telling me to keep going, and Dad, for your unwavering support.

Finally, Adam, without whom I wouldn't have started this book, let alone finished it. Thank you for encouraging me to pursue my dream, for cheering me on during the highs and offering endless solutions-based advice during the lows. And to F, L and B, who fill my life with joy.